Foreordained

Aaron N. Hall

Dedicated to those like Jason
Who may need just
A little more
Faith

CONTENTS

PROLOGUE

Today would not be a choice day for the Holy Dragon to bless the kingdom of Nezmyth.

Lightning... a murky black sky... a raging downpour... the weather this evening reflects the spirits of the people of Nezmyth. There is a surplus of misery and uncertainty and hope seems to have deserted them long ago.

But tonight, the Dragon has breathed a spark of hope.

Legend is about to take shape.

* * * * *

Every few gallops, a horseman would shoot a panicked glance over his shoulder. Soldiers are everywhere, and the King's spies are even more plentiful.

The rider had been by the Cathedral dozens of times, waiting for that blessed parcel to fall into his empty hands. He had almost abandoned hope that this glorious day would ever come, let alone on a night like this.

The horse galloped with wild haste down the drenched streets, panting heavily, its smoky breaths erupting from its nostrils. The rider squinted to fight the torrent blurring his eyes as he careened through the darkness. Raindrops ricocheted off his leather hat—the rest of his clothes soaked to the bone.

Could it possibly be true?

The rider gripped the reins tighter and yanked with all that he was. The horse cried out a startled whinny and scooted to a shaky halt. Directly to the left, a monstrous mansion hung below the Nezmyth City skyline like a studious giant. Even among the more poetic and large buildings of Upper City, it demanded authority.

The horse rider threw his leg over the horse's side and leapt off the saddle, hitting the ground running for the thick steel gate that ran the perimeter of the fortress. He jammed his fist around a bar and shook it violently while shouting as loud as his lungs would allow. His eyes darted from one rooftop to another as his quivering frame turned about in every direction.

"Peace, peace!" A gatekeeper stood under a small shack by the gate. "What is it you want?"

"I need an audience with the Chief Patriarch immediately," the rider said while sparing another glance behind him.

"Master Ferribolt? At this time of night?" The gatekeeper said. "I doubt—"

The rider thrust his shaky hand through the window and grabbed the gatekeeper by the collar. The gatekeeper's eyes popped with surprise and he fumbled for the dagger by his side. The rider glared at him wildly, his nose mere inches from the gatekeeper's.

"*He has been called,*" The rider breathed.

The gatekeeper slid a numb, awestruck stare at the rider. As the rider gripped his collar, he noticed something upon his middle finger that made his heart skip a beat. A ring, emblazed with a brilliant orange stone lay just below his nose, signifying a Foreordained servant of the Dragon. His eyes grew. Immediately, the gatekeeper knew who this man was.

The rider continued brusquely. "I am a Blessing Bearer. Time is of the essence. *Let me in!*"

Without another word, the gatekeeper released his dagger and pulled a concealed lever from inside the shack. The mechanisms that held the gate slackened, and the gate crawled and squealed open after a brief shudder. The rider released the gatekeeper and wriggled through the first crack of an opening wide enough for his slim body.

As he soared down the drenched walkway and up the stairs, the gatekeeper found his tongue, "*Thank the Dragon...*"

The rider slid to a halt in front of a pair of wooden doors. He threw his shaking fist against the door thrice.

The knocks reverberated off the inside hall. As he stood panting, he shot more paranoid glances about him. He leapt across the porch and planted himself directly behind a pillar, shielding himself from the sight of the streets. A minute hadn't even passed, but it felt as though it were eons before the door finally creaked open.

"I'm sure this news could have waited until morning," a clean-cut butler wiped his eyes and answered the door. His eyes became curious as he noticed the rider perched behind one of the stone pillars several feet away.

"No, it couldn't, sir," the rider replied, not moving a muscle. "I have to see the Chief Patriarch *right now.*"

The butler eyed the rider curiously, then his expression became hard. The words he wanted to say seemed to have trouble leaving his lips. *Do I dare ask?*

"Are you a... *Blessing Bearer?*" he almost whispered as he nervously scanned the rainy landscape, as if fearful of listening ears.

The rider nodded stiffly. The butler's jaw clenched and he quickly stepped aside. The rider sprinted the three steps to the threshold and the butler slammed the door behind him. A thick, exhausted sigh left the rider as his heart rate slowly decreased. The uneasiness of the package he held still clung to him.

"Wait here," the butler said, already marching away. "He could be awake reading the Ancient Text, as he sometimes is..."

As the butler scooted away, the rider scanned the interior of the fortress. He could nearly see himself in the polished stone tiles, sprawled in a perfect grid across the floor. The high, cathedral-like ceiling was painted with depictions of angels, dragons and other creatures in great battles or lolling about in meadows and streams. Crystal chandeliers hung single file down the pristine hall. Elegant staircases curved up the far wall onto the upper floors. In the middle of the hall, an enormous statue of the Holy Dragon stood triumphantly crying out to the sky, with mighty claws, a strong curving back, and wise eyes.

In a matter of moments, Master Ferribolt himself came bustling to the door. His rotund build seemed to swell with jovial energy with a content smile to match. His circular spectacles rested on the bridge of his nose, directly in front of his soft gray eyes. The hem of his robe floated around his ankles as he paced, and it was matched with a nightcap perched atop his bald head. A ring with an orange stone, nearly identical to the rider's, was upon his finger.

"It's a little late to be out riding horses, eh?" He said. "And in this weather? Goodness, you're soaked. Jerem, take his coat."

As the butler slipped off the rider's coat, the rider rummaged in his satchel and revealed a rolled up piece of parchment. He held it gingerly, as if he held the very world in his hands. Master Ferribolt scanned it curiously before taking it from the rider's shaking hands.

"Is this what I think it is?" he asked.

The rider nodded.

Master Ferribolt's eyes became stone. "Come."

The Chief Patriarch turned on his heels and marched down the hall, the rider following closely behind. A large arch in the wall separated the main hall from the study. A lit fireplace on one of the far walls gave every bookshelf-lined wall a warm, orange glow. In the middle of the room, two plush armchairs faced each other, separated by a bear rug.

The Chief Patriarch nestled himself into the far one and insisted the rider take the other.

"Now..." Master Ferribolt unrolled the parchment and refastened his spectacles. As he opened the parcel, the rider swallowed hard in an attempt to flush the lump from his throat.

Master Ferribolt straightened out the battered parchment with white, wrinkled hands and the rider drummed his fingers on the armchair uncomfortably across from him. His eyes darted from side to side as he read the note, soaking up every word and every phrase, his gaze becoming harder and harder as they traveled down the paper. He scratched his head periodically. The rider shifted in the chair that had soaked up most of the water from his coat. Finally, Master Ferribolt finished and set the paper down carefully on his lap.

He looked up to the rider with a white-hot gaze. "You know what this message contains?"

"Yes, sir. I heard the Blessing myself... could it be true?"

"Every Patriarch in Nezmyth is completely inspired with each word they dictate in a Blessing of Fate," Master Ferribolt said. "There are no repeats or mistakes. The words come from The Holy Dragon itself. You, being a Blessing Bearer, know this better than most."

"Of course..." the rider said, rubbing his soaked hat in his shaking hands. "Then it *is* true... what do you make of the boy?"

"The boy?" Master Ferribolt said, his eyes not softening. "With any luck, this... Jason... may still be alive. But knowing King Barnabas"—he stole a glance to a rain-streaked window—"his spies have already caught wind of this, and they are hastening their flight to bring him this news. They must be stopped."

"What can I do?" The rider said.

"You?" said Master Ferribolt. "Stay here. Your life may still be in danger if you leave this house tonight. Guard this information with your life. I'll have my friends take care of your horse and show you to your quarters. Meanwhile, I'll attend to this matter," Master Ferribolt stood quickly, grabbing the coat that was slung over his armchair. "Goodnight, my friend. Your duty is fulfilled."

"Thank you. May the Dragon bless you," the rider said.

The rider stayed seated as Master Ferribolt briskly exited the room. He threw off the nightcap perched atop his silver head and thrust his arms through the sleeves of his heavy coat. With every passing moment, the King's spies had to be getting closer and closer to the castle. If the king caught wind of what has happened, he wouldn't hesitate in snuffing the life of this young boy. His lust for power had only grown stronger in passing years with no sign of diminishing.

"Gaston, assemble the coach immediately!" Master Ferribolt shouted. It wasn't long before a second butler emerged from around a corner with a pair of boots.

"Please sir, I just finished polishing the floors today and I am very tired," he said pleadingly. "Couldn't this wait until morning?"

"Absolutely not," Master Ferribolt said firmly. "I cannot elaborate how absolutely vital this issue is. There are things at stake here that are much bigger than you or I, my friend."

"Where are we going?" the butler said with rising interest.

Master Ferribolt bent his eyebrows, "Nezmyth Castle."

The butler's eyes grew wide. He opened his mouth to speak, but the words got caught.

"Yes," Master Ferribolt said. "A young boy received his Blessing of Fate just minutes ago. It won't be long before Nezmyth has a new King."

1 THE BOY

Jason flew backward and slammed against a wall with a mighty *thud*. The wooden sword in his hand escaped from his grasp and landed a few yards away. He slid down the wall into a sitting position, his eyes tearing up rapidly.

"Pay attention, Jason!" His battle instructor shouted. "If you would have done that on the battlefield you would be dead!"

Jason shook his head, staggered to his feet and tried to peer through blurry, swollen eyes. He stood backed into a wall on the side of a large square room built for sparring, equipped with racks of practice weapons and a padded floor. Other fifteen-year-olds lined the walls perpendicular to him, cheering and pumping their fists to the air.

Tarren stood several yards before Jason, a victorious grin slashed across his thin face. Tarren flicked a strand of greasy blonde hair out of his purple eyes in a way Jason recognized all too well. It made his stomach churn.

Tarren lifted up his arm in Jason's direction. A little ball of light began to emit from his palm and grew rapidly in size until it was the size of his own fist. Jason's heart rate spiked as he reflexively spun out of the way. He felt the heat from the ball of magic energy fly just inches behind his back before it dissipated into the wall.

As soon as Jason had spun full circle to face Tarren, he mimicked his move and shot a blast at him. He saw Tarren's face flicker with shock before the blast hit him directly in the sternum, sending him tumbling into a backward somersault.

"Nice jeroki, Jason!" The instructor clapped approvingly. The other teens in the room roared with approval.

With no time to spare, Jason dove for the fallen sword. Just as he pushed off the ground, Tarren had recovered and thrown a wooden dagger at him, soaring through the air and missing just above Jason's right shoulder. Jason landed hard and wrapped his hand around the wooden blade's handle before scrambling to his feet. Sweat dripped from his hair, his nostrils flared and his eyes like fire.

Tarren staggered to his feet. The devious grin was long gone, leaving nothing but an irritated scowl. When Tarren pointed both palms at him, Jason's adrenaline punched again. He dug his feet into the ground and sprinted toward Tarren, gripping the wooden blade with both hands. Dirty sweat coated his burning cheeks.

Tarren's jerokis popped in a rhythm one after another, alternating hands as they pelted toward Jason. Jason slashed his sword at each blast, slicing each ball of magic into oblivion as he bolted toward the attacker. He could feel the heat brushing his face from every blast he destroyed.

The teenagers roared and cheered at Jason as he blew past every jeroki. Jason had found his rhythm, and he and his blade had become one force.

Jason reached Tarren—the end was at hand. He lifted his sword high, ready to strike the final blow. Everyone was on their feet, chapping and jumping excitedly. In a split second, Jason's victory would be secured.

Right as Jason was about to go in for the finisher, he felt something poke his stomach. He looked down and his heart sank.

Tarren had withdrawn another wooden dagger from his pocket and shoved it in Jason's belly. His eyes flashed. Jason let out a cry of suppressed rage and threw down his sword.

He ran his fingers through his matted brown hair, nearly pulling out fistfuls of it. As Tarren stood up, the battle instructor walked up to them and placed a hand on each of their shoulders.

"Another victory, Tarren! Very resourceful! If Nezmyth ever sees war, we'll be blessed to have you in our numbers," he said. He looked at Jason. "Jason, don't get discouraged. You fought valiantly today. Dismissed!"

Words of comfort... but the hollowness of defeat still wasn't filled.

* * * * *

The chair Jason sat in squeaked as he sat poking the meat on his plate. His father, Tomm, sat at the head of the table jotting down notes for the next day of work while he blindly stabbed at bits of meat strewn across his plate. He stroked his chin with a burley, callused hand and pushed up his glasses before continuing with his notes.

Jason's mother, Kara, chewed on a slice of fruit silently on the other end of the table with a look on her face that seemed contemplative. Her deep brown eyes dreamily gazed down to her plate and her hard-working hands pinched her utensils with an air of modest elegance. Her long, brown hair fell down onto the dress she had washed over and over again— the dress that gingerly held her slender curves despite her age.

Dim light poured through the murky windows of the one-room cottage. The fragrance of cinnamon filled the old, wooden edifice—just another scent from the modest collection Kara stored in a chest close by. A faint fire flickered in the stone fireplace against the far wall to provide some heat to the three inhabitants. In the corner next to it, a hammock for Jason, pinned into the walls. In the other corner, a hay-stuffed mat just large enough for Jason's parents.

Not a word was spoken. A dark emptiness resided in Jason since the match earlier that day. Kara glanced at him briefly, sighing deeply when she saw the glove still on his right hand.

"You know you can take that off in the house," she said matter-of-factly.

"I know," Jason said. The silence ensued for a brief moment before Kara spoke up again.

"So how was your battle today?" She asked cheerily.

Jason's lip tightened. "I lost again. He stabbed me in the belly with a dagger right as I was about to strike."

"Oh... well... don't worry. You'll beat him eventually. We all learn from our mistakes."

Then I should know everything by now, Jason thought.

More silence followed until Kara spoke up again, "I've heard His Majesty might raise the tax again."

"Predictable..." Jason thought out loud. "The fiend is never satisfied..."

Immediately, his mother and father froze and threw a look at Jason as if he had just confessed murder. His father shook his head and went back to writing, trying to forget the taboo that just spilt from his son's lips. His mother, however, was not so forgiving. Her eyes darted from window to window before she leaned over the table angrily.

"Jason!" She hissed. "Be careful what you say, especially with you being who you are! You don't know who may be listening!"

It doesn't matter, Jason thought bitterly, continuing to poke at his plate. *Why he would want to be King of a kingdom like Nezmyth, I don't know...*

The story of Barnabas' Kinghood was a mystery that was whispered about in fruit stands and corner shops all throughout Nezmyth. He was once a reputable man of great respect—the Chief Captain over the Nezmythian Army under the rule of the previous ruler, King Thomas. They were best friends. King Thomas was a kind and decent soul that was loved by everyone for his kind spirit and fair judgment, and Captain Barnabas was always eager to serve him.

King Thomas didn't have a Queen, so he prayerfully selected Captain Barnabas to be his Inheritor, if King Thomas were to ever die while serving on the throne. Years passed, and Nezmyth dwelt in peace… but Captain Barnabas didn't. Months before the passing of King Thomas, his countenance changed. His eyes became colder, his heart became stone, and the people he once served grew to fear him like they would an angry boar. Suddenly, on a bitter winter's night, King Thomas mysteriously passed away, and Captain Barnabas rightfully took his place at the throne as His Majesty's Inheritor.

No one knows for certain how King Thomas died—details that make it past the castle gates are few—but only two things are certain: the passing of King Thomas was no accident, and speaking ill of King Barnabas is forbidden.

The silence continued. The soft prodding of wooden dishes and the scribble of Tomm's writing stick were the only sounds that occupied the dust hanging in the air. Jason's mind brooded over the fight earlier that day. He rehearsed every action and endlessly corrected himself. A frown contorted his face. He knew he should be thinking about something more positive, but due to recent events and the mention of his unwanted Kingship, he set down his fork and knife and stood from the table.

"Jason?" Kara asked concernedly.

"I'm going outside…" he replied.

The sulking of his beating heart carried Jason's feet to the battered door on the edge of the cabin. With a sharp tug, he unlatched the rusty lock. The sun spilt harsh light on him as he walked out and slammed the door behind him.

Although it was bright outside, a chilling wind swept the warmth of the sun away as Jason slunk his way around the edge of the cabin. Duos of Nezmythian soldiers—one in blue, one in red—patrolled the dusty street like hawks. The derelict people of Lower City avoided their eyes as they uneasily scurried by. Jason tried not to glare.

Leaves crunched under his feet and the surrounding trees dwarfed him as they reached toward the sky. The faint sounds of drunken shouting and dogs barking echoed from the slums of Lower City.

At the back of the cabin, hidden from the street, a familiar wooden bucket lay overturned against the side of the wall. Jason absentmindedly walked over and sat on it. He folded his arms and stared blankly ahead of him, leaning back against the wall. In the distance, beyond the bustle of the Market Triangle and Center Court, Nezmyth City sloped up to a hill that comprised the aristocratic Upper City. Elegant mansions graced the edges of the winding cobblestone streets like sugary sweets studding a wedding cake. At the very top of the hill, an enormous palace the hue of charcoal stood like a shadowy beacon against the skyline. It seemed to glare at Jason from miles away, a looming reminder of inevitability— Nezmyth Castle.

Jason tore his eyes from it. His attention shifted to the glove on his right hand. He turned about. No one but the whistling wind kept him company. Satisfied and comfortable that no one was watching, he carefully slid the glove from off his hand.

The hand was pale and supple compared to his left... evidence of the lack of sunlight it received. Jason balled his fist and extended his fingers in and out repeatedly. All the while, his eyes remained fixated on his palm. Just at the root of his index finger, three scars formed a triangle just bigger than his fingernail with one side of the triangle slightly bigger than the others. Inside, the skin shimmered with a glossy hue of burnt orange.

Jason's thumb grinded the strange mark... as if rubbing it hard enough would wear it away. Still, it glimmered with a polished sheen, resistant and steadfast.

A sigh billowed from his nostrils. Looking blankly ahead, he reached into his left pocket and pulled out a wooden flute no bigger than his hand and as thick as one of his fingers. Five holes dotted the top, with another hole on the bottom.

Jason let out another sigh has he placed his fingers on the holes and pressed the flute to his lips.

Soft, melodic whistles lightly flittered into the sky. Jason closed his eyes, blocked out the world. In his own artificial darkness he played and let the notes swell from his soul and out of his body. The shouts and noise of Lower City seemed to fade into nothingness. The stress... the frustration... the uncertainty... they mounted the backs of the flittering notes and rode with the wind, free and unhidden. Jason drank in the feeling.

"You always play your flyra when you're upset."

He nearly jumped out of his skin. Around the corner of the cabin, Kara had been observing her son silently. A rolled up piece of parchment with orange ribbon protruded from her hand. Jason glared at it with utter disdain. She smiled with worried eyes, trying to pick up the emotions that emulated from Jason. She came around the corner and pulled a small box next to Jason's bucket. As she sat down, Jason sternly and silently slipped the glove back on his hand.

"Maybe it's a special mark from the Dragon..." she said.

Jason frowned. "Perhaps." *Along with other unwanted things...*

"I'm sorry for the way I spoke to you earlier," Kara's voice softened. "But you must understand how delicate your situation is. We don't know if even the King knows that you've been Foreordained to take his place." Her voice died down to a whisper. "What do you think would happen if he knew?"

"He'd kill me," Jason said bluntly.

"That's right. And Nezmyth would continue to smolder until another King is Foreordained. And how long would that be? Another twenty years? Would Nezmyth even last that long?"

"But why does it have to be *me*?" Jason continued in a whisper. "I'm nobody! I'm just a Lower City rat that's always second at best! How am I supposed to lead a kingdom? Don't you think that the Dragon makes mistakes? That's how Barnabas became King."

"We don't know how Barnabas became king," Kara's eyebrows tightened. "No one knows for sure. But you and I both know the Dragon wasn't in it. The Dragon *never* makes mistakes. You were called for a specific purpose to be King, and although you don't understand it right now, someday you will."

Jason said nothing. A dark fist had wrapped itself around his heart, constricting it from feeling. Kara gazed upon him silently with a desperate hope that the words that she had said had sunk in to any degree. She let out a heavy exhale, closing her eyes, thinking. Finally, she opened her eyes and looked at Jason, her expression serious.

"How long has it been since you've read this?"

She was referring to the rolled-up piece of parchment in her hand. Jason refused to look at it.

"Long time," he said.

The parchment crackled and coiled as Kara straightened it out, as if it had been sleeping and was just waking up. Lines of jagged, hastily-written characters filled the page completely from top to bottom. The faint breeze wafted over the aging smell of ink.

"Do you remember the day we received this?"

"Yes…"

Kara half-smiled. "Your twelfth birthday, just over three years ago. You were so nervous… your father and I were sure that there was nothing to be concerned about. Whatever would come of you, the Dragon would be in it. And what a blessing it was to learn that *our son*… our precious Jason… was Foreordained to be the next King of Nezmyth."

The clenching feeling surrounding Jason's heart didn't dissipate. Kara cleared her throat and skipped to the bottom of his Blessing of Fate, where she read the last paragraph just loud enough for only Jason to hear.

"You will be a magnificent light that shines upon the world of Wevlia. You will imprison the vulture. You will restore the kingdom of Nezmyth to harmony and peace. Your blood is the blood of the next King of Nezmyth."

"I still don't understand why it has to be *me*, though..."
Jason said. "I'll never be ready to be a King..."

"Yes, you will. As long as you're doing what's right," Kara
rolled up the parchment and tied the orange string around it
again. "The Dragon has a way of preparing us for things to
come. Jason..."

She pulled her box around directly in front of Jason. He
knew that all to well—it's what she did whenever he tried to
lock her out of his heart. She looked deeply into his eyes as
she spoke. "You may not recognize it, but you have the
purest heart out of anyone I've ever met. You're kind...
you're wise... you may not understand why you were called
to do be King... but I promise that as you learn to put your
trust in the Dragon, someday you will."

Jason saw the reflection of his own eyes in his mother's.
The love that emanated from them was contagious, almost
enough to break down the stone barrier he had built around
himself. Her eyes sparkled, and her soft lips bent into a
smile. She ran her fingers through his matted brown hair,
pulled him close, and kissed him gently on the forehead.

"I love you, my son."

She brushed his hair one last time before getting up and
returning to the cabin. And once again, Jason found himself
alone. Through the love of his mother, the anger boiling
inside him had simmered down... and now only uncertainty
remained.

2 THE JOURNEY

Oblivion seemed to echo from the ancient walls of the Nezmyth City Cathedral. Dozens of pews lined themselves from the back wall to the front, silent and completely devoid of anxious churchgoers. All was still. At the front of the Cathedral, a podium stood where the Patriarch would regularly conduct sermons. Torches and candles occupied every wall, sending thin trails of smoke floating up to the vaulted ceiling. Crystal chandeliers hung single file and glimmered in the sunlight pouring through stained glass windows.

Several feet behind the podium, a platform rose to the height of a man, and on the platform three golden rods formed a triangle. One corner of the triangle pointed to the front wall, where a massive painting of the Holy Dragon hung, triumphant and eternal.

Master Ferribolt knelt on the platform. His knees and toes touched the floor as he sat on his heels. A silky orange robe spilled over his legs, and his strong hands rested upon his knees. His head bowed in reverence.

He breathed in... exhaled... then spoke.

"O Sacred Dragon... my spirit calls to thee this day. I can't help but feel a stirring within this city, and it causes me to feel... perplexed. Something is about to happen. The his eyes and his mouth began to water. A soft grumble emitted from his empty belly.

His lips curled into a grateful smirk and he said, "It's better than starving. Come on in."

Tarren withdrew into the shop and Jason crossed the threshold behind him. As he stepped inside, he noticed the potent smell of varnish that permeated from the flutes, pipes and drums hanging from the walls. He drank it deeply through his nose and let it out through his teeth.

The shop was slightly on the small side—several paces from wall to wall. A filthy desk and two dusty stools served as the only furniture in the entire room. Jason could see a smaller, darker room at the back with a straw mattress, waste bucket and water bowl.

"How did you get this?" Tarren inquired, lifting the bread in his hand.

"Golan back at the shop is very kind," Jason said. "He's from Upper City and his parents bake for the His Majesty occasionally. Whenever they throw out old bread or pastries, he brings it into the shop for us. He tries to get as much as he can before his parents give the rest to their other Upper City friends. It's never much... but like you said, it's better than starving."

"Isn't that typical?" Tarren said as he slunk over and sat down behind the desk. "A couple of Lower City rats like you and me picking up the crumbs of the Upper City folk." He stole a glance at the window before continuing on in a slightly lower voice. "The King keeps his helpers wealthy and demands payment from the rest of the kingdom. I heard it wasn't like this during King Thomas' reign."

Jason shushed him and peered over his shoulder out the window. It wasn't likely that soldiers would be patrolling down a remote alleyway, but Jason wasn't open to running the risk of being caught and thrown into prison. Meanwhile, Tarren scanned the haphazard array of tools strewn across his desk until he found a knife. He placed the bread on the desk and began to eagerly saw away at it, showering the desk with crumbs as he went. Jason stared absentmindedly out the window.

"Catch," Tarren said.

Jason turned just in time to see half of a loaf of bread soar toward him, wrapped in the same cloth he had given to Tarren. The chunk of bread fell right in his lap between his hands. He slid Tarren a disapproving look.

"Tarren, I had a biscuit on my way over. I don't need this——."

"Yes, you do," Tarren said. "Save it for later. You deserve it."

"I can buy half a loaf of bread."

"At the expense of what else?" Tarren retorted. "I know you're struggling just as much as I am, Jason. I can hear your stomach growling from across the room. Take it."

The bread rested like a soft stone in Jason's lap as he glared at Tarren. He knew there was no use arguing. It never changed the outcome any time before. He sheepishly smiled and said, "Thanks."

Tarren winked. "What are best friends for?"

With that, Tarren dove into his bread and munched on it greedily. Jason found his mind wandering... *How many weapons do we have to sell in order to make the King's tax this time? After it's paid, will we all have enough to eat? Pay for our lodging? How many people will be cast into prison, and how many will have to flee to the southernmost parts of Lower City?* In a flash, it seemed, Tarren had completely consumed the morsel and continued on to wipe his lips with the back of his hand.

"I think we need to celebrate on the occasion of this feast," he said. "Do you have your flyra?"

Jason nodded and reached inside his left pocket, "Always."

From beneath the desk, Tarren withdrew a blue flute about the length of his forearm that appeared to be decades old. It wasn't glossy or even painted, and black marks worn in by thick fingers were visible around the sound holes. Jason propped his tiny flyra between his fingers and held it to his mouth.

weapons we would be making Blocks more… have you been telling your friends at the combat gym about us?"

"Everyone I know," Jaboc replied. "But no one from Upper City trains at the gym I go to. Too ragged."

"Just trust in the Dragon, and things will turn out," Golan said with a hopeful grin and bright eyes. He had been standing on the other side of Jason, quietly listening.

Jason sneered at the comment as if it were a dim-witted joke and slipped his sword onto his back. *Trust in the Dragon…* All he said was, "I'll lock up tonight."

One by one, they all filed out of the shop, dragging their feet as they went. As Jason stepped outside, he locked the door tight and gave the bars on the window a shake. Still solid. He returned the keys to his pocket and began walking down the cobblestone street.

As he sun retreated behind the western horizon, he noticed other vendors and shop owners packing in for the night. Street vendors rolled up their rugs or picked up their carts, wearing expressions mixed with worry and fear. Jason knew that they too were thinking of the Harvest. His eyebrows creased as he paced and an unsettling feeling resided in his stomach, result of the abundance of uncertainty. *Who of these are going to prison this month?*

Finally, he reached a large brick building facing a street corner that branched into Lower City. The building was obviously decades old—mortar cracked between some of the bricks and the windows were foggy and dank. Two trees, equidistant to the stone walkway that led to the front door, budded with small leaves and gave a pleasing, symmetrical look to the derelict housing. Jason thought nothing of it as he made his way up the walkway and unlocked the creaky door.

A hallway met him as he crossed through the threshold and closed the door behind him. Dull floorboards creaked beneath his feet as he made his way to the end of the hall, where a ladder ascended to the floor above. Battered doors barely hanging on their hinges stood like tired soldiers against each wall, with the occasional muffled chatter sounding from the other side.

The people on the other side must be talking about the Harvest, too... Jason thought.

With each rung, Jason's mind swam around the Harvest as he ascended three floors of ladders. With each step, he felt like he was trying to push down the thoughts that kept trying to rise in his mind. When he reached the top, he turned right. He pulled his keys out of his pocket as he trudged down the hall. A thick sigh escaped his lips. At the very end of the hall, a battered door just like the rest appeared on his right, and he unlatched it with his key. He stepped inside and closed the door behind him, leaving the out the rest of the world.

He let out another heavy sigh as he surveyed his quarters. One square room, with a musty straw mattress pushed into a corner, a wooden chair, and a chest full of his belongings were his only company. It wouldn't be four paces before he would run into the far wall. He slipped off his sword and leaned it against the wall by his bed, followed by his jacket, which he threw on his trunk.

The chair creaked irritably as he plopped himself down in it. He closed his eyes and rested his head on the wall.

*Four hundred and eleven Blocks this month...*he thought to himself. *Enough for all of us to pay the soldiers for the Harvest, but barely enough to pay for all of our essentials after that. And what about the next Harvest? What about Tarren? I hope mum and dad have enough, too... there's no way they would survive if they had to flee to the southernmost parts of Lower City... it's dangerous down there...*

The dark feeling in his stomach didn't subside. He opened his eyes and stared out the small, dusty window on the opposite wall, seeing nothing but a sky full of stars. Jason pushed himself out of his chair and made his way to the window with slow, thoughtful steps.

"Nezmyth..." he thought out loud. "The Dragon has called me to lead you... I know you want a new King, someone to restore hope to you, someone to take away the tyranny and the fear…"

He propped his forearm against the window sill and put his nose just inches from the glass. Two moons and an array of sparkling stars hung in the black sky as they stood watch over the city. Smoke trickled upward from chimneys that stretched as far as the eye could see, emanating from cabins and huts with candles flickering in the windows. Jason blinked and exhaled.

"…but it's not me."

He turned about and slid down the wall into a sitting position, his mind still bogged with weary thoughts of the Harvest and his Foreordination. He pinched the middle fingertip of his right hand and slid the glove off, wiping his sweaty palm on his pants. His feelings beckoned for some mode of release. His hand was just about to reach into his pocket to retrieve his flyra when a knock came to the door.

Knock knock knock.

Jason froze and looked at the door. His eyebrows furrowed uncomfortably. *A visitor…? I never get visitors.*

"Hello?" he called.

No response.

He slipped the glove back onto his hand and picked up his sword. It found its way onto his back and he rubbed the sheath uncomfortably. When he unlatched the door and flung it open, his heart stopped.

Two Nezmythian soldiers, armed with swords and full armor, filled the doorframe with stony faces. Jason held his breath and he felt himself go pale, silently he was amazed that he didn't hear them coming up the ladder. The one on the right was the first to speak.

"Are you Jason?" he asked with a voice as deep and cold as a grave.

Jason's eyes darted from the right one to the left. *I haven't done anything wrong… the Harvest isn't for days… why are they here?*

He gulped and forced out, "I am."

Before he could react, the soldier on his left pulled back a fist and launched it at Jason. Jason felt the blow connect with his cheek like the kick of an angry mule. He felt the world disappearing. His legs slackened and his eyes rolled into the back of his head. Everything faded into black, and he fell to the cold, unforgiving floor, unconscious.

3 THE FORTRESS

A wasteland, cold and devoid of life, stretched to the horizon in every direction. Gray clouds that never breathed rain billowed in the sky, choking the sunlight that would peer through and give warmth and life to the earth. The air itself mixed with the smell of death and fear.

A mile away, a dead tree with writhing, white branches stood atop a lonely hill, casting a gloomy shadow over the parched soil. On the top branch, a vulture gazed out upon the wasteland, scanning the horizon as if something were to disturb his perch on the hill. Its icy eyes shielded the raging inferno inside its feathered head.

Suddenly, in the distance, the clouds retracted and a thin beam of sunlight shot to the ground like a golden thread that stretched to the sky. The vulture's eyes grew in horror as it looked on, its cragged beak falling open in wonder and fear.

Within the golden beam of light, a single seed, no larger than an acorn, slowly descended like a heavenly gift. As it approached the ground, the soil beneath it retracted open as if pulled by an invisible hand, making a small home for the seed to grow. The seed nestled into the tiny crater, and the soil pushed back over it again by the same invisible hand. The clouds closed, and the beam of sunshine dissipated.

Immediately, the vulture cried out in rage. It pushed itself off the branch, its eyes focused on the exact spot where the seed had been planted. It flapped its wings furiously, the inferno in its mind raging, the need to destroy, to uproot, completely overtaking it. It hadn't flown a hundred feet before an unseen force collided with it in midair.

A black eagle, valiant and strong, dug its claws into the vulture's body as it dive-bombed, sending the two birds plummeting toward the ground. The vulture fought and struggled, but the eagle's claws had dug in deep. Faster and faster they plummeted... the eagle only released its talons just moments before collision. The vulture crashed into the earth, kicking up a cloud of soil and dust while the eagle flapped gently to the ground. The vulture gasped and sputtered, its eyes filled with the purest loathing and disdain. The eagle stood on top of it, looking into its eyes intently.

"*I'll kill you!*" The vulture screeched. "*Do you hear me? I'll kill you!*"

"How will it be this time?" The eagle replied smoothly. "You've tried so many times before, but you lack the foresight that I have. Your anger has made you reckless."

"Anger makes one more powerful!" the vulture retorted. "Something a pathetic bird of principle like you will never understand."

"Oh, clearly," The eagle said. "But it is also apparent that your hatred has not impaired your judgment. You know what will become of that seed as well as I do. No matter... you can muster all the anger in the world, but I will not let you destroy that seed. This wasteland has stayed dry for long enough. It's time to breathe new life."

"It is *my* land," the vulture tried to stand, but the eagle pushed it back down. "And you cannot stop me from destroying it. I've come too far to be stopped by a mere seed."

"But it won't be simply a seed you are combating. You saw what took place. The seed is a gift from Above. You are battling forces beyond your control."

The vulture squinted. "Nothing is beyond my control. You will soon learn the consequences of underestimating me."

* * * * *

Jason's head swam and the left side of his face felt tender. Images of eagles and vultures became blurry and distorted. The grayness of the wasteland slowly faded into memory, replaced by something large and blue that took up his entire vision.

The ground shook softly and a faint crunching sounded in his ears, along with the sound of horse's hooves. It was still dark out. He felt something soft on his face. It didn't take long for Jason to recognize that he was lying on his side, but he wasn't on his bed back in his room. As he tried to sit up, he realized that his hands were immobile behind him, bound tightly with rope. Thankfully, he could still feel his sword strapped to his back.

"Good," a voice came. "You're awake."

Everything was still a blur. Jason couldn't match a face to the voice he had just heard. Grunting, he pushed himself up with what little strength he had. As he blinked hard, his starry eyes became clearer and he was able to pick up his surroundings. He sat in a bumping, jolting carriage on a bench that had to have been stuffed with feathers and upholstered with the finest cotton. The entire interior of the carriage was different shades of blue, from the curtains, to the benches, to the intricately-designed wallpaper. He heard the wheels crackle as they turned on the cobblestones of Nezmyth City streets.

Across from him, a man sat in crisply-polished armor, with a royal blue cape that fell from his shoulders to his calves. Wavy silver locks poured from his scalp and his burning red eyes were fixed on Jason. His right hand rested on the hilt of a sword that was fastened to his waist, and upon that hand, a ring with a blazing orange ruby graced his ring finger.

Jason tensed. Immediately, he knew who this man was. The ring is a symbol of a Foreordained servant of the Dragon, and only two people in Nezmyth are authorized to wear capes.

*The King wears a red cape…*Jason thought. *So this has to be the Advisor… and I'm in his royal carriage.*

Jason almost didn't move his lips. "Are you…?"

"The Advisor to His Majesty, King Barnabas," The Advisor didn't blink. "Yes. And your name is Jason, correct?"

Jason stiffly nodded his head.

The Advisor looked at him as if examining an insect of a strange species. "Very interesting…"

Cold sweat began forming on Jason's brow and the hair on the back of his neck bristled. *How does he know my name?* His eyes darted about, his head still swimming and his palms moist. The sleepy buildings of Nezmyth crept by as the carriage jittered down the road. *It looks like we're on the Southern Market Street…*

Jason eyed the Advisor nervously, "…Where are we going?"

"Nezmyth Castle," the Advisor replied.

A lump grew in Jason's throat. He wanted to ask why, but the greater part of him didn't want the answer. He silently hoped that it wasn't what he was thinking. However, the Advisor's next comment confirmed his fear.

"We know who you are, Jason," he said. "The knowledge of your Foreordination has evaded us for quite some time, but this night it has finally been brought to our attention. His Highness demands an audience with you immediately."

Jason's blood turned to ice. He almost lost consciousness again. His heart rate jumped and panic rose in his system like water over a boiling cauldron. *What is the King going to do to me? Kill me? Cast me into prison to be tortured for the rest of my life? What will he do to make sure he keeps the throne?* Immediately, he tugged at the ropes that bound his wrists together like a defenseless cub caught in a trap. His breaths became shorter. He tried to keep himself from shouting.

"*I'm sorry! I don't want this! I never wanted it!*" He cried. "*Please let me go, he can keep the kingdom! I'm not fit for the throne—!*"

Suddenly, he felt his tongue stick to the top of his mouth, stopping any words from escaping, the Advisor's red eyes fixed on him.

"There are traditional ways in which this meeting is carried out. It is my duty as His Majesty's Advisor to see to it that those rites are carried out as they have been for generations. I will escort you personally to the chamber of the King then it will be His opportunity to explain to you what must come to pass in the next year. Until then, you will refrain from speaking."

Jason felt his tongue release and his body slumped numbly into his seat. His head felt light again and a few times he felt reality start to fade. Not a word escaped his lips. Still, his heart felt like a beating war drum. Nezmyth City continued to crawl by in the carriage window. Jason stared at it, feeling very much like a trapped animal.

The next year? What is he talking about?

The carriage started to turn. Jason kept his eyes fixed on the window. He could feel his wrists starting to become raw from the rope. As the carriage continued to crawl, he could tell they had turned onto the Northern Market Street—the Market Street closest to Upper City.

The shops weren't the same brown, shanty, square shops that Jason was accustomed to on the Southern Market Street. These shops had intricately crafted signs and fine molding along the windows and doors. Expensive clothing and exotic flowers were seen on the other side of the windows. Flickering lanterns radiated an orange glow over the dark street. Even the iron bars over the windows seemed finely crafted.

Jason silently marveled at the sight. Although it was only a distant walk from one side of the Market Street to the next, he felt as though he had entered a different world. He imagined what it would be like to see well-dressed upper classmen shopping about the posh Northern Market Street in the middle of the day, with well-washed faces, spotless clothes and smiling faces.

Minutes passed before the carriage turned once more, this time on a street with a slight incline.

We must be travelling into Upper City... Jason thought. *Closer to the Castle...* A chill swept down his spine and he clenched his teeth to keep them from chattering.

The houses in Upper City were extravagant with pillars and porches—the homes of decorated military leaders, successful shop owners, and other aristocrats. Almost every home had a gate with a well-manicured lawn, along with hired soldiers to keep guard during the eerie hours of night. Nearly all of their windows were dark, as the masters of their homes had retired to bed. More street torches flickered to light the way along the stone path leading to the castle.

The path seemed to incline steeper and steeper while the mansions stayed perfectly level. As the incline started to decrease, however, Jason knew that their final destination was only minutes away. Just as the hill leveled out, he heard a voice from outside the gates.

"Good evening, sire," the gruff voice said.

The voice was followed by the sound of massive, creaking gates squealing open as if they hadn't been oiled in years. The carriage didn't slow as the horses trotted through. As they passed, Jason looked out the windows and saw the gates pass by that marked the perimeter of the Castle grounds. The massive iron fence stretched for hundreds of yards on each side and was guarded by beastly Nezmythian soldiers garbed in red or blue armor every ten paces. His heart fought to break out of his ribcage and he struggled to control his breathing.

The bumpy grinding of cobblestone gave way to the smooth churning of wheels on marble. As they rode by, Jason brought himself to look upon the once-famous castle grounds. What he saw made his heart sink in disappointment. He leaned over in his seat, his mouth hanging open in crestfallen awe.

The castle grounds once had a reputation for being green and lush, miraculously, without the care of any gardeners or caretakers. Nezmythians would come from all over the kingdom just to get a glimpse of the tropical plants and vegetation that grew in the King's garden. The enchanting smells and sights bombarded the senses in a hypnotizing landslide of color and fragrance.

Children were allowed to come with their mothers to pick delicious fresh fruit for their families. Sometimes the King himself would even come out to mingle with the commoners. In King Thomas's case, the people would rush forward to shake his hand or kiss his feet.

Now it was all dead. Nearly all of it was cold, black soil, completely devoid of life. Jason shook his head and looked at the floor of the carriage bitterly, mouthing some words of deflation.

The carriage turned sharply and pushed Jason to the side of his seat. Jason peered out the window again.

In the middle of the road, a tall stone statue of a noble Nezmythian Knight pointed his sword triumphantly to the sky. The corner of Jason's mouth twitched upward. *At least there's one thing here that isn't dead.*

But upon further inspection, Jason discovered that it wasn't a statue at all—it was a fountain. The water had completely dried up. The parched work was nothing but a dusty statue that protruded on the stone road, halfway between the gates and the castle.

After more chilling silence, the carriage staggered to a halt. "We have arrived," the Advisor said.

A deathly feeling resided in Jason's stomach, bordering on nausea. The chill of the night felt unforgiving. The twinkle of the stars shed neither light nor warmth upon his worried heart. He felt trapped. And his fate was in the hands of another—one whose reputation was diabolical.

Suddenly, the carriage door flung open. A pleasant-looking man with lamb chop sideburns and a pipe exhaled a smoky breath as he tipped his hat to Jason.

"Good evening," he said.

"After you," the Advisor commanded.

Jason looked into those red eyes. They seemed to be as a brick wall, without feeling. He tried to sense some glimmer of humanity behind those eyes, but could feel nothing. He silently wondered how long he had been like this. *Had he been the Advisor during King Thomas' reign?* He looked away, ducked his head down, and stepped down out of the carriage.

Immediately, his breath escaped him. He had never seen Nezmyth Castle up close. It stood as an ancient behemoth, completely overtaking his vision, as it towered to the sky like a black, ghostly cathedral. A massive set of doors separated Jason from the inside, accompanied by a set of royal guards. Stained-glass windows dotted the walls of the edifice, and above the doors, the largest one—a Nezmythian Knight pointing an orange sword to the sky, much like the parched fountain in the middle of the castle grounds.

Jason tried to flush out the lump in his throat as the Advisor stepped out of the carriage behind him. He nearly jumped out of his skin when he felt the Advisor grab his bound wrists. Magically, the ropes slackened and fell from Jason's hands onto the marble walkway. The Advisor simply continued on by. Jason rubbed his wrists, trying to soothe the raw skin. He shivered uncontrollably and his heart fought to break out of his chest.

"How long has it been like this?" Jason asked as he gazed upon the dead grounds. He immediately flushed as he remembered that there was to be no more speaking until he confronted the King.

The Advisor stopped and looked back at Jason, as if debating whether or not to respond to the question. Jason felt himself shrink a few inches. After a long moment, the Advisor spoke.

"Twenty years," he said. "...And the castle was white."

Jason let that statement hang in the air. As he stood in the shadow of the castle, in the grounds dominated by death, he thought to himself, *It's like this place has been cursed... nothing wants to grow here so long as its governed by a ruler with a wicked soul...*

"Come!" The Advisor barked. Jason looked at the ground and followed behind.

The Advisor walked swiftly toward the castle doors. The castle seemed to grow taller in Jason's eyes as they approached it. He wiped the sweat off his forehead with the back of his hand and rubbed the sheath of his sword. When he looked back at the carriage, he noticed the driver sitting on his perch above the cabin, leaning back calmly and smoking his pipe. He noticed Jason's stare and lifted his pipe confidently in the air. It was hard to distinguish, but he also thought he saw him wink.

Jason teased a half-smile. Part of him thought it amazing that the man could be so positive in a place like this, and the larger part of him thought the man was completely daft for being so oblivious to the horror that awaited just beyond those doors.

Finally, they reached the doors. Both soldiers nodded at the Advisor.

"Good evening, sire," they said in unison.

The Advisor nodded in return. One soldier bent down to pick up an exceptionally large mallet that had been lying by his side. Jason looked on in awe as the soldier hoisted the giant hammer off the ground and swung it three times against the door.

BOOM... BOOM... BOOM...

He could hear the sounds reverberate in the inside hall. Each breath that came and left was shaky and uncomfortable. Jason knew that King Barnabas... the dictator he was born to replace, the culprit behind the fear, the poverty, the tyranny, was directly behind that door. And he was utterly alone, on the top of a shadowy hill with no one to comfort him. He gripped the sheath of his sword as if holding on to life itself.

Like a giant awakening from slumber, the doors slowly began to open. In that moment, the Advisor turned around to face Jason.

"Do not speak unless requested to do so," he said. "It is customary that you shall walk in first, followed by me closely behind. When you approach the throne, kneel on one knee, head bowed, and do not rise until His Majesty permits it. And whatever you do"—those red eyes became even more fierce—"do not say *anything* that could possibly upset the King. He is growing tired of cleaning the blood from the floor."

The Advisor turned back around. Jason nearly vomited.

Dragon, help me, he thought.

emotion as they rested upon Jason. He carried on the King's lecture:

"The Year of Decision is the year in which every Foreordained King must make their final decision on whether or not to rise to their Foreordination. Yours starts tonight. If you so choose to accept your Foreordination, one year from today you will be established as the new King of Nezmyth. But that is not all that the Year of Decision entails."

King Barnabas' icy eyes became sharper, and he took over again:

"During your Year of Decision, we will be testing you in various ways to be sure you possess the qualities of a King of Nezmyth. You must be wise... brave... virtuous... just. If you fail any of these tests, you will be disqualified for the throne, and I will continue my rule as if you were never called. Your standing will be measured through this..."

The Advisor approached the veiled pedestal that stood beside the Throne. With one swift movement, he swiped the purple sheet off, revealing a stone pillar reaching to the height of his elbows. On top of the pedestal, three prongs held up a glassy orb the size of Jason's head, and inside the orb, pale blue smoke billowed and swirled as if it were a living thing. Jason's felt something mysteriously swell inside him as he gazed upon it, as if the orb were trying to tether with him somehow.

"The Oracle Stone," the Advisor said. "As old as the kingdom of Nezmyth—an unbreakable device forged and blessed by the Patriarchs of Old. It generates a link between itself and the Foreordained Kings at the beginning of their Year of Decisions. The hue of the smoke will change depending upon the purity of your heart—a radiant white if your heart is pure or black if your heart has surrendered to darkness.

"In order to create the bond between you and the Oracle Stone, you must hold it and gaze into its depths. You will do so now. After which, you will not be allowed to view the

Oracle Stone until the day of your coronation. If you do manage to view it before then, you will be disqualified for the Throne."

King Barnabas pushed himself up from the throne, stalked over to the Oracle Stone, and slowly slid his hand underneath it. As he lifted it up from the prongs that held it still, the smoke inside the Stone became agitated and began swirling violently. The pale blue color dropped rapidly to a dark, murky purple. Inside, Jason felt sick. He could *feel* the Oracle Stone, however faintly, tremble with fear in the hands of the King. He wanted to cry out, to tell the King to stop whatever he was doing to it, but the pain the Oracle Stone experienced was caused by the filthiness of the King's soul, not by anything he was currently performing.

King Barnabas made his way over to Jason and eyed him loathingly before dropping the Oracle Stone into his hands. Jason looked deeply into the smoke, his hands cradling the perfectly smooth surface. It was surprisingly light. The link the Stone had already been trying to forge from a distance instantly became palpable. Jason swore he felt it breathe a sigh of relief as it found itself in a pair of new hands. Faintly, a deep, soft rumbling distantly sounded like the echo of a sleeping giant and instilled peaceful warmth into Jason that he didn't consider possible.

The purple smoke dissipated, and in its place, a calm cloud swirled silently, deep and yellow like an egg yolk. Jason had indeed felt as though the very essence of his soul had been read and copied into the inner depths of the Stone, cast into something visual and measurable through the hue of the yellow smoke.

"So during the next year," King Barnabas yanked the Oracle Stone from out of Jason's hands. The peaceful feeling left Jason, but the Stone maintained the deep yellow color even as King Barnabas marched back and returned it to the pedestal. "We will be maintaining a close eye on you to make sure you are passing these tests. The Year of Decision is considered to be one of the most difficult years in the life of a

King, and rightfully so. You will not be warned beforehand, so you would be wise to prepare yourself for these challenges, as they will come as quiet as a street mouse, or as thunderous as an army. But no matter..."

King Barnabas turned around and stalked back in Jason's direction with eyes full of bloodlust. Jason felt frozen in his seat. He gripped his sword again. The King advanced closer and closer until his face was mere inches from Jason's nose. His burly hands gripped the armrest's of Jason's chair and he hissed through his teeth.

"You will *not* be King. I do not wish you to be King. You do not deserve to be King. You are nothing but a Lower City commoner... how could you possibly know the affairs of ruling a kingdom? Fools like Ferribolt may say that under the Dragon weaklings like you can become mighty, but your success will be just as fictional as that Dragon is. I promise you, I will maintain my throne by *whatever means necessary*. You have my word."

Jason felt all the color leave his face. King Barnabas painfully released the armrests of Jason's chair and stepped back onto the platform, still glaring at Jason with unfiltered disdain. A thousand things ran through Jason's mind as he sat with a wearily-beating heart, and a clenched jaw trying to chatter.

But I don't want *to be King! What are these tests going to be? And if I don't want to be King to begin with, does it matter if I pass? And what does he mean by 'whatever means necessary?' Does that mean he's going to kill me...?*

"Do you have any questions?" The Advisor said monotonously.

Many, Jason thought. *But none I want to ask out loud.* The glowering gaze of King Barnabas made Jason seal his lips shut. After a moment's hesitation, he shook his head, not making eye contact.

"Good," the King said. "Now leave me. I wish you luck, Jason, but mark my word... you will *not* be King of Nezmyth. I swear it."

With that, the Advisor left his spot by the King's side and stepped down from the platform, flicking his wrist as a signal for Jason to follow as he walked by. Shakily, Jason pushed himself out of his chair and slipped his sword onto his back.

Just as he had turned about to follow the Advisor, an eruption of cracks and snaps echoed through the hall. Jason leapt as he realized the sound came from right next to him. The chair he sat in just a moment ago lay in a heap as if crushed by a massive, invisible boot. Just yards away, King Barnabas sat in his throne with his hand outstretched toward the wreckage, his eyes focused on Jason. His lip curled.

"Also..." he seethed. "You are to tell *no one* of your Year of Decision, or I do the same to you. Understood?"

Jason's heartbeat didn't slow. Trying to flush out the lump in his throat, he gulped and forced out, "Yes, Your Highness."

King Barnabas lowered his arm while keeping his icy gaze fixed on Jason. Jason followed a few yards behind as the Advisor made his way down the narrow red carpet. The massive doors cracked open with the heave of the soldiers, spilling out the night air. Every soldier watched as Jason and the Advisor left the cathedral of shadows and walked out into the night, the doors closing behind them.

5 THE MENTOR

The last few hours passed like a dream—a terrible, terrible dream. The Advisor dropped off Jason without a word back at his residence on the rim of Lower City. Jason felt conquered by a mix of fear and confusion. His mind repeatedly played back every word that came from the mouth of King Barnabas about the Year of Decision and the trials that lay ahead. The questions hadn't ceased. He stood numbly staring at the faded bricks of his home for several minutes until he feared some unknown marauder sent by the King to kill him, which made him sprint for the door and escape to the shelter of his room.

He tried to sleep. He stared for what felt like hours at the ceiling, trying to calm his mind, trying to speak counterfeit words of comfort to himself. The room that he abode in had lost all feeling of rest, but instead had taken on the aura of a small wooden cell. No longer private. No longer safe.

Who could be watching me right now?

His heart yearned for solitude—an absolute haven, far from the reaches of the King and the Year of Decision. *But where?* King Barnabas had cast a dark sheet of fear and control over the entire kingdom. Where could he go that would be away from his watchful eyes? Jason thought that this must be like the feeling of a small animal, trapped in a cage under the eyes of a greedy poacher.

What will tomorrow hold? What trials are just around the corner? What is he going to do? Will anyone I love get hurt? Is it worth putting them in danger when I don't even want to be King to begin with?

Too many questions... no answers. A dark entity blossomed wider inside Jason's heart. King Barnabas has all the kingdom's resources in his disposal in order to eradicate Jason's chance of becoming King... and Jason has nothing.

It's impossible...

What, then? Surrender? No... the Year of Decision goes for the next year, whether I want it or not... *But I can't just sit here, waiting for the first trial to come... what then?*

Jason sat up.

...Escape.

Where? I could stay with Kristof in the southern region of the kingdom... but the King would still be able to find me there.

Flee the kingdom.

Jason froze. He had never been outside the kingdom before. Come to think of it, he hadn't heard much of anything concerning any of the bordering kingdoms as he grew up, just some of their names. Nezmyth is self-sufficient in terms of food and ore, so there has never been need to trade with other kingdoms. What lies beyond the border?

A canopy from the watchful eyes of the King.

Yes... perhaps that's the thing to do... I know that the kingdom of Unbuntye lies just to the west... I could travel through the southern pass... but what about those at the shop and Tarren? Mum and dad? They'll be worried about where I've gone...

Jason crawled over and threw his trunk open, sifting through the contents until he found a scrap of parchment and a writing stick. With quivering hands and a rapidly-thumping heart, he formed the words:

> Dear Friends and Family,
> Due to reasons I can't explain, I felt it
> necessary to flee the kingdom. Please know

that this decision was very difficult, but that I
felt it necessary for my own safety. I love
you, and I'll miss you dearly. Thank you for
all of the love and care you have always
showed me.

Jason

Jason folded the letter into thirds and left it on his bed.
I'm sure someone will find it when they come looking for me... His
heart felt torn into several pieces. On one hand, he felt an
overwhelming hand of shame hovering over him. The
cowardice of abandoning the kingdom—let alone his friends
and family—for his personal interest was despicable. But on
the other hand, his inevitability of failure loomed even closer
to his darkening heart. Escape seemed to be the only
reasonable option.

Everything was a blur. He slipped his sword onto his
back... he climbed down the ladder to the bottom level of
the building... he walked westward on the cobblestone
streets... he walked and walked through the bitter chill until
he reached the walls that marked the perimeter of Nezmyth
City.

The stone walls only stood a dozen feet high—they had
been erected thousands of years ago. Enormous watchtowers
of strong timber stood sentinel over the city walls, manned by
wary Nezmythian guards. They paid no heed to a single boy
trudging down the street toward the edge of the city. Jason
passed through a gap in the wall barely large enough to fit a
carriage, guarded by two Nezmythian soldiers that eyed him
threateningly but took no action.

Before Jason lie grassy hills as far as he could see. A
brittle breeze caressed the green, which swayed sleepily in the
pale moonlight. Birds cawed in the distance. A crusty dirt
road stretched on until it reached the crest of a hill, where it
disappeared from view. Jason pressed on, sure that it would
lead to his destination.

Jason imagined the faces of Golan, Jaboc and Bertus as they arrived at the shop the following morning to find Jason nowhere present. He imagined his parents worryingly discussing at the table why he would leave so suddenly, without so much as a goodbye. He thought of Tarren, utterly alone in his music shop, struggling to decipher how he would attain his next loaf of bread.

When Jason finally reached the top of the hill, the road split into two separate paths. A sign at the split marked the destination of each path. An arrow pointing left read "SOUTHERN PLAINS" while another, pointing right, read "WESTERN WOODS." A large rock big enough to sit on rested before the sign.

Jason turned about to gaze upon Nezmyth City. The castle in the far distance seemed almost hidden by the black sky. Not a single house, hut or cottage had a candle flickering in the window. All was still. The city slept, unaware that its prosperity hung in the balance, and that its one hope was walking away.

How could you...? You coward...

There's no way! It's hopeless!

But you're their only chance...

What does it matter? I'm outmatched in every way. It's hopeless.

The conflict within bubbled and boiled until it made Jason's eyes mist. His chin tightened and his jaw clenched. He felt the shame radiate and pour from every limb in his body until his gloved right hand shot for his sword, tore it out of its sheath, and threw it to the ground. It clanged in the dust, rebounding hazy moonlight into Jason's eyes. His fists quivered angrily.

"*It's not me!!*" he cried into the darkness.

"Oh, it's absolutely you. I read the Blessing myself years ago."

Jason nearly leapt out of his skin and flipped about. Mysteriously, a pudgy bald man that he hadn't seen previous was sitting upon the rock underneath the road sign, chewing on some grass and looking intently at Jason. His silver eyes twinkled behind a pair of round spectacles.

It took several gawky moments for Jason to find his tongue. *The only other person that would read my Blessing of Fate beside my parents would be...* "Master Ferribolt...?"

Master Ferribolt's eyes sparkled and a grin graced his rosy cheeks. "The last remaining Chief Patriarch on this dark world that we live in. If you're hoping to find refuge in the kingdom of Unbuntye, I would strongly advise against it. It fell to Darkness ages ago, along with every other kingdom in Wevlia."

Jason's heart sank at the remark. His eyes fell to the ground. "I just don't know what to do..."

"Well, at this point you have two options," Master Ferribolt continued, adjusting himself on the rock. "You can flee to the kingdom of Unbuntye, as you've planned, and discover what an awful, evil place it's become over the course of years. Or you can remain in the kingdom of Nezmyth and do what the Holy Dragon has called you to do."

"Well, Master," Jason said slowly. "Neither of those are good options... If I flee the kingdom, Nezmyth is doomed, but if I stay, Nezmyth is doomed anyway. It's me against King Barnabas, and he's so powerful. There's no possible way I can pass my Year of Decision, even if I wanted to be King."

"Oh, yes there is."

A staccato escaped Jason's lips. "Then I would love for you to explain! Because the way I see it, it's hopeless."

Master Ferribolt's eyes twinkled again. Jason had never seen eyes like that before. The peculiarity didn't come from the color or the size, but from the light that glowed from behind them. There was no guile, no treachery, just soft understanding and unbiased caring. It caused Jason to soften his heart a little, but only a little.

"Jason..." he began. "Long ago, we lived far away as spirits in a place called the First Life. In First Life, there was The Holy Dragon. The Holy Dragon created numberless worlds, including the world of Wevlia, which we now live. We lived with the Dragon in harmony and peace for eons as we waited for the day where we could experience mortality, but the time wasn't right."

Jason's eyes fixed on the Chief Patriarch. The story already rang a familiar bell in the inner banks of his memory.

"Over time, one of our leaders, The Guardian of the Night, grew a desire to rule the worlds that the Dragon created. The Dragon refused due to the Guardian's recklessness and pride, and out of jealous spite, the Guardian rallied as many of our kin as he could to defeat the Dragon. To aid him in his quest, the Guardian of the Night used the power of Darkness to taint the minds of our brothers and sisters in order to assist him in accomplishing his evil purposes.

"Thus, the War Against Darkness commenced. The followers of the Dragon—including you and me—battled against the forces of Darkness in an immense clash. At length, the Guardian of the Night and those who succumbed to his power were defeated, and they were cast out. Now their spirits wander the worlds that the Dragon created, including our world, invisible to our eyes.

"It was then that the Holy Dragon saw fit to send us to mortality, to learn and experience the things that only come with a mortal body—hot and cold, hunger and contentment, joy and pain. And now that we're here, the Dragon stands guardian over our world, the world of Wevlia, to watch over us and protect us from the forces of Darkness."

"Yes, the Legend of the Formation..." Jason thought out loud. "I remember hearing that story as a child. But how did the Dragon decide to protect us from the forces of Darkness?"

Master Ferribolt nodded and continued. "The Holy Dragon knew that we would be weak during mortality—imperfect, easily susceptible to corruption through the whisperings of those evil spirits that wander—so It organized a government of Foreordination. The Dragon chose men with righteous spirits, who would oppose the powers of Darkness, to lead the people before they were even born. Doing so would serve as a barrier, preventing men with evil hearts from ever obtaining positions of power."

"So how did Barnabas become King?" Jason asked with a creased brow.

Master Ferribolt's expression became serious. "Barriers can occasionally be broken, and the Holy Dragon will not interfere with the free will of others. Very rarely, evil men manage to slip through the cracks of justice and obtain the power they lust after, but very rarely. Every time, another noble soul is Foreordained to take their place, and their reign comes to an end."

"I don't feel like a noble soul, though..." Jason said. "After all, I decided to run away..."

"A rash decision, yes, made by someone who was frightened and confused, as we sometimes are," Master Ferribolt responded. "But you still haven't left, have you? You can still choose to stay."

Jason didn't say anything; he simply glared at the ground. Master Ferribolt leaned closer.

"Jason... every man, at some point in his life, is given a challenge, and with that challenge comes a choice. He can choose to yield to fear and let greatness pass by, or become something greater than he once was, and triumph."

"Become something greater..." Jason echoed. "But how? Barnabas is *King*. He has everything he could ever need to stop me from succeeding, even if he didn't have legions of soldiers at his command. I've seen him. I've seen how strong he is. I've seen the magic he possesses. What am I to all of that?"

"Have you been paying attention to anything I've said?" Master Ferribolt retorted. "The reason I'm sitting here talking to you is to teach you that the King isn't in charge of Nezmyth's fate, *the Dragon is!* The Dragon will give you power to overcome, but you *must* be willing to become what you must be. That is the only way!"

Jason paused, letting the words sink in. Finally, he looked into the Chief Patriarch's eyes and said, "...and if I don't want to?"

"Then you have doomed us all."

Silence. Jason's eyes dropped. The words echoed within Jason's mind, racking his soul with a mix of shame and terror. The two said nothing and didn't make eye contact. The sea of grass continued to sway in the moonlight as the distant stars sleepily trickled down their feeble light. It almost felt like two invisible hands were pulling Jason... one toward the neighboring kingdom, and one back to Nezmyth City.

"I remember feeling the same way you do right now," Master Ferribolt finally said with a feeble smirk. "Why me? That was the question I constantly asked myself. I didn't consider myself anything special, and I surely didn't consider myself a more spiritual person than the next. My Year of Decision came in my early twenties. The training to become a Patriarch was rigorous and demanding, and I wasn't even sure myself if I wanted it. After all, it was a lot of pressure. Patriarchs no longer exist in any other kingdom, so the Nezmythian Patriarchs are the last remaining line."

"What changed your mind?" Jason asked, his interest piquing.

Master Ferribolt inhaled and let out a thick sigh. "I finally had to learn to push myself aside for the greater good. The knowledge didn't come all at once, but over time. I'm just one man, and the Holy Dragon had given me a responsibility—a calling. I could rise up to that calling by learning humility and faith, or I could shrink and live the rest of my years in shame... haunted by my cowardice."

Jason felt like a bolt of lightning had ripped through his heart. Master Ferribolt had summed up all of his feelings for the past five years, let alone the past day. But he still felt both hands pulling him toward Unbuntye, and toward Nezmyth City. He knew he needed to rise up and be a man... but how, he wasn't so sure.

"But I'm here, aren't I?" Master Ferribolt's eyes twinkled again. "I learned to trust in the Dragon's power, and it has never failed me. Jason, it's time to forget yourself and rise up to who you are meant to be. The kingdom needs you—the *world* does. This next year will definitely not be easy, but I assure you, I'll be with you for every step as a mentor, and as a friend. You don't need to go this alone. Please... don't give up. It will only bring regret."

They both faced each other for several minutes, not speaking a word. The weight of the calling he held started to float down upon Jason, along with the Chief Patriarch's words swirling in his conscience. Failure seemed imminent, but the glow that came from the Chief Patriarch was contagious—like a spark in the heart of the deepest, darkest forest that has a small chance of catching fire.

I don't understand why I have to be King... I don't know if I ever will. But do I want to live the rest of my life in shame? What will happen to the kingdom if I leave? What will happen if I stay...? It's nice to have the Chief Patriarch for support, but will that change anything?

"Will you stay?" Master Ferribolt asked softly.

Jason didn't speak immediately, but after a long wait, he simply looked at the ground and nodded.

"I'll stay..." he breathed.

Master Ferribolt smiled, "Well done, Jason, future King of Nezmyth. You're a courageous man. Now please... take up your sword and kneel."

Jason had almost entirely forgotten his sword lying on the ground next to him. As he stooped down to pick it up, Master Ferribolt stood from the rock. Jason took a step forward and knelt in front of him, the point of his sword stuck in the ground and his gloved right hand firmly around the handle. Master Ferribolt placed his hands together, his thumbs and index fingers forming a triangle just inches above Jason's forehead. He breathed deep and exhaled.

"Jason," he said. "By the Dragon's Fire, I bless you with courage and strength, that you will be able to overcome the powers of Darkness in this coming year. Be strong, believe, and you will be victorious."

A warm, tingling sensation started at Jason's scalp and trickled down his body until it spilled out of his fingers and toes. The darkness evaporated from within him, and he was instead filled with peace, as if it were possible to bathe in spring sunlight. When the Chief Patriarch had released his hands, Jason stood and sheathed his sword, still not making eye contact.

"That was incredible. I've never felt anything like that before."

Master Ferribolt smiled. "Jason, I want you to visit me every week during your Year of Decision. My estate and the Cathedral are a refuge from the watchful eyes of the King, and there I will teach you the things and ways of the crimson cape. Agreed?"

Jason nodded.

"Wonderful," Master Ferribolt said. "Now return home and rest. Dawn will soon be upon us. I'll send a message to your friends at your shop so they won't be concerned as to your whereabouts. This next year will not be easy, Jason, but it is not impossible. That, I can assure you."

Jason thanked the Chief Patriarch feebly and slowly made his way back down the hill. As he turned about to look where the Chief Patriarch had been standing, he saw no one there. He had vanished as mysteriously as he had appeared.

When Jason returned to his room, the sun was just beginning to peek over the horizon. The note of his abandon still lay on his bed. After tearing it up, he slipped fast asleep.

His mind was still racked with uncertainty, but the warm feeling still hadn't gone from his heart.

6 THE BLACKNOTE

Flittering notes from Jason's flyra hovered to the ceiling of his cramped room. A hardened, half-eaten morsel of bread—the one Tarren refused to accept—rested on his trunk along with a half-empty jug of water. He sat with his legs crossed on his mattress, his eyes shut, closing out the dark uneasiness that coats the kingdom on every day of the Harvest. A small pouch with one hundred Blocks sat silently by his side, along with his empty right glove.

Eight months in a year, and the Harvest comes every four... He thought. *Who is going to prison today?*

Jason replayed and reflected on the events of the past few days over and over in his head—his abduction to the castle... the confrontation with King Barnabas... the Year of Decision... Master Ferribolt. It felt like a lifetime had passed. Three days prior, Jason had been living from day to day only focused on making enough money for the Harvest, but that version of him had gone, and he now fought a silent battle for the fate of Nezmyth. His Foreordination was no longer an unpleasant thought he kept stored in the back of his mind, untouched and undisturbed, but a blaring reminder of who he is and the obligation he held.

He couldn't help but feel like a stray mutt trapped in a cage, forced to fight another dog much larger and meaner than himself. Hopelessness was in great supply, and the only thing that kept him rooted in Nezmyth City was the promise of a wise Chief Patriarch that hope was still there.

One week, Jason thought. *And the King hasn't done anything to test me yet... what is he planning...?*

It had been hours of quiet waiting. Jason eventually grew tired of playing music and his legs had grown stiff. He pocketed the flyra and pushed himself onto his feet, giving his arms and legs a stretch. Bright sunlight shot through the small window on the opposite wall, illuminating the dust particles that floated in the air. He walked over and peered out.

A deathly hush had nestled over the city. Not a single commoner was seen on the street—everyone is commanded to stay inside their homes on the day of the Harvest. The only people that travelled were soldiers, in pairs, accompanied by money carriages guarded by more soldiers. Jason's eyes scanned the cityscape. He knew that no soldier would bother to visit the southernmost parts of Lower City—no one down there would possibly have money for the Harvest and the money carriages would be pilfered by the legions of street urchins, no matter how many soldiers stood guard.

As he continued to scan, he noticed a group of soldiers marching towards Lower City from the Southern Market Street. A large cart drawn by a horse was nearly half full of small boxes and pouches. By each corner of the cart, a red- or blue-armored soldier followed closely, eyeing his surroundings with weapon in hand. Another pair of soldiers followed them knocking on each door they passed by.

That's odd... Jason thought. *They usually have another prison carriage with them to haul away people that can't pay the Harvest...*

Jason watched the money-collectors approach a door. They knocked, and the door swung open slowly to reveal a ragged-looking man with a grim face. A woman who had to have been his wife stood closely behind. The man dropped a small pouch into the soldier's hand, speaking frantically and shaking his head. Jason's heart sank.

He doesn't have enough... Jason thought. *What are they going to do to him?*

After the man's plea, the soldier in red handed the pouch back and began speaking back to him. The soldier in blue left the door and went for the money cart. From the side of the money cart, he pulled out a small wooden sign with a large black dot painted on it.

The other soldier continued to speak to the two house owners and their faces became darker with every word. The soldier with the sign proceeded to draw a hammer and nail from a pocket on his side, and hammer the sign next to the door. When he had finished, the two soldiers left the house and promptly continued to the next door. The grim-faced man and his wife stood in their open doorway, sharing expressions of terror before the woman burst into tears. The door quickly closed in front of them.

Jason's eyebrows furrowed, trying to make sense of what he just saw. They weren't imprisoned or even beaten, but they seemed shaken up by the sign that had just been nailed to the side of their door. *What is it?*

Suddenly, he heard footsteps ascending the ladder out in the hallway—thick footsteps from heavy boots.

Soldiers... he thought.

He stepped over to his bed and slipped on his glove, along with his sword that had been resting against a wall close by. He rubbed the sheath of his blade and paced the floor, listening to the footsteps of the soldiers as they visited every door in the hallway.

At length, the knock finally came to Jason's door. With a perturbed haze drifting in his stomach, he crossed the floor and unlatched the door handle. Two soldiers filled up the doorframe, one in blue and one in red. Jason remembered the moment just days ago were a pair of soldiers knocked him unconscious at his doorstep, but the memory resided for only a fraction of a second.

"Harvest," the red soldier growled, his hand outstretched.

Jason dropped the pouch in his hand. "One hundred Blocks. All of it."

The red soldier nodded and handed the pouch to the blue soldier, who pulled the pouch open to inspect the quantity. Satisfied, he stuffed it away in a larger pouch he carried by his side. Jason expected them to leave without delay… but they didn't.

"An announcement from His Majesty," the red soldier said.

Jason's eyebrows bent.

"His Majesty, King Barnabas, has declared that after this day of Harvest, the tax will be raised to one-hundred and twenty Blocks as opposed to the previous one-hundred Blocks."

Jason's jaw fell and his eyes widened. The soldier continued.

"The King realizes this is an increase that may be difficult for some of the poorer class to pay, so he has devised a plan in his mercy. If you find yourself in the position that you cannot pay the tax in full, you will be Blacknoted. A sign will be placed on the side of your door indicating that you were not able to pay the full tax, and you will not be expected to pay for one more month.

"The penalty for failing to pay, however, is indefinite mandatory service at the gold mines of the eastern mountains. The service will be rendered by the head of the house. While at the mines, you will be provided with food and a bed, and will work from sunup to sundown. Any attempt to remove the Blacknote after it has been placed will result in immediate imprisonment."

He had heard of the mines before. Dozens of shanty villages carved out of mountainsides were the homes for the pale-skinned, burly men that live there. Stories and rumors surfaced in his mind of thick dust clogging lungs, insect-ridden beds, meager rations, and infrequent baths accompanied by backbreaking labor in cramped spaces.

Ice water flushed through Jason's veins. Immediately he thought of Tarren, his parents, and the others at the shop. *How are we all going to afford that? And how would any of us fare at those mines?* As he remembered that Tarren had been short of the tax a few days ago, his heart dropped into his stomach and he felt his face go white.

"That is all," the red soldier said. With that, they spun on their heels and backtracked down the hall, leaving Jason standing in the doorway with shaky hands and a light head. He stood like that, numb, until he heard the footsteps fade down the ladder and disappear into oblivion. His heart wanted him to race down the ladder and sprint all the way to his parents' home and Tarren's shop, but his head knew better.

I can't leave for the rest of the day, he thought angrily. *Unless I want to risk being beaten or thrown into prison... or both.*

He slammed the door shut and paced the floor again, his brain stewing.

This is so sudden... a twenty Block raise from the previous tax! That's absurd... unreasonable... it can't be coincidence... this has to be one of my trials. But how is this supposed to test me, and why would King Barnabas want to punish the kingdom further for my sake?

Again, too many questions, and no answers. Nothing could be done until the following day, after the Harvest had come and gone. Jason growled and kicked the chest by his bed. Although it was late afternoon, he silently resolved to try to sleep as much as he could. Once the sun had set and the moon claimed the sky, he would be able to leave his quarters. He crawled onto his mattress and closed his eyes.

The minutes crept by like hours. Jason lay on his side, trying to nod off but the churning in his brain refused to settle. He thought he caught himself drifting a few times... faint dreams of King Barnabas and black dots faded in and out of his subconscious. Hues of purple and orange started to swirl in the sky as twilight approached. He dreamt of the night not long ago when the Chief Patriarch had spoken words of council and left him with a warm glow emanating through his whole body. He silently longed to feel that again.

Jason's eyes flittered open as the blackened sky had filled with dim, twinkling stars. He gasped and sat up, wiping his cheek with the back of his hand. He scooted to the end of his mattress and slipped his boots on as quickly as he could before he grabbed his sword and sprinted out the door.

Nezmyth City was almost still in the dead of the night— just a few food vendors were out to serve those who ran out of food during the Harvest. Soldiers eyed Jason suspiciously as he bolted down the street, panting and dripping sweat down his burning cheeks. Every dozen or so houses, Jason would see a door with a black dot nailed to the side—victims of the Harvest. Jason could picture the ominous sign so well, nailed to the cabin where he grew up on the northern rim of Lower City.

His heart pounded, fighting to keep up with his legs. The small cabins surrounding the dusty street started to look familiar. A cabin to his left caught his eye—the cabin he had been racing toward with full gusto.

As he approached it, he scooted to a stop. A lantern flickered in the window. *They're still awake…* No black-dotted sign by the door. He would've breathed a sigh of relief if he wasn't gasping for breath. He trudged up to that familiar door and knocked it three times, his lungs still fighting for air.

There was a faint rustling inside as he heard Tomm and Kara exchange inquisitive remarks. A pair of eyes popped up behind the window, and upon seeing Jason, turned into bustling footsteps heading for the door.

Kara threw open the door, then threw her arms around her sweaty, dirty son. She spoke frantically.

"Are you okay? Did you get Blacknoted?"

Jason held her. "No, mother. I'm fine. I had enough."

Tomm stood in the doorway and exhaled deeply, letting the anxiety leave him. His dusty glasses glared in the moonlight. Both of them were dressed as if they were ready to go somewhere—Tomm with his dagger by his side, Kara in pants instead of a dress, and both wearing a pair of boots.

"We were just about to come check on you," Tomm said. "We were afraid that you wouldn't have enough, with you living on your own and everything."

"All of us at the shop had enough," Jason said. "But just enough. And you?"

Tomm nodded. "Just enough."

Kara released Jason and he stepped inside, closing the door behind him. A single lantern on the table threw a dull, flickering glow through the cabin. Everything was right where they had always been: his parents' mattress, Jason's hammock, the fireplace, the table, and the chest of Kara's crafts, fabrics and scents.

"You probably need something to eat..." Kara went for a basket of fruit by the chest.

"No, mum, I'm fine," Jason wiped the sweat from his forehead.

"Don't be ridiculous, you look exhausted."

"Please, mother," Jason said forcefully. "I have enough for my needs. Save it for yourselves."

Kara ignored him and proceeded to grab an apple from a small basket of fruit on the table. She strode over to Jason and personally thrust the apple into his hand, looking him directly in the eyes. Their eyes were nearly a mirror image of each other's.

"Take it," she whispered.

She let go and strode back over to the table where Tomm had already sat down. Jason, defeated, sighed and followed behind her.

"It looks like lots of people have been visiting their loved ones this evening," Tomm said. "Looking out the window, we see people every so often hurrying down the street. We figure they had the same idea that we did."

"Do we know anyone that's been Blacknoted?" Jason asked, taking a bite of his apple.

Tomm and Kara suddenly became very grave. Jason's heart sank. Kara was the first to speak.

"Tarren's father just left before you arrived. He only made ninety Blocks for the Harvest, and the soldiers showed no mercy. The Blacknote is nailed to his door."

Jason's jaw fell, and the apple in his mouth suddenly tasted like sawdust. His stomach felt like someone had just punched it. The image of Tarren's father getting carried away to be slaughtered blared in his mind's eye. He tried to shake it out. "...Does Tarren know yet?"

They both shrugged.

"How is he going to pay one-hundred and twenty Blocks next month...?"

"Gulaf is resourceful," Tomm said, "And incredibly hardworking. I've known him since we were teenagers. He'll figure something out—at least I hope so."

"I hope so too..." Jason thought out loud. "That would practically leave Tarren an orphan, after what happened to his mother..."

There was a brief silence as they all sat around the table, stiffly pondering. The lantern continued to flicker light on all of them, casting large shadows against the walls. The crunching of boots on dirt sounded faintly from outside as soldiers patrolled down the street.

Finally, Kara asked, "Have you checked up on Tarren...?"

"I was planning on going there right after this," Jason said. "I saw him just a couple of days ago and he was short of the tax about eight Blocks. I'm really worried..."

"Well don't wait, we're fine!" Kara said. "Go! Then hurry back and tell us the news!"

Knock, knock, knock

All three of them shared puzzled glances as they heard the knock come to the door. Tomm pushed his chair back and crept over to the window cautiously. Kara and Jason looked on, not breathing. As Tomm peered out the side of the window, the anxiety dropped and he looked at Kara and Jason.

"It's Tarren!" He hustled for the door and threw it open.

Tarren stood in the doorway with his hands on his knees, panting just as profusely as Jason was minutes ago, his hair darkened with sweat. His work apron wasn't on, but instead, a leather belt was strapped around his waist, toting a pair of double-edged daggers.

He looked up at Tomm when he answered the door and gasped, "Is Jason here?"

Tomm stepped aside so Tarren could look in. Jason stood so quickly from his chair that it fell backward. He raced over to the door and pulled Tarren in, embracing him and ignoring the intense body odor that radiated from him. When they let go, Jason looked into Tarren's eyes with a white-hot intensity.

"Were you Blacknoted...?"

Tarren grinned and shook his head. "It was a complete miracle... someone came in and bought several flutes and drums just yesterday... brought me up to ninety-nine... then I threw in ten Bars and paid the tax..."

"The Dragon is looking out for you, Tarren," Tomm grinned and squeezed his shoulder. "You're a good man."

Tarren grinned broadly, still panting. "I'm glad you all are alright. It's welcome news after passing by my father's house..."

A stiff silence filled the room as Tarren absentmindedly stared at the floorboards beneath him. Jason and Tomm eyed each other uncomfortably. Kara stepped forward, her eyes glistening.

"So you saw...?" she whispered.

Tarren's chin tightened and he nodded his head.

Kara spared no time in throwing her arms around him. Tarren held her in turn, smiling and trying to speak words of assurance.

"Everything will be okay. He's always made work a priority above everything else. He'll be alright."

"If you ever need *anything*, we're always here," she said.

"You're the best, Kara," he said. "You're never going to stop being another mother to me, are you?"

"Never," she replied.

Jason smiled. *I'm so lucky to have such loving parents... it's amazing that Tarren has turned out as well as he has, especially with what happened to his mother and how absent his father is... I don't know how he manages to smile as much as he does...*

Suddenly, Tarren's reassuring smile faded. His eyebrows bent and his eyes filled with focus razor-sharp. Jason recognized that look all too often—the expression of dissatisfied justice.

"Barnabas has gone too far..." he seethed.

Kara released him from her grasp. Every eye in the room was on Tarren. Kara spoke gently, "Tarren, we know how you feel, but there's—."

"*A hundred and twenty Blocks!*" Tarren said, ignoring Kara. "That's insanity! Usually he raises it by a couple of Blocks maybe once a year, but twenty Blocks at once...? Why the sudden raise?"—Jason thought he knew—"King Barnabas just becomes more and more insane with each passing year!"

"*Tarren!*" Tomm bore his teeth. "*Not so loud!* Soldiers are still patrolling outside and you could get us all incarcerated!"

Tarren breathed in deep and exhaled, as if to flush out the darkness nestled inside him. He looked to the ground, then looked up at the three of them.

"So what do we do?" he asked.

"We trust in the Dragon that things will be alright," Tomm said. "Just like we always have. Whatever happens, the Dragon is in it. Agreed?"

Tarren and Kara nodded. Jason's eyes fell. His father's words seemed to be an echo from Master Ferribolt just days earlier. *Trust in the Dragon, and everything will be alright.* But his mind stretched in a dozen different directions. *Tarren's father has already been Blacknoted... how many hundreds of other people have been Blacknoted as well? All for what? For testing me...?*

Jason glared at the floor. In the wake of his father's question, he finally nodded in accordance.

Whatever happens, the Dragon is in it... Jason thought. *I sure hope so.*

"I'm glad all of you are okay…" Jason said. "Let me know if you hear of anyone else that's been Blacknoted. I'm going home."

"I should go, too," Tarren turned to Tomm and Kara. "Work still comes in the morning. Thanks for everything, all of you."

They all exchanged their goodbyes before Jason and Tarren exited to the night sky. As the door clicked shut behind them, both Jason and Tarren turned to the right and began walking up the dusty street to the Southern Market Street. Jason glanced at Tarren out of the corner of his eye—a left turn would have been a faster way for him to get back home to his shop. No soldiers were in sight, but regardless, he spoke in a hushed tone, sure of where this conversation would lead.

"Taking the long way home?" Jason said.

Tarren's eyebrows were bent. Fumes seemed to emanate from his head. Jason knew that he must be stewing over the sudden change in the Harvest.

"Something just isn't right," Tarren replied hotly.

"It took you seventeen years to decide that?"

"You know what I'm talking about," Tarren continued. "Twenty Blocks all at once—that's almost everything I make in a month. It came out of nowhere. Why would Barnabas do that? We know he's greedy and evil and cruel… but don't you find it just a little bizarre? I think something's going on behind that castle walls that we don't know about. But what? What would make him want to raise the tax so drastically and suddenly?"

Jason swallowed and he felt cold sweat begin to bead on his brow. *It's because I'm Foreordained to be King and he's using this as one of my tests… did I mention that?* He tried to keep calm and act as though he didn't have a clue.

"Your guess is as good as mine," Jason breathed.

"How much longer does this need to go on?" Tarren said. "I have faith in the Dragon, but sometimes I honestly wonder… This kingdom is full of good, innocent people that are just trying to survive. When will we have another King? When will the Dragon call someone else to take Barnabas' place? Has someone already been Foreordained, but we just don't know it? *How much longer?*"

Jason kept his eyes locked forward as Tarren rambled. He didn't want to make eye contact. He didn't want Tarren to have the faintest chance of seeing through him, the faintest chance of discovering the secret which could get them both killed.

"I know," Jason said. "I don't know how we're going to survive. But we're out in the open and soldiers can appear at any second. Right now is not the time to talk about—."

As if on cue, a pair of soldiers appeared from around the side of a building, walking toward Jason and Tarren. Jason and Tarren sealed their lips shut as they continued on, not making eye contact with them. The soldiers' armor clanked and clinked faintly as they walked. Both of them toted spears.

"You two!" One of the soldiers barked at them.

Tarren and Jason stopped dead. Jason's heart dropped into his stomach and he felt himself go pale. Tarren tensed next to him, his hand twitching near the dagger by his side. The two soldiers marched up to them, their eyes locked on them like falcons eyeing a meal. Neither Jason nor Tarren spoke a word. Finally, the two soldiers stopped in front of them at about arm's length. Tarren matched the height and body type of the soldiers, tall and muscular, but Jason paled in comparison.

"Where are you going?" The soldier demanded.

"Home," Jason said.

"It's late. Where have you been?" The other soldier said.

"Checking up on our families," Jason replied, still not making eye contact.

"Is that all?" The first soldier probed.

"Yes," Jason confirmed.

Tarren kept his lips sealed shut, his eyes radiating with contempt, bearing into the soldier directly in front of him.

The soldier's eyes locked on to Tarren, trying to be threatening, but instead appearing slightly disconcerted. It isn't often that a soldier is confronted with a commoner his same size. Jason's heart beat thickly and he silently prayed that Tarren wouldn't do anything that would jeopardize their freedom or their lives.

"Why isn't your friend talking?" the perturbed soldier said.

Jason took a second to answer. "He's had a rough night."

Tarren's eyes narrowed. Jason knew what he was thinking. He was silently daring the soldier to make a move, to lift his spear, to give him an opportunity to strike back. Vengeance flashed in his eyes, and he would love nothing more than to get his knuckles bloody from a corrupt Nezmythian soldier. The tension in Jason's heart didn't settle.

"We heard you two talking..." the first soldier said. "Five Bars and we'll let you go. Otherwise, you're coming with us."

Tarren bared his teeth and wrapped his hand around his right dagger. Jason thrust his hand into his chest, signaling him to hold his ground. Tarren's hand slid off the handle, but stayed balled up in a fist by his side. Jason dug around in his pocket... but only managed to extract four Bars.

"All I've got is four," he said gravely.

"Good enough," the first soldier snatched it out of his hand and put it in a pouch on his belt. "Now go home." With that, they continued on their present course straight ahead, forcing Jason and Tarren to step out of the way.

The soldiers didn't speak a word as they continued their march down the Lower City path, their clinking armor become fainter with every step. Tarren looked on in disgust. He took a few steps toward them, then stopped. His fists were still tight by his side. Jason exhaled, not feeling much better about the situation. They stood in tense silence until they were certain they were out of earshot.

"There are good ones and bad ones..." he said.

"We could have taken them both," Tarren said, stroking the hilt of one of his daggers.

"You *alone* could have taken them both," Jason replied. "I don't know a better fighter. But it's never just two when you deal with soldiers. You might as well challenge the entire Nezmythian Army."

"They're supposed to *protect* people…"

There was a pause. Then, out of rage, Tarren ripped a dagger out of its holster and tossed it, moonlight rebounding off the blade as it hurtled through the air. It stuck itself flawlessly into a wooden pole nearly twenty yards away. Tarren slowly lowered his arm, his eyes locked on the pole, his mind's eye picturing his dagger lodged between the eyes of the King. Jason looked on helplessly, wishing there were some way he could soothe the rage that bubbled just below the surface, but it's difficult when your family has been destroyed by corrupt royalty.

"Tarren…" Jason said. "Come on. Let's go home."

Tarren's shoulders deflated as he dragged his feet to the pole where he had thrown his dagger. With some effort, he managed to extract the blade and slip it back into its holster.

The walk home continued in silence. Fumes of anger and frustration still radiated from Tarren. Jason couldn't help but think how close they had both gotten to being thrown in prison. If he wouldn't have had four Bars on him, the Year of Decision would have come to an end.

Whatever happens, the Dragon is in it.

Jason bid Tarren goodbye and patted him on the back as he reached his home on the corner of the Southern Market Street. Tarren absently returned the gesture and continued on his way, the Market Street lit by the dim stars that twinkled above. As Jason ascended the ladders to his room, his brain continually circled through all of the events in the day.

This is how King Barnabas wants to test me? Is it even a test…? How will I know? How many people are going to be condemned to the eastern gold mines next month? How is that going to affect the kingdom?

As he unlatched his door and crossed the threshold, he slipped off his boots and his sword. Sleepiness groped at his eyes and his back longed to be reunited with his bed. He plopped down on the mattress, and as he did, he noticed something peculiar.

A small piece of fine parchment was folded into thirds on his bed. His brow creased. *Strange... I tore up my abandonment note a week ago... but this parchment is too high quality to be mine. Where did it come from?*

Cautiously, he reached out and unfolded the note. As he pulled it open, his jaw tightened and he glared at the parchment intensely. It was a single sentence, accompanied by the royal insignia stamped in red wax.

IF YOU WANT TO END THIS, COME SEE ME.
  -KB

An ember started to grow within Jason. His mind rehearsed everything that had happened in the past week—Nezmyth Castle, the outskirts of Nezmyth City, his parent's home... along with all of the feelings that accompanied each event. His Year of Decision definitely had begun with a rocky start, especially with the Blacknote and the tax raise. *What else is around the corner?* His eyes locked on the note for what felt like hours as that fire started to grow within him, that one sentence repeating in his head over and over. *"If you want to end this, come see me."*

End what? Jason thought. *The Blacknote? My Year of Decision? What does he mean by that?* He continued to stare at the note. *Do I dare? What will he do if I come? What will he do if I don't...?*

Finally, after a long while, he folded the note back up again and shoved it in his pocket. He reached for his sword, slipped in on his back, and reached for his boots.

7 THE SPARK

Morning light seeped through the stained-glass windows of Nezmyth Castle, casting multicolored fragments of light onto the ancient floors. King Barnabas sat in the throne, his icy eyes glossy and a greedy smirk painted across his face. A scrawny, bearded man slapped a drum in rhythm not far away, filling the hall with percussive echoes. A woman with chocolaty dark skin, beautiful and shapely, danced on the throne platform wearing a sparkling outfit that revealed much and left little to the imagination.

The Advisor stood silently a few steps to the right of the throne with his hands clasped primly behind his back, looking forward as if he didn't notice the spectacle. Soldiers stood across the edges of the hall like statues.

BOOM... BOOM... BOOM...

The thunderous crushes reverberated throughout the hall. The glossiness in King Barnabas' eyes vanished, replaced by fiery irritation. The drum continued to sound as a group of soldiers heaved the massive doors open at the other end of the hall. The King watched the doors crack open, silently demanding to know who would have the audacity to interrupt him at a time like this.

A small hoard of Nezmythian soldiers filed in. In the middle of them was a boy of about seventeen with sword was slung over his back and a glove on his right hand. The corner of King Barnabas' mouth twitched as soon as he recognized the boy. He leaned forward and set his elbows on his knees, looking hard into the face of the young boy. The Advisor blinked and the dancer ceased her gyrating, turning about to see the commotion.

The posse made its way down the red carpet and stopped within a few dozen feet of the throne platform. The soldier at the front reached back, grabbed the boy by his bound wrists, and threw him to the floor in front of him.

"Your Highness," he began. "We found this boy at the courtyard gates. He possessed a note with the royal insignia, requesting his presence at the castle."

The soldier withdrew the note from a pouch on his side and held it to the air so the King could see the red wax insignia. King Barnabas' expression didn't change.

"Is this request authentic, Your Grace?" The soldier asked.

King Barnabas stroked his chin, not taking his eyes off the boy. He stowed his Advisor a sour look which was returned by a blank glance. Silence. After a deep breath, King Barnabas' eyes shifted to a stationary soldier by the wall.

"Take her to my chamber. We will continue this shortly."

The soldier complied, marching up next to the throne platform and escorting the damsel and the drummer quickly to a door on a side of the hall. Small bells on her scanty outfit tinkled and chimed as she walked. The soldier threw the door open and led the two through it, who stowed glances over their shoulders at the strange young boy.

The King looked back at the soldiers who had interrupted his entertainment. "Leave us. I will deal with him myself."

The soldiers looked on for a short second, flabbergasted that the King would desire to discipline a commoner personally, but quickly regained their composure. The foremost soldier tossed the note on the floor next to the boy before they turned about and marched back up the red carpet. The boy still laid on the red carpet, hands bound tightly together, breathing heavily and not looking toward the

Throne. He didn't move, even after he heard the doors creak to a mighty close. When the *boom* had dissipated through the hall, King Barnabas spoke.

"This was sooner than expected. I must admit, Jason, I had my doubts that you would hearken to the opportunity I left you, after how timid you appeared the last time we met…"

Jason felt some invisible force lift him back onto his feet as if he were a puppet. When he finally found his footing, the rope on his wrists mysteriously fell to the ground. He rubbed his wrists, trying to sooth the burning redness.

The King continued, "…But curiosity overtakes me. I believe I know the cause of your heated spirits, but I would love nothing more than to hear it from your lips. Please, feel free to speak your mind."

Jason hesitated for a moment, trying to place the words together. He gazed at the floor, his head swimming. His palms were sweaty by his side. As he stood before the King, images not far past flashed in his mind—black dots nailed by doors as he barreled through the streets of Lower City, Tarren's solemn countenance upon hearing the news of his father…

"…It's all for me, isn't it?" he croaked.

King Barnabas watched him, as if expecting him to continue. Jason's chest rose and fell with every laborious breath. He silently wondered what words would get him the answers he wanted, and what words would cost him his head.

"The tax raise and the Blacknote," Jason repeated. "It's one of my tests, isn't it?"

The King didn't answer right away. His eyes locked on Jason like he were something curious and miniscule. He shifted in his chair, rearranging his cape.

"Perhaps. Perhaps not. If it were, I wouldn't tell you. Does it matter? No. Honestly, I was hoping for something a little more—."

"Leave the rest of the kingdom out of this!" Jason said. "This is between me and you, no one else! You have no right to trivialize the lives of others for the sake of testing me!"

Something erupted behind the King's eyes. A thick shiver slid down Jason's spine as he realized that he had both interrupted the King and issued him a command in the same sentence.

"*Have no right?*" King Barnabas seethed. Immediately, he leapt up from the throne and bellowed, "*I own this kingdom, whelp!* Do you honestly believe you can waltz into my castle and tell me how I can and cannot run this kingdom? *Fool!* On any other day I would kill you for having the audacity!"

Jason bent his eyebrows, "The Three Unbreakables. Never lie, never steal, and never kill in cold blood. Even *you* have to abide by the Ancient Laws—"

"I do not believe in those foolish traditions!" King Barnabas continued to rant. "They are suggestions as far as I'm concerned, nothing more! The only Law I believe in is this one…"

King Barnabas reached his hand behind the throne and ominously pulled out his sword. The Advisor stayed as still as a statue, watching the two with vacant eyes. Jason tensed and rubbed the sheath of his blade as he looked on. King Barnabas brought it up to his face and gazed as his own reflection in the flat of his sword, rotating it casually as he inspected the craftsmanship.

"This is how a man attains his desires," King Barnabas spoke lowly. "Power, wealth… he fights his way through this world and achieves what he has only by the use of his prowess." He paused. "In ancient times, men slaughtered dragons with swords much like this one, and today, I am the greatest warrior in all of Nezmyth."

His eyes narrowed as he glared down at Jason from the throne platform.

"And if your Dragon ever did exist," he said. "I would stab it through the heart."

King Barnabas' eyes darted to the nearest soldier.

"You!" He barked. "Come here!"

The soldier turned on his heels swiftly and marched up to the throne platform. As he walked up, Jason watched him. He thought he caught a shot of unease in the soldier's face as the soldier stopped abruptly with heels together at the edge of the throne platform, waiting for further instruction. King Barnabas dragged his sword by his side as he walked up to the soldier.

"Tell me," he said. "How many citizens inhabit the kingdom of Nezmyth?"

"Numberless thousands, My Liege," the soldier replied promptly.

"How many soldiers are there?"

The soldier swallowed hard. Jason could see him start to tremble where he stood.

"Hundreds upon hundreds stand at your aid, Your Highness."

"So what is one compared to hundreds upon hundreds?"

The words were caught in the soldier's throat. He desperately tried to push them out, but his lips wouldn't comply. King Barnabas' eyes filled with impatience.

Finally, the soldier croaked, "Nothing, sire."

"I agree."

King Barnabas turned around as if he was going to walk back to the throne, and the soldier exhaled a controlled sigh of relief. He hadn't been excused to resume his post, so he remained standing firmly in place.

In an instant, King Barnabas spun on his heels and drew up his blade with lightning-fast speed, swinging it horizontally as his body turned about. The soldier didn't even have a second to react. His severed head leapt off the shoulders and toppled to the ground with a sickening thud, followed by the rest of the body, which limply collapsed to the floor behind it.

Jason felt the bile in his stomach creep up his throat and his legs became rubber. He made an effort not to drop to his knees and to stay conscious. There was a Nezmythian soldier, dead—headless—directly in front of him, blood beginning to pool, murdered without conscience or second thought. Jason's teeth ground together. The injustice boiled so intensely that his body shook and steam filled his eyes.

King Barnabas exhaled deeply, scanning his dark blade disgustedly. He lifted a finger and stroked the blade, removing it to examine the soldier's blood on his fingers.

"How revolting," he whispered to himself. He barked at the next soldier down the line. "Take this. Wipe it and polish it. And find someone to clean up this mess."

"Yes, Your Highness." The next soldier marched up, took the blade and briskly walked out of the Hall.

Jason felt numb. The last thirty seconds had sped by as if he were in a nightmare. King Barnabas had killed one of his own soldiers in cold blood, and then ordered the next soldier to clean his sword—a sword stained with the blood of a murdered comrade. He hung his head and wiped his eyes with his gloved hand, baring his teeth in anger and helplessness, not wanting the King to see.

"This, Jason," King Barnabas continued on casually, "Is a precursor to your Year of Decision. That is, if you plan on doing things *your* way. There is a way this can all change…"

King Barnabas leered at Jason as he strolled his direction. Jason lifted his eyes to the King, trying to push down the lump in his throat and subdue the steam in his eyes. King Barnabas slowly came to a halt directly in front of Jason, less than an arm's length away. He was a full head taller than him. A devilish smirk adorned his face.

"Promise me now that you will denounce your Foreordination at the end of your Year of Decision, and I will lessen the trials I give you. I will lower the tax back to one hundred Blocks per Harvest, and all Blacknotes will be revoked. Why should more innocent people suffer, Jason? You have the power to save them. Simply denounce your Foreordination, and things will return to normal."

A sickening, lurching darkness coagulated within Jason with every word that came from the King's mouth. *Should I*

trust anything he says? I witnessed him break the Third Unbreakable just seconds ago… why should he have a problem lying? He's probably lying to me right now. But what if he's not? Is it worth the risk…?
He wanted to believe it were true. He wanted to believe that the King would hold to his word, but Jason couldn't deny the lurching feeling he felt within him.

Just trust in the Dragon, and things will be alright… what would the Dragon want me to do…?

Jason said nothing. King Barnabas' eyes continued to bear down on him, but Jason refused to open his mouth. After several moments of that, King Barnabas' sneer faded to the typical loathing scowl that Jason expected. His voice died down to a whisper, his nostrils flared and his tone was venomous.

"I am not going to kill you, Jason. I am going to *destroy* you. I am going to tear your world apart from around you until you return to this throne pleading for mercy. Until then, I will see to it that *your* Year of Decision is the most difficult that any King will ever endure in the history of Nezmyth. The Blacknote is only the beginning. As I said before, you will *not* be King of Nezmyth. When you find yourself ready to give up, come see me. Now leave."

King Barnabas spun on his heels, his cape snapping, and retreated back to his throne. He plopped down, glaring at Jason, clearly baring his teeth behind his oily lips.

Jason turned slowly around to exit the castle, and as he did, the body of the murdered soldier caught his eyes. He felt sick again. He clenched his teeth and swallowed, his fists clenched by his side. He walked two steps, then stopped.

Jason turned his head over his shoulder, catching the sight of the King just out of the corner of his eye. He spoke softly.

"A week ago, I didn't want to be King. I didn't understand why *I* had to be the one to take the throne—I still don't."

He paused. King Barnabas continued to scowl. Jason took a breath, and let it billow out of his teeth.

"…But I think I'm starting to."

With that, Jason looked forward and made his way down the red carpet. The massive doors cracked open, and he walked out into the sun.

8 THE LESSON

"Excuse me, I'd like an audience with Master Ferribolt."

Jason stood outside the elegant Upper City mansion as the sun was just climbing the crest of its daily journey. It cast down brilliant light upon the kingdom, illuminating the splashes of red, orange and brown that began to spread through the trees. A brittle breeze wafted by, causing Jason to shiver and tense in his jacket. The gatekeeper stood comfortably beneath a shaded shack by the front gates, blinking at Jason.

"Do you have an appointment?" the gatekeeper said.

"No..." Jason replied. "But he told me a couple of weeks ago that if I ever needed anything I could come see him."

The gatekeeper, puzzled, dropped his gaze to a sheet of parchment tacked to a table inside the edifice. "Your name?"

"Jason, son of Tomm the printer."

Suddenly, the gatekeeper's eyes popped open curiously. "Of course... he's made a note of it right here. Right inside, please."

The gatekeeper pulled a lever inside the shack and with a shudder, the gates squealed open. Jason nodded to the gatekeeper in gratitude and made his way through. The lawn and stone walkway were perfectly manicured beneath his shoddy boots. Birds chirped in the hedges that were trimmed into perfect cubes.

Jason marched up the stone steps to the porch and through the stone pillars that stood sentinel beside the steps. He knocked on the door three times and threw glances over his shoulders. Not far in the distance, Nezmyth Castle towered to the sky. He tore his eyes from it, revisited by the memory of his most recent visit, and scanned the door in front of him. It was riddled with uniform squiggles and jagged lines that he couldn't decipher.

A loud click sounded from the other side. The door swung open, and before Jason stood a butler with a pointy nose and perfectly pressed suit. It was a peculiar contrast— Jason, with his repeatedly-stained pants and shoddy boots, and the butler with his prim, pristine uniform. It made Jason feel out of place, to say the least.

The butler eyed Jason for a moment before asking, "You are... Jason?"

"Yes, sir," Jason said, confused that the butler knew his name.

A flicker of something flashed across the butler's eyes for a fraction of a moment. It had to be something between wonder and amazement, but Jason couldn't place it. The butler regained himself quickly and put on its most professional face possible.

"The Master has been expecting you," he said. "Right this way."

Jason's eyebrows bent, *Expecting me?*

The butler motioned for Jason to come inside. As he crossed the threshold, Jason's jaw fell. Positively everything in the mansion was as pristine and organized as a cathedral. The entire ceiling was painted with glorious depictions of meadows and valleys. Paintings of Chief Patriarchs past lined the walls. A statue of the Holy Dragon protruded from the center of the hall in majestic glory.

"Good afternoon, Jason!" Jason heard Master Ferribolt call from an adjacent room to his right. "Come in, come in, let us have a chat!"

Jason gave the butler a sheepish smile and a nod as he walked toward the noise. As Jason walked through the giant arch leading to the Chief Patriarch's study, the butler looked on in awe, as if the essence of hope had entered into his presence.

The smell of mahogany and yellowing pages coagulated in the Chief Patriarch's study. Master Ferribolt sat in a plush armchair in the middle of the room, his face buried intently in an ancient, leather-bound book. He waved his hand without taking his eyes off the book, motioning for Jason to come hither. Jason slipped the sword off his back and sat in the opposite chair facing the Chief Patriarch. A bear rug silently growled at his feet.

The Chief Patriarch didn't look at Jason for a matter of time, let alone speak. Jason's eyes scanned the walls, analyzing the rows upon rows of books. More paintings of past Chief Patriarchs hung intermittently throughout the room. An elegantly-crafted desk on the far side of the room was neatly organized with parchment, writing sticks, quills and ink.

"Isn't the Ancient Language fascinating?" Master Ferribolt said, still scanning the pages of the book.

Jason shifted in his chair, "I've never bothered to study Ancient Nezmythian, Master."

"Well, that is about to change, my boy," he grinned, "Because you must be fluent in the language as a King, Advisor, or Patriarch. There are many lessons to be learned in the Ancient Text, and I will take it upon myself to teach you in the coming year."

A pause. Master Ferribolt must have expected Jason to be more excited at the news, because the silence in response caused him to lift his gaze from the pages. Jason absently stared back at the bear head that rested by his feet. Master Ferribolt snapped the book shut and set it on the floor by the side of chair. He fixed his eyes on Jason, wise and understanding.

"You haven't come to visit me since we first spoke," he said. "It's been two weeks."

Jason kept his gaze toward the floor. "I know. I'm sorry."

"Why is this?"

Jason shrugged.

"Nothing in particular was bothering you?"

A staccato escaped Jason's lips. *Bothering me?* The thought was almost laughable. With the recent events on the raised tax, Blacknotes, the Year of Decision and everything that came along with it, there had in fact been a lot of things bothering him. For the first time in his life, Jason felt the weight of the kingdom upon his shoulders in a very real way, and pressing forward on nothing but a sliver of hope was straining to say the least.

Jason took a deep breath. The eyes of the Chief Patriarch stayed locked upon him. He leaned forward in his chair, his spectacles glistening.

"Jason," he said. "The best remedy for the weary mind is an unfiltered confession. You needn't keep your fears and insecurities locked inside. If you do, it can destroy you. I can help you, but first, you must tell me what's wrong."

Jason took a deep breath again, and this time looked up into Master Ferribolt's eyes. Those eyes had a special power. Not an ounce of darkness abode therein, but love and conviction radiated from them like the sun spreading warmth upon an eerie wasteland. It made Jason feel smaller, but gave him the desire to grow larger—larger in caring... courage... confidence.

"I visited the castle last week," Jason said.

Master Ferribolt's brow creased curiously. "The King summoned you again?"

Jason nodded. "In a way."

Master Ferribolt leaned forward in his chair. Jason proceeded to rehearse all of the things that took place at the castle one week prior, everything from the soldier's murder, to the King's bargain, to Jason's tactlessness. Master Ferribolt never blinked through the whole story, but would occasionally scratch his chin or fasten his spectacles. Finally, when Jason had concluded, he rubbed his hands together and gazed upon Jason with eyes white-hot. Jason looked on, tense, waiting for what was to come.

"Well Jason…" the Chief Patriarch said quietly. "I'm glad you didn't trust the King. That was very wise of you. I think you and I are both certain that he will stop at nothing to assure he retains the Throne at the end of this year. Therefore, he is not to be trusted."

Jason nodded.

"But from the sound of things, you were also extremely tactless during your conversation. That was *very* risky, and you could have been killed. Never do it again. Agreed?"

Jason nodded again.

Master Ferribolt leaned back in his chair. "Jason, you have a passion for justice. That is good. But I can guarantee that the King will try to use that against you at some point in the coming year. You *must* restrain yourself. If you give him whatever grounds necessary to kill you, he will without hesitation, and the kingdom is lost."

"What he's doing is *wrong,* though!" Jason said. "He's making the entire kingdom suffer even more just for the sake of testing me! It's like he's holding the kingdom for ransom!"

"Jason, I'm just as disgusted about this as you are," Master Ferribolt said firmly. "He's continuing to be the selfish, arrogant swine that he is. Is there anything we can do at the moment? No. Will more innocent people suffer? Yes. But the Dragon always deals swift justice at the proper moment. Meanwhile, we need to be patient and have faith. Evil men always get their just rewards."

Jason's eyes darted to the windows at the slew of words that just came from the Chief Patriarch's lips. *Is he insane? Who could be listening right now? He could get us both killed!*

"As I mentioned before," Master Ferribolt said, reading Jason's anxiety. "My estate will be a haven from the eyes and ears of the King. You needn't worry about what is said behind these walls—you're protected here. Think about it. Can you imagine the uproar that would be heard among the kingdom of King Barnabas were to imprison the Chief Patriarch? He would fear rebellion. He may be reckless, but he's not stupid."

Jason felt himself relax just slightly, but only slightly. His thoughts still hovered around the Blacknotes and the words of the King just a week ago. *"I'm not going to kill you. I'm going to destroy you."*

"I just don't know what I'm going to do..." Jason said.

"The answer is simple!" Master Ferribolt said. "Move forward with faith!"

"How can you say that?" Jason retorted. "Master, with all due respect, I still *don't want* to be King! And it's hard to move forward based upon something I don't fully understand."

"But that is precisely what faith is," Master Ferribolt said. "Tell me Jason... what proof do you have that the sun will rise tomorrow?"

Jason's eyes narrowed impatiently. "It always does."

"That still doesn't answer my question. What *proof* do you have that the sun will rise tomorrow?"

Jason thought for a moment. "...None, I guess."

"But you believe it still will?"

"Of course."

"Why?"

"Because it always has!"

Master Ferribolt's eyes became sharp. "So what you're telling me is that you believe the sun will rise tomorrow because you've experienced it so many times before. You have no proof that it will happen again tomorrow, but regardless, you *strongly believe* that it will. Am I wrong?"

"No..." Jason conceded. "But I still don't see how that's supposed to help me during the next year."

Master Ferribolt lifted his gaze to the ceiling... thinking. Jason sat adjacent to him, wondering what could be going on inside his head. They sat in silence for several moments. Jason rubbed his hands on his pants anxiously. Finally, Master Ferribolt looked at Jason with a very satisfied smirk.

"How about we try a demonstration?" He said. "Jason, stand up please."

Jason slipped his sword onto his back as he pushed himself out of his chair. Master Ferribolt's clever smirk never faded.

"Now," Master Ferribolt continued as he pushed himself up and began to stroll across the room. "Stand perfectly still for the next few seconds. *Metula.*"

Suddenly, everything went black. Jason twitched in surprise and let out a startled yelp. He waved his hand in front of his eyes furiously, hoping to see some trace of it, but it was like someone had pulled a black sheet directly over his face.

"*I'm blind!*" Jason said.

"You're very observant," Master Ferribolt said amusedly.

Jason stretched out his hands in front of him, feeling for something to hold on to. "Give me back my sight! This isn't funny!"

"This isn't a joke, Jason, it's a lesson!" Master Ferribolt replied. "Now please stand still! This is going to be very complicated..."

Jason let his arms hang to his side with a huff, and for a second, everything was silent. But slowly, gradually, like an advancing army, sounds of rumbling, crackling and shifting came from all around him. Jason kept perfectly still through it all. It sounded like an earthquake was going on around him, but the ground didn't so much as shiver. *What is Master Ferribolt doing?*

The rumbling and shifting noises lasted only for a matter of seconds. When it was over, Jason heard Master Ferribolt speak from the other side of the room.

"Alright Jason," he said. "I want you to walk toward my voice. Do you understand?"

"Okay..." Jason said.

He proceeded at a cautious pace, with his hands held just in front of him. Right foot... left foot... right foot... Jason silently hoped that he wouldn't step on anything to make him trip. He walked for only a few seconds before the Chief Patriarch shouted, "Stop!"

"What?" Jason said irritably as he came to a halt.

"...Turn just a little to your left."

"You want me to turn to my left?" Jason said.

"Yes. Turn to your left."

"Why?"

"Do you trust me?" Master Ferribolt inquired.

"Who else can I trust right now?"

"Yes or no, Jason."

Jason sighed. "Yes."

"Then turn to your left, and keep walking."

Jason twisted ninety degrees to his left and continued his slow, methodical stride. His heel didn't pass his other foot with each step—slow and steady. Occasionally, he felt himself begin to lose his balance, but when he did, he would bend his knees and straighten his back to reclaim his center of balance.

"Okay Jason," Master Ferribolt spoke up again. "You're going to want to crouch down in the next few steps... alright... ready... now!"

Jason crouched down as he waddled through the darkness. *What is he doing...?*

The next few minutes continued as such. Jason kept his hands up to his chest, just a few inches in front of him, and he crept through the dark, heeding the Chief Patriarch's every command. The Chief Patriarch had him turning, twisting, and sidestepping through the darkness while he continued to rack his brains for the purpose of this escapade. After what felt like too long, Jason could tell that he was directly in front of the Chief Patriarch.

"Well done, Jason," he could tell he was smiling. "*Telumay.*"

Suddenly, the world came back into Jason's view as if someone had yanked the dark sheet from off of his face. Master Ferribolt stood backed up to one of his bookcases, which was mysteriously missing about half of the books. He held out something in his hand, no larger than his palm, round, and bright and yellow like the sun. Jason eyed it curiously.

"Here is your prize," Master Ferribolt said.

"A guabo?" Jason asked.

Master Ferribolt nodded. "Juicy and delicious. Now, look behind you."

As Jason turned about, he gasped with a "*Whoa!*"

Somehow, Master Ferribolt had transformed his entire study into an obstacle course. Pillars of books ten feet high dotted the entire room. Some books and chairs formed small archways and narrow passages that required intricate instruction to navigate blindly. Jason could almost trace the path that he took as he ogled at the sight, his jaw hanging loosely on its hinges.

"...How did you do this?" Jason slowly took the guabo from Master Ferribolt's hand.

"That's not as important as how you made it through," Master Ferribolt said. "So... how did you make it through?"

"I just listened to your voice," Jason replied. "Even when you told me to do things that I didn't understand... it felt pretty ridiculous at the time, but now I understand why."

"What would have happened if you wouldn't have listened to me, and just walked directly toward me?"

"I would have made a real mess," Jason said, his eyes hopping to each precarious tower of books.

"Correct," Master Ferribolt said with a wide grin. "What you just experienced is a metaphor of our lives, Jason. Often we just want to walk directly to our goals, but we aren't aware of all of the obstacles that stand in our way. We need to listen carefully to what the Dragon would have us do; otherwise we'll tend to make a big mess, like you said. That is always the best way."

Jason nodded. He felt something like a warm glow start to flicker and glow through his head and heart. Clarity. Everything felt right, and it made sense as Master Ferribolt explained it.

"So how do I 'listen to the Dragon's voice?'" Jason said.

"You give heed to the feelings of your heart," Master Ferribolt replied. "As you fill your life with goodness, and earnestly learn skills to prepare yourself for the throne, the Dragon will prompt you in your heart and in your mind as to what you should do."

"Sounds easy enough."

"Sometimes," Master Ferribolt said. "But the Dragon has a way of testing the limits of our faith. You must be prepared to do whatever you feel is right, not just what is easy. And that is a skill that you must continue after you take the Throne, because remember... the Dragon is the one who ultimately rules the kingdom, not the King. You are simply the steward. Acting upon those feelings must become second nature."

Jason let that sink in for a little. He was starting to become more and more discomfited with the fact that his Year of Decision was going to test his limits in every way thinkable. The time of simply worrying about the Harvest was long gone. And on top of watching his back everywhere he went, he knew he had to focus on ways to improve himself as he prepared to be King.

With a grin, Master Ferribolt walked passed Jason, heading back to his plush armchair some ways away. He snaked his way carefully around the stacks of books that he had intricately constructed, occasionally stepping on loose papers that had made their way to the floor. After a few seconds of watching, Jason followed behind, continuing to his own chair.

"Do you want some help cleaning all of this up?" Jason inquired.

Master Ferribolt laughed heartily. "No thank you, Jason, I'm quite alright. I'll put all of these back on their shelves after the conclusion of our lesson. So tell me..." They both plopped themselves down into their opposite armchairs and Master Ferribolt laced his fingers together. "How are you going to better yourself for the Throne?"

Jason shifted in his chair slightly and drummed his fingers together. His eyes traced the edge of their sockets as he racked his brains. *I'm from Lower City and all I've ever thought about was how to pay the next tax… what* would *I do to prepare myself to be a King? What would a good King do?*

Come to think of it, the only King he had ever known was King Barnabas, as he took the Throne just a few years before Jason was born. He knew that King Thomas had been a great King, but nostalgic whispers between commoners in the southern Market Street weren't much to build a sure knowledge upon.

"Well…" Jason said. "I suppose I should start sparring again… King Barnabas is a great warrior, so I should be too."

Master Ferribolt nodded in approval. "It's a good start."

"But I don't know how I'll be able to grow more patient or wise or anything…" Jason thought out loud.

"*That* will come in time," Master Ferribolt said, "Through the trials that the King will give you, and through the lessons that you learn in this very room. As I said earlier, I will take it upon myself to teach you Ancient Nezmythian during this next year. This is so you will be able to read the Ancient Texts and learn the lessons within."

Master Ferribolt picked up the ancient book he was reading as Jason first walked in the door. He stood from his chair just enough to reach over and hand it to Jason, who took it gingerly. The cover seemed to be an organized grid of squiggles, jagged lines and dots, much like the door to the Chief Patriarch's mansion. As he cracked open the cover, he discovered the yellowed, frail pages of the book had more of the same on each page.

"There are many tales from past Kings and Patriarchs found in the Ancient Text," Master Ferribolt explained. "At the time, they wrote them down for the benefit of future Nezmythians. I'm sure you've heard stories like *The Battle at the Plains of Nomori* and *The Prophesy of the Final King*, but there is much subtler power to be found in the detail of the Ancient Language. Not to mention, all of Nezmythian Law is written in the Old Language."

"How long will it take to learn?" Jason asked with a discouraged air to his voice. The army of dots and lines on the pages seemed overwhelming to his already-weary mind.

"I myself am still learning all the facets of the Ancient Language," Master Ferribolt's eyes twinkled. "But you will have no problem learning the basics within the year."

Another long pause as Jason absorbed everything that had been said. He carefully folded the cover back over the pages and traced his finger around the characters in the title. His finger picked up traces of dust that had nestled into the leather over the years. He flicked the dust off his finger and looked up at Master Ferribolt.

"So when do we start?"

Master Ferribolt replied, "Immediately."

9 THE UNKNOWN

Dawn sprinkled over the eastern mountains as the sun climbed ever slowly into the sky. Sleepy clouds absorbed the golden sunlight on their bellies and drifted through the blue like ships in the sky. The paleness of early morning nestled in Nezmyth City as spring slowly gave way to autumn.

This morning, a satchel was slung around Jason's shoulder, opposite to the shoulder that always carries his sword. He had just less than an hour to get to the shop, which gave him plenty of time to shop for food with what little money he had. Most of his time was spent along the fruit stands and carts that had parked themselves along the edges of the southern Market Street. Lower City gardeners lucky enough to have sufficient property to grow produce usually abode in the area. Soldiers slowed their pace as they walked by, predatorily scanning the crowd.

Jason reached for a loaf of bread at the current cart and turned it about curiously. It was getting hard, but still edible. An elderly lady with thin, stringy hair watched Jason from behind the cart with eyes keen and hopeful. Finally, when Jason had satisfactorily inspected the morsel, he lifted his eyes to the old woman and put a hand in his pocket.

"How much?"

"Three Pieces," she replied. Her voice was frail and quivery.

Jason's brow bent and he stopped feeling for change in his pocket. "It was only two last week."

"The Blacknote changes things..." she replied, her voice trailing.

Jason's gaze dropped to his boots. "I understand... but that means I can only afford half of a loaf today."

The old lady nodded. "One Piece and five Shards."

Jason extracted the money from his pocket and dropped it into the woman's wrinkled hand. He took the bread from her other hand and dropped it into his satchel. *Looks like I need to be more careful about how much I eat now...*

Several others in his vicinity wandered from cart to cart, obviously on the same mission as Jason. Jason kept a weary eye out. It's not uncommon for street urchins to pilfer the sacks and totes of those innocently shopping for produce. He remembered a time as a small child where he stole an apple from the basket of a woman shopping on the southern Market Street. When his mother and father found out what he did, he wasn't allowed dinner for days. He made sure he never stole again.

It's been almost a month, Jason thought. *Eight months in a year, just seven more to go. I wish I knew what the King was planning. But just trust in the Dragon and things will turn out, right? This whole faith thing is hard... it's like walking in the dark.*

He had browsed his way over to another cart loaded with little fruits that Jason wasn't familiar with. They appeared to be something halfway between a grape and a tomato... about the size of the tip of his thumb and a succulent reddish-purple. No one seemed to be accompanying the cart. *Maybe they left to go get something... that's a little foolish. It's amazing this cart still has any fruit on it.*

Jason picked one of the fruits up and rolled it around in his fingers. *What does it taste like? I don't want to just steal one, though...* He dipped his hand into his pocket and pulled out a Shard, sure that it would cover the price of one of these little morsels. He placed the Shard on a table behind the cart, and popped the fruit in his mouth.

The fruit exploded its juice in Jason's mouth. It was tangy and sweet—unique to anything he had ever tasted. His eyes lit up. It was delicious. His eyes darted about the crowd, looking for anyone who may appear to govern this small fruit stand. *What are these, and how much are they?*

"Booshum berries," a lovely voice from behind came up, "Very delicious, rare, and expensive."

Jason turned about, and what he saw made his jaw hit the cobblestone. A girl just a few inches shorter than him walked up and stood next to him at the cart. Her hair spilt over her head and shoulders like a golden waterfall, and the area around her nose was lightly peppered with freckles. Dimples creased her smooth cheeks as she grinned with sculpted lips. The dress she wore was spotlessly white—free from any stains or lint—and they hugged her fit, slender frame.

Jason nearly choked on his booshum berry as he forced it down his throat. *There's no way she's from Lower City...* The girl seemed to ignore him as she picked booshum berries out of the cart and placed them in a basket around her elbow. Jason's heart beat thickly.

"Expensive...?" he forced out.

"Mmhm," the girl replied. "One booshum berry can sell for as much as an entire Piece, depending on where they grow."

"*A whole Piece?*" Jason exclaimed, shielding his mouth as if to pull the berry out of his stomach and place it on the cart. Silently, he wished he could do so.

The girl giggled amusedly. "You don't have anything to worry about. These are grown here. I know the man who grows them, and he usually sells each one for one Shard each. So I think you're safe."

She turned and winked at him. Her eyes were silver. Jason's heart jumped into his throat. With a twinkling grin and a short laugh, she placed her hand on Jason's shoulder. Jason really hoped that she couldn't feel his heartbeat.

"Don't eat too much, mister."

With that, she patted his shoulder twice, dropped some change on the table behind the cart, and disappeared into the crowd.

Jason stood, mouth agape, facing the crowd where the girl had disappeared. The exchange had only lasted a minute, but it was enough to make Jason's head swim in some sweet nectar he wasn't familiar with. As he thought about the encounter, he silently reprieved himself for his lack of speech. He would have given ten Blocks for her name, but she had vanished into the crowd as quickly as she had appeared. *What was a girl as beautiful as her doing here...?*

"Booshum berries?"

"Huh?" Jason twitched as if awoken from a dream. A younger man had somehow appeared at the cart behind the booshum berries and was eying Jason expectantly. Flecks of grey peppered his short, dark hair, and his clothes were neat and tidy.

Jason's eyes jumped from the booshum berry salesman to the crowd where the girl had mysteriously faded. He craned his neck to try to get a better view of the crowd, but to no avail. She was gone. His lips pressed together and exhaled through his nose.

If I ever run into her again, Jason thought. *I'm going to get her name.*

* * * * *

"Jason, *gaytah emglay?*"

"*Elu mayteshu,* Master Ferribolt."

"Good," Master Ferribolt said satisfactorily. "That is 'how are you' and 'I'm doing well.' Remember, using the prefix *may* before the adjective indicates your temporary state of being. If you were to say *elu teshu* that would imply that you're doing well constantly. The same goes for whenever you describe your feelings."

It had been a few weeks since Jason first started learning Ancient Nezmythian from Master Ferribolt. An enormous book filled with those unfamiliar dots and squiggles rested on his forearms and covered his lap. He felt as though his brain was trying to mentally push a cart up a hill. *This is what I have to look forward to for the next seven months?* The armchair in Master Ferribolt's study was starting to become more familiar to his body, and although it was considerably more comfortable than anything he was used to, it was usually associated with strenuous work and study. His sword leaned against its side.

"Try asking me a question, Jason," Master Ferribolt said, leaning back in his armchair and grinning expectantly.

Jason looked up from his book, which looked just as confusing to him as it did last week. "...In Ancient Nezmythian?"

Master Ferribolt nodded with rosy cheeks radiating with confidence.

Jason breathed in deep and let the air seep out his nose. In his mind, he tried placing the vowels and consonants together, like putting together a puzzle that you don't have all the pieces to. He stared blankly ahead as he did so. There were only a handful of characters in the Ancient Language, but the process of placing each one together into words and mentally translating it to Modern Nezmythian was taxing. Finally, he opened his mouth.

"*Shoo emglay...* uh... *beedeesh...*"

"Who do I go...?" Master Ferribolt looked on quizzically.

"No—sorry, um... *tahlo emglay beedeesh... oon guabo?*"

"Where do I go for a guabo?" Master Ferribolt grinned and his eyes twinkled.

"Yes! That's what I meant!"

Master Ferribolt chuckled. "Not bad, Jason! You may not think it, but you're making excellent progress."

"Thanks," Jason said with a sheepish smile.

"I think that will conclude our lesson for the day. You've worked hard and I can tell you're exhausted."

Jason silently thanked the Dragon and snapped the book shut in front of him. As he held it on his lap, he couldn't help but tease a smile at the Chief Patriarch's praise. What he didn't notice was Master Ferribolt staring at his right hand. Master Ferribolt eyed it like an abstract sculpture or painting—trying to decipher its meaning. Curiosity filled his gray eyes.

"Tell me, Jason," he said. "Every time I've seen you, you've been wearing that glove, no matter what the setting. Is there a particular reason? It seems a little impractical to me."

The flattered smile quickly faded from Jason's face. His hand involuntarily slipped to his side, between his leg and the chair's arm. He thought briefly about making up some bogus story as to why he wears it all the time. The probing questions had come all too often from those that didn't no him well, and frankly, he never felt like giving the straight answer. *I can't lie to the Chief Patriarch, though...*

A sigh left his lips. Jason set the book down on the floor and began tugging at the tips of his glove.

"I don't like showing this to people..."

Master Ferribolt looked on intently. The glove came off, and Jason's milky-white hand was revealed. The orange, triangular scar showed itself just at the root of his index finger. He held out the palm of his hand to display it for Master Ferribolt.

"This has always bothered me," Jason said. "I don't know why. It's just such a peculiar birthmark that I can't help but feel like it's something more—like I've been branded for something. And as you've already noticed, I don't exactly like being *branded* for things. So I wear a glove so I don't have to look at it all the time. I know it sounds strange, but that's it..."

Master Ferribolt never took his eyes off the mark as if the glossy orange inside the triangle had locked in his gaze. He stroked his chin. Jason looked back at him uncomfortably, perplexed as to what could be going on behind those spectacles and those gray eyes.

"That's very interesting, Jason," Master Ferribolt said.

"Do you know if it means anything?" Jason asked.

Master Ferribolt didn't answer right away. He leaned back in his chair, his expression softening just slightly. "If it did, I would let you know. It could be nothing more than a peculiar birthmark. It's not uncommon."

"I'm not so sure…" Jason said, his eyes bearing into his hand as he slipped the glove back on.

"Jason, that mark on your hand is the least of your troubles right now," Master Ferribolt said. "What you need to focus on is learning Ancient Nezmythian and bettering yourself for the Throne. The Oracle Stone won't get whiter if you just wait for the end of your Year of Decision to come. Have you had the opportunity to begin sparring again, as you mentioned weeks ago?"

Jason sighed. "No…"

"Jason…" Master Ferribolt leaned forward in his chair. A sudden change swept over his countenance as if a shadowy curtain had been pulled over his face. A hint of distress came over Jason as this happened, for he rarely saw Master Ferribolt out of his whimsical, intelligent facade. Master Ferribolt's eyes hardened and his jaw clenched lightly—like the expression of a stern parent. The words that slipped from his lips were ominously sober.

"…Have you considered the possibility that you will have to battle the King before your Year of Decision concludes?"

Jason's heart dropped into his stomach, and he suddenly felt nauseous. The thought was like a hammer to his insides. He pictured King Barnabas towering over him just as he did one month ago, with rippling muscles and a powerful square jaw, lifting his dark blade high above his head, ready to strike. What would Jason do when that time comes? Could he possibly defend himself? *Nezmyth's greatest warrior… against me.*

Jason tried to force down what felt like a grape lodged in his throat. His heart felt like it had stopped beating seconds ago, and his eyes fell to the floor, considering the horrifying possibility.

"Jason, I'm not telling you this to frighten you," Master Ferribolt said. "I just don't want to see you fail. I want to be there when Barnabas is forced to step down from his throne, and I want to be there when you begin to rebuild Nezmyth into a prosperous kingdom. Victory *is* possible Jason. You need not fear, but you must act."

The words barely slipped into Jason's ears, almost like his head was under water. The image of King Barnabas lifting his sword above his head kept replaying in his mind. In his heart, he knew it could happen. *The King said he would stop at nothing to maintain his throne… what would stop him from killing me himself when the time came? But how can I possibly prepare myself to battle against the greatest warrior in Nezmyth?*

Jason voiced that question to the Chief Patriarch. Master Ferribolt's answer came quickly, resolutely, and firmly.

"The Dragon didn't set you up for failure, Jason. If you're to be sure of anything, be sure of that."

That answer struck Jason like a light that suddenly lit up in his heart and rose up to his head. It made perfect sense… but like anything else, that one remark wasn't enough to settle the uncomfortable mist that coagulated inside him. He knew he had to begin sparring, but how to go about it… he wasn't sure. His thumb involuntarily found the hilt of his sword and stroked the pommel, as if rubbing the ruby on it would polish Jason's mind into conjuring a solution. Master Ferribolt looked on like a concerned parent.

"Is there anything else on your mind, Jason?"

Jason shook his head. *Just the usual.*

"Well, you better be off then," Master Ferribolt pushed himself out of his chair. "It'll be dark before you are home, and I don't want to have another encounter with soldiers like you did the day of the Harvest."

There was a dark pause as Jason followed suit, pushing himself out of his chair and slipping his sword onto his back. Master Ferribolt walked by his side, escorting him to the door. Jason stared at his boots as he walked. The disheartening realization was beginning to come to him...

"Tomorrow is the day of the deadline, is it not?" Master Ferribolt asked gravely.

Jason nodded.

"Is there any word on your friend's father?"

Jason let out a deep breath. "No. I haven't seen Tarren in a while."

"I shall pray for him and his father," Master Ferribolt replied. "What will be will be. I will ask the Dragon to give him and all other victims of the Blacknote special protection. We will see in time how this affects the rest of Nezmyth."

Jason thanked him as they approached the front door. Gaston, Master Ferribolt's butler whom Jason had grown accustomed to greeting each week, turned the ancient handle and pulled the door open. Jason clutched his jacket tighter as he bid the two farewell and crossed the threshold.

The hedges and flowers of the Chief Patriarch's estate swayed gently in the twilight breeze. It blew the soft, sweet fragrances into Jason's nose, caressing his senses as if to comfort his weary soul. Purples and oranges illuminated the sky like a watercolor painting as the sun retreated over the western horizon. It wouldn't be long before the street side lanterns illuminated the ascending, winding streets of Upper City.

Jason kept his hands in his pockets as he walked. He looked at the enormous, beautiful homes that lined the street from left to right as he descended down the hill.

No Blacknotes on any of them, he thought distastefully. *Successful businesspeople and scholars... they have no problem paying the Harvest whenever it comes around. It's probably like pocket change to them. Meanwhile, the rest of us go hungry and scrape whatever we can to stay out of prison.*

He knew it was wrong to complain—Upper City was sure to be full of decent people with good hearts. The division in the classes wasn't any fault of their own success. The true culprit of the problem was as well known to Jason as it was to anyone else in Nezmyth—maybe a little more so.

The walk home wasn't a short one. Jason had to trudge to the very foot of Upper City and come partway down the posh Northern Market Street before coming to the familiar territory of the Southern Market Street. All the while, the probing eyes of patrolling soldiers didn't make the journey any easier. It usually took about an hour before reaching his flat on the corner of the Southern Market Street and Lower City.

When he finally did, he slipped off his boots and his sword and crawled onto the straw mattress. Squiggles, dots, and jagged lines, along with images of Blacknotes, circled through his mind as he slowly drifted to sleep.

* * * * *

Tarren's eyes stayed glued to the floor, trying hard to force back the mist that was growing in them, trying to be strong. Jason found himself at a loss of words. He would open his mouth as if to speak some golden nugget of confidence and comfort, but stopped himself each time, sure of his incompetence to console the heart of his troubled friend. The Cranny seemed especially hollow and quiet today. The instruments hanging on the walls seemed to mourn along with their master.

They sat like that for several minutes, in silence, before Jason spoke up.

"When did they come…?" Jason asked, barely breathing.

"It had to have been in the dead of the morning," Tarren replied, "Because I ran there right as the sun was coming up. He had to have still been asleep. At least the soldiers had the decency to let him write a note before they took him."

Tarren pinched a half-torn piece of parchment on his desk and held it out to Jason. Jason stood from his usual stool by the door, walked over and retrieved the note. The handwriting was scratchy and hap-hazard, as if it had been written in a hurry. He held the note with both hands, holding it at an angle to catch the light from the window.

> Tarren,
> Not enough money for
> Blacknote. Short two Blocks.
> Don't worry about me. I love
> you, son.

Jason's stomach felt like it had been punched when he read the last sentence. He had never heard once the words "I love you" come from Gulaf's lips, and it was tragic that the one time he vocalized his affection is through scribbles on a parchment, shortly before being hauled away indefinitely. He looked up at Tarren. Tarren had torn his eyes away from the floor and was looking at Jason with an expression that was mixed several feelings—mostly dread and uncertainty.

"The worst part about all of this is not knowing if I'll ever see him again..."

"You will see him again," Jason tried to sound reassuring as he placed the note back on Tarren's desk. "It's just labor in the Eastern Mountains, not execution."

Besides, Jason thought. *If I take the throne, I'm going to obliterate the Blacknote first of all.*

"But how long will it be?" Tarren said. "Weeks? Months? Years? First, my mother, and now this... I don't know how much more I can take, Jason. Something needs to be done."

Jason shushed him and peered out the window. Seeing that the coast was clear, his voice died down to a whisper. "I agree, Tarren, something needs to be done. But now isn't the right time."

"*Then when?*" Tarren nearly shouted.

At that moment, the sound of hurried footsteps came bustling down the alleyway. They both exchanged glances, both thinking of the peculiarity of someone coming down to The Cranny, let alone in a dead run. Jason craned his head to get a look out the window, but he could only make out a dark silhouette through the smudges on the glass. Tarren stood from his desk and brushed off his apron, hoping that the rushed footsteps were a customer.

The door unlatched and burst open. In the doorway stood Tomm, with glasses hanging on the bridge of his nose and dirty sweat coating his neck and cheeks. His strong hand stayed on the door latch with white knuckles and his expression was hard. Jason stood from his chair quickly, a sense of alarm rapidly growing inside him.

"Father...!" Jason gasped. "What's going on?"

"I knew I would find you here," Tomm panted. "I just came from your flat—you didn't answer the door—and your shop isn't open yet—so I knew you'd be here..."

"What's wrong?" Tarren's eyes darted between the two of them.

"I'm not sure yet," Tomm said. "Something is wrong with Kara. She's sick. Come with me."

Jason and Tarren didn't hesitate. Tarren threw off his apron and bounded out the door as quickly as Jason did, making sure to lock the door behind him. The three of them hurried out the other end of the alleyway, bursting into the dusty streets of Lower City. They made no chatter as they went. Leery looks of townspeople met them as they made their way through the maze of Lower City streets, along with the occasional glare of soldiers. All of the Blacknotes had been taken off of the houses where they had been previously nailed.

Finally, they came upon the familiar cabin where Tomm and Kara lived. Their feet carried them quickly to the front door, which Tomm threw open as soon as they were upon it. The cabin wasn't accompanied by the familiar smells that Jason was used to. No cinnamon, no spices... nothing. His eyes darted about the cabin, but it wasn't long before he saw the horror.

To his left, Kara rested on her straw mattress, but her outward condition made Jason's face twist and his stomach lurch. The hue of her skin had deteriorated to a pale green, with brown splotches all over her legs, arms and face. A prim white dress adorned her slender frame, slightly spread out as if to sooth her decaying skin. She looked up as the three of them burst into the cabin. A smile graced her parched lips.

"Hello there…!" her voice was raspy and weak.

A man was already hunched over her by the side of her bed. His dark brown hair was neatly parted on the side and he toted a large case of vials, containing liquids of different colors and consistencies. Jason recognized the man. He had showed up to his family's cabin whenever he had the cold or a hacking cough. He remembered a few of the vials that the man made him drink from in order to make him feel better, and how awful they tasted.

Tomm stooped down next to him by his wife's bedside. "Do you know what's wrong, Lartok?"

Lartok didn't answer promptly. He shuffled through a few vials in his tote and let out a pensive breath. "I have theories, but I can't offer a clear diagnosis at this time. I'll do my best, Tomm, but this looks extremely rare. You might have to hire a doctor from Upper City."

"You know I can't afford that…"

Lartok didn't reply. From his tote, he extracted a long needle and a tiny glass cup. Jason eyed it uncomfortably.

"Kara," Lartok said. "I need to prick your finger to extract a sample of your blood, okay? You're going to feel a little pinch…"

He took her hand gently and slowly pressed the needle into her skin. Kara looked up to the ceiling and didn't so much as tense. Jason silently marveled at her self control. It only took a moment before crimson blood started to bead around the tip of the needle. Lartok withdrew it, wiped the tip off with a rag and some clear fluid, and started squeezing drips of blood into the tiny glass cup. Kara continued to look up to the ceiling, her eyes glossy as if she were dreaming. Lartok bandaged up her finger when he had concluded.

"What's that for?" Jason asked.

"A sample of her blood has to mix with one of my solutions for a week," Lartok said, not looking at Jason. "Depending on what color it turns, we'll know if my suspicion is correct."

"What's your suspicion?" said Tomm.

"Kara might have something called *Ipoklime*," Lartok explained. "It's not contagious. It's a very rare skin disease. No one knows how it's contracted, but it usually comes on very suddenly and dwells for a long period of time."

"How long?" Tarren said.

"Months," was Lartok's reply. "Sometimes over a year." He started placing all of his vials and tools back into his tote. "We won't know for sure if she has it until after my sample has time to mix."

"So it could be months before she gets better...?" Tomm asked gravely.

Lartok stood after he had placed all the tools back in his tote. He took a deep breath and exhaled, as if to flush out the uneasiness from his system. He didn't look up. "I don't know, Tomm. If it is *Ipoklime*, there is only one cure, and it's rare, expensive, and illegal."

"Why is it illegal?" Jason asked with bent eyebrows.

"Because it contains several substances that will either cure her, or kill her," Lartok replied. "Most doctors refuse to use it because its success rate is so slim."

A dark hush fell upon the room as every heart sank. Jason's eyes slid to his beautiful mother, trapped on a mat with insufficient strength to stand. The *Ipoklime* had tainted her, doomed her to decay, helpless and immobile, for the rest of her life—however short or long it may be. Jason's eyes dropped to the floor and his eyebrows bent. *How much more can this family take...?* He was sure Tarren was feeling the same way. After all, Kara was a second mother to him.

"Thank you, doctor," Kara breathed. "Everything will be okay."

Lartok teased a half-smile. "I sure hope so, Kara."

Tomm inserted his hand to his pocket to pull out some money, but Lartok stopped him. "No, Tomm. This one doesn't cost you anything."

Tomm pulled his hand back out. His chin dropped and he whispered a barely-audible thank you.

"I know with the raised tax you're going to need every Shard you have," Lartok said. "So don't worry about the payment now. I just hope as well as you all do that Kara gets better."

There was a short pause. Finally, Lartok bid the three farewell and crossed the floor, making his way for the door. As he unlatched the door and slammed it shut, the three remained suspended in gloomy silence. None of them looked at each other, let alone spoke.

At length, Tomm dragged his feet over to the bed and stooped down, taking Kara by her gnarled, splotched hand. He rubbed her hand with his as if doing so would get the disease to dissipate. Worry filled his eyes.

"I love you, my dear."

Kara's eyes twinkled and he cracked lips pulled into a smile. "Everything will be okay…"

Jason and Tarren exchanged looks. Tarren dropped his eyes and breathed deeply, inwardly speaking words of comfort to himself. Jason's mind started considering the possibilities. *Could this be one of my trials?* He recalled the words that King Barnabas had spoken to him over a month ago.

"I am going to tear your world apart from around you…"

His jaw clenched and he flexed his hands. He knew this had to be a trial, but how King Barnabas could make Kara contract a rare disease, he didn't know.

"When you find yourself ready to give up, come see me."

Is it worth it if the King destroys everything I love? It hasn't been two months… how much more of this can I take?

Jason looked upon the frail, sickly countenance of his mother and thought to himself, *If she knew what I was going through, she would want me to be strong. Everything will be okay…*

10 THE BRUTE

The vulture adjusted itself atop the dead tree on a hill, its powerful talons groping a branch below as it gazed over the wasteland with arrogant satisfaction. Miles away, a sapling protruded from the ground just under a foot high. Its thin stem and leaves swayed gingerly in the hollow breeze that wafted over the wasteland.

On a lower branch, the black eagle's sharp eyes focused upon the sapling. From its perch, it could make out all of the follicles in the leaves, the small fuzz upon the stem. It would sometimes watch the sapling for hours like a sentinel, all the while keeping a close eye on the vulture to be sure it wouldn't didn't try anything rash.

The vulture chuckled inside itself. The eagle ignored it, but continued to look on.

"Everything is going according to plan," the vulture sneered. "It will not be long before the sapling has browned and withered. Your efforts will be in vain."

The eagle's eyes stayed fixed on the sapling. "You cannot see it as well as I do. It sways and dips with the changing of the wind, but its leaves stay healthy and green. The wasteland will see life again. Your arrogance will be your downfall."

The vulture dismissed the reply. "The tragedy is that you believe you can protect it, even with all my power and cunning."

"Your power is an illusion," the eagle replied coolly. "And although you may be cunning, you simply dwell in the shadow of one who is greater. And I believe you still know that, despite the darkness that dwells within your heart."

Finally, the vulture's satisfied expression faded. Silence ensued, then the eagle looked up and said calmly, "The simple and pure will rise up to thrash the mighty. You will see that in time."

The vulture scowled and held its tongue, but only for long enough to conjure a reply. "I suppose we will."

* * * * *

A blob of sweat slid down Jason's cheek and dropped down to the red-hot blade below. It sizzled and evaporated in a tiny puff of steam. His left hand kept a firm grip on the handle—still crude and unfinished—while his right wrapped around the handle of a metal hammer. The hammer crushed the blade into shape with every blow as it rested on the anvil.

When the blade had been pounded into adequate shape, Jason carefully took it by the handle and dipped it into a barrel of water by his side. Steam sprouted up from the water, coating Jason's arm, which was already drenched in sweat. With his left hand, he wiped his brow with the back of his hand. Then he threw the sword into a barrel full of identical ones, the handles sticking out from the top.

"Closing time!" Jaboc called over the machines.

Indeed, the shadow had fallen over the red line at the back of the front desk. Outside, the Southern Market Street had fallen into full autumn swing. Trees rich with red and gold shivered in orange sunlight and the townspeople that walked by sported thicker clothing made of wool and fur. Autumn was always a beautiful time of year for Nezmyth, but as of late, Jason's mind had been caught up in other things.

The four shop workers hastily got to work turning off the machines. Each machine sputtered and churned to a gradual halt, and the shop became oddly silent. Footsteps sounded louder across the old wooden floors.

Bertus tipped his head back and glugged from an enormous canteen he had crafted. Dirty sweat dripped off his burly face and arms like lightly falling rain. Golan pulled a towel from his pocket and wiped his face with it. Jaboc let the sweat drip from him as if it stood as a testament to another day of hard work. He smirked satisfactorily.

Jason rubbed a towel across his face and hair and tossed it on the back of a chair to dry. He couldn't stop thinking of his mother... there hadn't been word yet on her sickness from Lartok. He also couldn't stop thinking of his Ancient Nezmythian lessons or the fact that he *still* hadn't come up with a way to start training. And he had grown tired of Master Ferribolt's reproving expressions for the past month.

"It's the end of the week," Jaboc called. "And I am *ready* for it."

He had made his way to a coat rack at the side of the shop where all of their jackets were hung and their weapons leaned up in a corner. One by one, they all crossed the floor to the coat rack after Jaboc.

"I am as well," Golan said. "I haven't had much time at all to spend with Tarmanthia since the Blacknote. I hate spending so much time away from her..."

"You still live in Upper City with your parents!" Jaboc sneered. "Why do you need to worry about the Blacknote?"

"Because he still works with all of us," Jason said as he slipped his jacket on. "And paying the Blacknote requires all of our efforts."

Golan, trying to dispel the rising tension, redirected the conversation. "What do you have planned, Bertus?"

"Go play some music in Center Court," he shrugged. "Hopefully some Upper City folks with throw me a few Pieces."

"That's not a bad idea," Jason said. "Maybe I'll join you sometime."

Bertus half-smiled. Jason always had a hard time telling whether or not he approved with his suggestions. Although Bertus was by far the biggest and strongest of the bunch, he was very agreeable and thoughtful, and never impolite.

"What are you doing, Jason?" Jaboc asked.

Jason shrugged and shook his head. "I'm not quite sure yet."

"Well, *I'm* going to the combat gym down the street," he said. "I haven't been in weeks and I can feel it." He squeezed his arm and smirked again. "I need to be sure these stay beautiful..."

Bertus and Golan rolled their eyes, but something inside Jason's mind flared up. The scoffing remarks from Master Ferribolt... the fear he felt upon considering the possibility of a Kingly battle... they both erupted from the back of his mind and made his eyes pop. *Why didn't I think of it before...? Now is my chance.*

"Wait!" Jason said, focusing on Jaboc. "Jaboc... how often do you attend a combat gym?"

"I used to every day..." Jaboc said slowly. "But not since the Blacknote. What does that have to do with anything?"

"Nothing," Jason said hastily. "I—uh... I've just been trying to find the time to spar lately. Mind if I join you?"

Jaboc chuckled amusedly. Jason didn't break his gaze off of him. Bertus and Golan exchanged looks. After an awkward pause, Jaboc's smile slowly fell. He said, "...You're serious?"

Jason nodded with stiff eyebrows.

"Um... Jason," Jaboc continued uncomfortably. "I don't think you're really the type to be sparring at a combat gym..."

"Why not?" Jason said. He was starting to wonder if Jaboc's toned muscles had gone to his head.

"Well," Jaboc looked like a very sensible reply was right on the tip of his tongue, but every time he opened his mouth to say something the words came out stuttered and broken.

Jason's eyes bore into him accusingly. Finally, Jaboc let out a defeated exhale and said, "You'll see. Come with me, but don't say I didn't warn you."

Bertus and Golan buttoned up their jackets and walked around the front desk to escape the conversation. Jason eyed Jaboc as he slipped his sword on over his jacket. *He's never seen me spar before... who is he to think that I can't handle myself at a combat gym? Growing up, the only one who could beat me in my sparring group was Tarren, and he's the best fighter I know. Jaboc will see soon enough.*

Jaboc and Jason made their way around the front desk and exited out the door in silence. Jason locked the door latch and gave the handle a tug, satisfied when it didn't budge. He pocketed the key. Jaboc stood to his right with his hands impatiently in his pocket.

"You sure you don't want to drop that off at home?" Jaboc said, referring to Jason's sword. "They have practice weapons there."

Jason shook his head. "Nope. Let's go."

Jaboc puffed out his lower lip with a hum, and then jerked his head, signaling Jason to come with him. He kept his eyes straight ahead as he walked, while Jason had a tendency to look at his boots. Vendors on the sides of the street cast sheets over their handcarts and their wheels crunched softly on the cobblestone as they concluded the work day. Soldiers eyed everyone they passed by, as usual.

As he looked down, he noticed that Jaboc didn't have any weapons attached to him—not even a knife. His eyebrows creased.

"Why don't you carry any weapons?" Jason asked. "Isn't that dangerous?"

Jaboc scoffed and smirked at the remark. "I'm fast. Someone with a sword or an axe can be disarmed, but you can't disarm someone from their fists."

"But every Nezmythian child is supposed to train with at least one sort of weapon while growing up," Jason said. "You know... in case of war."

Jaboc nodded. "I trained with a sword. But it never did much for me. I can land three punches before I can swing a blade."

Jason tried to picture Jaboc on a sparring mat opposing a brute with a sword, bobbing and weaving through each slash, then disarming the foe and bringing him to his knees with his bare hands. It wasn't exactly hard to imagine. Jason was sure Jaboc could hold his own on the sparring mat against someone of any size.

As they walked, Jason spotted an old fruit cart loaded with a vast array of colorful, freshly-harvested snacks. An old, frail-looking man stood at the foot of the cart, his hands behind his back and looking pleasant despite his tattered apron and weathered, flat shoes. *Everyone is turning in for the day… maybe he needs the extra money, so he's staying out longer.*

Jason's stomach growled. He slowed his pace.

"Hold on," Jason said to Jaboc as he strolled up to the cart. "This'll only take a second."

Jaboc sighed irritably and came to a halt as Jason approached the man. His wrinkled lips pulled into a smile.

"Good evening," the old man's quivering high voice replied. "What would you like today?"

"I'll have one guabo, please."

The old man retrieved a ripe, golden guabo from his cart as he asked Jason for seven Shards. Jason extracted the change from his pocket and dropped it into the man's hand as he took the guabo from the other. He didn't hesitate in taking a large bite out of the side of the fruit. Delicious nectar spilt into his mouth, sweet and tangy.

Jason hummed in delight, and through a full mouth said "Thank you! One of the best guabos I've had."

"You're welcome," the old man said sweetly. "Come again soon!"

The old man turned around and flipped a canvas over his fruity handcart, retiring for the night. With that, Jason joined back up with Jaboc and finished the rest of his guabo in silence. Chitchat was minimal and bland as they walked down the Southern Market Street. Eventually, they turned left as if to travel to Center Court, but stopped halfway down the road. Jaboc nodded and motioned with his hand.

"This is it," he said.

They both stood at the foot of a massive, square facility with several stories, built of faded red brick and chipping mortar. Above the door, a sign read 'THE CROSSING BLADES COMBAT GYM' in eye-watering yellow letters. A silhouette of two men crossing swords and baring their teeth was painted on the full length of the gnarled door. Jason's heart rate increased as he looked at it. Muffled shouting, smashing and thumping sounded from the other side.

As Jason stood gawking at the outer wall, questioning silently if this was really the best way to become a better fighter, he rubbed his hands together apprehensively. He thought that Jaboc was still by his side until he heard a loud click and a slam, and realized that Jaboc had walked in without him. Quickly, he jogged up to the door, wrapped his hand around the door latch and threw it open.

The smell of sweat and leather hit him like a wall and clogged his lungs as he entered. He coughed slightly into his gloved fist as he tried not to hunch over. The muffled shouts and bellows now reverberated with clear resonance off the walls. If he had walked two more steps, he would have ran right into Jaboc.

Right inside the door and to the right, a large square opening at about chest level was cut into the wall. A short woman with shoulder-length red hair and a long scar down her cheek sat in a chair on the other side. It looked to Jason as if she was in charge of whoever signed in to spar. Racks of wooden practice weapons lined the walls in her room. She was filing her fingernails, sighing occasionally, her dull, brown eyes full of boredom. Jason blinked.

"Hello, Kari..." Jaboc said while leaning through the window, his charming smile stretched across his face.

"Jaboc," she replied with her eyes fixed on her nail file. "Sorry, but all the mats are taken, so unless you can find someone who will share a ring with you… you're going to have to go home. Sorry."

"Please," Jaboc said playfully. "I come prepared, Kar'! Bobby's already here. He'll let us spar with him and we'll probably find some other guys to tangle."

Who's Bobby? Jason wondered.

"Us?" Kari finally looked up. She leaned sideways in her chair to peek around Jaboc and caught Jason's eye. Jason half-smiled sheepishly. Her nose crinkled and she sniffed loudly. She raised an eyebrow at Jaboc, who tried to maintain his charming pretense, despite the fact that Kari was obviously immune to it.

"I work with him," Jaboc explained. "And he insisted… I tried to warn him."

Kari chuckled to herself and shook her head as she resumed filing her nails. "Did you tell him you can't bring real weapons onto the sparring floor? Then again, from the look of him, he might need it… kind of stringy-lookin'."

Jason frowned. An awkward silence clung to the air for just a second before Kari tossed her file aside and stood from her chair.

"You can't take that in," she said, looking Jason in the eye. "You can trade it in for a practice weapon here, and I'll keep your sword safe in a chest along with some others. Otherwise, you can't go out on the floor."

Jason eyed her suspiciously, and the sword suddenly felt glued to his back. He rubbed the sheath uncomfortably. He didn't even have to hand his sword over when he went into the castle or Master Ferribolt's home…

"Jason," Jaboc said. "It'll be fine. Just give it to her."

Jason paused, and finally, he pulled the sheath off his back and handed it through the window. A strange feeling came over him, as if he had handed a small piece of himself to a stranger. He watched her carefully as she bent down, unlatched a lock by her feet, and set his sword inside. When she came back up, a wooden sword of a similar size was in her hand. She extended it to Jason.

reflexively. He brought his sword and sent it straight upward into the brute's foot.

Bobby roared as he hopped on one foot, cradling his injured other. It gave Jason the time he needed. He scrambled back onto his feet and seized the moment. He leapt into the air in an aerial kick, attempting to connect with Bobby's chest and topple him, but his foot didn't connect. It was snatched out of the air by the brute.

"Stupid little—!" He bellowed. His face had changed from a cocky grin to an enraged, teeth-baring scowl.

All that Jason saw was a blur, but what Jaboc saw was Bobby spinning backward, holding Jason over his shoulder like a large sack, and swinging him over his head and onto the ground.

Jaboc cringed horribly. The loud *thud* of Jason connecting with the mat was deafening. Upon his victory, Bobby the Brute craned his neck to the sky and bellowed savagely, flexing his arms and hands. When he was done, he slowly turned about and lumbered to the edge of the mat.

"*Next!*"

Jaboc sprang up to the mat and jogged over to Jason. He bent over to get a good look at him. He looked like he had just been thrown around by an angry gorilla. His left eye was blackening. His shoulder blades were probably bruised. He couldn't feel his left leg. His breathing was labored. He looked up at Jaboc through his half-closed, watery eyes. Jaboc shook his head disappointedly, sighing deeply.

"I told you. Your leg looks like it's broken. Just lay still here... some people will come fix you up soon," he said. He hesitated, and added "...and maybe you should train with someone else for a while."

Jason tried to lift his head up off the ground, but only managed to lift it about two inches before exhausting his strength and dropping it again. The last thing he heard before losing consciousness was Jaboc saying:

"Sorry, Jason."

11 THE REQUESTS

Jason awoke later that night still lying on the combat mat where he had been knocked out earlier. Fresh moonlight crept in through the dusty windows and casted pale squares on the gymnasium floor. He tried to recount what had happened, but every event that partook within the past few hours were blurred and hazy. A vague memory of being tossed around by Bobby the Brute was the only thing floating around in his joggled head.

His eyelids seemed like they were magnetized together, but he forced them open and the blurry image of the gymnasium ceiling slowly came into focus. With great effort, Jason set his hands to his sides and pushed himself into a sitting position on the mat. Stars fluttered around his vision and every muscle in his body was pulsing uncomfortably.

I thought Jaboc said some medics would clean me up, Jason thought bitterly as he felt the sensitiveness of his shoulders and shoulder blades. His left eye felt tender, too—it had probably blackened by now. He kept thinking about the pulsing pain in his shoulder blades when the thought occurred to him.

He looked to his right briefly, and to his surprise, someone had laid his real blade right next to him, sheath, strap and all, ready to be picked up when he gained consciousness. Jason reached out and wrapped his hand around the sheath, bringing it onto his lap and caressing it carefully.

Jason forced himself to stand. He groaned as his legs pushed his torso higher. He felt like a statue that had just gained mobility after being inanimate for a century. Obviously, his left leg must have been broken when Bobby threw him over his shoulder. The leg felt brittle and hollow, like how broken limbs usually feel once they've been healed by a magical bone-mending technique. Jason concluded that the medical staff must have cleaned him up after all. He made a mental note to take it easy on his leg. It would probably take all week for it to fully heal.

As he slipped his sword onto his back, he growled in frustration, but the noise just echoed off the stubborn, lifeless walls. His entire upper back seared sensitively when it came in contact with the sheath. Stars fluttered in his eyes. Moonlight flooded into the shanty hall, and he was the only amateur limping around to collect his things and go home.

He eased himself off the edge of the mat and set himself down gingerly to the ground. Out of the corner of his eye, he spotted a murky mirror on the far wall, just beside the set of stairs leading to the basement. It took him a few minutes to hobble over and face himself.

His eye had blackened—it was swollen and his eyelid hung loosely over it. Jason turned around and took his sword and shirt off to face his reflection once again. Sure enough, his entire upper back was black and blue, surely from the final blow that Bobby the Brute executed. His hair was sticking up in odd angles. He felt an exceptionally large goose egg on the back of his head. The back of his forearms were scraped up from where he slid on the mat.

He felt like a defeated, derelict soldier. All he wanted was rest.

I can't go home now, he thought to himself as he put on his shirt and sword again. *Thieves and robbers will be prowling, not to mention suspicious soldiers... But if I don't go home, where will I sleep?*

He looked out one of the windows that was perched just below the ceiling and saw the stars glittering in the endless black. It didn't take him long to debate. He was too tired. He would just find someplace here to sleep until morning.

If the gym people would leave me here after closing time, they might as well have me for rest of the night.

Jason limped to the nearest mat. Easing himself down gently, trying to be as ginger as he could to his black and blue shoulders and head, he slid his body onto the edge and rested his head. Rolling onto his side, he curled up slightly, his arms wrapped around his sword like a child and its stuffed bear. Jason fell asleep within seconds—tired, cold, and alone.

* * * * *

Jason's flyra carried his thoughts and feelings with each whistling note. The sky had turned a bright shade of red with the sunset, which complimented the orange and brown trees. But even with all the beautiful scenery, Jason couldn't keep his mind clear. Jaboc's words echoed in his head from the prior week: *"...maybe you should train with someone else for a while."*

Jason and Tarren each sat on their familiar stools in The Cranny. Jason pulled the flyra away from his lips and craned his neck to look out at the sunset. He sighed to himself. Tarren sat at the desk, meticulously tuning a newly-crafted instrument with his strong hands, his hair streaming down passed his eyes. Jason spoke just loud enough to be heard across the room.

"That's a beautiful sunset," he said.

Tarren didn't look up. He probably didn't even hear Jason—his hearing became very selective when he became involved in a task. Jason continued on as if he were sure he was listening.

"It's very interesting that the most beautiful part of the day comes at its close... after the haze of the morning and the sweat of the afternoon. It's almost like a reward, if you think about it... like a brand new painting every day, to us,

from the Dragon… congratulating us for enduring yet
another day."

"I'm sorry?" Tarren's head finally popped up.

Jason smirked half to himself, "Never mind…"

"What's the news on your mother?"

Jason bowed his head. "The solution mixed for a week…
and it didn't change color, so it's not *Ipoklime*. It's so strange,
though. She's showing all the signs of it, but her blood is just
fine. I'm not sure what to think."

"Maybe she'll be alright, then." Tarren thought aloud.

"Maybe…" Jason echoed. *Or not…*

Tarren went back to his work. Something else was on
Jason's mind besides his mother's illness. Flashbacks from
last week's match with Bobby the Brute revisited him over
and over again along with Jaboc's words, "*…maybe you should
train with someone else for a while.*"

He took another deep breath and tried to organize his
thoughts into complete sentences. He mentally rehearsed the
following question in his mind, trying to configure the words
in the best way possible. Finally, he leaned forward on his
stool and traced the holes in his flyra with his fingers.
"Tarren, there's something I've been meaning to talk to you
about."

Tarren looked up again. "Is it important?"

"Very."

"Well, go ahead."

"It's nothing bad. Uh… It's just the reason I wanted to
come see you today was because I have a question for you."

"Okay…" Tarren tilted his head.

"Well… I went to a combat gym last week…" Jason
began, biting the side of his lip. *How am I going to put this?*
"I've realized that I need a lot more practice in battle
and…"—Jason inhaled deeply—"I want you to teach me to
spar again."

Tarren's eyebrow shot up. He gawked at Jason skeptically.

"Are you joking?" he said with a nervous chuckle. "Why?
You're already an amazing fighter."

"Liar," Jason said, furrowing his eyebrows. "I just went to a combat gym last week and got beaten unconscious. There's only one person I know that could teach me to fight those kind of brawlers, and that's you."

While Jason was talking, Tarren put his hands on his knees and shook his head. Jason could almost hear the gears cranking in his head.

"You remember the last time I tried sparring with you privately?" he said coldly and calmly. "After our combat lessons we took together?"

Too well... Jason thought to himself as his blood ran cold. He caught the rusty memory of blasting a hole through a wall after he got mad at Tarren for beating him so badly. He still wasn't positive that Tarren had fully forgiven him.

"I remember... but I'm more patient now," Jason said hastily. "Besides, I'm trying to learn for different reasons now—more important reasons. I wish I could explain them to you but it's... complicated..."

He hoped—*prayed*—it would never come to it, but he had to be ready to fight King Barnabas if the time ever came. He couldn't risk the safety and wellbeing of the entire kingdom solely because he neglected to learn when it could have been the difference between life and death.

The only thing in the way was Tarren. Tarren could probably have handled Bobby the Brute and Jason simultaneously—maybe even the more elite fighters at The Crossing Blades. If he would teach Jason, it would make a world of difference... but the hole in the wall incident was enough to dismiss it without thinking twice, and Jason wouldn't blame him.

"I don't know..." Tarren replied by rubbing his chin and looking at the floor.

"Tarren, please!" Jason said, his blood was beginning to freeze.

"Why is this so important to you right now?" Tarren shot, looking into his eyes.

Jason didn't know what to say. He couldn't tell Tarren of Master Ferribolt, King Barnabas and his Year of Decision... otherwise it would all be for naught. But lying definitely wouldn't make the Oracle Stone any whiter. He looked down, then sighed.

"It's just a feeling," he said, "A strong feeling. It's something I need to do."

A long pause. The gears turning in Tarren's head were almost audible. He traced circles on his desk with a grease-smudged finger. Jason looked up into his eyes, and Tarren looked back. Finally, Tarren sighed and continued on with his work, taking his eyes off Jason.

"I'll think about it."

* * * * *

The loud hums and churnings of machines were eerily absent from Kristof's Weapons and Crafts. Their order list lacked something they needed to keep work going: orders. Bertus, Golan and Jaboc were all doing their usual things when there's not a thing to do. Bertus was playing with his ponytail. Golan was whittling something small and round out of some scrap wood while he rested his steady hands on the table. Jaboc's arms rested across his chest as he leaned back in a chair, his head tilted back and snoring softly.

Not much was spoken to each other—there wasn't much to say. No one had walked through the front door since the four of them that morning. Finally, it was Bertus that broke the silence.

"Are we on track for the next Harvest?" he asked Jason.

Jason's hands were behind his head, looking up, counting the number of boards in the ceiling. "No. I counted this morning. We're behind about a six Blocks. Everyone has been saving their money since the tax raise. And let's face it, most people already have weapons they carry with them, so ordering new ones won't be important to them."

Bertus exhaled and scratched his chin. Jaboc twitched and smacked his lips before resuming his crackling snores. Meanwhile, Golan remained fixed upon his work, whittling away the small token with expert precision.

"What are you carving, Golan?" Jason asked.

Golan looked up at him, then turned back to his work as he realized his cheeks went pink. "Um… a ring."

Jason's eyebrow cocked musingly, "Is it for—?"

Suddenly, a feminine voice from the front of the store echoed through the silent shop.

"Hello?" She rang the bell. When Jason got up from his chair to check who it was, Jaboc awoke with a snort.

"Who's there?" He asked with fluttering eyes.

"Go back to sleep," Jason said, patting him on the shoulder and walking around his chair to the front desk. *It sounds like a woman up front… the last thing we need is Jaboc chasing away our only customer today with his flirtatious—*

Jason's jaw fell.

It was *her!* The freckled girl from several weeks ago stood patiently at the customer desk while Jason walked up to meet her. Her form-flattering white dress looked like it had just been washed. She blinked at Jason and smiled a flawless, dimpled smile, her long eyelashes emphasizing her sparkling silver eyes. A brown satchel was slung over his shoulder.

Jason's heart thumped as he walked up to her. The voice inside his head repeatedly told him to remain calm and professional. He cleared his throat. His hair was untidy and his clothes were just as filthy as usual, but he tried to project confidence with every footstep. It was difficult as he realized how shoddy he looked in contrast to her radiance.

"Hello," She said brightly. "I'd like to place a custom order. You can do that, right?"

Jason's face lit up. He could have kissed her—the thought crossed him more than once. He quickly grabbed a writing stick and paper out of a nearby drawer and slapped them on the desk.

"Yes, we do!" Jason said excitedly. "Just let me know the specifications and we'll get to work on it immediately."

She smiled broadly. "Perfect! Do you have much experience making long staffs?"

"Yes, we do," Jason said.

"Excellent! Now, I'm sorry, but I'm really specific about what I like." She brought out a folded-up piece of paper she had been storing in her pocket. "First off, I would like it made from Golden Oak, which is pretty rare—it only grows in the deepest parts of the Ancient Woods…"

Jason tried to pay attention to the specs the best he could. He couldn't keep himself from shooting glances at her silver eyes as she leaned across the table. Jason tried to pay attention through nodding and saying things like "yes" and "absolutely" and "we can do that," and he silently prayed that he wasn't so distracted that he was missing any important details.

Suddenly, her voice trailed off and she stopped talking. Jason quickly realized this and looked at her quizzically. She bore an expression of curiosity and enthusiasm, as if something important was just dawning on her. She continued to ogle at Jason and he became more and more nervous.

Shakily, Jason asked, "What?"

Her eyes squinted, "I've met you before haven't I? You seem *very* familiar."

Jason's heart thumped louder, and his lips pulled into a sheepish grin. "Yes, only briefly… we were both buying fruit on the Southern Market Street less than two months ago… at the booshum berry cart."

"*That's right!*" her face lit up and she stood up straight. "I'm sorry, I can't believe I didn't have the decency to introduce myself!"—she stretched her hand out to Jason— "Saryan. It's a pleasure to meet you again."

The corners of Jason's mouth touched his ears as he took her hand and shook it. Her handshake was firm and spirited, but her hands also felt soft and gentle. He hoped that she couldn't feel his pulse through his hand. *Saryan... what a unique name...*

"Jason," he replied, still wearing a big, dumb grin. When he realized this, he cleared his throat and tapped the parchment he had jotted the specifications on. "This is pretty elaborate. It might take a while to get the materials and construct it, but I want to say we'll have it done within a month." He paused. "...You're not from Lower City, are you?"

Her eyes twinkled and she shook her head. Jason suddenly became serious.

"You should be careful," he said. "There are a lot of people down here that would love to rob an Upper City girl. Why are you coming down here for your errands? It's dangerous for you here."

A sly expression suddenly slid across her face. She peeked over her shoulders, out the window, checking for soldiers. When she saw that the coast was clear, she leaned over the table and looked directly into Jason's eyes. He gulped, and he felt his heart rate kick up again.

"For your information," she whispered. "I'm ordering a custom staff because I'm a battle instructor, so I can take care of myself. Besides"—her voice died down even more—"I know how the Blacknote affects you people down here. Most of us in Upper City have no problem paying it, and some of us want to come down and buy from Lower City people to help them pay the tax. We're all people in the same kingdom. We know you need the help, and we're just as unhappy about the King as you are."

That's debatable... Jason thought. Still, he couldn't deny the girl's giving spirit. It was admirable. And truthfully, the complicated order she had just placed would be expensive, and it would be a great help for the four of them to pay the tax in the next two months.

Impressed and corrected, Jason asked, "...is that all?"

"No," she said dreamily. "I also need about a dozen practice swords. Shorter ones. My students are all fairly young."

Jason recorded that on the parchment, then she asked what the total would be. When Jason gave the answer, she seemed pleasantly surprised at how reasonably it was all priced.

"Can you take deliver it to my arena when it's ready? I don't want to impose—."

"It's no trouble," Jason said. "Where is it that you teach?"

"In the basement of The Crossing Blades. It's between Center Court and the Southern Market Street. Just enter through the backdoor and there's a set of stairs."

Something like a shiver slid down Jason's back as she repeated the name of the gym where he got thrashed two weeks prior. He was very thankful that the mention of a backdoor… the last thing he wanted to do was show his face to Bobby the Brute again—at least anytime soon.

"Alright then," he said. "All we need is the material fee and you can pay the rest after we've delivered it. We'll get started immediately."

Satisfied, Saryan dropped her satchel on the desk, rummaged through the contents for a moment, then extracted a small pouch of money, which she dropped on the desk with a shimmering thud. Jason picked it up and placed it in a drawer under the desk. *There must be at least thirty Blocks in here…*

Saryan smiled wide, showcasing her dimples and her perfect teeth. She shook Jason's hand again, expressed her thanks, and her eyes sparkled.

"I'll see you soon."

Jason's heart swelled again. And with that, she was out the door and gone.

For a moment, Jason stood swaying in place, still soaking up the moment. He clung onto her last words. *I'll see you soon.*

He sighed, grinning ear to ear. He looked at the order form closely in his hands. *Wow...* not only was he excited about getting another order, he was completely energized about finally getting her name. *Saryan...* He couldn't pull the corners of his mouth down. It wasn't long before the others came up.

"Do we have another order?" Bertus said with pressed lips.

"Yes, we do!" Jason said without taking his eyes off the form. "It's a long staff. A girl named Saryan just ordered it. She's from Upper City, so she's rich... and the design is intricate."

"An Upper City girl!" Jaboc piped up, realizing that a golden specimen had drifted right under his nose whilst he dozed away.

"Why didn't you have me come sketch it?" Golan asked, puzzled.

Jason looked at the floor briefly. "Sorry. I kind of forgot."

Bertus pushed his lips together, compressing an amused snicker. Jason caught his eyes and squinted slightly.

"What?" He said defensively.

"I saw her," Bertus said musingly. "She was beautiful. I would have lost my focus too, if I were you."

Immediately, every employee's face brightened into an entertained smile. All eyes were on Jason. He felt himself flush and his cheeks burned crimson. Each coworker suppressing laughs, excluding Golan. He merely smiled genuinely.

"Did you call on her?" Jaboc shot.

Jason's eyebrows bent. "No!"

"Good," he replied. "Then I'm going with you when you deliver the order. I'll call on her if you won't."

"No, you're not," Jason's face became hot. Jaboc snickered, as if he had gained a small victory from witnessing Jason's protectiveness. "Okay, knock it off everyone," he continued. "All I did was take her order. That's it. Leave it." Bertus and Jaboc looked at each as if they were hungry to harass Jason more, but settled on shaking their heads and letting out small chortles. Jason looked at Golan and raised an eyebrow. "What, don't you think it's funny, too?"

"Well, kind of…" Golan said truthfully. "But it's also kind of neat. Maybe you really found someone special."

"Like I said, all I did was take her order," Jason tried desperately not to grin, but couldn't stop his eyes from flashing. "And I'm sorry about forgetting to grab you. It was a big order, too."

Golan continued. "It's alright. We'll get more. At least you'll get to see her again when we deliver the order. That would give you the chance to call on her."

"*I'm not going to call on her!*"

"I will!" Jaboc's face brightened.

"Shut up, Jaboc!"

"You should, Jason," Golan said plainly. "Won't you regret it if you don't?"

Jason let out a mighty exhale. He knew he would regret it if he didn't, and he knew he wanted to, but he didn't like being put on the spot by everyone else in the shop. He tried with much difficulty to find a way to transition the conversation into a different direction. At the same time, however, he was trying to imagine *how* exactly he would call on her when the time came… he had never done it before.

"That's the least of our problems," Jason said coolly. "What we need is several more custom orders like that. That'll be the only way we can afford to pay the tax in two months. As for right now, we can get started making those practice swords before the end of the day. Let's go."

Jason didn't wait for the other three's vote of agreement before he retreated back into the shop and started up the machines. Twelve wooden practice swords wouldn't take the four of them long at all. The rest of them followed suit, shaking their heads playfully and exchanging snarky remarks under their breath.

Still, Jason couldn't take his mind off the order from earlier. He had finally gotten her name… *Saryan*… and he replayed their conversation over and over in his memory. What were the odds that she would suddenly turn up in his shop? He couldn't forget that dimpled smile and those silver eyes.

Could the King have sent her here...? It is very coincidental. No... she's helping us pay the tax, and King Barnabas wouldn't want that at all. Very strange... but I don't mind.

He looked out the window. The sunset threw brilliant colors onto the horizon, like a painting from the Dragon.

It was beautiful.

12 THE BAIT

Jason's hands jammed into his jacket pockets as he strolled down the declining Upper City street. Tiny streams of water snaked through the cobblestone—it had rained while he was inside studying with Master Ferribolt, which made the air heavy and moist. He mumbled Ancient Nezmythian to himself, having a conversation with some imaginary person beside him.

"*Elu choreeloh...leh, moosh paylet racar tishu...*"

He had become somewhat comfortable with Ancient Nezmythian small talk. Now after having studied it for two months, he had a firm grasp on the basics and found himself very capable in maintaining an adequate conversation with Master Ferribolt, although he often became confused and slightly frustrated when Master Ferribolt would begin speaking at a quicker pace to test him. His biggest weakness remained a limited vocabulary.

"Go to the city library," Master Ferribolt had suggested. "They have a small collection of Ancient Nezmythian texts, and there you can brush up on terms and phrases."

Jason met the suggestion with gratitude, but politely dismissed it, assuming that he didn't have the time to go. The library was on the east side of Center Court, and he was sure they wouldn't let a Lower City commoner into the Ancient

Nezmythian section. The books are centuries old, and likely to be very valuable. Master Ferribolt shrugged and told Jason that he wouldn't know unless he tried.

As Jason rounded the corner of the Northern and Southern Market streets, he noticed something extremely odd. As far as he could see, the street was completely empty. No Lower City commoners, no marching soldiers… not a soul was out. Jason's eyes hardened and his heart thumped, thinking of the foreboding peculiarity of the setting.

He didn't notice the person sitting against a wall to his left.

"Psst! Mulak flowers. Two Bars each."

Mulak flowers. A sliver of ice slid down Jason's spine. His eyes darted to his left, where he caught the gaze of the shady salesman. The man's hands were buried in the pockets of a massive coat. He had a gnarly grin and a milky blue eye, accompanied with a long, thick scar down his matching cheek. A dark chuckle escaped him as he caught Jason's gaze.

"Two Bars each," he man echoed. "Soar higher than the clouds. See things you always wanted. Come on, chum."

Cold sweat thickened on Jason's brow. He would only need one. He could grind it up and feed it to his mother… after all, she had showed all the symptoms of the *Ipoklime…* maybe Lartok's concoction was wrong. He had two Bars in his pocket…

He took a step toward the man… then stopped.

This is wrong, Jason thought to himself. *Why are there no soldiers on the street? The King could have spies anywhere around here. For all I know, he could have planted this man here to sell me the Mulak flower, so the King could have a reason to imprison me. After all, the flower is illegal.*

Jason's jaw clenched and he flipped on his heels.

"Don't talk to me again," he said firmly as he strode away.

The shady flower salesman chuckled. "I'll be here… case you change your mind."

* * * * *

"Thank you," Jason said as two men with thick arms and leather gloves dropped an enormous stock of Golden Oak on the desk. One of the men gave him a grunt and a swift nod and held out his empty hand.

"Oh! Of course…" Jason said. He reached under the desk and pulled out a medium-sized leather pouch before he handed it over to the delivery man. "There should be thirty-five Blocks in there."

"Much obliged," the delivery man slurred as he pulled open the drawstrings and peered inside. He tipped his hat. "No offense, but I'm s'prised ye can afford this wood, workin' in a place like this. 'Ave a nice day."

Jason returned the gesture and the man swiftly walked out the door. Through the window, Jason could see the grizzly driver of the large delivery coach snapping the reigns and shouting at the horses. After a few shouts, the horses whinnied and set off at a steady trot to the next customer.

Bertus came up from behind, and together, he and Jason hoisted up the Golden Oak and laboriously walked it over to a saw table. The stock had to be seven feet long and a foot thick, and it was incredibly heavy—even Bertus was straining under its weight.

"It's supposed to be really strong," Bertus grunted. He and Jason dropped the stock on the table as soon as it was possible. "My cousin's brother-in-law's father's great aunt has a walking stick made of Golden Oak. It's been handed down and reused in their family for generations, and they think it'll still last another few hundred years."

"No wonder it was so expensive," Jason said. "Hopefully we don't break any of our equipment trying to shape it. I figure we'll cut it down into several sections so we can have spares, just in case…" Jason trailed off comically.

Over at one of the other work tables, Jaboc was nailing a bronze plate onto a plaque. Swinging vigorously on the last nail, he missed and the head of the nail and the hammer came smashing down onto the tip of his thumb.

He leapt into the air and yelped like a startled animal and began to dance in place while cradling his injured thumb, which was reddening and pulsing with pain. Bertus and Jason snickered silently at the desk as they watched him.

"So are you going to deliver it to her?" Bertus asked with a smirk.

"Who, Saryan?"

"Yes, Saryan."

"Probably," Jason responded. He smiled faintly. "After all, Golan suggested it."

"Make way! Make way!" An unfamiliar voice called from outside.

"What's going on?" Jason said, turning to Bertus. Bertus shrugged his beefy shoulders.

Golan was adjusting the display case in the window when he called into the shop, "The King is coming through town! Hurry! Come outside!"

Bertus and Jaboc hustled and weaved around the room and slipped out the front door.

Jason's blood turned to ice. A cold sweat formed on his brow as his mind once again began to shift into full power. His neck and arm hairs bristled.

King Barnabas? What's he doing out of the castle?

After a moment of hesitation, Jason forced his feet forward to the exit. His heart pounded and his mind was a hive of angry bees swarming and hypothesizing what King Barnabas was doing out of the throne. He got the dark, sinking impression that this had to be no mere coincidence. He and his Year of Decision had to be related to this… there was no question about it.

Jason shielded his eyes from the blinding noonday sun, the shadow of his gloved hand falling onto his eyes. He rubbed his arm as the autumn breeze nipped at his lean torso. As he looked to his left, King Barnabas himself came into view about fifty yards down the cobblestone market street. He was sitting atop a black stallion, wearing his usual charcoal-black garbs and sporting a smug grin, trotting along leisurely as the townspeople cheered at the sight of him and bowed reverently.

It's almost like he has no idea that every man, woman and child in this miserable kingdom thinks he's disease, Jason thought bitterly.

King Barnabas was accompanied by what seemed to be half the castle. The Advisor trotted just a few feet behind him and to the right on his own white stallion, appearing emotionless as ever. Nezmythian soldiers marched with dignity along the procession, ready to force back any madman with the audacity to throw a dagger or jeroki. Further down the line, dancers with ribbons and musicians with flutes and horns trailed behind, along with carriages full of distastefully beautiful women.

As King Barnabas was about to pass Jason's store, it was like Jason's head was swimming in ice water. The vibrantly cheering crowd seemed distant and hollow to his ears. King Barnabas blinked and slowly turned his head… and while scanning the crowd, found Jason.

Their eyes locked. It had been over two months since he had seen those icy eyes, but he still hadn't forgotten them in their most discomforting detail. They looked down on Jason just as they did before—with loathing and unimportance. But this time, they were riddled with something else… what was it? Whatever it was, it felt dark and uncertain, like having a deep dark abyss in your soul.

Jason's gaze was razor sharp on King Barnabas under pointed eyebrows. Neither of them blinked. Barnabas stared at Jason expectantly—Jason knew what he wanted. He had noticed that Jason was the only one on the street that wasn't clapping or cheering. King Barnabas continued to leer expectantly. Jason did nothing. His defiance and undying distaste for that tyrant ran deeper than any sword that could pierce him.

King Barnabas saw it on Jason's face. He wasn't going to give him anything. An amused chuckle slipped his lips, and he waved his hand as if to command a dog to sit down. Suddenly, Jason felt his legs buckle as though invisible hands had clipped his knees from behind. His knees hit the ground roughly, and he found his gaze equal to that of every other commoner on the street—under the subjection to the King on the horse.

Jason bore his teeth behind closed lips as he glared at the King. King Barnabas leisurely pressed on, satisfied with the small victory he attained. However, as Jason surveyed the rest of the crowd, he found something peculiar.

Right in the King's way—about a hundred yards up the street—an old man struggling with a heavy cart was frantically trying to push his rig off the street. He would strain and push with all of his might, but to no avail. He looked oddly familiar to Jason… he kept browsing all of his acquaintances in his mind, but struggled to make the connection. It wasn't until he was looking closer at the cart that he noticed it was stacked to the top with colorful fruits of all varieties, and it struck him like a club.

The guabo man from the day I went to the gym! Jason gasped. *Why isn't anyone helping him?*

Just as Jason pushed himself up to jog down the street, he noticed a couple of characters already walking briskly to assist the man's safe exit. Jason slowed down, but as he continued to watch. They didn't look like any other person on the street. One was wearing a blue outfit and the other, red. Suddenly, it came to him.

Those were Nezmythian soldiers.

Oh no, Jason thought gravely. The cheering crowd had all eyes and ears fixed on King Barnabas. Jason looked around frantically. *Am I the only one watching this?* He watched in unfiltered anxiety as the soldiers shouted something inaudible at the old man, who took it frightfully. It wasn't within a minute that they had finished their shouting and grabbed one side of the cart. The old man did the best he could to run away, but stumbled to the ground in the process, unable to push himself up.

"*Hey!*" Jason bellowed. The soldiers, in one swift move, threw their arms up.

With a thunderous crash, the fruit cart toppled onto one side. Fruit tumbled onto the street in a landslide of colors. The crowd's festivities didn't even hiccup. It was almost like it never even happened.

The cold sweat on Jason's brow was still there. *Is no one else seeing this?*

Jason tore through the crowd in an attempt to make it to the cart before the King. The thought of the frail old man lying helplessly in the side of the street with his entire stock of fruit strewn across the King's path made Jason shudder. *What will King Barnabas do if he doesn't move?* He weaved and hustled through the townsfolk the best he could, but the crowd was congesting the street sides like a mindless herd of cattle. Bumping every other person's shoulders, the crowd became thicker and thicker the further down the side of the street until it was nigh impassable.

This is ridiculous! Jason thought hopelessly. He was gaining on the precession, but at the rate it was going, he would never reach the old man and clean up the wreck in time.

Then a thought came into his head... a sickly, reckless, stupid thought.

But would it work? Jason thought. *It's an enormous gamble... but is this coincidence? This has to be another trial, it has to be... Well, if Barnabas wants to know what a future King would do, the future King would probably do anything he could to help that old man... So here it goes!*

In a flash, Jason tore through the crowd into the middle of the street, flying between two royal guards whose attention had faltered. They both shouted at him as he pumped his arms in front of him as furiously as he could. Just as he had sped up past the Advisor and King Barnabas himself, both of their horses let out startled whinnies and began to panic. The Advisor quickly got control of his horse, but King Barnabas shouted out a few choice words and his black stallion began to buck. Jason didn't stop to apologize. His heart raced. He bolted up the street to the old man with the cart.

As he ran, the crowd slowly transformed from a cheer to grave murmurs and shouts. Jason knew they were all wondering about the maddened teenager peeling down the street. He's going to get himself killed! Only time will tell.

Jason screeched to a stop in front of the wreckage. The old man fought desperately to push himself onto his feet, but the years had robbed him on his strength. Jason quickly folded onto his knees next to him and grabbed him by the shoulders. When the man realized another pair of hands had stopped to help him, he turned to see who was insane enough to do so.

He looked the same way he did just a month ago; frail, old, but with gentle eyes full of innocence. As Jason hoisted him up onto his feet, his eyes moistened, and through trembling lips, he formed two words:

"Thank you."

"Don't thank me yet," Jason said. "Just get out of the street. I don't want to—."

Suddenly, an enormous force crashed into Jason's back. He toppled to the ground helplessly, his hands and face scraping the cobblestone. He flipped over where he lay, finding two Nezmythian soldiers towering over him, spears pointed at his sternum. Just seconds later, the King and his Advisor were also upon him.

King Barnabas sat perched on his saddle, fists clenched with rage and his face as red as a radish. His chest rose and fell heavily and his hair was matted and untidy like he had wrestled a bear. The Advisor leisurely trotted up beside him, looking curiously upon Jason.

All the music had stopped. The eyes of everybody in Nezmyth City were on Jason—as still and silent as a graveyard.

"YOU—WHELP!" King Barnabas growled barbarically. "How dare you run past a royal precession to assist a withering, lowly peasant? *Does your stupidity know no bounds?*"

Jason involuntarily went into mental lockdown. His entire body froze over, starting at the head and quickly migrating to his hands and toes. No one so much as breathed.

"Take him!" King Barnabas shouted at the soldiers. "The procession is over. His fate will be decided at the castle."

In a split second, Jason had a guard on either side of him feverishly forcing his hands behind his back, tying a rope tightly around his wrists and leaving plenty of slack for a leash. They tied another rope around his mouth to keep any sound from escaping, and they walked onward. One of the soldiers took the leash that held Jason and forced him to walk in front of him.

The townspeople looked on gravely as Jason was carried away to the castle.

13 THE CLOAK

"Reckless! Juvenile!" The King spat. His face contorted and twisted with unfiltered rage as he stalked around Jason's chair in circles. Jason gulped hard. His throat felt dry and harsh. He flexed his wrists to loosen the ropes that kept him bound to the crude armchair, but to no avail.

His heart pounded as he withstood the endless verbal abuse that erupted from King Barnabas' furious teeth-baring grimace. He was still shocked that Barnabas hadn't sent his blade through him yet. He waited for it with sweat dripping down his cheeks and onto his quivering lap.

"...*what* in your right mind would make you *dare* interrupt a royal procession?" King Barnabas barked savagely.

"Please, Your Highness," Jason's words came out shakily and with great effort. "I thought it was a trial. You see, I saw the soldiers come out and throw the cart over and I assumed—"

"And now you see what happens when you make *assumptions!*" King Barnabas interrupted. He paused unnervingly—Jason thought he saw a spark of fear run across his face, but King Barnabas quickly regained his composure. "Were you *afraid* of what I would do to that old peasant if he did not move out of the way? Is *that* it?"

Jason silenced himself. The truth is that's exactly why he did what he did. Barnabas would probably have thrown that old man into prison for not making way … or worse.

"You thought I would *kill* that man?" King Barnabas seethed.

Jason tried to push the word "yes" out of his mouth, but the King interrupted.

"*Do you think me a fool?*" He bellowed. "I would never make such a decision with—" He stopped abruptly in mid-sentence and his face turned ghostly white. He quickly shut his mouth and took a deep breath to collect himself.

Jason blinked. He opened his mouth to speak again, but was quickly thwarted.

"Silence!" King Barnabas spat in a whisper. "These things do not concern you! Now…" He slunk his way back to the throne, turned around and ominously sat down. He laced his hands together and propped them to his lips, glaring with eyes white-hot. "Now you are all alone… and I decide your fate."

Jason swallowed hard. The image of King Barnabas decapitating the Nezmythian soldier from two months ago resurfaced in his mind. His hands began to shake and sweat as his heart pulsed harder and faster. The dark blade was leaning on the throne next to his left hand.

King Barnabas slowly stood from the throne. He picked up the blade. Fire came into his eyes like a glowing furnace of hatred and desire. He opened his mouth to speak as he stalked toward Jason, that evil blade scraping and sparking against the floor.

"I swore that you would not be King," he said softly. "Now I fulfill my oath."

Jason's eyes widened with terror. His throat closed up. King Barnabas gradually picked up the pace from a walk, to a brisk walk, to a slight run.

"You knew this day would come, Jason!" he shouted with triumph, lifting his blade off the ground and holding it over his head. His eyes overflowed with madness. Jason's heart was fighting to break out of his chest. "Long... live... the *Ki*—!"

Just as Jason was about to scream in horror, a gust of wind streamed through the Hall, followed by a deafening smash as the great doors flew open and slammed against the ancient walls. Shouts and grunts of the soldiers that guarded the door sounded as they were knocked unconscious.

King Barnabas' fury remained untouched. Instead, his gaze reverted from Jason to the end of the hall. He pointed a shaky finger and shouted, "*You!* I told you to stay away from here!"

Jason tried to turn around in his chair, but the ropes around his wrists constrained him too tightly. He heard groaning from the end of the room coming from the beaten guards.

"Barnabas, I must have a word with you," the deathly low voice echoed through the hall.

The King could have ground his jaw into powder. His face contorted with even more rage than just a moment before with an unmistakable shade of red.

"Later!" He spat. "I am busy with the boy!"

"It regards the boy," the deathly voice came again. "And he mustn't be here to listen."

Feeling his golden opportunity to kill Jason slip through his fingers, King Barnabas shouted, "*NO!* He's mine! I command you to wait outside the while I finish hi—with him!"

"Barnabas," the voice returned. "Please. Bridle yourself for one moment and listen. This cannot wait."

Defiantly, King Barnabas lifted his sword and gave a swipe at Jason's throat. All color left Jason's face. But as the blade connected with his jugular, it clanged as if his very skin were made out of steel. Jason sat in eerie wonder, and King Barnabas in livid incredulity, as the deathly voice spoke once again.

"Let the boy go. If he's guilty of anything, it's selflessness. Leave him be."

King Barnabas was going to explode. His eyes shot from
Jason to the intruder. His face crunched and creased with the
resemblance of an angry bull, and he stood hunched over in
front of Jason, bearing his teeth and clenching his fists. Each
rise and fall of his strong chest seemed more and more
labored. Finally, he uttered to Jason with venom:

"*Go.*"

Confused, Jason looked up into his face. He didn't even
notice that the ropes tying him to the chair had somehow
become undone. *Did he just tell me to go?*

"I said…" He jumped backward a few feet. "*GO!*" He
shoved his hand forward and launched an enormous, purple
jeroki at Jason.

It was so large and so fast that Jason didn't have any time
to react before the blast connected with his entire torso,
sending him flailing backward. Such force! It was so much
more powerful than any other jeroki that he had been hit
by—even Tarren's. The room was spinning and tumbling
around him as his body bumped and slid across the stone
floor, battering and bruising his body. Jason finally stopped
spinning as he was at least ten yards away from the angry
King. He didn't even think before scrambling to his feet and
bolting toward the door.

Jason pumped his arms and stretched out his legs as fast as
he could—adrenaline made the process second nature. As he
came closer and closer to the exit, he could see who was
talking to the King more clearly.

The tall figure was completely masked in a dark cloak.
The hood hung over his eyes and face so that he was
completely unrecognizable. Jason wanted sincerely to thank
the mysterious figure for saving his life, but the fear for his
own life kept his feet moving past him.

Jason peeled through the enormous doors and passed the
soldiers that lay unconscious by the threshold, not stopping.
Just as his feet found the castle grounds, the double doors to
the castle slammed shut just as quickly and violently as they
had opened. The sound seemed to reverberate off the distant

mountains. Jason stole a glance over his shoulder as he continued to run.

What was THAT? He thought.

He didn't stop running for miles. It wasn't until he was a good distance down an Upper City neighborhood that he stopped to catch his breath. He turned to face the castle—the black cathedral on a hill—and stroked his throat, which should have been slit just minutes ago.

Who was that man in the dark cloak? Why did he save my life? Was the fruit man really another trial? It had to be! Just look at how King Barnabas got so nervous after I mentioned it...

Not much was certain, but one thing remained clear.

If I survive the next five months, it'll be a miracle.

14 THE DELIVERY

I'm so glad I don't have to enter through the front of this building...

In one hand, Jason carried an intricately-crafted staff made from Golden Oak, and kept his other hand (his right) tucked safely in his pocket. Behind him, Bertus lugged a small wagon loaded with a small array of wooden practice weapons.

"Have you figured out what you're going to say to her yet?" Bertus asked. Even though he couldn't see him, Jason knew he was grinning.

Jason's ears went pink. "None of you are ever going to let this go, are you?"

Bertus chuckled. The door that stood between them and the interior of the Crossing Blades was very similar to the one in front—battered and brown. Nervousness coated Jason's lungs as he mentally rehearsed exactly what he *would* say to Saryan when the time came. It didn't become any easier the more he thought about it.

He unlatched the door and pulled it open, revealing a wide but deep flight of stairs descending to a basement level. The wagon filled with practice swords barely slipped through the door, and Jason and Bertus both had to assist in carrying it down to the bottom. As they hobbled to the base of stairs, they were met by another door.

Jason looked at Bertus. Bertus grinned and stepped back as if avoiding an amusing dare.

"I don't want to open it! This is *your* delivery."

Jason grinned sheepishly in reply. His heart thumped. *Why am I so nervous about this? I've confronted the King of Nezmyth three times! Nothing should bother me by now...*

He knocked. There was barely a second of silence.

"The door is open!" Saryan's muffled voice returned.

Jason pushed the door open and crossed through, followed by Bertus toting the practice swords. They found themselves in a vast room with a relatively low ceiling, all constructed of large bricks. Light poured in through small windows all along the walls, which cut illuminated squares on the padded floor and revealed the dust particles floating in the air.

Saryan didn't notice them at first. She was on the far side of the room hanging stuffed dummies on a rack—most likely for jeroki target practice—with her back facing the two. Her golden hair spilled halfway down her back, and her black sparring outfit spread halfway down her arms and legs, glorifying each curve of her toned body.

Jason's jaw hung open. Bertus cleared his throat.

At the sound, she flipped around, and seeing Jason, her eyes lit up. Jason could see the silver from across the room.

"Jason!" she said delightedly. "Just in time!"

Jason didn't know of the oafish grin spreading across his face as she jogged toward him. Bertus looked on with lips pressed, like a teenage boy watching a romantic play he found more amusing than engaging.

"Hello, Saryan," he said with a smile. "This is your staff! Uh—well, obviously"—he laughed awkwardly—"it's *your* staff. Who else would it belong to? We don't just make staffs randomly and bring them to people... you paid for it."

Bertus' palm connected with his face.

"Excellent timing!" She said with an ear-to-ear grin. She reached out and gently took the staff from Jason, who had been holding it out stiffly. As she took it from Jason, she held onto it with both hands and weighed it mentally.

She scanned it carefully. "Excellent work! You even got all of the engravings I asked for in just the right places. I hope it wasn't too difficult. Golden Oak is an amazing fiber. Incredibly strong."

"It's true…" Jason said. *We broke a saw blade and several knives in the process of making it…*

She politely stepped back and started swinging the staff around her body like a windmill. She tossed it in the air, caught it and brandished it one more time before jamming it in the padded floor. Her eyes flashed.

"It's perfect! Thank you," she said. She brushed her hair out of her eyes. "I'm sure the practice swords are fantastic, too."

Jason had almost entirely forgotten those. Immediately she went over to the wagon to inspect them and found them just as satisfactory as the custom staff. All of them unloaded the wagon and propped the practice swords against the wall by the door. When they were done, Saryan turned to the others.

"Would you two like to stay for class?" she said. "I teach in the next few minutes, and it would be great to have someone else with me who is older and more experienced. Most of my students are very young."

Something inside Jason twanged uneasily. "I'm not sure…" Anxiety gripped him. *I want to call on her… but I don't want to do it in front of Bertus… He'll tell the others and they'll never let me live it down. How would I even ask her?* "I think we need to get back at the shop. We've got things we need to take care of."

"Mmhm," She hummed skeptically, folding her arms. "I saw you and your little friends three weeks ago. 'Things you need to care of…' like sitting around and hoping that orders will come? It really takes all of you for that?"

The word "uh" escaped Jason's lips. He suddenly felt very vulnerable as he knew she could see right through him.

Bertus took a step forward and put his hand on Jason's shoulder.

"Don't worry, Jason," Bertus sneered. "The three of us have it covered. You can stay for a little while."

Nothing but air left Jason's tongue—unsure of how he should react. Saryan was the next to speak.

"Great!" She said, clapping her hands. Her silver eyes twinkled. "The children should be here any minute. If you could just have a seat over there…" she pointed to the wall near the door.

After a deep breath, Jason awkwardly shuffled his feet to the edge of the room and sat down, resting his head against the brick wall. Bertus expressed his thanks to Saryan, took the wagon and exited the room. He sat quietly, stealing glances at Saryan as she paced the room dreamy-eyed, twirling her new staff. Minutes passed. Jason drummed his fingers on his knees as he watched.

He cleared his throat. "So what do you want me to do…?"

Saryan responded with a sly glance from the corner of her eye. Her lips curled into a smirk and she shrugged.

"Maybe a demonstration. Are you a decent fighter, Jason?"

A flashback of Bobby the Brute over a month ago passed over Jason's eyes. He ignored it.

"I used to be the second best fighter in my training group," he replied. "Only my best friend Tarren has ever beaten me. He's incredible."

"What's your weapon?"

"A sword."

"The standard choice. What's his weapon?"

"A pair of daggers."

Her eyebrows popped. "That's impressive. He must be agile."

Jason nodded stiffly. "And strong."

Suddenly, the door opened and Jason could hear an adult female voice mumbling before a small boy walked in with charcoal-black hair and spectacles.

"Hello, Miss Saryan," he said monotonously.

"Hello, Jonny," Saryan said. "If you could just have a seat next to Jason while the rest of the students arrive that would be wonderful."

"Yes, Miss Saryan," Jonny said. As he turned around his eyes widened with shock at the sight of Jason. The last thing he was expecting was to find another person at least seven years older than him at this class. Jason grinned uncomfortably at Jonny, but Jonny immediately became fascinated with his own boots and studied them as he walked over and sat several paces from Jason.

The rest of the students in Saryan's class came in steadily and in all shapes and sizes. A girl named Silvia with dark hair came in showing off her new sparkling bracelet to anyone who would look. A pudgy, loud boy named Harmo stuffed his face with sweets as he walked in and nearly fell on top of a smaller, scrawnier child who had inadvertently planted himself in the way. All and all, there were probably about fifteen to twenty students, all dressed nicely in recently-washed clothes.

Upper City children... no one else gets taught battle procedures this young. Jason sat feeling much like a donkey in a stable of horses. He could feel all of their beady eyes darting on and off him. As he looked around them, most of the kids would look away out of shyness or keep staring from curiosity.

Harmo was the first one to speak up boldly, "Who're you?"

Jason was about to explain himself, but Saryan beat him to it.

"That's my friend, Jason," she spoke loudly as she walked up. Her arms rested on her staff, which was lying across her shoulders.

Jason grinned.

"He came by to deliver a staff I ordered three weeks ago," Saryan continued while shaking the staff in her clenched hand. "He's very sweet so I expect you to treat him as an honored guest."

"Miss Saryan is a prewife!" An anonymous student piped up. Immediately, all the students dove into laughing fit. Saryan rolled her eyes with an amused smirk, brushing off the juvenile comment that she and Jason were romantically involved. Jason blushed furiously as he looked at the floor between his boots.

"I'm not his prewife," she assured. "He's a friend. But it doesn't matter what I say to you because I can tell by the looks on your little faces that you're not convinced. But that doesn't matter now. Do you know why? Because it's time to run! Everybody get up!"

Saryan dropped her staff. The class moaned as they staggered up from the wall and began jogging around the perimeter of the room. Jason remained seated against the wall, drumming his fingers again and quietly observing. The feeling was a little strange to him—school was so long ago and sitting in class being taught by the most intoxicating girl he could think of gave a feeling of déjà vu with a strange twist.

He felt free to let his mind wander on various things: his still unanswered question to Tarren… his sick mother… the Year of Decision… his empty stomach. Occasionally his wandering trail of thought was broken as Saryan would command the class to jump, dive, or roll. Harmo seemed to have the most difficult time with the jumping and diving parts.

Saryan jogged merrily along, not breaking a sweat as she led the pack. As she came around the room one more time, she made eye contact with Jason. He grinned sheepishly. She smiled wide. As she passed, she bent down and grabbed his wrist, yanking him onto his feet. Jason felt his heart skip a beat as he staggered into a jog, leading the rest of the pack along with Saryan.

They ran side-by-side for a short while. Jason smiled wide but didn't notice. They almost ran around the complete perimeter of the room. As she and Saryan made eye contact, her eyes flashed and she called out:

Jason shook his head and looked down, "I don't know. I didn't come here expecting a fight. And I don't want to hurt you."

Saryan's eyebrow popped. She turned her head and opened her mouth wider as if to say something, but closed it instead. Her aura became devious. Jason gulped.

"Okay, Jason." She said. "If you don't want to, you don't have to."

Jason didn't know what to say. Something inside of him told him that this wasn't the end of the matter. He didn't like the feeling.

"But would you mind standing up to help me with a little demonstration?" She said.

Jason glared up at her, trying to read what was on her scheming mind. He then peered around the class to see every child's eyes full of expectancy and anticipation. He glared up at her again. Her face radiated craftiness.

"Sure," he said cautiously.

"Thank you," Saryan said. "Just stand a few feet away… yes, right there is perfect. As I was saying before I was so rudely interrupted,"—she shot a look at Harmo, who was glowering at Jason—"today we are going to discuss the vital attack areas of the body! These are places that are sensitive and always handy to attack because they are more likely to make your opponent double over in pain, giving you time to run away or attack them another time. Like so!"

Jason was standing watching the class with his arms folded and his legs slightly apart. Before he could think, Saryan had jerked the staff off her shoulder, rammed it between his knees and yanked it upward.

He doubled over immediately and let out a startled yelp, clenching his hands and putting his forearms between his thighs. The class jeered and laughed at Jason's clenching pain while Saryan slung her staff back over her shoulder.

"Would you care for another demonstration?" She hollered.

Her class shouted in vibrant unison, giggling and clapping their hands.

"Alright, you know what?" Jason grunted passed the pain. "I'll take you up on that offer."

Saryan raised her eyebrow, "I accept! Choose your weapon and meet me in the middle of the floor."

She motioned at a rack of fake weapons against the far wall, then to the large square in the center of the room. As she sauntered to the square with her staff slung over her shoulder, Jason tried to ignore the pain and stand up straight. He slid his sword off his back and set it down where he was sitting. It was much labored, but he walked over to the rack of wooden weapons and grabbed the double-edged sword. By the time he had stalked to the square, most of the pain had subsided.

Saryan stood lazily on the opposite edge of the square, swaying her hips absently and humming to herself. She smiled and winked at Jason again. He shot her an annoyed look but tried to flush out his irritation and replace it with concentration. He brandished his fake blade, his eyes searing hot. He slipped on a confident smirk.

"Well, aren't you a smug one?" He said. "Remember, you asked for this. So don't complain when the tip of this sword reaches you."

"I wouldn't," she said dreamily. "But that won't happen. Try not to act surprised when I have you pinned."

Jason smiled and tightened his grip.

Saryan winked at him again while sticking her tongue out, then she hollered at one of the students without taking her eyes off Jason, "Say when!"

Jason hunkered down in his fighting stance, ready to pounce. Saryan spun her staff and crouched, mimicking Jason's stance and eyeing him like a panther eyes its prey.

Suddenly, the student with a high nasally voice called out. "Bow to your opponent!"

Jason put his feet together, put his left fist in front of his shoulder and bowed his head in the Nezmythian Dual Stance.

Saryan bowed comically by jumping overzealously into the dual stance and bowing her head quickly that all her hair fell in front of her face. Her class snickered with delight.

"Ready..."

Jason gripped his blade tighter. Saryan still showed no sign of concentration.

"*Go!*"

Immediately, Saryan leapt forward like a lion and thrusted her staff at Jason. Jason reflexively parried the attack while spinning out of the way. Saryan stopped for a split second to size him up.

"Nice!" Saryan said enthusiastically. "Your reflexes are pretty impressive!"

Jason bowed with a wide grin, "And we've only just begun."

Saryan laughed haughtily and lunged forward again. Jason bent his knees and blocked the blow with the flat of his sword, but Saryan thought quickly by leaping forward and kicking Jason in the sternum. Her class shouted for their teacher's victory while Jason staggered backward.

He rolled out of the blow with a backward somersault. Saryan grinned with delight and attempted another forward thrust on him. Jason barely saw the attack as he came up from his somersault. Thinking quickly, he sidestepped, drew his sword upward and knocked Saryan's staff out of the way. Following that, he grabbed her forward wrist, pulled it downward, and kicked her leg upward, sending her unto a clumsy front flip.

Saryan yelped something indistinct and landed hard on her back with a resounding *thud*. Jason picked his sword back up and strolled over to Saryan. He stood right over her head, looking down on her half-closed, buzzing eyes between his boots. Her hair was strewn all over her face.

"You should really consider tying up your hair before you spar," He said.

Unexpectedly, Saryan's groaning stopped and her eyes snapped open on the alert. They weren't surprised... they were devious. A smile leapt onto her face.

In a split second, Saryan pulled her knees to her chin, placed her hands by Jason's boots and launched herself upward, sending her toes right into Jason's chin. Jason caught air and fell onto his back, his jaw throbbing with pain and his tongue cut from the bite.

Saryan poised herself in a handstand until she gracefully placed her feet back onto the ground. Her class cheered. She cocked up her staff and pounced on Jason to pin him down and win the match.

Jason recovered swiftly and rolled out of harm's way. The staff stabbed the ground right where his chest would have been. Jason bounded back into a standing position after a few side rolls and pointed his left hand's palm at Saryan. In a second, a glowing white ball illuminated his palm and shot toward Saryan with ferocious speed. Saryan's reflexes saved her. She immediately jumped out of the way in a dive roll.

Jason repeatedly shot jerokis at her, pumping his arm as fast and hard as his body would allow. Saryan kept dodging them like a lightning-fast dancer, moving farther and farther backward with every spin and roll.

Her eyes were white-hot with focus on Jason's last jeroki. As the jeroki left his hand, Saryan raised her arm and cupped the ball of burning magic out of midair, spinning herself around and launching it back at Jason.

"*Whoa!*" Jason quickly ducked as his own jeroki soared just over his head and into the far wall. Just as he turned back around to face Saryan, the end of her staff came across his face.

Saryan had gotten Jason right where she wanted him, and now he was her punching bag. Blow after blow, he became more and more disoriented. His eyes teared up. Finally, she sent one smashing blow into his chest and sent him tumbling in a backward.

Finally, Jason stopped tumbling and found himself feeling very sore and bruised. He groaned loudly. She had done a really good job thrashing up his head and torso and his head was still spinning. As he shook his head and tried to fight the mist out of his eyes, he could see a dark blob moving quickly toward him.

Saryan leapt above Jason, her staff pointed right at his chest, ready to pin him down. Jason reflexively swiped his sword above him. He successfully smacked away the down-coming staff and Saryan immediately lost her balance in midair. She clumsily fell on top of Jason, both of them grunting in pain as they connected. Jason spat her matted hair out of his mouth. Saryan scrambled to get back to her feet.

Jason beat her to it. He grabbed her shoulders, found her stomach with his feet and launched her over his shoulders. She flew once again through the air like a rag doll, landing hard on her back.

She groaned hard and picked some sweaty, splitting hair out of her mouth, hollering at Jason who was lying on the floor a couple yards behind her, "What is it with you and throws?"

"If you don't like them," Jason replied hotly on his back. "Quit setting yourself up for them!"

The class was now cheering wildly. Most of them were on Saryan's side, but a couple of them were even cheering for Jason by this time. Both of them lay on the ground a few feet away from each other, panting hard and lacking the energy to get back up.

Jason spoke through panting breaths, "How do you feel about calling it a draw?"

Without a word, Saryan somersaulted backward onto her feet.

Guess not, Jason thought.

He leapt up with a kick. The instant they both got up, they turned about and swung their weapons, blocking each other's individual blows flawlessly. The children's madly vibrant cheers rebounded off the walls.

Jason swung his sword upward, but Saryan deflected the blow effortlessly. She spun around and tried to bring her staff down on Jason's head, but he parried also. Jason backpedaled as they took turns swinging, striking, dodging and parrying blows at each other, each of them beginning to sweat and pant heavier.

They had parried and attacked themselves to the center of the room when they each swung simultaneously. Their weapons connected. They both pressed forward in an attempt to overpower the other. Their faces were inches apart, twisted with exhaustion and competitive fury, glaring deeply into each other's eyes. Saryan's chest rose up and down quickly and her teeth showed through her lips. Jason's hair dripped with sweat.

"Do you do this to all the guys you meet?" Jason grunted.

"Nope," Saryan panted. "Just the special ones."

Suddenly, without warning, her face swiftly reached through the gap between her staff and his sword, and she planted her lips on Jason's cheek.

Whoa! Jason was so focused on his leaping heart that he had lost the grip on his sword. Saryan seized the moment and smacked Jason's hand with the edge of her staff, sending a burst of pain into his hand and launching the sword from his grip.

Defenseless, Jason was kicked to the floor and pinned down by a staff in the chest.

"*Ha!*" Saryan grinned ear-to-ear and poked the staff into Jason's chest harder. Her class hollered and jeered with glee as they leapt to their feet and clapped their hands. Jason's chest rose and fell with each frequent breath. His hand, head, and torso were completely throbbing with pain and the sweat dripping from his hair was starting to get into his eyes.

Sweat dripped off Saryan's nose and chin, her hair completely distressed and her brilliant silver eyes wild with victory. She panted like she had just ran across the city.

"You did that on purpose!" Jason said.

She knelt down victoriously and looked Jason square in the eye. Baring her teeth in a triumphant ear-to-ear smile, she said, "Yes, I did! And I still won, even if I had to kiss your sweaty, smelly cheek! Now what are you going to do?"

There were a few words he had been meaning to say, and he wondered if it was the right time and place for them, then decided there would never be a better situation. He felt like, somehow, he had gotten to know Saryan much better in the brutal past minutes... and he liked what he found.

"Well... can I call on you?"

15 THE TRAP

Tarren laughed haughtily when Jason finished the story, "You got beaten by a *girl!*"

"She's been sparring since she was four!" Jason retorted. "Besides, she caught me off guard."

They strolled through a remote alley somewhere between Center Court and the Southern Market Street. Three-story buildings of brick and cement towered over them from both sides, keeping the alleyway shrouded from the sun. Tarren walked ahead of Jason. Jason kept his hands in his jacket pockets.

"Oh, and that's your first lesson in duel sparring—actually, that's just a general lesson in sparring." Tarren stated matter-of-factly. "Always stay about a dozen steps ahead of your opponent." He paused for a second. "It's about time you asked for her courtship, though."

Jason grinned.

They finally reached a weathered door with a rusty latch after walking for several minutes. Tarren grabbed the latch and firmly jostled it as he attempted to push open the door. After a few strenuous seconds, the latch scratched open with a loud *clack*, and the door swung open on rusty, screeching hinges. They walked through.

The entire building was a massive, empty hall. Torches were nowhere present—the only light came from the large windows along the top of the walls. Several pillars stretched from floor to ceiling throughout the room. It smelled incredibly dank and dusty. Best of all, the floor was loaded with several sparring mats and racks of old, half-beaten wooden dummies.

Jason looked on in awe. "This place is perfect... how did you find it?"

Tarren latched the door behind him. "You know my father is a mason. He helped build this place many years ago—just before King Barnabas' reign. Obviously, it used to be a combat gym, but after so many tax raises the owner went broke and got put in prison. He hadn't arranged to pass it down to anyone, so it's been abandoned ever since. My father and I used to come here to practice together when I wasn't in school."

Jason hummed. Tarren clapped his hands and rubbed them together. The sound echoed off the dusty brick walls. "Well, what do you say we get started?"

"Okay," Jason complied.

"Now," Tarren began casually as he walked to the center of the room. "The first thing I want to talk about today are jerokis. Tell me everything you know about them."

"A jeroki is a magic ball of energy shot from the palm of your magic hand," Jason began as he walked closely behind him. "Your magic hand is the opposite hand that you use your weapon with. Anyway, you aim your jerokis by where your fingers are pointing, not your palm. You have to thrust your arm forward as they form or they won't shoot forward. And you can destroy an oncoming jeroki by slicing through it or turning your hands into a wedge and splitting it. And you can redirect them, too, apparently..."

"Not bad," Tarren said. "Jerokis are the most basic of magical attacks, and probably the most reliable. You can get into some intense intermediate-level magic with paralyzing curses and such, but the most advanced magic is rarely ever practiced. Only the rich can afford instructors that know the techniques, and most of it is too over-the-top for typical sparring."

"Do you know any advanced magic?" Jason asked.

"I've always been poorer than you, Jason," Tarren slid him a look. "But let me show you something I've been working on. You know how normal jerokis are just like a super-powerful long-distant punch? Well I got thinking... what if you can actually make them *burn*? Watch."

Jason stepped back as Tarren set his arm parallel to the floor. He pointed his palm toward a wooden dummy at the end of the room and slowly, a jeroki charged in his hand until it was bigger than his head. Tarren pulled his hand back, and launched it.

The yellow ball of light erupted into a bright blue beam as lit up the room. It shot with breakneck speed and toward the dummy, which exploded into pieces, sending bits of debris and wood pelting in every direction.

Jason ducked and shielded his face with his forearms. He heard several pieces of wood land around him and when he lifted his eyes, he saw the bits of the wooden dummy lying in varied places across the combat mat, smoking and charred. An empty chain where the dummy once hung jingled on the rack at the edge of the room.

All Jason could think to do was whistle quietly.

"Mmhm," Tarren said. "What I did is this: while you're charging your jeroki, think of fire, heat, burning things, and concentrate on them with all your might. Then right as I threw that jeroki, I spun my palm and stuck my hand straight out, fingers together. I don't know how it works, but it turns the jeroki ball into a beam, it travels faster and actually *burns* what it touches. And from the look of things"—he glanced around the rubble—"it's a lot more destructive."

"When do I try?"

"Not here," Tarren said with finality. "You blew a hole through a wall with a normal jeroki. Besides, this took me months to perfect. It's so hard to control! You have to force it to go straight and aim it just perfectly so you don't end up blowing up something you don't want."

"...oh," Jason said flatly.

"Yes," Tarren said. "I figure we'll spar a couple of times and call it good for today. Is there anything else you want to know?"

Jason shook his head. "No."

"Good," Tarren replied. "There are some practice weapons over there. Let's get started."

* * * * *

Another sleepless night.

The stars were shy to shine their light through Jason's bedroom window. A murky black sheet covered the sky as Nezmyth slept below. The moon barely shone through. All was still.

Jason filled the room with soft notes coming from his flyra. He sat upright on his bed with the instrument protruding from his lips.

Something wasn't sitting well inside of him. It wasn't a feeling of sickness from something he might have eaten, but almost as though something was crawling, lurching inside him. The dark cloud within him kept him awake and refused to give him rest.

It's almost been half a year... Jason thought. *Why am I still alive?*

The dark cloud was growing stronger. A filthy hand was inching closer and closer to his heart.

Jason frowned and stopped pulled the flyra away from his lips. He set it beside his bed and frowned at the floor, analyzing the feeling inside of him. His hands laced together by his knees.

"Something isn't right..." he thought out loud. "But what?"

"*Jaassoonn...*"

Jason perked up like a dog at the sound of a whistle. His neck hairs stood up and he scanned the room. His sword lay by his bedside, less than arm's length away. He waited for a long, tense moment, fully ready to spring for his sword at the first sound of anything else. Moments passed…

Nothing.

Maybe I'm just hearing things…? It's late…

Then the whispering came again, this time louder and sounding as though it was calling from some distant cavern.

"Jaassooonnn…"

Jason's hand went for his sword and ripped it out of its sheath. He scrambled to his feet and bent his knees, ready for any attack, eying every corner of the dark room. More echoing whispers came one after another, hissing some incoherent garble Jason couldn't decipher. His eyes darted about in his sockets, searching for any slithering darkness creeping up on him.

It was then that he noticed the water bowl. Its surface was shimmering as though it were rippling glass in the filthy moonlight. A dim light flickered at the bottom of the basin like some lonely blue candle.

Jason cautiously crept over to the bowl, eying it like a wolf eyes a steel trap.

Why is the surface rippling? Jason thought uncomfortably. *I haven't touched it in hours.*

As Jason scooted closer and closer to the bowl, he began to see flickers of shapes in it. He reached his head closer and closer to it, trying to discern the shapes that danced around in the bottom of the water.

He felt himself slipping. His mind was sliding away from his body. Reality was melting from underneath him. His nose was an inch above the water and his eyelids had fully retracted into his head.

"Yoouu… aarree… MINE!"

He was in a white room—spotlessly white and enormous. At first he felt relaxed and alone, but suddenly an enormous black snake materialized out of midair, growing to be as wide and long as a street. Its icy blue eyes locked on Jason and he felt terror course through his body like ice water had replaced his blood.

The snake slithered and struck, swallowing Jason completely.

A million sensations hit Jason at once. He felt his throat being slit and his hot, sticky blood splattering through the air. His heart erupted inside his chest and blood filled his lungs. He coughed, struggling to breathe, but a black, withered hand was around his face, growing until it completely consumed him.

Suddenly, he was falling. The wind of freefall snapped at his hair and clothes as he hurtled into an unknown abyss.

As he was falling, four figures dangled in the distance, closing in faster and faster at breakneck speed. They were hanging by ropes, it seemed... as they came in closer, Jason recognized who they were.

Saryan, Tarren, Kara and Tomm's vacant eyes stared back at Jason lifelessly. Nooses were around their necks. Across their bodies were letters slashed across them with their own blood.

"LONG LIVE THE KING."

Jason tried to scream, but just as he did, he hit water. He felt it enclose around him, squeezing him, choking him. He furiously swam for the surface and broke through coughing and panting for breath.

As he sputtered out what water had lodged itself in his lungs, he frantically looked around. He couldn't see six inches in front of him. He treaded water, shaking with cold and fear, the darkness palpable.

The surface of the water quivered and contorted like an enormous sheet. Waves rippled and crashed over Jason as if the water had grown arms. The waves pummeled him with giant fists, keeping him beneath the surface, stealing any chance for a breath.

Jason's fingers turned into snakes that struck and slashed at his arms, lacerating them with poisonous gashes.

His skull was squeezed by giant hands, ready to break.

Flashes of sickly images ran across his mind: Nezmyth City engulfed in purple flames, chariots of black horses trampling Nezmythian children, the slaughtering of Jason's parents and loved ones by invisible hands.

"*What is happening to me...?*" Jason thought's echoed in the abyss.

Amidst all the horrifying images that relentlessly bombarded him, Jason saw one that stabbed into his consciousness. A man in a red cape stood hunched over a table with a water basin, muttering words in a diseased tongue. His icy blue eyes were razor-sharp with concentration as he watched images warp and contort in the water.

Jason's lips twisted, "*YOU...*"

The water receded and Jason was again standing in the white room. His breathing was labored. In a haze of black smoke, King Barnabas formed, stalking his way up to Jason with his black blade. The image of his bloodthirsty scowl barraged Jason forward and backward, invading his field of vision.

"*You are MINE...*" the King's voice echoed and cut Jason's very soul as he advanced closer. "*Your only exit is to YIELD!*"

Give in... the thoughts whispered loudly to Jason. *The nightmare will be over... you will be at peace... don't be afraid...*

Jason was about to comply, to surrender, but something stopped him—something inside that disagreed. He stepped backward involuntarily. "I—I..."

King Barnabas cocked his sword and thrusted it forward, stabbing Jason in the belly. Jason felt the blade rip through him. He gasped for air and fell to his knees, staring at the blade stuck through his body. The black blood seeping out of his stomach crawled and stretched over his entire body, encasing him in some oily murk.

"*I control this world...*" King Barnabas growled distastefully. "*And even in the face of death you refuse to yield...*"

The image of King Barnabas crouching over the bowl flashed against Jason's eyes again. Then the image of his quiet, dim bedroom sparked across his vision.

"This isn't real..." Jason muttered as his body seeped into nothingness. "It can't be..."

Against the dark oil coating his eyes, Jason saw the image of his friends and family hanging by nooses again. They all spoke simultaneously with King Barnabas' voice.

"*You are in here for as long as I desire... if you desire to escape... YIELD!*"

Every fiber in Jason's body wanted to cry out for mercy. He felt constricted... immobilized... trapped. King Barnabas was in control.

I'll do it... Jason thought. *Just make it stop... end the horror... I can't handle this... no more...*

"...with that challenge comes a choice."

Master Ferribolt's confident grin was the only cheerful thing Jason had seen for what felt like hours. His eyes were full of hope... trust... love. He remembered getting a blessing by the Chief Patriarch in a starlit field... the warm glow he felt in his heart that night. They put a dim spark into Jason's body that he felt had been lost forever.

"...he can choose to yield to fear and let greatness pass by, or become something greater than he once was, and triumph..."

Abruptly, Master Ferribolt's face twisted into the black, blue-eyed snake, flicking its tongue at Jason, stealing the light in his body.

"*YIELD!*" King Barnabas commanded from the black.

Jason felt the scream rise out from inside him, "*GET— OUT—OF—MY—HEAD!*"

The serpent recoiled as if it had been dealt a mortal blow. It twisted and writhed like a worm until it disappeared into oblivion.

Jason felt the fire inside him building. The image of King Barnabas hunched over the water basin was different. He was rocked. His knuckles were white on the table, struggling to stay upright.

"*You are NOTHING!*" The King Barnabas in Jason's head grew to the size of a building. The blade in Jason's belly was gone. Barnabas' overgrown foot lifted over Jason until he felt himself underneath its shadow. The foot came down and crushed Jason, severing nearly every bone in his body.

"*YIELD or DIE!*" The King' voice was like thunder. Jason screamed.

"I need…" Jason thought desperately.

Suddenly, Jason felt something in his hand. As he turned and looked, he recognized that it was his sword. He gripped it tighter, and with a mighty cry, thrust it in the boot of the King.

Light erupted from the wound. King Barnabas cried out in pain and shrunk back to normal size. Jason scrambled to his feet and marched back toward him, blade shaking in his hand, the broken bones only an imagination. Different images flashed less frequently. The tangibility of the nightmare realm began to deteriorate. Jason's teeth chattered and his heart thumped. Another image flashed of the real King Barnabas staggering by the water basin, desperately trying to stay standing as if a bear were sitting on his shoulders.

"*This is MY world!*" the dream version of the King screamed with thunderous malice. "*And you will DIE before you ESCAPE!*"

The snake materialized—this time, hundreds of them. They all slithered toward Jason at lightning speed, the lust for his blood in their icy eyes. They would be upon him in seconds.

Master Ferribolt's voice echoed again from his memory. "The Dragon will give you power to overcome, but you *must* be willing to become what you must be…"

"I'm willing…" Jason thought.

Jason lifted his sword and cried out with the mightiest voice he could muster, "Dragon, consume my enemies! *Crawl back to your hiding place, tyrant! RELEASE ME!*"

Light shot from Jason's sword. King Barnabas shielded his eyes and let out a cry of pain. The snakes hissed and squirmed painfully, but still slithered with bloodlust toward Jason. Death was still eminent.

Jason inhaled and released another cry from the raging inferno of his heart:

"RELEASE—ME!!"

Fire erupted from Jason's sword and filled up the air until it consumed all the serpents and the King's agonized body. All of the horrifying images Jason had seen evaporated into nothingness after one last terrible pass.

At the castle, King Barnabas' body snapped rigidly. He swayed and toppled to the ground like a falling tree, overcome and unconscious.

The nightmare world dissolved. Jason found himself lying on the cold wooden floor of his room, shivering and drenched in sweat. He laid there for several minutes, curled up, his strength completely gone. His sword lay just a few feet away. The contents of the water basin had spilled across the floor.

It was all Jason could do to reach up onto his bed and pull the sheets over his cold body before he fell back asleep.

The dark feeling was gone.

16 THE INVITATION

"So what is bothering you," Master Ferribolt said, "other than the usual fare?"

Jason shifted his feet. The fireplace in the Chief Patriarch's study was lit, permeating the room with a soft, warm glow. They both sat in their usual spots, facing each other with the bear rug separating their chairs. Overcast dominated the sky and snow gradually trickled past the foggy windows. They had just finished their Ancient Nezmythian lesson and Jason had filled in Master Ferribolt on the details concerning his recent sparring practice with Tarren.

"Have you ever had… nightmares?" Jason asked.

Master Ferribolt slid him a puzzled look. "Well, everyone experiences nightmares from time to time, Jason."

"Well, of course," Jason said. "But this one was different… it was so life-like and so horrifying… I woke up on the floor completely soaked in sweat. I was playing my flyra late at night because I couldn't sleep, and I heard something calling my name from inside my room…"

Master Ferribolt leaned forward in his chair and his eyes became hard as he keenly followed each word.

"…but it was coming from my water bowl. When I leaned over and looked inside, right away it was like something caught me and was trapping me in a nightmare world. All of my worst fears popped into my head and seemed to be fighting against me…"

Master Ferribolt's eyebrows were furrowed.

"But that's not the strangest part," Jason continued. "Amidst all of the terrifying things that I saw"—his voice died down to a whisper and he glanced at the windows—"I saw King Barnabas leaning over a table with a water basin on it, speaking some evil language I've never heard before…"

Master Ferribolt's eyes widened. Immediately, he pushed himself up from his seat and briskly walked over to a nearby bookshelf. A small cupboard was built into the bookshelf with a lock on it, and the Chief Patriarch produced a key from his robes as he approached it. Jason remained seated, feeling uncomfortable at the sight of the suddenly-distraught Chief Patriarch.

"Do you know what it could mean?" Jason said.

"I might," Master Ferribolt said uneasily as he turned the lock. "But I dearly hope that I'm wrong."

The door swung open on squeaky hinges. Jason craned his neck to see what was inside. From out of the small, wooden cell, Master Ferribolt extracted a large black book. The ancient leather had an oily sheen to it and locked in yellowed, wrinkled pages. It had to be centuries old. He carried it in both hands and hurriedly walked over to Jason, extending to the book to him.

"Take it," Master Ferribolt said.

Jason hesitantly reached out his hands and held the book. Instantly, he felt something inside him lurch uncomfortably. He got the distinct impression that he was holding something diseased.

"*Tepnoh Edomah*," Master Ferribolt said darkly.

"That sounds like Ancient Nezmythian…" Jason said, badly wanting to set the book down.

"It is," Master Ferribolt said. "It means '*Magic of Darkness*.' For goodness sake, put that book down before it starts growing on you! I can hardly stand to look at it, let alone touch it."

Jason complied without hesitation, thrusting the book to the floor like it was vermin. Master Ferribolt glowered at it as it sat atop his bear rug.

"Every Patriarch in the world is trained to understand and recognize *Tepnoh Edomah*," Master Ferribolt said, his eyes fixed on the dark book. "It's a positively diabolical entity. It's said to be the very seed of the Darkness conjured by the Guardian of the Night—the same force that battled against you and I and the Dragon in the First Life."

"What does it do?" Jason asked, feeling a sliver of ice slide down his back.

"Grants you overwhelming power," Master Ferribolt continued. "It's extremely powerful and easy to learn, which is probably why King Barnabas has taken to it. But there is one damning factor to its capabilities…"

"What?"

"It robs you of your emotions," Master Ferribolt locked his fiery eyes at Jason. "It numbs your capacity to feel happiness and contentment. The more you dabble in the arts of *Tepnoh Edomah*, the more rapidly your positive emotions drain from within you. In its place, fear, anger and revenge prevail. Joy ceases to exist.

"Jason, I do believe you've confirmed the suspicions I have had for many years," Master Ferribolt said gravely. "I have had reasons to suspect that the King had dabbled in the arts of *Tepnoh Edomah,* but until this day had no evidence. The King used to be such an honorable, pleasant man those many, many years ago… *Tepnoh Edomah* must have caught his eye and he began to experiment with it. That would explain the downward spiral in his character those many decades ago… the transformation into the monster he is now…

"What he used on you was a Dreamslayer spell. He contacted you miles away through the water bowl in your bedroom, and as you looked in to inspect it, he trapped you like an insect. He told you your only means for escape was to sacrifice your will—to yield—did he not?"

Jason nodded, his eyes wide.

"If you did, your mind would be lost at this moment. You would be a puppet in his hands... do anything he desires... including kill yourself."

Jason's jaw fell. Every phrase came at him like a speeding jeroki aimed at his brain. *Tepnoh Edomah...* losing your emotions... robbing Barnabas of his character... it all fit together so perfectly, and the knowledge was overwhelming.

"So how did you escape?" Master Ferribolt asked. "How did you fight your way out of the Dreamslayer spell?"

Jason looked at the ground. His legs shook, "I'm not so sure... all I remember is that among all the terrible, awful things I saw, I briefly saw you, and remembered the words you said to me the night I almost fled the kingdom—things about relying on the Dragon for strength and becoming something greater than I am. I think that's what eventually saved me."

"And that is the *only* way to defeat *Tephnoh Edomah*, Jason," Master Ferribolt said. "*Never* forget that. *Tepnoh Edomah* is seductive and insurmountably destructive because it's the embodiment of the Guardian of the Night's lust for power. Do not *ever* dabble in it. If you do, you will become just like King Barnabas."

A hush fell over them. But it only lasted for a moment before Master Ferribolt continued.

"More importantly, I want you to remember that your faith saved you. There will come times—very soon—where you will have to battle more against the forces of Darkness and *Tepnoh Edomah*. Remember that the Dragon will grant you strength and power if your heart remains pure. But you must stay on the path that you are now. Doing what is right is rarely easy, but the rewards are always worth the adversity."

Jason teased a smile, echoing the words in his mind. *Your faith saved you...* Suddenly, he remembered another thing.

"Oh! I had another dream..." Jason said. "It was about a vulture and an eagle and they were fighting over some tree... do you think that could mean anything?"

Master Ferribolt raised his eyebrows curiously, "It doesn't sound like the work of *Tepnoh Edomah* to me. You've been dealing with a lot of stress, and those dreams could be a reaction. Focus more on continuing your study of the Ancient Language and bettering your battle skills. These dreams could be a passing thing."

Jason grinned feebly.

* * * * *

Kara's flaky, cracked lips pulled into a smile as Jason took her splotched hand. She shivered faintly, despite the thick, wool blanket draped over her frail, sickly body. It was the middle of the day, and Tomm was away at the printing house, busy at work, trying to find more opportunities to make money and pay the Harvest as his wife lay sick in bed. Jason sat cross-legged at her bedside. The floorboards grew colder as winter approached. Jason's eyes filled with worry, but Kara's eyes, however, shined as they always did. They fixed on Jason.

"You seem different…" she breathed.

"Different?" Jason asked, puzzled. He was beginning to think the *Ipoklime* was affecting her sight.

"Yes…" Kara returned. "Your eyes are brighter. They haven't been that way since you were very young."

Jason grinned feebly. He didn't say anything. A lot of things had happened lately that had caused change within him, but he wasn't in a position to elaborate. He finally said, "But I've never seen you like this before. I hate coming home to see you like this." He sighed. "I'm so sorry, mother…"

"Don't be sorry," she said. "It's not your fault."

But I think it is… Jason thought. *If only you knew.* "There has to be some way. There has to be a cure. If there were some legal way to obtain a Mulak flower—"

"Jason," Kara wheezed. "Even if I never get better... and I die right in this very bed... death isn't the end. You haven't forgotten that, right?"

Jason rubbed her hand between his.

"You were too young to remember when your grandfather died," she continued. "He and I were very close... always had been, and his death was very hard for me. But before his spirit left his body behind, he pulled me to his bedside and told me a story."

Jason leaned forward, still grasping his mother's hand.

"Once, a long time ago, there was a great race. It wasn't like any other race... this race stretched not down a street, not across a city, but across the *entire kingdom*. Thousands of people trained for this great race, for the chance to achieve fame and glory beyond measure.

"Among these were three friends. They knew each other all their lives, and loved each other like brothers. They decided they would enter the race, and they trained for hours each day to run it. Finally, when the day of the great race came, they were as excited as could be. Everyone in the kingdom had come out to watch! Each brother looked forward to hearing the starting whistle with great anticipation.

"All of the racers took their marks. The official sounded his whistle, and the three brothers took off. They ran, and ran, and ran... they ran for days. The race wasn't easy, oh no. There were lots of hills, tall grass, and rocks that would sometimes make them trip and fall. But they always got up, and pressed on, determined to reach the finish line.

"One day, one of the friends became weary, and had to stop.

"'Go on!' he told his friends. 'I'll find a wagon that will take me to the finish line! Keep running!'

"They were disappointed and sad that their friend had grown weary so soon, but the two friends kept running, knowing they would eventually see their friend at the finish line.

"More days passed. Their legs burned and they were hungry and tired, but they continued to run. Suddenly, only a few days from the finish line, the second friend also grew weary as they passed through a small village.

"'This is where I stop, my friend!' he called as his friend kept running. 'I shall replenish my strength here with supper and a bed. I will see you at the finish line soon enough!'

"The third friend continued on. It was very lonely, not having anyone to laugh with or talk with as he ran, but he ran anyway. Days passed, and he finally reached the finish line. The entire kingdom celebrated. They cheered for their countrymen who valiantly ran the race.

"But best of all, when the third friend crossed the finish line, his other two friends were there to greet him, embracing him and showering him with praise. They were united once again. They had all ran the race, and although the two had grown tired and had to quit running, they were all together again at the finish line."

Jason's eyes hopped from his mother, to the ground, to his mother again. Kara squeezed Jason's hand and looked him in the eye, her eyes brighter than ever.

"I'm getting tired, Jason..." she said. "But even if I have to quit the race, I'll still see you at the finish line. Death isn't the end—our spirits will always live on, and we will always be a family. It's just the postponing of a sweeter reunion. Don't forget it."

* * * * *

Jason pulled at his collar and knocked on the door in front of him. As he waited, he sniffed the charming white flowers he held in his gloved hand. He was amazed that these flowers were still on the market, especially since winter was so swiftly approaching. His heart beat thickly as he considered who was on the other side of that door. He cast his eyes about him and observed his surroundings. It wasn't often that he simply got to stand around in Upper City and observe the grandeur of the mansions surrounding him.

The house was just as noble and majestic as the other ones on the sloping street. Jason tried not to look at the shadowy castle in the distance—he instead decided to examine the quaint iron fence that rose up to his hips and ran around the perimeter the property.

The gardening that hugged the walkway and the edge of the fence was exquisite. Flowers in various cheerful colors painted the area vividly, trying to splash as much color as possible before the snow snuffed them out. A healthy green lawn filled the remaining area. Pillars ran around the edge of the white stone porch.

Suddenly, Jason heard the door swing open behind him.

"Good evening!" Saryan's eyes twinkled as she closed the door behind her. She buttoned up her thickly padded jacket to protect herself from the late-autumn dusk. She flicked her hair back with gloved hands.

Just as Jason saw her, he felt tacky in his own clothes. He had to dig endlessly in his trunk to find a clean shirt and it was impossible to remove the grease from his pants. His filthy brown jacket had random patches in it, but he did manage to find a cleaner glove for his right hand. As he held out the flowers, Saryan's face lit up.

"Oh, thank you!"

"I'm glad you like them. They're not as beautiful as these, though…" Jason said while motioning to the garden. "…Do you do all of this yourself?"

"Not all of it," Saryan conceded as she sniffed the flowers dreamily. "Mostly it's the gardener. She's worked for my family for years, so I've picked up a few things from her as I've watched her. Just let me put these inside, I'll be right back."

Jason blinked and broke a half-grin, "Sure."

As she hurried inside, Jason finally realized how hard his heart was beating. His smile faded and he inwardly coached himself on how to behave. *Just be a gentleman… that's what*

*mother always taught me… be courteous, be kind, be considerate…
don't do anything foolish…*

In a matter of moments, Saryan was back outside.

Jason cleared his throat, "I hope you don't mind a simple
walk through the city."

"I think that sounds perfect," her eyes sparkled.

Jason's lips pulled into a smile, and his heart didn't stop
throbbing. They walked down the walkway and closed the
gate behind them. Jason kept his hands firmly in his pockets
and his eyes on the ground as they walked. Saryan followed
suit and walked shoulder-to-shoulder with Jason. A short
period of silence ensued as they ventured down the Upper
City street… Jason wanted to say something, anything that
would start a conversation with the girl, but didn't want to say
anything that could make him sound remotely foolish. So
instead he kept quiet.

"So…" Saryan said. "How are things at your shop?"

"Good," Jason said. "Well, okay, I suppose… we've had
more orders… but I'm still not sure yet if we'll have enough
money for the Harvest next month. But something tells me
we'll be alright. At least I hope so."

"I hope so too."

"You probably don't have to worry about the Harvest
much, do you?" Jason asked, looking at her.

Saryan shook her head. "My father is a Captain in the
Nezmythian Army, so we're exempt."

"A Captain," Jason echoed, his eyebrows raised. A few
things popped into his head all at once. Firstly, he felt
irritated that anyone at all in the kingdom was exempt from
the horror of the Harvest. Secondly, he was slightly
frightened at the idea that her father was one of those in King
Barnabas' close circle. He took a mental note to keep his
guard up. *What if King Barnabas has made her one of my trials
somehow?*

"Wow…" he said. "No wonder you're such an incredible
fighter. It's in your family."

Saryan smiled. "It's true. He's had me sparring since I was four. I don't love it, though... it's just something I'm very good at. Look."

They were quickly approaching the Northern Market Street, and snow was beginning to softly trickle from the sky. A tall, beautiful cathedral towered to their left as they walked by, adorned with ornate stained glass windows and mighty wooden doors. Saryan grinned proudly as they strolled along.

"That's where I attend Cathedral each week," she said. "Patriarch Willows is a wonderful man. I always leave feeling inspired by his words."

Jason creased his eyebrows curiously, looking at her.

"Yes, I agree..." Jason said almost dreamily. "He ministered at the Cathedral I used to attend down in Lower City... back when I received my Blessing of Fate..."

"Used to?" Saryan echoed.

Jason took his eyes off the Cathedral. "I haven't attended in a long time."

"Why?"

"It's a long story... Lately I've been feeling like I should go, though."

Saryan moved in closer and put her hand in Jason's arm. Their eyes met. The silver of her eyes sparkled brighter than ever against the contrast of the falling snow. Her sculpted lips pulled into an innocent, delighted grin. Jason could almost count each of her freckles.

"Come with me," she said. "It would be a lot better than going alone. And you could see Patriarch Willows again."

Jason's heart leapt and his lips pulled into a congruent grin, but he somehow felt a conflict of thought coagulating in his mind. *She could definitely be a trial in some strange way... but would a trial be trying to get me to go to Cathedral? That doesn't make sense. Maybe she's not a trial? Or maybe she's just being very sly...*

Jason's answer wasn't immediate. "You mean your father doesn't go with you?"

Saryan's smile quickly faded, and her eyes lost their sparkle. She looked at the walkway ahead as they passed by the Cathedral. "He's away on a trip for now… visiting the villages around the edges of the kingdom. I never know when he'll be back… sometimes he'll be home for a day or two, then have to leave for another couple of months. So I'm all alone for now."

"You're very close to him," Jason said.

"Especially after my mother died," Saryan replied. "We've had to rely on each other ever since then. I was only six, and he taught me how to be strong. There isn't anything I wouldn't do for my father."

A short pause. Then Jason said, "I'm sorry about your mother."

Saryan squeezed his arm and smiled. "Don't be. It happened a long time ago. And I think it's helped me to become who I am now. Besides, it's not like she's far away. I think she looks down and tells me she loves me every day… in very small ways."

Jason couldn't help but grin. It was then that their street connected with the Northern Market Street. The elegant mansions of brick and stone gave way to classy shops with expertly crafted signs and displays with merchandise Jason could never hope to afford. The aristocrats that would normally wander this market street were few as the snow continued to drift down from the darkening sky. However, most shops still had lanterns hanging outside.

Saryan shivered slightly and huddled closer to Jason. Jason's heart thumped a little harder for a second.

"Goodness, aren't you freezing?" Saryan asked while glaring at Jason's jacket.

Jason's gaze dropped to his jacket. It had been in his possession for years. Come to think of it, it had belonged to one of Kristof's prior apprentices before Jason showed up. He was allowed to have it because the previous apprentice had left it behind. Some of the edges were frayed. Like most of Jason's other clothes, it was eternally stained in some areas. And he had to sew some of the seams back together on a few occasions.

"I feel okay..." Jason said.

"We need to get something to warm up," Saryan said. "I know a great place nearby where we can get some hot cider. Come on."

"Saryan..." Jason put all of his weight in his boots to resist Saryan's tugging. "I can't afford anything on this street. I still don't know if I'll be able to pay the Harvest."

"I'll pay for it!" She said, tugging harder. "Come on, I'm cold! And we should probably get you a new jacket, too. That one is disgusting."

Jason didn't quite know what to think, let alone say. He had never had anyone want to buy him anything, really. All he had ever known was to feel lucky that you had the necessities. It was all a very strange feeling... He finally succumbed to her tugging and she led them to a small shop just a hundred yards down the Northern Market Street. Elegant ironwork criss-crossed over the windows, and a dangling sign above them read *Sue's*. Saryan opened the door and Jason followed behind.

As they stepped inside, a wall of warmth and fragrance collided with them. A roaring fire crackled at the far side of the shop, past several circular tables accompanied with three-legged stools. A pleasant-looking woman stood at a counter in front of a wall with several jugs of colorful liquids, two iron stoves, and a large ice box. Lanterns hanging along the walls radiated a cozy glow across the polished tables and floorboards.

Jason stood in awe, diagnosing all of the materials used in crafting this interior and calculating their cost in his head. It wasn't long before it would be wiser to just give up.

"Evening, Sue!" Saryan called to the woman. "Two mugs of hot booshum cider, please!"

"Of course, Miss Saryan!" the woman nodded. "You two take a seat and I'll bring it to you when it's nice and hot."

The place was empty. Saryan picked a table with two stools right by the window, and Jason sat down with her. The view outside was picturesque with the snowfall, street lanterns and upper-class shops, but he couldn't help but stare inside.

"Have you ever been in a restaurant, Jason…?" Saryan asked amusedly after seeing Jason's reaction.

Jason shook his head slowly. "Never. All of them are here on the Northern Market Street. I never imagined I would ever have the money to come in one."

Saryan hummed. "I feel like we've talked a lot about me tonight." She propped her elbows on the table and rested her chin on her fists. "Tell me about you."

"What do you want to know?"

"Everything."

Jason inhaled deeply and shifted in his chair, keeping his hands between his knees. *First off, I can't tell you everything…* He shrugged. "I don't know… I feel like you know most there is to know about me. I'm a craftsman. I live in Lower City. That's it, really."

"Do you have any talents?"

Jason had to think for a moment before he could answer. He definitely didn't consider sparring a talent of his… but then he remembered. "I've played the flyra for many years." He reached into his pocket and extracted the small flute, placing it on the table and prodding it gently. "It's what I do when I want to be alone with my thoughts."

"You're musical!" Saryan's eyes lit up. "You *must* play me something. Go ahead!"

"Are you sure this is the setting?" Jason felt himself shrink just a little bit. His eyes hopped out the window and about the store. Sue was busying herself wiping off dishes. A small pot steamed on the stove behind her.

Saryan smirked. "There's no one else here, Jason. Go on!"

Jason forced his lip to curl into a half-smile before he picked up the flyra and placed his fingers on the sound holes. Slowly, he brought it to his lips then searched through the library of songs in his head. He chose a short one that was relatively easy, but had special meaning to it. Shakily, he inhaled, and played.

The notes from the flyra almost made the interior of *Sue's*
seem a little warmer. The whistles left the flyra and floated to
the ceiling, dancing and gliding as they went. Sue stopped
and looked at Jason for a brief moment, as if the song called
something familiar from a distant memory. Saryan's eyes
softened to a misty glow as she watched him. Jason closed
his eyes, blocking out the environment, allowing himself to
be one with the music. He played on.

Finally, the whispering, glowing notes died down. Jason
removed the flyra from his lips and opened his eyes. Saryan
hadn't broken her gaze on him. She breathed deeply and
exhaled, as if doing so filled her soul with warmth and let
whatever darkness was there seep out.

"That was beautiful..." she said dreamily.

Jason nodded and put his hands back between his knees,
flyra still in hand. "Thank you... it's called *Mohkoh Mohlay*.
It's about a man who is forced to leave his family behind to
go to war—forced to leave behind what he wants in order to
do something he's been commanded to do..."

"I love it," Saryan smiled.

Jason smiled in return. The sky had grown completely
dark and the snowfall was getting thicker. The Northern
Market Street was now covered in a thin blanket of snow.
Saryan and Jason exchanged looks.

"It'll be hard to climb the street back to your home,"
Jason said. He chuckled for a second. "That's probably why
this place is empty."

"You're right," Saryan returned. "We should get going."

It was just then that Sue came over with two piping mugs
of booshum juice. Jason and Saryan exchanged looks again.

"I'm sorry, Sue," Saryan said. "We were just about to
leave."

"Oh, it's not a worry, Miss Saryan," Sue said with an
unfailing grin. "Why don't you take these with you? The
night is only going to get colder. Keep yourselves warm."

"Oh, you're too kind!" Saryan said, taking the mug from
Sue's hand. Jason took the other. Saryan then extracted what

looked like several Bars from her pocket and slipped them into Sue's hand. "I'll bring the mugs back tomorrow morning."

"You're a treat, Miss Saryan," Sue's eyes sparkled. She turned to Jason. "And you sir, have a special gift with that instrument. That song was a whisper from the Holy Dragon."

Jason grinned sheepishly and expressed his thanks.

They both got up from the table and slipped back outside, expressing their thanks to Sue once again and sipping from their mugs. The booshum juice was exquisite. It splashed their insides with lovely warmth and tickled their tongues with a sweet tanginess. They continued to chat and laugh occasionally as they made their way back up the Upper City streets. Snow continued to fall and wet their hair and street lanterns lit up their way as they trudged through the thin snow.

Finally, they made it to the gates of Saryan's home.

"Thank you for tonight," Jason said as he opened the small gate for Saryan.

"Jason, I had a wonderful time," Saryan said as she trudged up the walkway, Jason following on her heels. "I hope we can do this again very soon."

Jason's eyes beamed. "I hope so, too."

As they approached the door, Saryan took Jason's empty mug from his hand.

"I'm sorry we didn't get you a new jacket tonight," Saryan said with a smirk. "You better not freeze to death before I see you next time."

Jason grinned. "I won't. And you don't need to worry about getting me a new jacket. I've always managed."

Her eyes glimmered. "So will you come with me to Cathedral soon?"

Jason didn't have to think long for a reply. "...I think I will."

She smiled. Jason was about to tell her goodnight, but before he could, she leaned forward and pressed her flawless lips against his frozen cheek. Jason could feel his face flush and his heart forgot to beat.

As Saryan withdrew herself, she smiled widely and blinked her long, dark eyelashes. Her cheeks were rosy too, whether it was due to the cold air or the recent kiss, Jason couldn't tell.

"Goodnight, Jason," Saryan waved softly, opened the door, and closed it, leaving Jason standing alone in the chill outside her house. In his mind, Jason recited every wonderful moment for that evening. He let out a deep sigh of contentment and smiled to himself broadly.

He spoke as if remembering a heavenly dream, "Saryan…"

17 THE RETURN

Jason recoiled hard, nearly tumbling onto the floor as Tarren's foot connected with the side of his face, sending his saliva flying through the air in a fine mist. He spun out of the attack and blindly took a swipe at Tarren with his wooden broadsword, but Tarren ducked underneath the blow effortlessly.

"Too slow, Jason!" Tarren shouted.

Jason mimicked Tarren's roundhouse kick as he kept spinning. This time it connected flawlessly with Tarren's cheekbone.

"What was that? 'Too slow?'"

It was within a second that Tarren had recovered from the blow and took a swipe at Jason with the wooden dagger he held backwards in his right hand. Jason dodged by reflexively bending backward. Tarren threw a few more slashes at him as he forced Jason further and further to the edge of the combat room, all of which Jason dodged or blocked with the flat of his sword.

When Tarren had finally backed Jason into a wall, he tried one more swipe at Jason's neck. Jason ducked and rolled out of the way, kicking at Tarren's feet as he swept across the floor. Tarren's balance was lost and he fell onto the floor, face up and grunting loudly as his back connected with the padding.

Jason slid back up to his feet and attempted to stab Tarren in the chest and win the match, but Tarren rolled out of the way, threw his legs up past his head, and rolled backwards into a kneeling position to block Jason's next swing with his armored forearms.

Jason stepped backward and Tarren jumped to his feet, spinning around to face Jason. The both sidestepped around each other, their eyes full of fire and sweat dripping from their hair. Breathing came in great bodies of air.

"Your reflexes are amazing," Tarren panted. "…Getting better every week."

Jason smiled hotly, "Thank you."

Tarren smiled. Without warning, he jumped back, twitched his hand and shot a quick jeroki at Jason.

Jason's body gave itself a quick dose of adrenaline. *Let's try this…*

Jason quickly jumped sideways and out of the way of the oncoming ball of magic. He extended his left arm outward and cupped his hand. As the jeroki sped into his palm, Jason could feel the heat as if it was a miniature sun flying through the air. He spun around, trying to change the direction while still maintaining the speed of the jeroki, and he actually felt it resting in the palm of his hand for a moment. Halfway through the spin, however, he lost control of the jeroki and it jumped out of his hand. It soared into the far wall and dissipated.

Jason nearly laughed as he kept his eyes on the wall, a smile stretching across his face. *Whoa! That almost—*

While Jason wasn't aware, Tarren had leapt forward and drilled his foot into his back. Jason fell face-first onto the floor and tried to scramble back to his feet, but as soon as he was facing upward, Tarren was on top of him with a fake dagger at his throat.

Jason groaned loudly and Tarren merely frowned at him with his eyebrows raised, his sweaty blonde locks hanging down from his face. Jason was panting as if he had sprinted laps around the room all afternoon. Tarren wasn't.

"You lost," Tarren said.

"I know."

"Why did you lose?"

The words stuck to Jason's throat. He sighed irritably, "Because I lost focus."

"Right you are," Tarren said, getting up and blindly throwing the dagger across the room next to the other fake weapons. "It wasn't when you tried redirecting that jeroki that it cost you the match, it was when you kept thinking about it after it disappeared. If you would have turned and looked at me right after it had got out of your hand, you would have seen me coming and had enough time to dodge the kick—maybe even counter it."

"I'm getting better though," Jason sat up on the padding and wiped his brow with the back of his hand. "I can tell. Maybe I'll beat you someday." Tarren walked to the side of the room where a couple of canteens sat on a table. He grabbed one and threw the other one to Jason.

Tarren chuckled. "Absolutely," he uncorked the canteen and took a deep gulp of water. "Right after you're crowned King of Nezmyth."

The water that was sliding down Jason's throat leapt back out, sending him into a coughing fit. He looked at Tarren, his eyes wide and the hairs on the back of his neck feeling prickly.

"You shouldn't joke about things like that." He coughed and covered his mouth. "This warehouse is remote—cough—but you still don't know if soldiers could be walking by."

"It was a harmless joke, Jason," Tarren rolled his eyes. "You need to stop being so tense. No one is going to arrest me for that."

Jason shoved the canteen back into his mouth, trying to flush out the harshness caused by his hacking cough. When his throat was finally soothed to the point where he could talk normally, he asked, "The Harvest is in less than a month. How are you doing?"

Tarren didn't look at him as he unstrapped his arm plates. "Not good."

"How behind are you?"

"Thirty-eight Blocks."

Jason's heart dropped into his stomach. He wanted to speak words of comfort, words of hope and assurance, but nothing seemed to come.

"Let's be honest Jason," Tarren said. "I'm going to be Blacknoted this time."

"Don't say that," Jason's eyebrows bent fiercely.

"Maybe it's a good thing though," Tarren chortled. "It means I'll finally get to spend time with my father... merrily working in the gold mines of the eastern mountains. Maybe they'll even let us share a room, if there already aren't a dozen slaves in each one."

"*I said don't say that!*"

"*Wake up, Jason!*" Tarren spat. "I don't know if you've noticed, but the entire kingdom has been falling apart for decades! Don't pretend like you didn't know this was going to happen to you or me sooner or later! It's time to just accept it. It's hopeless."

"There is still three weeks left before the Harvest," Jason said. "And even then, you'll still have a month to make more money and pay the tax after it passes."

"Unless the King changes his mind about that," Tarren said. "It could happen. The fool is as greedy and ruthless as he is powerful."

"Don't talk like that!" Jason said, praying there weren't soldiers patrolling outside. "Soldiers could be listening! Would you prefer to work at the eastern mountains or get beaten every day in prison?"

"Is one option really better than the other?" Tarren seethed. "Maybe I'd have a better chance dying in prison. That'd be a quicker way to escape this nightmare of a kingdom."

Jason's eyes snapped and something like a stake lodged into his heart. His eyes stung and his hands shook. No sound was able to escape his lips. After a long, painful, frozen moment, Jason turned on his heels and bolted to the door. The padding muffled his footsteps, keeping them from echoing in the massive building. His throat tightened with each step. He grabbed his sword and jacket as he escaped out into the frozen air.

He slammed the door behind him and trudged through the snow, clenching his jaw and sniffing occasionally. He wiped his eyes before the tears could stream down his burning cheeks.

Mother is sick and dying... he thought bitterly. *Father is struggling to pay the Harvest... Tarren isn't going to make it either... what's next?*

"I'm going to tear your world apart from around you..." the words from King Barnabas echoed in Jason's mind.

As he turned a corner, the castle came into view between two buildings. It stood atop the Upper City hill, lodged between the white of Upper City and the grey of the winter sky. Jason stopped. He could picture King Barnabas right now... idly sitting in this throne, leering at another dancing damsel, utterly careless of the thousands of lives that struggled to survive directly below him.

His jaw clenched harder and his anger boiled higher. To release his fury, Jason charged a large jeroki in his hand and launched it to the sky, directly at the castle. It traveled only a hundred yards through the air before it dissipated.

Jason's anger evaporated into emptiness. His chin fell to his chest... and his knees dropped to the snow. His sniffs gave way to sobs, and he let the tears flow freely.

* * * * *

Master Ferribolt's prodding had finally gotten the best of him.

"Jason," he had always said. "I *strongly* recommend you study Ancient Nezmythian outside of my home. You've grown surprisingly proficient in the three months we've studied together, but your vocabulary is still lacking. That should be accomplished through your own studies."

Jason always met the remark with a huff, but you can only turn down the Chief Patriarch's friendly advice so many times before you feel like you're flat-out sinning. He knew how to get to the city library, so directions weren't necessary.

"I beg your pardon?"

The librarian pulled her rectangular reading spectacles down to the tip of her nose and looked hard at Jason with probing black eyes. Her thin, wrinkly lips were pursed in curiosity.

"I want to get to the Ancient Nezmythian literature section of the library," Jason repeated.

"You are... studying the Ancient Tongue?" the librarian scanned Jason's messy garbs skeptically.

Jason nodded. "Yes, ma'am. For over three months now."

The librarian pulled anxiously at the shoulders of her pale dress and her eyes darted to her desk. She tapped her hair bun squeamishly with her palm, then immediately began to rummage through the drawers below, muttering to herself, "If I can find that key... ah! Here it is."

Her hand reappeared with an old-fashioned metal key that was partly caked with rust. Jason looked at it oddly and took it from the librarian's outstretched hand. She looked at Jason closely, "The books with the Ancient Language are on the top floor inside the gated region. None of the books there are available for lending. Remember to bring the key back when you are finished."

Jason nodded and bid his thanks as he walked into the library. Outside, it appeared to be a crusty old building that hadn't been refurbished in too many years, but once he stepped inside, the smell of pages upon pages of old paper and ink was almost thick enough to taste.

There weren't any walls—every crevice, nook and cranny was covered with a bookshelf stuffed to the brim with books. Tables, oil lamps and chairs were plentiful and a few of them were filled with casual readers or small study groups as they hunched over pages and intensely soaked up information.

Shelves jutted out of the wall to create small hallways and sections for different topics. A balcony wrapped its way around three fourths of the massive hall and could be accessed by a few flights of stairs. Jason's eyes darted from bookshelf to bookshelf, corner to corner. He silently marveled at the centuries of records that were kept in this very hall.

Jason located a flight of stairs on the far right side of the room. He briskly walked over to it and started to climb. The wooden steps creaked as his body weight came down upon them, but Jason could feel that they weren't about to break any time soon. He climbed higher and higher until he reached the balcony, which he discovered held more bookshelves. He briefly scanned the area, but didn't see any gated door. The spirit of exploration moved him forward.

As he made his way across the first side of the balcony, he loosely examined some book titles that stuck out to him on the shelves to his right. He had to have been in the history section, because the titles were things like *Great Conquerors of the Ancient World, Uchlov the Fearsome: The Biography,* and *King Clements: Master of Laughs.*

As he rounded the corner to walk down the next stretch of balcony, he noticed something odd in the corner of the room where two bookshelves stood just a few feet apart from each other. He moved in closer, his eyes hard and probing.

It was a gate. A crude iron gate only two feet wide stood between the grand library of Nezmyth City and a small room with a few dusty bookshelves, a desk, a lamp and a chair. On the gate, near Jason's gloved hand, was a small lock.

This has to be it, he thought to himself. He took the key out of his pocket, inserted it into the lock, twisted, and heard a click. He withdrew the key and pushed on the gate, which squealed loudly. Jason cringed and pushed the gate slower, muffling the ear-scraping squeaks.

The first thing Jason noticed about the room was the dust. It was everywhere: on the table, the chair, the shelves, even on the tiny window sill. *It's obvious this place doesn't get many visitors...*

Jason walked up to the chair and caressed the seat with his hand, wiping a thick layer of dust off, then he took a big gulp of air and blew hard on the table. A cloud of dust and dirt jumped into the air, and immediately he started coughing and fanning the debris away from his face.

An old lantern stood quietly at the edge of the table. Jason lit it and steadily fed it more oil until it had a cheery glow to it. He took the lantern in his hand and used it to brighten up the titles on the dusty books that clung to their spots on the shelves. Most of the squiggles, dots, and jagged lines were familiar to him, but he could only make out fractions of the titles.

He frowned. *This is going to take some work.* He finally decided to settle on a thick book with the word "Crafting" in the title. He plopped down into the chair, set the lantern on the table, and placed the book down beside it. As he opened the leather cover, yellow pages filled with squiggles and dots revealed themselves under the glow of the lantern.

Here we go... he thought to himself.

* * * * *

Saryan's hand had found its favorite spot around Jason's forearm. She walked perfectly in step with Jason as they made their way down the Upper City street, along with nearly a hundred other townspeople. Everyone was dressed formally. Saryan had clipped her hair stylishly, and her powder-blue dress hugged her curves until it flittered past her hips and down to her ankles. A coat of mammoth fur shielded her from the cold, and long, white gloves almost entirely covered her arms.

Jason gulped and his heart thumped, but it had nothing to do with the beautiful blonde by his side.

How many years has it been? He thought. *Over five? What will Patriarch Willows think?*

He wore his usual dingy jacket because it was the only one he owned, but he did his best to wash it in preparation for today. Saryan let him borrow her father's old formal wear because Jason couldn't seem to find his. The flowing white sleeves billowed down to his wrists, and the brown cotton slacks were perfectly pressed. He had to admit… he felt cleaner than he usually did.

The bell tower of the Cathedral sounded—three bongs, signaling that the sermon would start very shortly. Jason exhaled a shaky breath. Saryan pulled herself in as they walked.

"It'll be fine," she said. "You'll be glad you came."

Jason thought of smiling for her, but instead only the corner of his mouth twitched.

The crowd was beginning to bottleneck at the front doors of the Cathedral. Their pace slowed down to a penguin-like walk, slow and cramped. Perfectly-trimmed bushes were like shelves for snowfall at about elbow's height. They sandwiched a walkway several paces wide, and this led to the entrance of the Cathedral.

At the entrance, a delightful-looking man in orange robes, tall and thin, vibrantly shook hands with those who walked by, asking them about their families and friends and wearing an ear-to-ear smile. Gray hairs were starting to sprout throughout his burnt black hair and his eyes were just as dark. Jason cleared his throat as he saw the man. Saryan grinned. He avoided eye contact until they were almost upon him.

"Hello, Brother!" Patriarch Willows said as he snatched Jason's hand.

His eyes had a mysterious power on Jason. Jason's eyes wanted to avoid them. He wanted to avoid those seemingly all-knowing eyes, shield his soul from them. And something inside him crawled, knowing he was shaking the hand of the person that pronounced upon him his Blessing of Fate, his curse and calling.

Jason finally forced himself to look into Patriarch Willow's eyes. There was no trace of contempt in those big, black eyes—only unconditional brotherhood. Jason felt comfortable to force a half-grin, which was all he could muster.

"Hello, Patriarch Willows," he muttered.

Patriarch Willows leaned in slightly. The smile gradually spread wider across his face, and something like wonder and joy overtook his aura.

"Jason…" he said almost reverently. "It's been quite a while, my young friend. How have you been?"

"Better," Jason said truthfully. "Better than the last time."

"Good," Patriarch Willows said. "You don't know how happy I am to hear that. It looks as though you've become acquainted with Miss Saryan. How wonderful. Please, take a seat inside. The Dragon's fire will keep us warm this afternoon."

He squeezed Jason's hand firmer before he let go, shepherding Saryan and Jason into the Cathedral. The building was magnificent. Stained glass windows pelted colorful light onto the ageless stone floors as they depicted Patriarchs and Chief Patriarchs from ages past. Chandeliers hung in a perfect row down the vaulted ceiling and dozens upon dozens of pews faced the pulpit up front. A platform with a golden triangle was just a few feet behind the pulpit. At the head of the Cathedral, occupying almost the entire wall, a massive painting of the Dragon hung, snaking through the sky with powerful claws and eyes that comprehended the eternities.

Saryan tugged Jason along, and they slid into an open spot next to some pleasant strangers. Jason rubbed his hands between his knees and tried not to look at them. Saryan slipped off her fur coat and greeted them like close acquaintances.

The Cathedral hissed with the reverent whisperings of hundreds of Upper City folk, all catching up with each other on the week's events and discussing what the Patriarch's sermon might be. Jason frowned. He was sure that none of them were fearfully whispering of the outcome of the Harvest. All he saw was oblivious, smiling faces at every turn.

After several minutes of this, the double doors crawled to a close, and the windows and torches were all that were left to illuminate the Cathedral. The hall fell silent. Patriarch Willows bustled down the aisle, his orange robes flowing behind him and his usual smile still stretched across his face. Jason shifted in his spot, making the pew creak.

When Patriarch Willows finally made it to the podium, he grabbed it with both hands and peered over the crowd.

"My friends!" he called. His voice was impressively loud. "It's a joy to have you here in the sanctum of the Holy Dragon today. I hope you will find joy and inspiration as I attempt to convey what the Sacred Dragon would have me say."

He paused. All eyes were upon him.

"I have prayed very heavily over this matter for the past week," he continued. "These are very uncertain times. The Harvest arrives again next week, and although most of you present enjoy the blessing of your wealth, there are thousands of others that are not as fortunate. It is needless for me to say that we must reach out and help those people in any way that we can. The Perfect Dragon has commanded us to serve and to uplift from the beginning of time, and that commandment is just as strongly in force today as it always has been. Do your duty to your fellow Nezmythians."

A few whispers whisked throughout the congregation. Jason grinned and exhaled.

"But today I felt inspired to teach you of endurance!"

Jason's eyebrows bent.

"My friends... brothers and sisters under the Dragon... it is all too easy to look upon our lives and ask 'Why me? Why is this happening now? What did I do to deserve this?' The answer, sometimes, is that you deserve it because the Dragon loves you and is trying to help you!"

Jason sat up straight, his eyebrows still bent.

"Trials and adversity come to all of us. That is part of our mortal existence. But with all of these trials—tests, you might call them—we can make a choice. We can either choose to give up and surrender to the forces of Darkness that are so eager to take us, or we can lean on the Dragon, call upon His mighty strength, and overcome!"

Flashbacks of Master Ferribolt's lectures flooded out from Jason's memories, along with the recent memory of the Dreamslayer spell. The only reason he escaped it was because he called upon the Dragon for strength.

"Brothers and sisters, trials are an opportunity to grow. The way to get the purest silver is to refine it with flame over and over again, and it is the same with us! If you're feeling lost, if you're feeling beaten, if your feelings are that you cannot go any further, it is because the Dragon wants you to lean upon Him. He wants you to become stronger! And in doing so, you will become a mighty instrument of truth and virtue upon Wevlia, and you will be greeted one day with the Dragon's words of, 'Well done. Rest from your labors.'"

The last four months had been full of challenges... and Jason knew there were more to come. The Blacknote... his sick mother... the Dreamslayer spell... and all of them were supposed to be for his good? His mind told him it didn't make sense... but something deep within him, some small, stirring spark, seemed to agree. He had grown stronger in these past four months. He had felt it. But that made him wonder...

What else is to come?

18 THE THREAT

Harvest day had arrived.

Snow pelted the winding streets of Nezmyth City, where, as usual, no one was about except for small battalions of soldiers and their money carts. The window of Jason's flat was dank and foggy and the room wasn't heated. He kept his jacket on as he sat on his straw mattress and shivered, blowing thin notes through his flyra.

He couldn't stop thinking of everybody. Tomm was just seven Blocks short of the tax... it wouldn't be a problem to achieve that much more with the next month after the Blacknote. That was a miracle in and of itself, especially considering that Kara wasn't strong enough to sew and sell dresses as she sometimes did.

Tarren however, was a different story. Jason hadn't spoken to him since his dramatic exit at sparring practice two weeks prior. He prayed that Tarren had managed some way to achieve the tax... or at least enough that he could possibly make the Blacknote deadline. But prospects looked grim.

He shivered again. The sun hid behind thick, gray clouds, making the time of day uncertain. Jason was sure it had to be late afternoon.

A small pouch sat next to Jason on the mattress. Inside it rested one hundred and twenty Blocks. The only reason it was there was because of his last conversation with Saryan.

"Do you have enough for the Harvest?" she had asked just a few days earlier.

Jason sighed coldly and shook his head. "No... just short. But it's okay. We should all be able to pay it after we're Blacknoted."

"I don't want to risk it," she shook her head vehemently. "You don't know if the King will change his mind on the policy. I'll be over to your shop tomorrow with whatever more you need. You and whoever else is there."

"Saryan, I couldn't possibly ask you to——."

"I'm giving it to you," she said with fire in her eyes. "And there's nothing you can do to stop me. If I want to, I can find out which soldiers will be patrolling all of your streets and give it to them anyway, so you might as well take it. Don't you dare argue with me."

Jason knew it was no use, so he didn't. He tried to negotiate an exchange for labor of some sort, but her scowl melted to a smile, she kissed him on the cheek and told him his kindness was enough. They had spent nearly every day together since the night of their first courtship. He didn't mind... every opportunity to spend time with her was an escape from the troubles of being a poor Lower City boy facing his Year of Decision.

The one thing he was still getting used to was her showering of gifts. He found it embarrassing to walk into the shop occasionally with a new shirt or pair of gloves, because he would then have to endure the juvenile prodding of Bertus and Jaboc concerning his budding love life. He endlessly tried paying back Saryan in small ways, like a small bouquet of flowers or sweets, but she would insist that it wasn't necessary. He continued doing it anyway.

With the more time he spent with her, the more convinced he was that she was not a trial sent by the King. *She's helping me pay the tax and encouraging me to attend Cathedral...* he would think. *That's* helping *me become King. It wouldn't make sense.*

Despite these thoughts, he still felt it necessary to keep his guard up. He kept a portion of his heart locked up and secure... just in case. At this point, it would be dangerous to assume complete safety.

Suddenly, he heard footsteps. He inserted his flyra into his left pocket and pinched the top of the small pouch. In his mind, he traced the path of the soldiers as they stopped at the other end of the hall and slowly made their way toward his door, stopping to collect the tax from each tenant as they went. When he heard them finally approach his door, he slipped on his sword and pushed himself up off the mattress.

They knocked. Jason pulled open the door and two Nezmythian soldiers filled up the threshold. Jason was sure it was the same ones from four months ago.

"Harvest," the one in blue growled.

Jason dropped the pouch into his outstretched hand and asked, "Are there any changes to the Blacknote policy?"

The soldiers ignored the question as they scanned the contents of the pouch. Jason flexed his hand, on the verge of demanding an answer—demanding to know if the fate of his loved ones had changed.

At length, the soldiers slipped Jason's pouch into a large pouch, satisfied with the amount contained. The red soldier looked Jason in the eyes and said:

"No."

With that, they turned on their heels and left. Jason closed the door in front of him. As the door latched shut, he closed his eyes and rested his head against it, his weary mind breathing a fresh sigh of contentment. *Everything could be okay... they have an extra month to pay... it'll be alright...*

But when he opened his eyes, he saw something that made every hair on his body stand straight. His blood froze and his heart jumped into his throat.

King Barnabas was standing in his room.

His hands were behind his back, and his icy eyes were fixed on Jason like a hawk eying a field mouse. His red cape billowed to the heels of his perfectly-polished boots, and his dark blade was sheathed across his back.

Jason turned slowly about to face him, as if any sudden movement would cause him to lash out in an attack. Cold sweat was quickly forming on his brow. His gloved hand reached for the hilt of his sword.

Before he could touch it, King Barnabas rumbled, "That would not be wise."

Jason's hand numbly fell to his side. Silence filled the room. The King hadn't made a single sound as he had entered the room, which horrified Jason even more than his presence alone. His sanctuary had been violated. If he had the ability to suddenly appear where he wanted, where else had he been?

His throat felt as harsh as a desert, but Jason managed to croak, "...why are you here?"

"To congratulate you," King Barnabas said. The expression on his face didn't change. The corners of his mouth seemed perpetually glued into a grimace and his eyes could have frozen a forest fire. "I must be frank... I did not believe you would last this long. Your Year of Decision is halfway to its conclusion, and you have somehow mustered the ability to endure your numerous hardships. Congratulations."

Jason didn't blink. He knew that wasn't it. He knew there had to be more. King Barnabas took a single step and he was instantly upon Jason, towering over him. His hands stayed clasped behind his back, but his eyes were now closer, and Jason could make them out in every excruciating detail. He tried not to shiver.

"These past four months have been challenging, have they not?" he breathed.

Jason swallowed and tore his gaze away from the eyes that were bearing into him. He said nothing.

"A lot has happened," King Barnabas stepped back and started pacing in circles. "You have begun visiting with the oafish Chief Patriarch on a weekly basis, learning the Ancient Language... amusing, but misguided. You have sought to sharpen your combat skills with your friend... foolish and futile. You have found a lovely girl of a superior social class you wish to pursue... tragically vain. And above all of this, your dear mother is dying, your father struggling to make ends, and your best friend on the verge of slavery. And it is all thanks to you."

A pause. The King closed in on Jason to where his face was just inches from his own. Jason tried to steady his quivering hands.

"You could have ended this months ago," the King said. He now started prowling around Jason. "Would you like to know how many slaves currently labor in the eastern mountains? There are *thousands*. Your best friend's father is one of them, you know. I gave you the option, Jason, but you refused. I wish you could hear their toil in the daytime, then hear the tearful wailing cut through the night. It is positively unforgettable. Would you like to know how many have *died* in those mines because of you...? How many fathers? Husbands? Brothers?"

Jason's eyes stung and his chin tightened. His fists stayed clenched by his side, shaking. He could hear them now—the whips cracking, the son weeping over his father, the husband sobbing over his lonely, helpless wife. And it was all because of him.

"This visit serves as a final warning," King Barnabas seethed. "I have been very lenient with the trials I have given you because I believed you would opt out of your Year of Decision quickly. But this marks the end of my clemency, and I refuse to play games with you from this point on. Denounce your Foreordination now, or you and the kingdom will suffer like never before."

Jason's knees went weak. His lips refused him to speak, and the silence hung like a dangling corpse. The King's eyes continued to lacerate him. Upon Jason's speechlessness, his eyes lit with rage. His lips pulled apart, revealing gnarled, grotesque teeth in the form of an enraged scowl.

"*Why?*" King Barnabas hissed. "I *know* you do not want the Throne! I have watched you for months and I *know* you want to go on as a peasant! *Why do you persist? I demand an answer!*"

After a tense, shaky moment, Jason finally found his tongue. He pulled his trembling lips apart and breathed:

"Because I need to. For everyone."

King Barnabas closed his mouth. And as he did, his eye twitched. He stepped back.

"So be it..." the words slid off his lips. "The Oracle Stone has not changed, Jason. Your stubbornness has cost innocent people their lives, and you have now incurred the fullness of my wrath. There are forces beyond your sight that have been protecting you, but no more. I have things into plan that even they have not foreseen. Your fate is secured."

With that, the King disappeared in a flash of purple mist, leaving Jason alone, the image of those icy eyes branded once again onto his conscious. His mouth dangled open and his knees finally buckled, dropping him to the cold floor. He brought his knees to his chest and wrapped his arms around them, shaking, reflecting on the horrific words that were just spoken. Tears, one by one, streamed down his cheek.

What have I done...?

* * * * *

Jason hadn't felt this small in months.

The fluffy white snow had become slushy along the Upper City street where the Chief Patriarch resided. Exquisite white deteriorated to a filthy grey as it was bombarded by carriages and boots of bustling aristocrats. The cold was more bitter than bracing. The faces of Nezmythians seemed sunken and pale as they wrapped themselves with scarves and gloves.

At this point, all of the flowers and shrubs in the city had surrendered to the onslaught of snow that masked them. Green was gone, only to be replaced by whites, grays, and browns.

Throughout Lower City, signs with black dots were nailed to every tenth door.

The gray snow hardly crunched under Jason's feet as he made his way up the winding street to the quarters of Master Ferribolt. When Jason reached the gate, the gatekeeper tipped his hat with a nod before pulling the lever. The gates shuddered and slowly creaked open and Jason made his way through.

He stroked the sheath of his blade and exhaled through his nose, watching the cloudy breath billow out as he made his way up the steps. He knocked on the door, and it was a matter of moments before Jerem was at the threshold.

"Good morning, Master Jason," he said crisply. His uniform was just as sharp as ever.

Jason asked, "Is Master Ferribolt here?"

"Yes, he just arrived," Jerem said while stepping aside. "Please, come in."

Jason stepped inside and Jerem held Jason's sword as he took off his coat. He stomped the snow off his boots and slipped his sword back on before Jerem took his coat and hung it on a nearby rack. The massive statue of the Dragon made eye contact with Jason. He ripped his eyes away from it, as it seemed to twang something uncomfortably inside him. Jason then dragged his feet to the study, breathing deeply and shakily as he went.

The study was just as it always was: a fire was lit, sunlight streamed through the windows and the books and artwork along the walls were unchanged. The only thing different was Master Ferribolt. Instead of sitting in the armchair or at his desk, he knelt in the very center of the room, with his head bowed and his hands on his knees. As Jason edged closer, he could make out the words he spoke.

"…and O Holy Dragon, grant thy servant Jason with strength, wisdom and courage as he endures the remaining months of his Year of Decision. Help him feel thy warming fire each day, and accomplish this mighty task for the better of the kingdom."

Master Ferribolt's head lifted, then slowly swiveled about. When he caught Jason out of the corner of his eye, his face softened. Jason swallowed. Master Ferribolt pushed himself off the floor, strode over to Jason, and thrust upon him a fatherly embrace.

Jason wasn't sure how to react. He didn't lift his arms, but let them dangle by his sides. Master Ferribolt buried his face in his shoulder.

"I've sensed your worry these past few days," he said as he let Jason go. He kept one hand on his shoulder. "How is your family? And Tarren?"

Jason looked at Master Ferribolt's feet. "Mother and father were Blacknoted, but they should be able to pay it when the time comes. Tarren is most likely Blacknoted too, but I haven't spoken to him in a while. He probably won't be able to afford it when the soldiers come again next month."

"We mustn't lose hope," Master Ferribolt replied as they both migrated to the armchairs. "The Dragon always provides to those who ask."

Jason said nothing. He slipped off his sword as he sat down, and his eyes gravitated to the bear rug between him and the Chief Patriarch. Master Ferribolt's eyes locked onto him through his spectacles, as if probing his feelings and thoughts.

"Why didn't you visit me earlier?" he said. "The Harvest was almost a week ago, and you should have visited me the next day."

Jason propped his sword on the side of the chair and laced his fingers together. He leaned forward and looked at the ground as he spoke.

"I've been doing a lot of thinking…"

Master Ferribolt stayed silent, expectant for an answer. Jason's hands shook.

"...I think I'm done. I'm going to tell King Barnabas that I can't take it anymore. I'm just one person—a Lower City boy. I can't... I just—can't."

The quiet was palpable—not even the fire crackled. Master Ferribolt didn't blink and Jason refused to match gaze with him. It continued for what felt like hours.

"So you're giving up...?" Master Ferribolt breathed.

Jason stared at his boots, his hands still laced together. He nodded.

The hush perpetuated. Master Ferribolt leaned forward and rubbed his hands together. After a deep breath, he asked slowly, "Is it because you feel it's the right thing to do? Or something else?"

It happened in an instant. Jason's teeth grinded together, he leapt from his chair, shoved his sword onto the floor, and thrust his hands above his head.

"*I don't know!*" he cried. "There is so much I *don't know!* For half a year I've had to go on not knowing! And look at what's happened! What's next? How is the King going to destroy my life even more? Other people's lives? Who else is going to suffer because of me? It's not fair! And it's *all my fault!*"

Jason kicked a chair over with his last exclamation, then after a moment, dropped to his knees. Master Ferribolt kept his mouth closed and watched. Silence fell on them once again. Jason's body stayed turned to the Chief Patriarch.

Master Ferribolt wordlessly pushed himself from his chair and strode over to Jason. He eased himself into a cross-legged position facing Jason's distressed countenance. His eyes were swollen and red and he wiped his nose with his gloved hand. Neither of them spoke a word.

After a sniffle, Jason finally asked, "Was it this hard for you?"

Master Ferribolt shook his head. "No. King Thomas wasn't bent on keeping me from being a Patriarch when my time came."

Another sniffle. Master Ferribolt's face became hard.

"This is a very sudden decision, Jason," he said. "What brought this about? You were making such great progress."

Jason proceeded to describe King Barnabas' unexpected visit on the day of the Harvest. As soon as the King was mentioned, Master Ferribolt's brows stiffened and his jaw tightened. Jason's shuddering and sniffing died down. He tried to repeat everything that King Barnabas had said to the best of his memory.

"...and now he said the kingdom is going to suffer like never before," Jason finished. "Master, this year has already been so hard. If he's going to make things even worse, maybe I need to denounce my Foreordination... for the best of everyone."

"Do you honestly believe in your heart that is the best for everyone?" Master Ferribolt asked.

Jason didn't know what to say. It seemed like he didn't have much of a choice. What more was the King capable of? What more could possibly happen? Would the kingdom be prepared for it?

"With every challenge comes a choice, Jason," Master Ferribolt said. "You remember that."

"I thought just deciding to go through with the Year of Decision was my big challenge," Jason replied. "But this goes so much farther beyond that. I didn't know so many people would suffer because of me."

"You're not the one instigating the suffering," Master Ferribolt said sharply. "King Barnabas is. Don't give into the lies that the forces of Darkness are whispering to you. This is not your fault in the slightest." A pause. Then Master Ferribolt continued, "Months ago, did you believe you would make it this far?"

"No," Jason answered.

"I did," Master Ferribolt tried to match Jason's gaze. "And I know you can sit in the throne of Nezmyth, too. You're over halfway there. It would be a tragedy if you were to give up now."

"King Barnabas told me the Oracle Stone hasn't even changed, though," Jason said crestfallenly. "That's what measures my worthiness as King."

"He's never given you a reason to trust him," Master Ferribolt said flatly.

Once again, Jason found himself lost for words. Master Ferribolt put his hand on his shoulder.

"Jason," Master Ferribolt said. "When you finish this Year of Decision, you will be considered a legend. Heroes are forged in the fieriest of furnaces. This is your furnace. Your name will be revered for years to come. But you must *endure*."

Jason still didn't look at him. "I don't know, Master. I just don't know. It's hopeless."

Master Ferribolt deflated. His eyes sunk to the floor and his body seemed to lose its resilience, but his firm grip on Jason's shoulder didn't let up. The weakened silence lasted briefly, then something like a spark leapt across the Chief Patriarch's eyes. His gaze snapped up and astonishment splashed onto his face. Jason was too busy staring at the floor to notice it. Master Ferribolt tightened his grasp on Jason's shoulder and his tone was serious, but full of wonder.

"Jason," he said. "The Sacred Dragon has just struck me with inspiration. You need to go to the library to study Ancient Nezmythian immediately."

Jason looked up, perplexed.

"Master," he replied. "I've been going to the library frequently for almost a month. I've tried reading almost half of the books in their collection."

Master Ferribolt's eyes could have burned a hole in Jason's head. "Jason, go now. You may find an answer tonight to one of the questions of your soul. Do not postpone this."

Questions of my soul? Jason thought. Master Ferribolt pushed himself to his feet and lifted Jason up by the armpits. Jason wiped his eyes another time while Master Ferribolt picked up his sword from the floor and handed it to him. As Jason slipped it on, Master Ferribolt steered him by the shoulders out of his den.

"Master, I don't understand," he protested as he scooted along.

"Usually it's not until afterward that we understand, Jason!" Master Ferribolt said almost cheerfully. "But there are very few coincidences. Everything has a purpose. And if the Dragon wants you to go to the library *right now* to study Ancient Nezmythian, there must be a purpose!"

Jerem eyed the two curiously as they hastened to the door, and Master Ferribolt nearly shoved Jason outside when he had the chance. Jason staggered onto the porch and Master Ferribolt threw his jacket onto his head.

"Come by tomorrow and tell me the outcome of this!" he said jovially. "Don't lose faith, Jason!"

With that, the door slammed shut. Jason stood gawking at it for several seconds. As he slipped off his sword to put on his jacket, he pondered on how peculiar that short chain of events was.

Snow trickled from pale clouds that coagulated across the skyline. A carriage trotted by, heading down to the Northern Market Street. It wasn't even afternoon, and there weren't many orders to fill at the shop, so Jason wasn't all too concerned about being late. His trust of Master Ferribolt was almost as strong as his fear for the King, so there was only one thing to do.

I guess I'm going to the library, he thought. The trip took nearly an hour—descending down the Upper City street, across the Northern Market Street then down into Center Court.

The giant, triangular court had Nezmythians bustling in every which way with carriages, carts, and bags of goods from the numberless shops and stands that made up its edges. It had to be the only area where Lower City and Upper City folk could be found in the same place, although the Lower City folk usually came as beggars.

Thousands of red bricks engraved with the names of past Kings were completely masked by a packed layer of snow, while several statues of some of the greats stood intermittently throughout the Court. Several pairs of Nezmythian soldiers staked this as their territory and eyed everyone suspiciously as they marched.

In the very center of the court, the statue of the Holy Dragon had been removed decades ago. Instead, a giant marble representation of King Barnabas was erected. Stubborn pigeons that refused to fly south gathered on his shoulders. Jason watched one land atop his head and defecate its runny, white waste upon his scalp. He sneered and thought to himself, *I'm certain we all feel that way.*

The library was on the eastern side of Center Court—an incredibly large stone building with massive pillars guarding the entrance. Jason weaved his way through oncoming townspeople as his feet crunched across the plaza.

"The usual spot?" The librarian asked, not taking her face out of her book.

"Yes ma'am," Jason replied.

The librarian blindly reached into a drawer, pulled out the rusty old key and handed it to Jason. Jason took it graciously, and within a couple of minutes, he was in the small, dusty Ancient Nezmythian section.

He pulled out his chair and mulled over the rows upon rows of books, some with titles he couldn't easily decipher. Frustration gathered in thin layers within him. *What am I possibly supposed to find here? I came to the library so I could increase my vocabulary… how am I going to find an answer to a 'question of my soul?'*

One by one, he began pulling books off of shelves and skimming through them. The first book was something about plants. It had to have been a scientific manuscript from hundreds of years ago, and most of the writings in it were too complex for Jason. He put it back on the shelf quickly. The second book was a history of battles, a book he had picked up on a previous occasion. He didn't find anything new within the pages, just a vast collection of dots, squiggles and jagged lines he only partly understood.

This ensued for nearly an hour—book after book, page after page. Irritation gradually bubbled higher until Jason was slamming books shut and thrusting them back into their spots on the shelves. He thought of the time he could be spending doing other useful things, but instead, the Chief Patriarch sent him on a wild goose chase through the pages of the Ancient Text.

He was about to leap up from his chair and storm out the gate, but something inside coerced him to open just one more book. He sighed thickly to through his teeth and snatched a title that he didn't understand, dropping it on the table and sifting through the pages.

More of the same… page after page… some words he could pick out here and there, but nothing stuck out—until he reached a scratchy illustration that made his eyes pop and his blood run cold.

The image was that of a sickly individual, lying on a table with decaying, splotched skin. An eccentrically-dressed man stood over him with his mouth wide open, as if singing a hymn or song, with his arms stretched to the heavens. The eeriest part of the picture was the black murk that seemed to evaporate from the victim's mouth, like something dark inside him was being sucked out.

Jason's jaw dangled as his face drew closer to the image. On the opposite page, the title read *Reeshmah Edomah*.

"*Bane of Darkness*," Jason translated out loud.

Quickly, his eyes darted down the description. There was much he didn't understand, but he felt as if he understood the gist of it. It explained how evil men in times past used *Tepnoh Edomah* to inflict illness upon those who had crossed them, sometimes resulting in a slow, painful death. The following, *Reeshmah Edomah*, was a spell concocted by

Patriarchs and magicians to extract the dark spirit that overtook the body.

Interestingly, the spell was in the form of song. At the bottom of the page, a straight line with accompanying lines and dots represented the pitches and durations of each note.

Several thoughts snapped into alignment all at once: King Barnabas, his sick mother, the Year of Decision, *Tepnoh Edomah*. Jason's heart jumped into his throat and his body shook. He frantically searched for some loose parchment and a writing stick. He felt his pockets—nothing. He threw open the drawer under the desk—and found a half-torn sheet of parchment and a stub of a writing stick. His heart thumped madly as he copied the music onto the parchment with shaking hands and wild eyes.

When he had finished his hasty print, he threw the writing stick down and bolted out the gate, sprinted down the stairs and toward the exit, passing a very annoyed librarian.

The scrap parchment snapped in the breeze as he pelted through Center Court, garnering the curious gaze of several townspeople. Several soldiers watched him oddly, but decided not to pursue him. Down a street he went, and emerged onto the Southern Market Street, where fewer people gathered to buy and sell.

Jason's heart pulsed like a war drum inside him. It had been three months since Kara had first contracted *Ipoklime*... but was it really *Ipoklime*? Or was it something that simply appeared similar in order to fool Jason into buying a Mulak flower? No wonder Lartok's solution confirmed it wasn't *Ipoklime*... After surviving the Dreamslayer spell, Jason knew that King Barnabas was dabbling in the dark arts of *Tephnoh Edomah*. The book at the library described her condition perfectly. Everything made sense. And the solution was literally in his hand.

Sweat dripped from Jason's hair—he hadn't stopped running since the library. Breaths came in bursts and his lungs were on fire. At length, he finally found himself at the door of his old Lower City home, with a small plume of smoke billowing up from the chimney.

Jason threw open the door to find the usual scene. Kara lay in the same bed she had for the past three months, with Tomm sitting next to her, cradling her splotched hand. His eyes darted to Jason at his hasty entrance. As he latched the door behind him, his heart started to settle bit by bit.

Tomm's face became hard and he stood up and stormed over to Jason. He didn't stop until he was nearly nose-to-nose with him. His eyes were fierce through his dusty glasses.

"I looked all over for you!" he hissed. "You weren't at your flat, or the shop, or even Tarren's. Lartok just left a few hours ago. He said that she only has a few days left."

The last statement was hollow and shaky, and Tomm's eyes started to mist. Jason met him with a shake of his head.

"No, father," he said. "I found a cure."

Tomm's misty eyes sharpened. "Jason, tell me you did *not* get a Mulak flower… with you being who you are—."

"No," Jason said, his heart still thumping. "I didn't. Just watch."

Wasting no time, Jason hustled to Kara's bedside and dropped to his knees. He smoothed out the hastily-written sheet music on the bed and extracted his flyra from his pocket. He put it to his lips, but before he played, he took one final look at his sickly mother.

She looked as awful as ever. Her optimistic resilience seemed to have abandoned her, and her eyes were closed as if her illness had doomed her to eternal sleep. Her chest rose and fell under the cover very slowly. She shivered.

Jason's eyes locked onto the *Reeshmah Edomah*, and he played.

The melody was haunting. Although it came from the bright whistling of a flyra, it swayed and bent in such mysterious ways that stirred the inner mechanisms of the soul in a dark way. Inside Jason, something swirled peacefully, but firmly.

Kara's body shuddered. Jason's heart lurched, but he forced himself to play on. Kara shuddered again. Tomm stepped forward, who had been watching from a few steps back, his eyes full of fear.

"Stop," he pleaded.

Jason ignored him. The haunting, hypnotizing melody filled the chilly cottage. Suddenly, a sickly gasp fled out of Kara's lips, and her mouth opened to the sky.

"Jason, stop!" Tomm said more forcefully.

Jason didn't hear him. He could *feel* the *Reeshmah Edomah* working inside him... he could *feel* the dark spirit being uprooted from his mother's body... Tomm couldn't feel it because it wasn't the sickly one, or the one playing the song. He had to go on.

Gradually, a thin, hazy smoke started billowing out of Kara's mouth. It curled and coagulated into a dark, sinister smog and hovered for several seconds, churning, lusting after the body it had inhabited for three months. *Reeshmah Edomah* forbade it from entering back in. Jason's eyes bore into it as he played. The flyra was his sword, and the *Tepnoh Edomah* was the enemy.

Finally, as the song reached its final note, the black smoke let out a silent cry of rage and darted through the nearest wall, disappearing for good.

An eerie hush fell upon the cottage. Tomm and Jason's eyes locked upon Kara. They didn't breath. They just watched. The seconds felt like hours. At length, Kara coughed and sputtered before her eyes flittered open. Incredibly, she sat up, and Jason noticed that the normal color was already beginning to return to her arms and face.

She looked around and said dreamily, "What *was* that?"

Tomm's eyes couldn't have gotten wider. He flew past Jason and fell to his wife's bedside, holding her tightly and uttering words of disbelief. Jason folded the sheet music back up and inserted it in his pocket, along with his flyra. He looked on in bewilderment, as if the eerie happenings that had just taken place had been a dream.

He watched his father cradle his mother in his arms. This part of the nightmare was over. She was sitting up in bed, speaking normally, the splotches on her skin disappearing. She was well again.

Master Ferribolt was right, Jason thought. *Sometimes we just don't understand the reason until afterward. If I would have ignored his advice...*he didn't allow himself to finish the thought.

At length, Tomm turned and stared at Jason, his face riddled with wonder. His lips pulled apart several times as if he were about to speak, but his words got caught each time. Finally, he forced himself to ask:

"How? How did you...?"

Jason half-smiled, recalling all of his visits with the Chief Patriarch, his Ancient Nezmythian training, and his visits to the library. All he said was, "It's complicated."

Tomm's eyes darted about, from Jason, to Kara, to the wall where the *Tepnoh Edomah* entity had dissipated through. His wonder turned hard, and his eyebrows creased.

"Jason, what's going on?" he said. "We've noticed you've been different lately, but this is incredibly strange. What have you been doing?"

Jason breathed deep, and his eyes darted out the window. He didn't care if soldiers were a mile away—it wasn't worth the risk of confessing everything he had done in the past four months. Too much is at stake.

"I wish I could tell you," Jason said. "But I can't."

"Why?"

"I just can't. Please don't ask me more. I would tell you if I could."

Tomm's eyes locked on him skeptically and Jason held his breath. The gears were turning in his mind—he knew what his son had been Foreordained to become, but he knew nothing of the Year of Decision or the trials that came with it. But something in Jason's tone and demeanor let him know that there was something in play much bigger than either of them. At length, Tomm's eyes fell to the ground, and he gave a gentle nod. Jason felt comfortable breathing again.

He still couldn't get his mind off of King Barnabas, however. *Things are going to get worse…* But then he looked upon his parents lovingly holding each other and thought to himself, *…but I just need to keep going. Maybe it's not time to give up just yet.*

19 THE MYTH

A small breeze carved its way through the writhing, dead branches of the tree. The small creatures that inhabited the wasteland were sound asleep in their underground holes. A dreary moon cast dim light over the landscape. Nothing stirred except the vulture, the eagle, and the sighing wind. The vulture's feathered breasts rose and fell heavily.

Some miles away, a tree that had once been a sapling had grown rapidly over a short period of time. Its trunk was thick and strong, and leaves had started to bud long ago, permeating the branches with green.

The black eagle that rested on a nearby branch exhaled softly. It shot a sideways glance at the vulture, which promptly ignored it as it usually did. Silence continued, but only for a while.

"How does it make you feel?" The eagle inquired.

The vulture said nothing.

"It's only a matter of time," the eagle continued as if it had heard nothing. "Look at its branches, its trunk… its leaves look greener every day. It is surely no longer a sapling."

The vulture's eyes narrowed, but it remained silent.

The eagle sighed. It listened carefully to the soft wind, as if it were whispering something, then said, "What will you do now that all of your methods have failed?"

The vulture didn't move, but said, "They haven't."

The eagle shook its head, "Don't you fear what fate will bring upon you for these abominable deeds?"

The vulture replied coolly, "There are few things I believe in this world, and fate is not one of them."

"Do you believe in justice?"

The vulture glared at the dark eagle with venom and scoffed bitterly, "Justice is simply the angelic disguise of vengeance."

"There must be some corner of your heart that isn't covered in black," the eagle said.

The vulture frowned hotly, "Leave me."

The eagle looked oddly at the vulture. Its eyes were marred with the scars of struggles past. It doesn't matter. Apparently, demons have no remorse—just plans. The eagle stretched out its wings leapt off the branch. It flapped its wings, pushing the air under it and soaring through the starry black night. The bird continued to soar, ever gaining speed, until it slowed down and perched itself on the ground, a watchful distance from the steadily growing tree.

The vulture growled disgustedly. It blinked several times as it gazed at the eagle a mile away. Surely, it was a safe distance. The vulture hopped off the highest branch on the tree and flapped its wings carefully, easing itself lower and lower until its powerful talons rested on the cold soil by the root of the tree. The wind nipped at its beak harshly. The vulture turned around and faced the trunk of the cold, lifeless tree, speaking lowly.

"It is gone," the vulture said.

Out of a nearly unnoticeable knot, a fox's head popped out, followed by a pair of paws, torso, legs, and finally a tail. Its bright yellow eyes shimmered in the pale moonlight as it silently slunk its way across the ground and stood face-to-face with the vulture.

"I am at your service, master," the fox said.

"It is time for you to act," the vulture said coldly. "Kill it, and make it look like an accident. The eagle must not know about this."

"I will succeed, my lord," the fox replied.

"Good," the vulture said. "Because if you do not, the eagle will know, and I will have to cover up this mess, presumably with your blood. A fox does not have much use once it has lost its head."

The fox's eyes grew then shrunk again, "Understood."

"You have two weeks," the vulture said. "If the tree is dead, you keep your head, otherwise... you die. Go."

* * * * *

Knock knock knock

Jason rubbed his hands together after he had rapped his knuckles on the door of The Cranny three times. Snow trickled down into the alleyway, which was thicker than on the Southern Market Street because there wasn't a steady stream of boots to pound it down. He shuffled his feet anxiously. He felt like he stood there for much longer than he really did. Next to the door, a small wooden sign with a black dot was nailed to the wall.

Finally, he heard footsteps on the other side—thick, slow footsteps. It wasn't long before Tarren opened the door in his usual greasy apron. His hair hid his eyes which were swollen and tired. Dark circles clung under them, and his shoulders sagged in a way that he had never seen before. Jason's lip curled uncomfortably at the sight.

"Hello, Tarren," he said sheepishly.

"Hello, Jason," Tarren returned airily. He jerked his head. "Come in."

It wasn't much warmer inside The Cranny than it was outside. The only difference was the bitter breeze that was kept out once Tarren had latched the door shut. Fewer instruments hung from the walls than Jason was accustomed to seeing. The smell of resin and grease wasn't as thick. Overall, the room seemed a lot emptier than usual.

"What do you need?" Tarren asked flatly as he landed in his usual chair.

"I need to apologize," Jason replied after he sat in his stool by the door. "I'm sorry I haven't spoken to you in so long. I've just had a lot on my mind lately and after our last sparring practice… it was all just too much. I wanted to check up on you and see how you were doing."

Tarren rubbed his face in his hands. "Jason, you know I didn't mean what I said. I didn't know it would make you as upset as it did. Are we okay now?"

Jason nodded, "We are."

Tarren rubbed his face some more, let out a sigh, then said, "Did you like my new addition outside? Didn't cost me a Shard."

Jason frowned. He figured now was definitely not the time to make a Blacknote joke. "No. I don't like it at all. Do you think you'll be able to pay in the next three weeks?"

Tarren shook his head.

A pause ensued, but only a short one. Jason got up from his stool and said, "Come. Apologizing isn't the only reason why I came over today. I want to show you something, and I think it could help."

Tarren pulled himself out of his chair and Jason unlatched the door. They both stepped out into the cold, and Tarren made sure he locked the door before they started down the alleyway.

"Mother is healed," Jason said as they walked.

Tarren's reddened eyes popped and he threw a look at Jason. "How? That's incredible!"

"It would take too long to explain," Jason said. "But I figured it would be a little bit of good news for you. Look."

They had reached the mouth of the alleyway, and they made an abrupt stop just before they appeared onto the Southern Market Street. Jason gestured to something that only rose to about his chest and was as wide as his arm. It was a sign. Propped up on the side of the street, it was emblazoned with eye-catching yellow letters and a big red arrow pointing into the alleyway.

THE CRANNY
MUSICAL INSTRUMENT
REPAIR AND SHOP
FINEST QUALITY AND SERVICE
IN NEZMYTH CITY

"I know it's not much," Jason said defensively. "I threw it together using some scraps. But I've had Saryan tell all of her Upper City friends about your shop, so now they'll know where to find it. You never know. I'm sorry. I should have done this a long time ago."

Tarren's jaw dangled. His eyes sped down the sign over and over again. Jason held his breath and looked expectantly for an answer. It came as a touched smile slowly spread across Tarren's pale, dry face. He didn't shed any tears, just short bursts of laughter popped from his lips. He shrugged.

"I don't know what to say," he said.

There was a pause, then Jason said:

"Can we start sparring again?"

Tarren slid Jason a raised eyebrow. "Yes. We can. Thank you, Jason. Every little bit helps."

Tarren wrapped his arm around Jason's shoulders and gave him a squeeze, a smile still stretched across his face. They set a time for their next sparring practice and said their goodbyes, and Tarren retreated back into the alleyway. Jason started up the Southern Market Street toward Center Court.

It had been just a few days since Kara had been healed. Jason had returned the following day to Master Ferribolt to report on all that had happened, just as had been instructed. The Chief Patriarch was positively giddy when Jason had explained everything.

"Does that not give you hope, Jason?" Master Ferribolt had asked with an ear-to-ear smile.

"It does," Jason replied. "But only a little. I still find it incredible that I just happened to stumble across that spell."

"You truly believe that was mere coincidence?"

Jason didn't respond right away, but when he did, the answer came more from his heart than his mouth. "No. I guess I don't."

"Do you remember the title of the book you found it in?" Master Ferribolt asked with his hands laced together.

Jason pictured in his mind the characters and sounded it out. "*Eeloh Pahlumay*. I don't know what that means."

"*The Sacred Arts*," Master Ferribolt translated. "You have stumbled upon a gem, my young friend! That book is an extremely valuable vein of knowledge. Full of legends... wisdom... you would do well to study more from its pages. I believe you would find it extremely useful."

"Is there more Ancient magic in it?" Jason asked.

"Certainly!" Master Ferribolt replied with a sparkle in his eye. "But it would be more valuable for you to discover it on your own, so I will leave you to that. What I will tell you, however, is that your capacity to perform those spells depends upon the strength of your spirit. After all, it is *The Sacred Arts*. Keep that in mind."

The library was a welcome shelter from the winter cold. After the librarian gave him the key, Jason made his familiar journey across the library floor, up the stairs, across the one side of the winding balcony and into the dusty old Ancient Nezmythian section. The chair he inhabited was becoming less and less filthy with every visit. The lantern cast a dim, flickering glow on the bookshelf as it hovered over, and it didn't take Jason long to find *Eeloh Pahlumay—The Sacred Arts*.

He extracted it from the shelf and carefully placed it on the table, then pulled the lantern as close as he dared without endangering the pages. Opening to a random page, his eyes hovered up and down the characters, catching a few words phrases and terms, but nothing too astounding. He thumbed through the pages, stopping whenever he found something that looked like a spell, and recorded them on some parchment he kept in his pocket. A couple he found particularly interesting was a form of meditation that hastened physical healing, and a phrase that made the blade of a sword burst into flame.

Of course only the rich can afford instructors that know advanced magic, Jason thought. *Advanced magic is directly related to Ancient Nezmythian.*

This continued for hours. As he continued to scan the pages, he fell upon an intricate sketch of a sword. Its double-edged blade was wide, with what looked to be tinted blade... not a standard steel-like material. Its hilt was completely encrusted with rubies, and on the cross guard a winding dragon slunk its way around the metal with its lips in a snarling roar.

His face moved in closer as he analyzed the legendary sword in its magnificence. He stroked his chin.

Incredible... Jason thought it awe. *Who could forge something like that?*

Jason quickly skimmed the squiggles and jagged lines on the adjacent page, looking for words he recognized. Surprisingly, the title, printed in large, bold letters at the top of the page, was easily understandable.

"Blade of Nezmyth."

Jason sounded out the words and hummed to himself. In the description below, he caught words like "sword," "Dragon," and "legendary," but not much else. He sighed.

This would be a much better story if I actually understood more Ancient Nezmythian... he thought to himself with a half frown. He was just about to turn the page when he saw something that made his blood turn to ice.

A gasp leapt from his lips and his hand slammed onto the page. His eyes darted out the window, then through the gated door. He glared at the book with incredulity, silently asking himself if he actually saw what he thought he saw. Slowly, he forced his hand off the page. At the bottom of the page, a familiar symbol was crudely jotted in the corner the page with an old quill and ink, separated from the much larger illustration of the Blade of Nezmyth.

It was a triangle with one side longer than the other and crudely filled with ink. Jason's eyes locked on it. He knew where he had seen that symbol before. His eyes again darted to the iron bar door, and when he saw no one present... he shakily reached under the desk and began to take the glove off his hand.

As the glove slid off his fingertips, the orange, triangular birthmark revealed itself in the quiet, dark room in the corner of the Nezmyth City library. Jason's eyes fixed on his bizarrely carved hand, nearly sending a shiver through his body. His eyes darted to the door again. No one was there.

Without breathing, he pushed his hand over the desk and set it on top of the page. The oil lamp flickered as his eyes darted from his hand, to the page, to his hand again. His heart thumped rapidly in his chest.

They nearly matched up exactly.

"Excuse me."

Jason nearly leapt of out his skin. His carved hand slammed into the table as it shot out of view, and his eyes darted to the left. The librarian was standing behind the door, bearing a tired and irritated frown.

"The library is closing," she said. "It is time to go home, Jason."

Jason gulped, quivering, as he quickly shoved the glove back on his hand out of view. "Right. Sorry."

The librarian spun on her heels and briskly walked out of view, leaving Jason alone in the room once again. Jason quickly shoved the glove back onto his hand and slammed *Eeloh Pahlumay* shut.

20 THE ASHES

Jason's most recent sparring practice with Tarren went reasonably well. They had both maintained their prowess over the month that they hadn't met on the sparring mat, and when they came together to practice it was as if nothing had ever changed. Tarren, of course, beat Jason time and time again, but Jason found himself growing stronger, more agile, thinking quicker on his feet. He just prayed that his sharper skills would never really need to be used...

It was just one week from the Blacknote deadline and Tarren reported on having a noticeably steadier stream of newcomers in The Cranny. Even Saryan pitched in by purchasing a couple of lavish flutes ("I've always wanted to learn," she had said). He was, of course, still unsure that he would meet the deadline, and if he did it would be by the skin of his teeth. It was too tough to call.

Jason took comfort in the fact that if he actually *did* acquire the Throne in three months' time, the Blacknote would be done away with. The slaves of the eastern mountains would be freed, and the heavy tax would be obliterated. But the words of King Barnabas from his unwanted visit three weeks prior remained stamped onto his mind. "*...you and the kingdom will suffer like never before.*" Would he even survive these next three months?

Tonight he would try to forget that, though. The sun was setting and cast a shadow over the red line at Kristof's Weapons and Crafts. All four of the craftsmen noticed it and began shutting down machines for the day. The hissing of steam deflated to silence and churning trickled down to oblivion.

"Has your sparring with Tarren helped?" Jaboc asked Jason as they retrieved their coats from the rack.

"Very much, yes," Jason replied coolly as he slipped on his sword.

"Good," Jaboc said. "Maybe in ten years you'll be ready to come back to The Crossing Blades!"

Jason squinted and punched him in the chest. Jaboc chuckled, but once Jason had turned his back to him, his face twisted and he rubbed his sternum. Bertus and Golan smirked.

"I'm going with Saryan to the theatre tonight," Jason said as he straightened his jacket. "I'd rather attend a boring performance with a beautiful girl than grapple with sweaty men for an evening. I hope you enjoy yourself."

"You and your rich woman," Bertus said. "How did you meet her again?"

"Destiny!" Jaboc fluttered his eyelashes and put his head on Jason's shoulder.

Jason pushed him off. "Something like that. But I need to go." He thrust the key into Golan's hand. "I need to meet her in Center Court before dark and I still need to change into my formals. You can give me back the key tomorrow morning."

"Always in a hurry!" Bertus said.

"Have a good time," Golan said genuinely.

With that, Jason shot out the door and hurried down the street, heading for his flat. He changed into his formals and bolted out of his room as quickly as he had left the shop, while making sure that he had locked the door behind him. He sailed down the ladders, and snow crunched under his worn boots as his feet flew toward Center Court.

The sun had finally set over the horizon as he found himself in the center of Nezmyth City. A lot of the shops and restaurants were beginning to close, but one enormous stone building with pillars and banners seemed to draw wealthy people inside like bees to a hive. Jason jogged to it. Horse drawn carriages dropped off well-dressed couples as they trotted by. Jason scanned the shuffling crowd for Saryan…

Finally, he spotted her, standing alone with her arms folded, looking about—looking for him.

A smile slid across his cheeks. He made a loop and snuck around one side of her. His greeting was wrapping his arms around her and whispering in her ear: "You're easy to spot in a crowd."

"Pardon?" the woman's voice wasn't familiar to him.

Jason jumped back and the woman turned about slowly, glaring at him oddly. Her hair was long and golden like Saryan's, but she had to be at least ten years older. Jason felt himself flush bright red.

"I'm sorry—I thought—I'm looking for—."

"Have anything you want to confess?" the singsong voice came from behind.

Jason turned to see Saryan with her arms folded, a smirk stretching to one of her dimples and an eyebrow cocked upward. He laughed, then turned to the lady and once again apologized for the mix up. She simply shook her head and walked away. Saryan laughed heartily as she came up and took Jason's arm.

"Looks like you blew it," she said. "She owns a restaurant here on Center Court. She's wealthy. And single."

"That was embarrassing…" Jason shook his head.

"Could've been worse," Saryan said as they joined the crowd heading inside the theatre. "You could have kissed her neck."

Jason's eyes squinted. "*We* don't even do that!"

Saryan laughed. Jason's eyes glossed over as he looked at her. She was bundled up in several layers of clothing, mostly fur, so her shapely figure couldn't distract from her radiant face. Her eyes positively sparkled in the dawning moonlight and her smoky breath softened her face in an intoxicating haze. Even though the cold nipped at his whole body, Jason's heart melted.

"You look beautiful tonight," he said.

Her lips pursed into a grin. "Thank you. You clean up pretty well, too."

At length, they reached the door and were met by a positively massive man—he had to be three times the size of Jason—with a stony face and hands as wide as Jason's chest. He was dressed crisply, almost identical to Master Ferribolt's servants, Gaston and Jerem. Jason felt himself recoil slightly at the sight of him. His voice was as deep as he was thick.

"How many?"

"Two, please," Saryan replied.

"Three Blocks."

Saryan extracted the money from a pocket in her fur coat and handed them to the behemoth. He slipped the Blocks into a deep pocket in his pants, which Jason was sure was filled with hundreds more. When he did, Saryan lifted her arm horizontally, her palm down. Jason followed suit, looking on curiously. The giant put a finger on the back of each of their hands. Jason felt a strange sensation for a brief moment... then it was gone. When the giant took his hand away, Jason realized that the man had magically stamped their hands with blue dot. His eyes locked on it incredulously.

"It won't disappear for a few hours," Saryan explained.

"You can't take that in with you," the giant motioned to the sword on Jason's back. "There's a man at a booth to your right who will keep that during the performance. You can retrieve it afterward."

Jason's heart shriveled just a little as he heard that. The last time he was asked to remove his weapon was the evening Bobby the Brute left him a broken mess on a combat floor. Saryan squeezed his arm reassuringly, then they were ushered into the main lobby.

The building was the most elaborately ornate display Jason had ever seen, even more so than the castle. Red carpet coated the entire floor and snaked up two ascending staircases to a balcony level. Crystal chandeliers sparkled and dangled from the ceiling and posters of current performances were encased in elegant frames hung throughout the lobby. And Upper City folk scooted along to the doors leading to the auditorium, eager to find their seats before the performance.

To the right, they spotted the booth. A toned, burly man dressed just as sharply as the doorman stood behind the counter and beckoned Jason over. Jason slipped off his sword and they scurried over. As they reached the desk, he reluctantly held out the sword, sheath and all, and the man expressed his thanks as took it gingerly. He slipped the blade partly out of its sheath so he could observe the make.

"A finely-crafted blade, sir," he remarked as his eyes glided over it. "I will keep it safely here during the performance."

Jason nodded sheepishly, then Saryan gleefully tugged him toward the large doors opening up to the auditorium. It was exceptionally large, with dozens of rows of plush chairs facing a stage ornamented with swirling, glossy woodwork around the edges. Upper City people buzzed with chatter and swarmed as closely to the front as they could. It looked to be first come, first serve. A thick, red curtain was drawn over the stage, which was illuminated by a row of flickering lanterns.

Saryan drew Jason as close as she could to the stage, and they shimmied into a pair of available seats. The room wasn't chilly with the legions of people, so Saryan slipped off all of her winter wear to reveal a silky red dress that spilled from her shoulders to her knees. Jason's heart swelled and his face burned for a second.

Jason wasn't quite sure what to make of the performance. It didn't start until the theatre was completely packed, which took quite a while. When the curtains withdrew, the stage was populated with a battalion of actors that all dressed in tights and frills that would surely get them laughed at if they were to wear in public. On top of that, their mannerisms and expression seemed so exaggerated that it was almost comical.

The plot was also very complex… Jason was sure there was a tale of murder and infidelity to be found somewhere, but the costumes and acting were so distracting that it got lost in the mix. Saryan had to nudge his leg several times to keep him from dozing off.

The final time Saryan nudged Jason, he lifted his head to find that the curtain was closed and the legions of Upper City residents had stood from their seats and were slowly exiting the auditorium. After he rubbed his face and stretched his arms, he turned to see Saryan's eyes bearing into him, with her usual eyebrow cocked.

"You think I paid a Block and five Bars for you to take a nap?" she said.

Jason shrunk in his seat. "Sorry…"

"Well, you missed out," she sighed. "It turned out that the wife was the killer, was trying to win her husband's fortune, and wanted to run off with the butler. I'm surprised you didn't wake up. Everyone in the theatre gasped."

Jason stretched again and stated absentmindedly, "I haven't been getting a lot of sleep lately. Besides, it was hard to take anyone seriously with the outfits they were wearing. And the way they talked was so strange… I just dozed off."

"They're *actors*, Jason," Saryan's eyes narrowed. "They have to speak loudly so everyone in the theatre can hear them. Unless you know some magic way to make them louder?"

I'm sure I could find out, Jason thought. "I'm sorry I fell asleep. Really."

Saryan closed her eyes and exhaled, as if it helped her deflate just a little. Then she said, "I'm just disappointed that you missed out on such a good story."

"How can I make it up to you?" Jason replied as he put his hand on her knee.

She looked at her hand and teased a smirk. "You can walk me home."

Jason got his sword back, just as promised, and it wasn't long before they were both trudging through the snow, heading toward the Northern Market Street and Upper City. Snow started trickling from the blackened sky just as they walked passed a dozen shops and turned onto an ascending Upper City street. The minutes seemed to fly by as they talked, and it didn't feel like long at all before they were on Saryan's doorstep.

"I'm sorry I wasn't better company this evening," Jason said as they stood outside the door.

Saryan chuckled and echoed, "Better company..."

"What?" Jason said, his eyes stiffening.

A sweet smile graced Saryan's cheeks as she explained, "Jason, there's something different about you. What is it?"

"What do you mean?" he replied.

"You're always trying so hard to serve me and make me happy and make me feel better when I'm sad. No one has ever tried so hard as you. Why?"

Jason hesitated before he answered. Because she already spends so much money on him? No, that's not the reason. If she were as poor as he was he's sure that wouldn't change anything. Her eyes would sparkle just as bright. Her laugh would be just as sweet. Her company would be just as warm. She would make him want to be better just as much. Finally, he whispered, "I suppose that's what people do when they love someone."

Saryan's face softened like her insides had completely melted. "I was hoping you'd say something like that."

She didn't hesitate. She threw her arms around his neck, pulled him down and pressed her lips on his. Jason's eyes shot open and his heart erupted—whether it was beating faster or slower, he couldn't tell. He was floating. It had to have only been a second, but all perception of time had evaded him.

When she pulled her face back, her hands found his, and she whispered, "I hope I never let you let you down."

Jason felt dizzy, but as he looked beyond her flawless, glowing face, he noticed something in the distance—a red, flickering entity. A murky pillar of grey rose from it, and it seemed to be coming from the upper rim of Lower City. His eyes squinted. As he mentally calculated the more specific location of the smoke, his heart sank lower and lower.

"Saryan," he said firmly. "I have to go."

"What's wrong?" she replied.

"Nothing, I hope," he said. "But I can't be sure. I'll let you know as soon as I can."

He took a step, one hand still in hers. As he did, it felt wrong to abruptly leave after such a magical moment. Their eyes met—her silver orbs were so full of worry. He stepped toward her and put his heart into one more kiss, again tasting her frozen lips, letting the moment hang. Then finally, he squeezed her hand one last time before he leapt down the porch.

His eyes repeatedly darted to the distance where he saw the fire as his feet shot down the descending street. Snow continued to fall, making the way slick and treacherous. Several times he nearly fell onto the cobblestone, but managed to catch himself before he toppled over.

Silently, he thanked his sparring with Tarren for increasing his endurance. The run from Upper City took a long while, passing down the Northern and turning onto the Southern Market Street. The plume as smoke became larger and more visible, and the fire grew in turn.

He knew where it was coming from—he knew from the time he saw it over Saryan's shoulder. It was a building on the corner of the Southern Market Street and a street branching into Lower City. His building.

Breaths came in bursts as he slowed down, joining a crowd who had gathered outside to watch the old brick building smolder. He recognized most of them as fellow tenants, looking on in despair and uncertainty. Devilish red flames completely engulfed the building, casting hazy black smoke into the starless sky and throwing cruel heat onto the onlookers, indifferent to their homelessness.

Jason glared. He caught some chitchat from a tenant a few feet away who lived on his floor:

"...happened less than an hour ago. Everybody got out, but everything we have is gone! I only had time to get my money to pay off the Blacknote..."

"Jason!" a familiar voice called from his right.

It was Tomm and Kara. They were dressed in their night clothes and heavy coats. Jason sighed and held his arms open as they ran up. Kara embraced him tightly. Tomm hung back a little, his face somber and seemingly older.

"I can't believe this happened to you too!" Kara said as she continued to squeeze her son.

Jason's heart sank lower. "What do you mean 'me too?'"

"Our house is gone too, Jason," Tomm said. "Everything. I don't know how the fire started, but it must have been from outside. We hardly had time to grab our coats and our Blacknote money and get out. We saw the smoke from down the way and wanted to check on you, too."

Jason didn't speak. He simply looked on to where he used to live, along with dozens of other Lower City folk. Anger bubbled inside him. The question of whether this was coincidence seemed irrelevant. It wasn't. This is exactly something King Barnabas would do. And for his sake, more people were now without a home. He breathed a deep, shaky breath.

"Is this where you live...?" a lovely voice came.

He hadn't even noticed Saryan come up on other side of him. Now she was in pants, boots and a lighter coat. The fire cast an eerie reflection off her silver eyes.

She must have seen the fire too and ran after me to see if everything was alright... Jason thought as he looked upon her and said, "It *used* to be."

"This is terrible," she said in a hushed tone.

Kara nudged Jason, retrieving his attention. She said, "Is this her?"

"Yes," Jason faltered, stepping out of the way. "Mother, father, this is Saryan, the girl I've been courting."

"Pleasure to finally meet you," Kara said half-heartedly as she reached out her hand. "I simply regret that it had to be under these circumstances."

"As do I," Saryan replied, taking her hand and shaking it. "I'm so sorry for both of your losses. Do you have a place to stay?"

The three looked on each other. Jason *could* stay with Tarren as he looked for another flat, but for all he knew, Tarren could be shipped off to the eastern mountains by the next week, and boarding with him in the back of The Cranny would be incredibly cramped.

"Gulaf's house is vacant," Tomm said. "He's been at the eastern mountains for nearly four months now."

"That's if everything inside hasn't been ransacked," Kara muttered.

"We could find an inn?" Tomm suggested again.

"You know we can't afford that," Kara countered.

"You can come stay with me for now," Saryan interjected. "All of you. There is plenty of room, and I'm sure my father wouldn't mind even if he weren't away."

The three exchanged glances. Jason was a little cautious at the offer, but Kara and Tomm were downright guarded. Skepticism was riddled across their faces. Their eyes jumped from Jason to Saryan, then to Jason again.

"Saryan," Kara said. "Would you excuse us for a moment?"

Saryan nodded, and the two motioned for Jason to come hither. They ventured off a few yards and huddled in a small circle. Kara took a deep breath and Tomm folded his arms across his chest, glancing from his wife to his son. Jason stayed silent.

"Jason…" Kara said. "Tell us more about this girl. Is she…"

The word seemed to escape her just as she was about to use it. Jason leaned forward, expectant. Finally, the word hopped off Kara's lips:

"...chaste?"

Jason would have laughed, but the seriousness of the moment restrained him. "Yes, mother, she's one of the most virtuous people I know. You know I've been going to Cathedral with her every week."

"But good people still make mistakes, Jason," Tomm said sternly. "I don't care if she's got a dozen guest rooms on the opposite side of her mansion, living in the same home with a woman you're not wed to is dangerous behavior for a *future King*." The last two words were barely a whisper.

"I agree, Jason," Kara said. "From what you've already told us, I'm sure she's a wonderful girl. But I think it's clear that your father and I are a little concerned about the situation."

"Well, we don't have much of a choice right now," Jason said. "Where else can we go? We have no other clothes or belongings except what we have on our backs. And her father is a Captain in the Nezmythian Army, so as long as we're living under her roof, we're exempt from the tax. We could use that one hundred and twenty Blocks to rebuild on where the house burned down."

Kara and Tomm exchanged anxious looks. Jason made a powerful argument... it's not that he *wanted* to live with Saryan, he agreed that good people still make mistakes, but it seemed like the best option by far. It would just mean that he would need to set stricter boundaries with her.

Finally, Kara sighed and said, "Alright. But you need to be *careful*, my son. Don't do anything that doesn't feel right."

The corner of Jason's mouth twitched into a half-grin. The brick building where he used to live started to crumble slowly, leaving a heap of ashes in its wake. From the sky, dirty snow contaminated by the smoke trickled to the ground, coating the cobblestone with grey.

21 THE INTRUDER

The notes from Jason's flyra flittered to the dark-stained boards in the ceiling. He found it hard to sleep in his guest room—everything was so clean and fashionable that he felt his mere presence was like a stain to the interior. The bed was incredibly soft and the covers were thick, which was much different than what he was used to with a scratchy wool blanket and a straw mattress. Paintings of beautiful landscapes like the northern shores of Nezmyth stared back at him from the walls. He played the flyra softly, even though he knew his parents and Saryan were on the other end of the house.

Saryan and Jason had set boundaries as long as they were living under the same roof. They were not to see each other after they both went to bed. If they were to pair off, they would go somewhere else. Kara's watchful eyes and sharp ears didn't make this difficult. It had been over a week, and neither of them had broken their rule, although Jason's heart longed to hold her by the fire and talk the night away. He was sure Saryan felt similar.

*Two and a half months left… It's so close…*he thought. *But what could happen in that time?*

His eyes darted to his right, outside the window. Judging by the position of the moon… it had to be a few hours before dawn. He exhaled.

An uncomfortable feeling ever since they had finished dinner hours earlier stuck inside him, thick and churning. It was something dark—something he couldn't put his finger on, very similar to the night King Barnabas attacked Jason with the Dreamslayer spell. Several unsuccessful hours of turning over in his mattress yielded very little rest. *What is it?*

Jason's forehead creased. He removed the flyra from his mouth and threw his legs over the side of the bed, putting his feet on the chilly floor. He set his hands on the edge of the bed and frowned deeply.

Something isn't right, he thought.

He stood up and walked to the door, grabbing his jacket and sword and pulling both on. He pushed open the door quietly and began briskly walking down the hallway, the feeling that there was something that needed to be investigated aching in his mind.

His feet were as quiet as a cat's across the floor, and as he came into the main room from the hallway, everything was silent and gray. Moonlight spilled through the massive windows, casting a pale haze on the plush chairs and couch that faced a stone fireplace by the wall. He looked around apprehensively. Everything was in its usual place—even he could see that in the dark of night.

He continued to walk through the main room and up the separate hallway that led to his parent's and Saryan's rooms. He kept perfectly quiet as he crept up, careful not to wake any of them. The door to his parent's guest room was open just a crack. He carefully reached forward and pulled it open ever so slightly.

Kara and Tomm were sound asleep under the covers, which shallowly rose and fell with every breath. Jason sighed. The door edged shut again, and he shimmied down the hall to Saryan's room. The door to her room was ajar, too.

The door squeaked quietly as he opened it enough just to poke his head in. Moonlight illuminated her sleeping face, and her hair poured across her pillows and sheets. She breathed peacefully—an angel at rest. Jason considered coming in and kissing her on the forehead, but remembered their promise and thought better of it.

Everything is fine... he thought.

Silently, he crept back across the main room on the way to his bedroom, but as he did, he stopped and stared out the window. Great snowflakes spilled from the blackened sky, coating the outer court in a liberal sheet of white. Perfectly manicured bushes and a magnificent statue centerpiece kept stoically still from the pouring powder. So serene... all that separated Jason from it was the back door.

My jacket is on, Jason thought. *It'd be a nice place to play. Hopefully, it'll help this feeling to go away.*

The door unlatched quietly and Jason was able to slip out without much of a sound. As he stepped outside, he was still under a small awning that shielded him from the snow. A wooden chair rested by the door. He grinned.

He slid into the chair and played for several minutes, his sword sheathed on his back, a little chilly, but otherwise protected from the snow. Neither Saryan nor his parents awoke. Just quietly alone in his thoughts, letting the whistling notes flitter through the snowfall...

Just then, an echoing crackle sounded through the air.

Instantly, Jason stopped playing. He listened for several seconds without so much as breathing. The crackle didn't repeat itself, but the cold that slid down his spine had nothing to do with the weather. The flyra found its way into his pocket and Jason drew the sword out of its sheath. The dark feeling in his stomach didn't let up.

He stepped barefoot into the snow and trudged his way across the courtyard, leaving thick footprints as he went. As he made his way past some bushes and the statue centerpiece, he noticed a well up against a tall stone fence which separated Saryan's property from the next. He eyed it oddly. The sound could have come from a small stone falling through its cavernous mouth… but who would have thrown it in?

The grip on his sword tightened and he edged his way toward the well. Closer and closer he crept… the snow bit at his toes, but he ignored the feeling. When he reached the mouth of the well, he peered over cautiously, expecting something to lurch out.

…Nothing. After several seconds, Jason sheathed his sword, satisfied that there was no danger.

Wham!

From behind, Jason was struck by a massive force that thrust his entire body into the well. With a yelp, he managed to put his hand out and grab onto the edge just before he was about to tumble into the abyss. His heart pounded. As he began to pull himself up, a dark figure arose and almost overshadowed him. The figure was large and incredibly strong, and seemed to be entirely covered by a long, continuous strand of black cloth. The black cloth even covered its face, but behind the cloth, Jason could feel its eyes bearing into him.

The figure clutched Jason's wrists. In one swift movement, Jason grabbed onto its wrists and planted his feet on the side of the well, refusing to be disposed of so easily. The figure grunted, and with a mighty heave, pulled Jason out of the well and launched him over its back.

Jason hit the snow with a powdery *thud* and scrambled to his feet, ripping the sword out of its sheath. The black figure stalked toward him, whipping out a pair of daggers and brandishing them as he went.

The figure threw a dagger. Jason ducked and felt it whir passed his shoulder. Reflexively, he shot a jeroki at the figure, which cut it out of the air with a single hand. The figure dashed forward, and in an instant was upon Jason. It was absolutely massive—over a foot taller than Jason and built like a warrior. It cocked a mighty fist and drove it into Jason's chest. Jason toppled backward and rolled several times, losing his precious sword in the tumble.

He again scrambled to his feet and tried shaking his head, but his vision was bleary and his balance off-kilter. He could make out colors—the green of bushes—so he darted around them, keeping his head down, hiding from the assassin.

The pops of jerokis started sounding through the air. Jason felt the heat of them fly just over his back as he snaked his way around the shrubbery. Slowly, his vision and his balance came into focus until finally, a jeroki connected with him and he again toppled through the snow.

Jason clutched the powder beneath him. *Who is this man...? He's obviously been trained...*

After a deep breath, Jason leapt up from where he lay and shot a barrage of jerokis at the intruder. The intruder's massive arms slashed and swiped viciously, cutting each one out of the air without a problem. Jason's eyes grew. It was like trying to beat down a brick wall.

The figure started at Jason, dodging around the bushes that separated them. Jason made a break for it—his objective was to find his sword. Until he found it, he was nothing but prey. As he darted through the snow, he kept his eyes peeled for a crack in the powder that resembled a sword, but the snowfall was making it difficult.

Finally, he spotted one. His heart leapt and he dove for it. When he yanked it out of the snow... he found that it was nothing but a broken branch the length of his arm.

His heart sank. When he turned his head, the attacker was upon him, and drove a kick directly into his ribs. Jason rolled over, still clutching the branch. His ribs now throbbed with pain and his eyes became misty again. Blindly, he brought the branch up to shield himself, and it was just then that the attacker came down on him with a dagger pointed in his chest.

Jason's arms quivered as he pushed upward on the branch, keeping the villain's weapon at bay, but the dagger was coming down inch by inch... Jason focused on *cayloon*, the Ancient Nezmythian word for "strength." He repeated it in his mind with all the energy of his soul, and he found it gave him power to push upward. Bit by bit he pushed, until in one miraculous thrust, he heaved the foe entirely off his body. In a split second, he shot a jeroki directly at its face, and it toppled over numbly.

It was only when Jason tried to push himself off the ground that he realized his sword was directly below him. His finger grazed something cold and metallic—he could recognize the pommel of his blade anywhere. He scooped it up.

His insides flared. The figure still lay on the ground yards away. He bore his teeth, scrambled to his feet, and shouted, "*Come on!*"

In an instant, he figure sat up and hurled the dagger at Jason. Jason's adrenaline spiked. With a swipe of the sword, he parried the dagger away, but as he deflected the blade its edge ripped through his shoulder.

A cry escaped his lips. His hand involuntarily shot for his shoulder, which was beginning to spill out blood. The figure planted its feet and leapt through the air like a panther, its massive fist prepped for impact. Without a second's hesitation, Jason released his shoulder and thrust his hand forward. A jeroki lit up and launched just as the figure was on top of it. This launched the figure backward in the same direction, kicking up a mound of snow that covered its body.

Jason ignored his bloody shoulder and hand, and a spell from *Eeloh Palumay* resurfaced in his mind. He swiped his hand across his blade, inches from the steel, and while focusing with all his might shouted, "*Mohlah Eelohda matah!*"

Instantly, the blade of his sword burst into flames, emitting a fierce orange glow. The figure forced itself onto its feet and shook its head. Jason couldn't see its eyes, but he could tell when it saw his blade engulfed in flames... it wasn't impressed. The figure hunkered down and put up its fists.

Jason glared at it. "The King sent you to kill me, didn't he?"

It was the first time Jason heard anything that could resemble a voice in the intruder. It chortled in its throat.

Jason's teeth bore harder and his blood boiled. Just at that moment, the fire that enveloped his blade went out with a hiss. Jason's eyes shot to it, and he almost missed the blue beams that shot from the intruder's hands.

They were just like the blue beam that Tarren fired months ago—more advanced magic. Jason dropped into the snow and the beams soared over his head, connecting with a house in the distance and blowing a chunk out of the roof. His jaw fell as he watched the debris fall to the ground.

As he lay there, catching his bearings, he suddenly realized that he couldn't move. His entire body was being constricted. He recognized this feeling—King Barnabas had done the same thing to him when he visited him at the castle for the first time. It was a Paralyzing Curse.

Jason's heart pounded harder. Out of the corner of his eye, he could see the figure's footsteps coming closer and closer. It slid another dagger out of a holster Jason didn't see before.

There has to be a way to break this! Jason thought frantically. *You broke the Dreamslayer spell, you can break this one! You have to!*

With his mind, Jason tried to push off the constriction and free his arms. He thought of every Ancient Nezmythian word or phrase that could possibly work. He could *feel* the weight in his mind, forcing his limbs to keep still. He thought of everything he could—even commanding by the Dragon's fire to release him. But this wasn't *Tephnoh Edomah*, and he was trapped. The silently prayed for some means of escape.

The figure bent down and put the point of the dagger into Jason's back. Jason closed his eyes, preparing for the end.

Suddenly, a rustling came from the bushes. The figure's head darted, and for a moment, Jason felt his arms and legs go free. Its focus was broken, and Jason stole the opportunity. Behind his back, Jason shot a jeroki directly into the foe's stomach. The enemy dropped its dagger and rolled onto its side, grunting in agony from the numerous point-blank shots it had already taken. Jason scooped up his sword, and in a blind slash badly wounded the foe's side. He leapt on top of the dark figure and pinned it down, pushing the edge of his sword into its throat.

Jason panted heavily. He had almost completely forgotten about his wounded shoulder—red blood had soaked into the snow where he had lay. From out of the bushes, the culprit of the rustling appeared. A brown rabbit, with innocent, beady black eyes, leapt out and bounded through the snow, leaving small paw prints as it went.

Divine intervention, Jason thought.

The dark figure was recovering from its brutal final blow. Blood began to seep onto the snow from the assassin. Jason could once again feel its eyes on him as he hunched over it.

"Go ahead," The figure growled in a deathly voice. "Kill me. I'm already a dead man."

"Did the King send you?" Jason shot.

"Yes," he figure replied. "He said to kill you and cover up. Boy... if you have any ounce of mercy you'll kill me now—I won't last one day here, and he'll torture me purely for pleasure before I die."

Jason sighed through his nose, "No. I'm not a killer." He bent in closer, still holding his sword at the assassin's throat. "Run. And don't stop until you've hit the borders of the kingdom. I've spared your life, and now you must swear to me that you'll never kill another man for long as you live. Do you swear it?"

"I swear it."

Jason removed his blade from the assassin's throat. The assassin slowly got up, wincing at the pain that shot from its side. The wound could be bandaged up and he could heal in time... but the assassin apparently had other plans.

"You still don't get it. There's no escaping this. You have a good heart... but so foolish..."

Jason was taken aback. After he had spared this man's life, that's what he had to say?

"The King's eyes are everywhere," the assassin muttered. "They're probably watching us now. You have no idea what he's capable of—how many legions of people he's killed. I'll never escape him like this. Even if you didn't wound me… there's no escape… why couldn't you have just killed me…?"

The assassin started to backpedal toward the mouth of the well. Jason's heart stopped beating and he looked on with wide eyes.

"I don't know who you are, or why he wanted me to kill you," the assassin continued. "But I won't be the last one. He'll send more. The King gets whatever he wants, and if anyone tries to stop him, he ends them. You're dead as well as I am. You hear me boy? You're *dead*."

With that, the assassin toppled backward into the well. Jason didn't hear him hit the bottom, but he knew that with his wound, there was no climbing out. It was a quicker death, with less pain.

His knees went out and he fell to the snow, shaken, his ears ringing with the things he had just heard. He felt like curling into a ball until it all went away—the Year of Decision, the trials, everything. It was the thought that he was currently being watched that snapped him back to reality. He had to get somewhere safer. There could be another assassin heading his way immediately.

It was also then that he realized that his left shoulder was thick with blood and his feet were completely numb. He sheathed his sword and quickly darted to the awning by the back door, clutching his shoulder in a futile attempt to stop the bleeding. He collapsed into the chair, and out loud muttered Ancient Nezmythian words that went with an ancient spell of meditation and healing.

Like the flickering of a candle, a glow began to develop inside him. His shoulder started to tingle ever so faintly.

22 THE GIFT

Master Ferribolt stared intently at the floor in his usual chair. As Jason sat across from him, he could almost hear the machines turning in his head. Finally, he rubbed his hands and looked into Jason's eyes.

"Well, it looks as though the King has held up his word," he said. "These months before you take the Throne are when you need to be especially on your guard. He had never made an attempt on your life until last night, am I correct?"

"Kind of," Jason said. "He tried killing me personally in the castle a few months ago. It was the day of the procession."

"Right, of course," Master Ferribolt stroked his chin. "Back then, he wanted the pleasure of ending your life personally. Now it looks as though he simply wants the job done, regardless of who performs the deed."

"Not exactly comforting," Jason muttered. "Some of the Ancient Nezmythian magic saved my life, though. It's amazing that I survived..."

"I agree."

"...but I tried using one spell that barely worked. It made the blade of my sword catch on fire, but it only lasted a few seconds."

"I believe I recall that spell," Master Ferribolt replied. *"Fire of the Dragon's Breath?* Yes. You see, Jason, there is a science behind the magic that we use every day. The level of magic we can perform is directly proportional to the strength of our spirit—you know this. You, having a righteous heart and pure actions, will only be magically strong so long as your thoughts and actions are good. A moment of anger or hatred can snuff out a spell like the *Fire of the Dragon's Breath*."

"Oh…" Jason suddenly recalled feeling a flare of anger toward the assassin after casting that spell. *It sounds like being magically strong requires a lot of self-control,* he thought. "So what about people like the King who experiment with *Tepnoh Edomah* and have a dark spirit? Why are they still able to use powerful magic?"

"A dark spirit can still be a strong spirit," Master Ferribolt said. "His selfish, evil thoughts and actions can be just strong as your virtuous ones, even more so. It's the indecisive spirit—the man that isn't sure whether he wants to be good or evil, selfish or selfless… that's the man that is magically small."

Jason hummed in recognition. It made sense. He couldn't believe that he wasn't taught this during his battle classes when he was younger… perhaps it was because his family is so poor. Good battle instructors are expensive.

Master Ferribolt leaned in and said, "What you must do, Jason, is be more good than the King is evil. If he ever does you battle, that will be your only chance of victory."

Jason's heart sank. "What I'm hoping is he *never* does me battle."

* * * * *

"There you are," Jason said as he held the newly-made mace forward. "Made to your exact orders."

"Excellent," a large-nosed butler from Upper City spoke with a nasally voice. "I'm sure the master will love his new weapon. He paid top Block for it, you know."

"And he got top quality for it, I assure you."

"Of course," the butler said. "Well, carry on then."

Jason thanked him. The butler took the mace and scurried out the door before hopping into an elaborate coach outside. Jason took the sack of Blocks the butler paid him and retreated into the shop. Out the window, a duo of chestnut-brown horses kicked up the snow and trotted away along with the carriage. Jaboc threw a couple more logs into the furnace in the far corner of the shop. The furnace accepted the new wood and roared happily. Outside, thin black smoke puffed up through a chimney that protruded from the roof of the shop.

Jason stopped at a lathe that held a half-finished combat staff. Next to the lathe, arrays of tools were strewn across the table. As he pumped his foot, the lathe began to spin the staff the Jason reached for one of the tools. Holding it firmly in his hand, he set the tool on the spinning rod, which carved it out as it spun and sent wooden imperfections flying out in a cloud of dust and debris. He squinted his eyes to protect them from the debris.

His shoulder tingled uncomfortably under the strain. Jason feared that he might have meditated the healing spell incorrectly, because a long scar now adorned his left shoulder from the battle with the assassin last week. He had disposed of his blood-soaked jacket and shirt as soon as he could, and out of the eyes of Saryan and his parents. The less they knew, the better. At least he wasn't too worried about the clothes— Saryan had bought him and his parents entirely new wardrobes after their houses burned down.

As the lathe spun to a halt, Jason heard the scurrying of feet coming up through the shop. He peered over his shoulder to find Golan hurrying up to him, panting rather heavily and peppered with fresh snowflakes. A scarf and hat protected him from the cold, and a satchel was slung over his shoulder.

"I'm sorry—that I'm back late—from my break," he said through great breaths. "I had to stop by the printing shop clear at the—opposite side of the Southern Market Street—to get something important."

"That's okay, Golan," Jason said, turning back to his work. "There hasn't been much to do today, anyway. But you did miss the mace customer coming back to pick up his order."

"Oh, no…" Golan deflated. "That was my best design too. Oh, well… this was much more important."

"What was it?"

The corner of Golan's mouth twitched into a sheepish smirk. He cleared his throat. Bertus and Jaboc were both diligently at their work stations on the other side of the shop, either unaware or negligent of Golan's return. Jason looked back over his shoulder, expectant for an answer. Finally, Golan reached into the satchel and pulled out a small slip of paper.

"I hope you can make it," Golan said. "I have one for Jaboc and Bertus as well."

Jason blinked a couple of times. He turned around completely and took the note from Golan's frozen fingers. He turned it around a couple of times as he scanned it curiously, finally getting the letters on it to face upward.

The letters curved and swirled elegantly around the slip of paper, and as Jason's eyes darted down the page, soaking up its contents, his eyes grew wider and wider. A smile spread across his face. Finally, he bellowed:

"You're getting *married?*"

Immediately, Bertus and Jaboc flipped around at their places. When they saw Golan's flustered face, their smiles grew and they hurried across the room to join Jason. The both huddled around Jason's shoulders, reading the note with wide, sparkling eyes and toothy grins. Jason laughed innocently.

"Today marks your Month of Merriment! So you'll be married exactly one month from today? That's wonderful! How did you present the ring?"

Golan turned pink, "Um… please don't tell Tarmanthia I showed these to you… I haven't even presented the ring to her yet. I'll do that tonight. But we've talked about it and we want to get married."

Jason let out a staccato and threw his hand forward. "Well congratulations, my friend!"

"Thank you," Golan said as he put his hand forward and shook Jason's. "I really hope all of you can make it. It would be a huge blessing to have such close friends attend, not just the aristocratic fare my parents will likely invite."

"I'm coming," Jason said. "I'll bring Saryan, too."

"You know I'll be there!" Jaboc said jubilantly. "And I'll be coming with *two* ladies. Jason can only get one."

"Shut up, Jaboc," Jason retorted with a punch to his shoulder.

"If there is food," Bertus added. "You will find me there."

They all laughed. Suddenly, a loud knock sounded through the shop from the front desk. The four looked at each other.

"I've got it," Jason handed the invitation to Bertus and he left the pack. As he twisted his way around the machines, he came into clear view of the front desk. What he saw made his face light up: a tall man with long, blonde hair and vivid purple eyes, appearing very tired, but happy.

"Tarren!" Jason said as he hustled to the front desk. "I've tried stopping by several times this past week—I was afraid they had taken you!"

Tarren forced a smile. He clutched a small box with both hands, and he seemed as though he could fall asleep where he stood. "I know. I'm sorry Jason… Lately I've been working through the night and sleeping all day. You see, after you made that sign for me, I didn't exactly get legions of new customers, but I got a few that needed a lot of things. They paid me in advance to make several sets of drums *and* flutes. So here I am! I paid the tax, and I'm still a free man."

Jason sighed. "You must be living your life right. The Dragon has blessed you with freedom. You should be very grateful."

"I am," Tarren said. "But I must repay the favor."

"No, you don't," Jason said firmly.

"Too late," Tarren smirked.

Tarren extended the small box toward Jason. Jason's eyes jumped from the box, to Tarren's weary eyes.

"Tarren," he said. "I didn't expect you to—."

"Will you hurry up and open it?" Tarren's eyebrow cocked. "I still have a lot of work I need to finish."

Jason paused, exhaled, then reached out with his gloved hand and took the box. Tarren had wrapped it nicely with brown string. After Jason had unraveled the string, he popped the top off the box to reveal a smaller wooden box amidst a crackly mess of tissue paper. He pulled out the box, unlatched its tiny lever, and opened it.

It was a brilliant new flyra. The maple wood was stained in a way that gave it a beautiful rosy hue, the glossy finish soaked up the light that made it grin with a dynamic sheen, and intricate carvings weaved around the sound holes. Needless to say, it was much different from the worn-out flyra that had stayed in Jason's pocket for several years.

"Play it," Tarren said.

Slowly, Jason placed the instrument to his lips. He had almost forgotten the taste of a brand-new reed… the wood was still fresh. As he blew, it didn't produce the hollow whistles that his old flyra did, but projected a warm, flowing stream of brightness. Jason couldn't help but chuckle like a small boy on his birthday.

"How long has it been since my flyra sounded like this…?" He said half to himself.

"Never," Tarren said proudly. "Your flyra is too old. Besides, it wasn't made with very quality materials to begin with. This one sounds loads better, and should last you for *much* longer if you take good care of it. I know you always keep it in your pocket, so that cover should keep it safe."

"Thank you," Jason said brightly. "I don't know what to say."

"Say that you'll keep being a great friend," Tarren replied. "I owe you my life, Jason. Your small sacrifice kept me out of slavery. So thank *you*."

Jason grinned. He carefully inserted the flyra into his pocket.

"Well, like I said, I have a lot of work to do," Tarren said. "But we'll spar later this week, agreed?"

"Agreed," Jason replied.

"May the Dragon bless you, Jason, son of Tomm the printer."

Tarren gave his trademark smirk and walked out into the bitter cold. Jason couldn't wipe the smile off his face. He patted the lump in his pocket that was his brand new flyra.

I guess a small act of kindness can go a long way for someone else, he thought.

23 THE PRYING

Jason quickly ducked and rolled away from the blow. Tarren continued to slash viciously with a dagger in each hand, in which Jason dodged barely, never taking his eyes off Tarren. Tarren slashed high, Jason ducked. Tarren would try a sweeping low kick, Jason would jump. Just as Jason was beginning to laugh, Tarren fooled him by lunging as if he was going to go for a stab but instead tried a low kick.

Jason caught the blow in the ankles, and he let out a startled yelp as he collapsed to the floor. He quickly rolled out of the way just before Tarren fell on top of him, and as he scrambled into a hunched standing position, Tarren did the same. They both backed away from each other.

Jason laughed playfully through shallow breaths, "You're losing steam!"

Tarren slid Jason a tired look, "You know I've been busy."

"I'll go easy on you if you'd prefer."

"Forget it. Let's dance."

Tarren tossed up a dagger in the air and shot a quick jeroki from the empty hand, which Jason felt wiz by his shoulder just inches from his ear. Tarren threw his other dagger through the air. Jason's eyes locked on it, and reflexively he swiped his sword upward in defense. The dagger connected with the sword flawlessly, but grazed Jason's shoulder on the exact spot that it had been sliced three weeks prior. His scar swelled in pain, and Jason bore his teeth.

Tarren had caught his first dagger and was darting toward Jason, ready to thrust it onto Jason's chest and win the match. Jason's reflexes grabbed the closest defense that shot into his mind. Jason bent his spine backward as far as it would go in the split second that he had. The dagger rushed forward, the edge barely grazing Jason's sternum as he fell flat onto his back. Tarren missed.

Jason landed with a thud, twisted his legs and swept at Tarren's ankles, knocking him cleanly onto the floor. Tarren fell on his back and coughed as the wind flew out of his lungs, uttering out some inaudible grunt, lying right next to Jason on the floor.

Jason looked at Tarren. Tarren looked at Jason. Then Tarren scrambled on top of Jason and tried to pin him down just as Jason was doing the same to him. They grappled with each other fiercely as they rolled across the floor until Tarren pulled his knees to his chest, placed his feet on Jason's torso and kicked him up over his back.

Jason flew through the air for a moment then landed roughly on his back, the wind knocked out of him. He shook his head and forced himself upward while taking deep breaths. It was only a second before he had recollected himself.

Tarren scraped up the dagger he had thrown earlier and got to his feet a few yards away. He quickly flipped around to face Jason, hunched down and brandishing a dagger in each hand, his eyes razor-sharp. Jason breathed in and out meditatively. He thought of race horses speeding down a track… a jeroki flying through the air… and he thought of the Ancient Nezmythian word "*tala.*"

He leapt forward. In the blink of an eye, Jason became a blur. Tarren's eyes popped open in shock right before Jason's speeding shoulder connected with his sternum, sending him tumbling backward. A grin flared on Jason's face for an instant, but he stayed focused. As Tarren was tumbling, Jason brandished his sword and waited for the perfect chance to strike and win the match. Just as he was swinging down, Tarren had tumbled onto his knees and held his armored forearms up, blocking the blow from connecting with his shoulder. His eyes flashed.

"*What was that?*" Tarren shot. "I've never seen anyone move like that!"

"It's fighting with your spirit, not just your body," Jason said.

Jason took his sword off Tarren's forearms and Tarren got up, breathing heavily. They both stood, bearing down on each other like animals, their eyes full of fire. A bead of sweat dripped down from Jason's chin. Tarren flicked his head, shooing some of the matted, sweaty hair out of his eyes.

In a split second, Tarren pocketed one dagger and dropped the other to the floor. Jason's eyes sparked. He raised his sword.

Tarren raised both palms forward and white balls charged inside them one after the other. Each jeroki flew forward consecutively: right hand, left hand. Each flew with ridiculous speed, but Jason found the rhythm and kept on it, slicing each jeroki skillfully as they flew toward him, dissipating into oblivion.

Jason started moving forward, first as a walk, then a brisk walk, then a run as he swung, slicing and dodging each jeroki that sped his way. His heart pounded. His face burned. As he closed in, the jerokis became harder to deflect. He tried to keep his breathing steady.

Finally, when Jason was only feet away, the jerokis stopped. Tarren's hand shot into his pocket and grabbed the dagger. Jason's concentration spiked. He thought of a flying bird. He thought of a spring releasing its compressed energy.

"*Sheelah!*" He shouted and pumped his legs into the ground.

Jason jumped higher than he was tall, the sensation of flying grazing his cheek and flowing through his hair. Tarren's quickly moving dagger thrust forward, but caught nothing. His mouth dropped in amazement as Jason flew over his head. Jason spun around as he flew through the air, his eyes keeping contact with Tarren's as he hung in the atmosphere. As Jason came down, he gripped the hilt of his blade tight.

His feet touched ground. Tarren flipped around reflexively. Jason thrust his blade forward and it found its mark right in the middle of Tarren's chest.

Tarren stood like a statue, the fake blade prodding into his chest and his mouth hanging open numbly. Jason's eyes flashed. He bore his teeth in an enormous, toothy smile while Tarren's hands fell to his side, his dagger dropping to the floor. Jason didn't say a word, he just continued to bare his victorious expression and keep the soft tip of the sword in Tarren's chest.

Tarren's lips barely moved, "I don't believe it..."

Jason stood up straight. His arms dropped to the side and his sword fell to the ground. The dusty light that poured into their derelict combat hall never seemed so bright. His heavy breathing was decreasing. Tarren sighed.

"I never thought I'd actually see it..." Tarren said. "And in just under three months of training, too. Wow..." he put his hands on his hips and shook his head. Jason couldn't stop smiling. Tarren looked off the ground and took a step forward, his hand outstretched. "Well, I think my little training sessions are over. You don't need me to teach you how to fight anymore. Congratulations, Jason."

A light inside Jason swelled. He grasped the hand and shook it, "Thank you. Then again, you have been very busy making instruments... maybe I wouldn't have won if you weren't so tired—."

"Nope," Tarren said flatly. "You beat me fair and square. Don't ruin the moment for yourself."

Jason laughed. Tarren continued, "How did you do those things, though? You moved so fast I could barely see you then you jumped clear over my head. I've never seen anyone do that. Did it come from those strange words you were shouting?"

Jason smiled mischievously, "Kind of. Maybe I'll teach you sometime."

Tarren walked over and grabbed their usual canteens, one in each hand. He tossed one to Jason, who caught it without looking. Tarren took a deep swig of his water and wiped his mouth, and Jason followed suit.

"So what made you start fighting again?" Tarren quizzed. "A year ago you wouldn't even think about going to a combat gym and suddenly, you wanted to start practicing at least once a week. And with your job and Saryan... you've been busy lately."

Jason pulled the neck of the canteen away from his lips. He quietly pushed the cork back into the neck and sat rubbing his hands together, a cold sweat forming on his brow lightly. Tarren blinked. Jason stared at the floor.

"Yes," he said. "I suppose I have been."

"But why?" Tarren said. "Is something coming up? You've got me curious."

Jason thought for a split second about telling Tarren about the Year of Decision, King Barnabas and his Kinghood coming up in just over two months, but only for a split second. He searched around in his mind quickly for a viable story that was still truthful.

"I just feel like I need to do a few things to improve myself."

"This is a lot of work for a few touch-ups," Tarren said.

Jason shrugged. He took a few more gulps from his canteen.

"Alright..." Tarren faded. A silence ensued for a few more moments before he spoke again. "Maybe now that you're a master in the combat ring, you could challenge the King so you can put him in his place."

Jason's freezing heart sank into his stomach. He knew Tarren was joking, but still, unknowingly, he had guessed exactly what Jason thought would be the climax of his Year of Decision. He held the canteen frozen in the air. His eyes darted around in his eye sockets. He cleared his throat.

"*Pff*, no!" Jason said with a quivering laugh. "That's an awful idea—suicide! He's the best warrior in all of Nezmyth! I mean—if you just saw his sword—."

Jason held his tongue, desperately wishing he could have taken those last few words and shove them back down his throat. Tarren's expression melted from jesting to incredulity in a matter of seconds.

"When did you see the King's *sword?*" he asked in awe.

Jason fumbled in his mind for words. He couldn't lie, but he *certainly* couldn't tell the truth. His mouth dangled open, forming words but no sound coming from his lips.

"Jason," Tarren's tone was serious. "What's going on?"

Defeated, Jason exhaled, looked out the windows and said, "I can't tell you."

"Why?"

"Because it's so much bigger than you and I," he said, his eyes still darting about. "And if I tell you, both of our lives will be in jeopardy, along with the well-being of the entire kingdom."

I've said too much, he thought.

If it were possible for Tarren's eyes to grow wider and his jaw to fall lower, it happened. The silence was palpable. Behind his eyes, Tarren was putting clues together, and Jason could see it. His eyebrows bent hard.

"Tarren," Jason said. "Whatever you're going to say, *don't.*"

Tarren's dangling jaw clamped shut. He opened it as if to speak, then closed it, then opened it again.

"Jason," he whispered lowly. "...you've been Foreordained to be something, haven't you?"

Something like horror and wonder flashed through Jason's mind. The promise of King Barnabas ending his life if anyone discovered his Year of Decision became vibrantly clear in his memory. This very moment here in the derelict combat gym could ruin the future of Nezmyth. Both of their lives were now in danger, and if Jason was killed, how long would it be before a new King is Foreordained? Jason prayed that no one was outside listening to their conversation, but he knew better… he must have spies watching him day and night, and it was only a matter of time before the King caught wind of it.

But what if he didn't…? He had to hope for that.

Before he could allow Tarren to say "King," Jason stormed up to him and fiercely grabbed him by the collar, pulling his face so it was mere inches from his own. Venom could have dripped from his lips.

"Tarren," he seethed. "Never, *ever* speak a word of this to *anyone*. You have now jeopardized both of our lives and the fate of the kingdom. You have to guard this information with your life."

Tarren went completely pale—he had never seen Jason with such audacity to grab him by the collar and demand things of him. But he knew that he had done something serious. How serious, he didn't know.

"I'm sorry," Tarren breathed.

"You haven't an idea how sorry you should be," Jason replied. "Just pray that this conversation is never discovered by anyone else."

Tarren nodded stiffly, "You have my word."

24 THE CONFESSION

Jason couldn't stop thinking about what happened at his last sparring practice with Tarren. *Does he know that I'll be King, or something else, like a Patriarch or Blessing Bearer? How long will it be until King Barnabas hears of it? Will he even hear of it? The combat gym is incredibly large and we were whispering in that conversation... with any luck it'll slip under his notice. But how likely is that?*

The sunshine during the day didn't do much to brighten Jason's spirits. Snow on the Nezmyth City streets had nearly melted into a crystal clear fluid as winter gave way to spring. The trees rebelled against the cold in budding sweet pink and yellow flowers on their once-bare branches.

However, it was now the dark of night, and Jason found himself in another unsuccessful night's sleep. He was still getting used to his new flyra—although it was much fancier than his old one, it didn't have the same sentimental value. So he chose not to play it. He sat on a rug before the fireplace in the main room of Saryan's home. A dim orange flame crackled, which Jason intermittently stoked with a metal stick. Mostly, he sat with his knees up to his chest and his arms resting on them.

Construction was going well on their new home on the rim of Lower City—it would probably be completed in a matter of weeks. The tax money that Tomm and Kara didn't need to pay was just enough to pay for the cheapest timber. Tomm and a few friends from his printing shop worked on the property after work hours.

Jason stoked the fire again. The warmth was just enough to keep his body warm, though his feet felt chilly, even on the furry rug below him. He swam in his thoughts, gazing absently at the flickering flame.

"Jason..." a sweet voice whispered to his right.

Jason turned to see Saryan walking dreamily out of the hallway. Her nightgown was rather short, only going halfway down her thighs, and even though her hair wasn't brushed and sleep plagued her eyes, she was lovely. Jason tried not to stare at her legs.

"Saryan!" he whispered back. "Saryan, what about our rule? It's late."

"I know, I know," she replied as she walked over. "I'm sorry. I just wanted to talk to you."

"It couldn't wait?"

She shook her head and brushed her bare arms as if to warm herself. She said, "I had a strange dream..."

She sat down next to him. Jason found himself with mixed feelings. They had established a rule—one they had mutually agreed one, one meant to keep them safe. However, she seemed genuinely distressed, which is something Jason had seldom seen. He stared into her silver eyes.

What's more important, Jason? He told himself. *One little rule, or her feelings? You can let it go for one night, you can trust her. She seems worried.*

Jason sighed through his nose and said, "What was it about?"

She curled her legs up and hugged her knees, similarly to Jason. She gazed into the fire and spoke softly.

"I dreamt that I was walking down a road—a road that I felt like I had long known before. The road changed as I walked. Sometimes it was paved with stone, long and straight, easy to follow. At other times, it twisted and curved in uncomfortable ways that made me very tired. On occasion the road was hard to see because it was filled with stones to climb over, or thick rain would cover me and make it hard to see. But somehow, I always stayed on the road.

"Suddenly, the sun stopped its light, and the sky filled with evil black clouds. I heard wailing in the distance that filled my ears and covered me—the voice of someone I know and love. My heart cried out to be with him, but he was taken from me.

"I kept down the road, silent and unsure. Slowly, the road became more beautiful… bricks placed carefully together with flowers growing on either side. It was lovely. But still, the black sky haunted me.

"Finally, I cried out to the air the voice of my confusion, hoping that someone would answer. And at that moment, a man appeared next to me, very sharp and striking. His eyes were dark and wise, with no ounce of contempt. They looked at me in a way that no one has looked at me before— full of love, but a love that was foreign to me, one that I had never experienced.

"I told him, 'I've been walking down this road for so long, but I'm not sure it's right. What should I do? My feelings betray me.'

"He said, 'You are to keep going. Your journey is not over. At times the darkness must cover you before you see the light.'

"With that, he disappeared. I had turned to look back down the path, but it was gone. That was when I woke up."

The two sat in silence for several moments. Jason locked his eyes on Saryan, not sure of what to say. It sounded like an incredibly bizarre dream. The fire cast a harsh glow on her face, which somehow made her seem older.

Jason reached out and took her hand, caressing it gently. Her gaze stayed fixed on the fire. Jason said, "I'm sorry. That must have been hard."

She didn't say anything. Jason desperately wished the love from his heart would transfer through his hand and melt away the sadness that coated her, but it stayed stoically fixed like a statue. They sat in silence like that for a while, his hand grasping hers, until finally, she spoke.

"Jason," Saryan's voice quivered. "Have you ever been forced to do something you *really* didn't want to do?"

A staccato leapt from Jason's lips. "Yes."

"What happened?" she asked.

Jason stroked her hand with his thumb. After a sigh, he said, "It would take too long to explain… I think I'm still kind of on that journey. Maybe someday I'll see the reason, but for now, I just have to go forward with faith. It can be really hard sometimes, not knowing what's around the corner. I'm still getting used to it…"

Saryan rested her head on Jason's shoulder. It was then that Jason noticed she was shaking slightly. His eyebrows creased.

"Saryan," he said. "Are you sure the dream is the only thing that's bothering you?"

"No," she relented. "I've been thinking about our relationship…"

A spark of something unpleasant shot through Jason. "What's wrong with it?"

"Nothing!" She said. "That's it, nothing is wrong with it! I've never been happier these three months that we've been seeing each other. Every day I wake up and look forward to the minute I'll see you again. I hope this feeling can last forever, and I don't want to ruin it." She paused before she said, "I never want to do anything to hurt you."

"I feel the same way," Jason reassured softly.

For the first time, Saryan lifted her head and gazed into his eyes. Her silver orbs were glistening with tears ready to fall— they seemed unsure, confused, even scared. Seeing them that way threw a wave of different emotions over Jason. His heart desperately wanted to cast the darkness out of the woman he knew to be so vibrant and strong. He would do anything.

"…Promise you'll love me no matter what?" She whispered.

Jason didn't have to hesitate on the answer. "I promise."

She teased a smile. She put her hand softly on Jason's cheek and leaned forward, kissing him softly on the lips. Relenting, Jason let his eyes close, brushing his fingers through her golden hair. *Maybe this is what she needs right now…* he thought. They sat like that for several moments, soaking up each other's company.

Their passion slowly started bubbling closer to the surface. Saryan shifted to her knees and knelt down as she held Jason's face with both hands and caressed his lips passionately. Jason tasted her lips and his heart beat increased. His hand rested on her waist.

A soft voice echoed in Jason's mind to stop and think—a fluttering of wings—but his rapid heartbeat and deep breathing drowned out the sound.

Saryan slid one leg over the side of Jason and sat down on his thighs, edging closer and closer toward his body. Their lips locked and held each other's hotly. Both of Jason's sweaty palms were on her waist now. Saryan's hands left Jason's face, found the bottom hem of his shirt and began pulling upward, slipping his shirt farther and farther up his body.

Again that voice came, a little louder, and Jason heard it sounding softly. His heart thrashed inside his chest and he ignored it.

The two's lips became disconnected as Saryan succeeded in pulling Jason's shirt completely off his back, but quickly met each other again. Jason breathed great breaths through his nose as he kissed her mouth, cheeks, and neck. Saryan moaned softly as her hands wrapped around Jason's head, her fingers sliding through his hair.

Her warm body scraped Jason's bare chest as she continued to moan and Jason's heart fought to break out of his chest. His hands slid down her waist, to her hips, down her smooth, exposed thighs. Her fingers left his face, traveled down his neck, his toned chest and abdominals, then reached the top of his pants. Her fingers fumbled at the drawstrings.

Jason's blood was ice, his heart was about to explode, but again the voice came, this time roaring like a lion.

STOP!

Jason's eyes shot open. With his hands on her waist, Jason involuntarily shoved Saryan off of him with a gasp. Saryan fell roughly onto the floor in front of him, looking extremely startled and numb.

Jason's eyes were wild. They darted from side to side in his eye sockets. His breathing came in great breaths. A thin layer of sweat coated his face and chest. He suddenly remembered the King's admonition to live to highest standard of virtue possible, or he would be disqualified for the Throne. His shaking hands came up and covered his face.

"Oh no..." he breathed, his voice shaking. In one fell swoop, he realized he had put the entire Kingdom's future on the line. If he would have let his emotions take control, in a matter of moments Jason would have failed his Year of Decision. King Barnabas would retain the Throne, and it would be all because of his failure to control himself. The reality hit him like a mallet to the head.

"What's wrong?" Saryan asked, looking up into his eyes.

Jason shook as he spoke. "I can't do this, Saryan... it's not the right time—I want to, but I can't... it isn't right. Not now."

"What's wrong with it?" Saryan shot defensively. "I thought you loved me! You said you would never do anything to hurt me." Her last remark was like ice.

"I don't!" Jason said. His heartbeat wasn't settling. "I wish I could tell you, Saryan, but I can't do this right now."

"Why?" she shot. "Why do you feel like you need to keep secrets from me? I've never offered myself to anyone like this. Doesn't that mean anything to you?"

"Saryan," Jason said, trying to smooth the tension. "You mean the world to me—more than the world to me—but I've promised to live a certain way and if I don't—."

"Then what?" she interrupted. "Is it really more important than what we have? All the hours we've spent together, the places we've been, the moments we've shared... is your little rule really more important than that?"

Jason found himself lost for words. Is the kingdom more important than his relationship with the woman he loves? Absolutely. Was it more important to *him* at that moment? No. But he knew he had an obligation, not to the King, but to the thousands of people living in the kingdom of Nezmyth. He had to keep himself virtuous, otherwise all would be lost. We wish he could tell it all to her.

The silence spoke volumes. Saryan's lower lip tightened. She got up from where she sat and looked Jason in the eye fiercely, almost as if she couldn't decide how to kill him. Jason's breathed slowly. With that, she turned on her heels and stormed out of the room. The only sound that came from her was her sniffles, in soft bursts that echoed as she retreated down the hall.

Jason let out a shaky breath and swallowed hard. His heartbeat was steadily settling back to normal. He looked at the floor and whispered to himself.

"What am I going to do...?"

He found his shirt next to him on the floor. He grabbed it and slipped it back over his body before he restrung his drawstrings and stood up. He crept slowly down the path that Saryan had walked, being careful not to wake his parents. Her doorway seemed colder and bleaker than it ever had before.

He exhaled as he stood behind the door, searching for the right words to say. He opened his mouth, and then closed it. He did the same thing again.

"Saryan?" He asked as he tapped his knuckle on the door. No response. Jason sighed.

"Saryan, I'm sorry…" he said. "I'm really sorry I hurt your feelings tonight, and I wish I could tell you the reason why I am the way I am, but I've made promises that I just can't break. I'm—."

Everything happened rather swiftly. Saryan silently pushed the door open, and as she faced Jason, there wasn't a spec of anger or hurt in her eyes. Instead, they reeked with urgency. She looked about anxiously and pushed her finger to her lips, signaling for Jason to keep quiet. She closed the door behind her, took Jason's hand, and led him through another door across the hall from her bedroom.

All the while, Jason couldn't seem to put the pieces together. *I hurt her feelings just moments ago, and now she seems troubled about something else… what's going on?*

Saryan closed the door behind them, leaving the room pitch black. With a click, a lantern by the door emitted a dull, flickering glow that cast a dim light over their surroundings. The room was an exceptionally large pantry, full of wine barrels and enormous burlap sacks of flour and grain. It also had no windows, so no one could hear or see them. Saryan folded her arms and sighed as she stood in front of the door.

"You're not the only one that's been keeping secrets," she said.

A pause. *How do I respond to that?* Jason thought. There wasn't any resent in her voice, but she didn't make eye contact. His eyebrows slowly stiffened.

"Saryan," he began slowly. "What are you talking about?"

"There's a reason you haven't met by father," she muttered as her eyes scanned the room apprehensively. "And it's not the reason I told you. He hasn't been visiting the villages around the borders of the Kingdom."

Jason wasn't sure he wanted the real answer, but he forced himself to ask, "Where is he?"

"Prison. The King is holding him there."

Jason's heart stopped beating for a moment and his blood went cold. This is when Saryan finally looked into his eyes.

Her jaw clenched as if she were inwardly in pain, and she tried to hold back tears—real tears.

"I'm done lying to you, Jason," she said. "You've been too good to me these past few months and my feelings for you are too strong. You deserve to know the truth."

Jason's jaw dangled. Saryan took a deep breath before she spoke again.

"It all happened several months ago. I woke up one morning to find that my father was gone. That wasn't unusual—being a Captain, he can be called upon at any moment to fulfill his duty—but when he didn't return for two days, I started to worry. It was then that I came home one afternoon to find a royal carriage parked outside my home."

Jason's insides tightened.

"I was taken to the castle where I was introduced to the King. He asked me if I knew where my father had gone. I told him no, and that I was very worried." She cleared her throat, trying to keep her voice from shaking. "It was then that he told me that my father was in prison, and would be kept there until I was prepared to fulfill a particular mission for him.

"Of course, I was mortified. I told him whatever it was, I would do it. My father is all I have left after my mother died, and I would do anything for him. So the King told me of a boy living on the rim of Lower City who works at Kristof's Weapons and Crafts—average height, deep brown eyes and sandy brown hair. He told me that I needed to convince him to fall in love with me, then seduce him. Only then would he release my father.

"I couldn't think of anything more appalling. Giving that part of myself to someone I didn't even know...? I asked him why this needed to be the terms of my father's release, and he wouldn't tell me. All he told me is that he would be watching me to make sure I finished the job, then commanded me to leave.

"You don't know how scared I was when I met you for the first time on the Southern Market Street. And I didn't really need a new staff, but I needed some excuse to see you again. Everything was going according to his plan… until I spent more time with you and saw how caring, and gentle, and selfless you are… you became my best friend, then I started falling in love with you.

"So I procrastinated. All I wanted to do was spend time with you, but in the right ways. The King would visit me occasionally and threaten me, and I would try to convince him that everything was going according to plan. Just before I met you at the theater last month, he told me of his plan to burn down your home. He ordered it to be burned so you could move in with me… because I was taking too long. It would give me a prime opportunity to lure you in, but you didn't give in. Now here we are…"

Finally, she couldn't hold back the sobs.

"Jason, I love you, and I wouldn't dream of forcing you to do something you shouldn't do, but I don't know what to do! Why is this happening? Why is the King making me do these awful things with you? I don't—!"

She didn't finish, and covered her face to hide her tears. Every word, every sentence thrashed Jason like a tidal wave. His suspicions from months ago were indeed true—she was a trial from the King, sent to hijack his virtue and disqualify him from the Throne. The knowledge crashed down on him. But here she was, confessing everything to him in tears of hopelessness and confusion. Amidst it all, Jason was torn.

I knew she was too good to be true, He thought. *She was preparing to steal my virtue all along. But she's risking a lot to tell me this right now. Everything.*

Jason wanted to wrap his arms around her, but his insides suddenly felt hollow—defeated, almost betrayed. Meanwhile, Saryan tried to control her sniffling.

"I know what they do to people in prison," she gasped through the sobs. "I've seen it. People are beaten… they're barely fed… and to know my father is there—."

It's all been for her father, he thought. *But I know she loves me. I know she does. But now what's going to happen to her? She's failed her mission, and King Barnabas will know...*

Jason forced himself forward and put his arms around Saryan's quivering body. She buried her face in his shoulder. Jason silently wondered if this would be the last time he would get to hold her. How long would it take before the King found out?

"I'm sorry, Saryan," he said softly.

"But *why*, Jason?" she said. "Why did the King want me to seduce *you* to release my father? It doesn't make sense!"

He wanted to tell her that he is Foreordained to be King. He wanted to tell her she was commanded to seduce him to disqualify him for the Throne. He wanted to tell her that he would release her father first thing if he survived the next six weeks. But he couldn't, and it pained him.

"Jason," she whispered. "I'm so sorry. For all of this."

"It's not your fault," Jason replied quickly, thinking of her father. "He forced you to do this. You're *so* brave for telling me, even now."

"Do you still love me?"

"Of course I do."

But it was different now, like a small hole had formed in his heart.

25 THE ALLY

It had been several days since Saryan's midnight confession, and nothing had happened to her yet. Maybe the King never caught wind of it? They were indeed very secluded during that conversation... not even his parents awoke for it.

It was interesting what it did for their relationship, though. For Saryan, it felt like a wall that was somehow invisible came crashing down. But for Jason, a wall had gone up. He tried to pretend it wasn't there, trying to convince himself that she still loved him, but he couldn't shake the knowledge that she was sent to seduce him. It's almost like they never should have met. A forced courtship.

But what would I have done in her situation? Her father is all she has. And now what's going to happen to her? What if the King decides to kill her father because Saryan didn't accomplish her mission? What do we do?

Today, Jason tried to forget those worries and fears. Maybe it was nothing to fret. After all, Tarren had nearly discovered his Foreordination and nothing had come of him yet. Today was a day to be in good spirits. Today was the day of Golan's wedding.

Saryan squeezed Jason's hand gently and nudged him, "That was beautiful."

"I agree..." Jason said. "I've never been to a wedding before."

"You haven't?" Saryan asked.

"I haven't," Jason said. "None of my friends have gotten married until today. I don't have any older siblings, or younger ones for that matter. I don't have any aunts or uncles, so today was my first."

Saryan's eyes sparkled.

Jason and Saryan's hands laced through each other's as they walked down the stone street of Nezmyth City, leaving the Cathedral and making their way to the Melding Hall. Several other couples and families surrounded them as they made their small trek through the street, everyone wearing their formal clothing and content smiles. An elegant white glove adorned Jason's right hand. Occasionally, he poked at a small, round parcel in his pocket anxiously. Pairs of soldiers passed left and right on the street.

Jason looked ahead as he spoke, "Have you ever imagined what your wedding day would be like?"

Saryan slid Jason a look. "Every girl in the world does, Jason. I always thought it would be a lot like this one," she continued. "My handsome groom waits for me at the door to the Cathedral, and as I come inside, he takes my hand as we walk down the aisle. All of my family is there, along with his. We kneel in front of the Patriarch's podium, and he explains the promises of eternal matrimony. Then we make our way to the Melding Hall to be locked together for time and eternity—two bodies, but one mind and one soul."

Jason's eyebrows jumped and he stiffened his lower lip, "Sounds like you have it all planned out."

Saryan smiled, "Have you ever thought about yours?"

"I have..." Jason conceded. "I've always thought more about the girl than the actual ceremony. What she'd be like."

"So what is she like?" Saryan asked.

Jason looked ahead. He couldn't make eye contact with her. Just then, Tarren, in his formals, zipped up from behind. Silently, he took Jason's other hand and leaned his head on his shoulder as they walked. Jason yanked his hand out of Tarren's before Tarren burst into chuckles.

"You're hilarious," Jason rolled his eyes as Saryan snickered next to him. "Shouldn't you be busy carving flutes or something? I didn't know you were invited to this."

"Sssh! I wasn't," Tarren said with a smile. He leaned in and whispered, "But Melding ceremonies always have free food. And Golan's parents are from Upper City! I bet they'll have pork, and cheese, and *freshly baked bread*. Oh! Is this her?" Tarren looked passed Jason and smiled at Saryan. He stretched out his hand. "I've heard so much about you! I'm Tarren."

Saryan politely put her hand out in front of Jason to shake Tarren's, "Oh, so you're Tarren! Jason's told me much about you, too. I'm Saryan. It's a pleasure to meet you."

"The pleasure is all mine," Tarren replied.

For a moment, Tarren's eyes glazed as he looked over Saryan's golden hair, silver eyes, freckles, dimples, and luscious figure. Saryan simply smiled back politely. Before Tarren's eyes could get too glossy, Jason cleared his throat to call him back to reality. Tarren blinked as if awoken from a very pleasant daydream.

"Well, it was nice to see you both," Tarren said. "I'll see you at the ceremony."

Saryan snickered some more as he awkwardly fell back into the crowd. "He must be very lonely."

"You could say that," Jason said.

"I have some friends I could introduce to him."

"They'll need to be some very special friends," Jason sneered.

Saryan sported her glowing white smile and patted Jason on the chest.

A massive, decorative building loomed over them on their right as the sun crept behind the mountains. The building was completely encircled by a stone and steel gate, which protected careless children from destroying the flawless green yard, well-trimmed shrubbery and vibrantly colorful garden.

The crowd walked through the open gates and strode down the stone walkway, entering into the exquisite building through tall, wooden doors. The brick exterior walls of the building were fading with age, but gave it a rustic beauty. Jason marveled at the sight, but Saryan merely grinned— Upper City girls have seen it all.

At the door, Golan and his dark-skinned, almond-eyed wife were dressed in their wedding formals and greeting the crowd. Jason grinned widely when he suddenly noticed a wooden ring adorning the wife's hand. People shook hands and hugged with great big smiles as they crossed paths, and it was no different with Jason and Saryan. After their round of congratulations and happy wishes they stepped inside.

As they entered into a banquet hall, the first thing Jason noticed was a band playing on a small stage in the far corner. Half of the entire hall was filled with round stone tables sporting plates, goblets and elegant flower centerpieces, and the other half was a polished ballroom floor. Dusk light from the tall windows crept in warmly. People slowly filed in and filled the tables. Saryan and Jason followed suit, walking down the length of the building hand-in-hand.

Jason pulled a chair out from the table and Saryan gracefully sat in it, thanking Jason as he pushed the seat in. Tarren jubilantly yanked a seat out next to Jason and sat down with his legs apart. A handful of sharply-dressed strangers jovially joined the three at the table.

Minutes passed as the crowd filled in and the carved sunlight crept across the stone floor. When the tables lost vacancy and the depth of crowd dispersed, the giant doors closed at the end of the building. The boom of the doors reverberated loudly and the crowd fell silent.

A lone man briskly walked across the ballroom floor as the band filled the hall with music. The delighted expression on his face was complemented by his swelling belly and his facial structure was almost identical to Golan's. He walked up the small staircase onto the stage and faced the crowd. His belly swelled once more with pride.

"Good evening, family and friends!" He bellowed, clasping his hands together in front of him. "It is my honor to preside over and perform the Melding ceremony of my son, Golan, and his lovely bride, Tarmanthia."

Everyone applauded. Golan's father's belly swelled again. "Would the couple please step forward?"

At the front of the tables, closest to the dance floor, Golan and Tarmanthia stood up. Golan took her hand, smiling sheepishly, and Tarmanthia returned the gesture by grasping his hand and smiling back. The two pushed their chairs back in and walked onto the floor. They stopped directly in front of a giant emblem in the middle of the room.

The band behind Golan's father stood silently on the stage, occasionally wiping their noses or shuffling their feet. Golan's father beamed.

"Son," he started. "I'm proud of you. I was nervous when you decided to choose a profession that wouldn't have you living in Upper City near your mother and I, but you chose something you loved, and I'm happy for you. Furthermore, you went on to find a beautiful woman that you can love with all of your heart, and now you stand here this day at the beginning of a beautiful and happy life together. Please step into the middle of the symbol."

Jason watched closely as Golan and Tarmanthia stepped hand in hand into the giant emblem. The emblem was covered by sunlight at this time, beaming radiantly from a well-placed window near the top of the building. Golan and Tarmanthia stood on the emblem, bathing in dusk sunlight and squeezing each other's hands tightly. Saryan sighed next to Jason.

"Guests," Golan's father continued. "If you haven't noticed, the symbol they stand on is a triangle enclosed inside a circle. It has great symbolic significance as the sunlight crosses it."

The crowd was hypnotically silent—every pair of eyes locked on the couple closely and every pair of ears hung on each word. Jason continued to poke at the tiny parcel in his pocket.

"The triangle is the most stable geometric shape," Mr. Terrace said. "May your marriage have stability and strength. The circle has no angles or sides. May your love continue through eternity. The sunlight... may you give each other warmth and joy as your bond perpetuates after death. Golan and Tarmanthia, from this day forth, you are both Melded together for eternity in the eyes of the Holy Dragon!"

After he said those last words, Golan's father pumped his fist into the air with his elbow bending at a right angle. The crowd followed suit.

"*For joy!*" Everyone shouted. It was followed by an eruption of applause and jubilant cheering. Golan and Tarmanthia turned to each other and kissed as they stood in the symbol.

"Thank you again for coming," Golan's father concluded. "Dinner is served!"

Golan and Tarmanthia retired to their table, all bearing enormous smiles as exquisitely-dressed waiters filed out to fill their empty plates. Each plate was quickly and efficiently filled with potatoes, roasted meat and steamed vegetables. Jason could hardly wait to dig in, but decided to be careful. Saryan, as she sat next to him, picked at her food and ate with extreme elegance, and Jason was very cautious not to look too sloppy sitting next to her. However, it was only a matter of seconds before Tarren's lips were covered with sauce and his mouth was filled to the brim with everything he could fit in.

The hall filled with the dull roar of conversation as the guests dined. Saryan and Jason exchanged words occasionally. Tarren was too busy stuffing himself. A few of the other guests accompanying them at their table must have been businessmen, because they constantly spoke of money and deals. Mostly, Jason ignored their conversation. He was never taught trade or business, only tidbits that Master Ferribolt had explained in passing during their Ancient

Nezmythian lessons. However, one part of their conversation leapt out to him as he listened to three of them.

"...wanted two hundred Blocks and eight Bars for it!"

"Over two hundred? Outrageous!"

"Well, he is the finest painter in the kingdom. He painted portraits for King Thomas years ago, may the Dragon give him rest..."

"I don't care how prestigious he is, if he asked that sum for a portrait that small I would have told him to pull up roots and move to Lunli Village!"

"You mean *Looney* Village!"

The three of them chuckled loudly with their mouths half-filled with food. Jason's heart contracted uncomfortably. He glanced at Tarren out of the corner of his eye. The three businessmen didn't notice it, but Tarren's gaze could have set them ablaze. He took a deep breath and wiped his mouth.

"I need some fresh air," he told Jason untruthfully. "Maybe I'll come back in when the dancing starts. With any luck, I'll find a nice girl."

With that, he pushed out his chair and stormed out. Saryan watched him concernedly as he escaped out a smaller side door on the opposite end of the hall. Jason sighed.

"Is he okay?" she asked.

Jason wiped his mouth with a napkin. "Don't ever mention Lunli Village around Tarren."

"The village where crazed people are sent to live?" she said. "Why?"

"Because that's where his mother is," Jason said.

Saryan looked like a wall of sorrow fell down on her. Jason leaned over and whispered as he explained:

"His mother was a seamstress—sometimes repaired uniforms for Nezmythian soldiers. One day, she was accused of speaking ill of the King by a random soldier seeking recognition. She was sentenced to prison. She was a sweet and gentle woman, a lot like my mother, but when she was finally released, she was... different. She would have visions of the guards still beating her. Months went by, and it kept getting worse and worse. When your son approaches to embrace you, and you run from him screaming, thinking he's a guard with a whip, you know there's nothing you can do. So they sent her to live in Lunli Village with others like her. It seemed like their only choice. He hasn't seen her in years."

Saryan was lost for words. Finally, she forced herself to ask, "How long was she in prison?"

"Almost a year."

Her eyes became glossy and worried. He knew she was thinking about her father. His heart panged at the sight.

He whispered. "I'll be right back, okay?"

Saryan nodded as he got up and left the table. He quickly made his way through the tables, dodging Upper City aristocrats and the occasional waiter. He was heading for the same door that Tarren had escaped out of, a smaller door that was much less conspicuous than the double-doors at the entrance of the Melding Hall.

He pushed the door open. He found himself on a brick pathway that snaked around the perimeter of the building. Along the walkway were perfectly-manicured trees and bushes, which were all budding leaves in the birth of spring. Tarren was just a few steps away with his hands on his hips. His eyes found Jason as he came through the door.

Jason was the first to speak. "Are you okay?"

Tarren shrugged. "I still miss her. And I hate it when people call it Looney Village... makes me want to throw a jeroki at their face."

"You should have," Jason smirked. "He could probably buy himself a new head anyway."

Tarren smirked in return. "So are you out here to comfort and console me in my time of woe?"

"No," Jason said. "I just needed some fresh air. It's a little crowded in there. And... there's been a lot on my mind."

"Like what?"

Jason went pink. He reached into his pocket and pulled out the small trinket he had been fondling all evening. It was a ring. The small band was just under the diameter of a coin—a well-polished silver, adorned by a modest blue sapphire Jason had purchased just for the sake of this project. He hadn't done much work with jewelry before, and this was his most expensive project yet, but it was also the work he had put the most love and thought into.

"So you're going to do it?" Tarren asked with wide eyes. "You're going to ask her to marry you?"

"I'm thinking about it."

"What do you mean *thinking about it?*"

"It's complicated."

Jason's heart was still sore from the night of her confession, and he found himself constantly second-guessing. Perhaps he should give himself time to tear down the wall that had sprung up, but how long would that take? King Barnabas' punishment could be just around the corner. Besides, he knew he wanted to spend his life with her. She was his best friend, and discovering her dire circumstances hadn't changed that. But complete forgiveness can be hard.

"Have you talked to her father yet?" Tarren asked.

"No," Jason answered. "Haven't even met him."

Tarren raised an eyebrow. "That's pretty risky."

"There are riskier things," Jason replied.

He handled the ring anxiously. He pictured himself bringing it out of his pocket in a balled fist, touching it against his beating heart and revealing it to the woman his heart called after, and as he did, his heart beat faster. He tried to control his breathing.

The crowd applauded on the other side of the door.

"Sounds like the dancing is about to start," he said with a thumping heart. He sneered at Tarren. "We need to find you some lovely Upper City girl to dance with."

"You mean I can't have yours?"

"No," Jason punched him softly. "Let's go."

As they both crossed through the threshold and into the main hall, Jason was astonished to see that every person was already on their feet in the ballroom. Saryan was sitting in the same place he had left her, twiddling a fork in her hand, staring off absently. Jason walked quickly toward her, trying hard not to let his knees knock together. When he finally approached her, he stretched out his hand, palm upward.

"May I have this dance?" He asked.

Saryan's eyes gleamed, "It's about time."

Saryan put her hand in Jason's and Jason led her carefully onto the dance floor, weaving through the many couples that elegantly floated across the floor as the band played in the distant corner. Jason silently hoped his sweaty palms and quickly beating heart wouldn't become too obvious, but knowing Saryan, it wouldn't be long before she read him like a book.

They found a spot amidst the crowd and stopped. Jason turned around to face her, and as he did, put his hand on her waist. Saryan placed her right hand gently on his left shoulder and their free hands clasped together. Jason looked deep into those sparkling silver eyes once more and gulped. Slowly, they shuffled their feet on the dance floor, not moving, but turning slowly in circles. Saryan blinked. Jason gulped again. He tried to clear his throat, but to no avail.

"Are you okay?" Saryan asked.

"Of course," Jason's throat was dry. "I'm fine."

Saryan's face became very sober, "You're upset from the other night. It's not hard to tell. Things have been different with us."

Jason didn't reply immediately. She was exactly right. He said, "Yes. Things have been."

She paused, looked down at their shuffling feet, then her eyes penetrated Jason's with unsettling openness.

"Jason..." she began. "I've been thinking... I understand if you don't want to see me anymore. You don't have to prolong this if you don't want to."

"That's not how I feel at all," Jason said seriously.

"The King will find out soon, if he hasn't already," she barely whispered. "I don't know if I'll even be alive for much longer. You and your family can live in my house—you've all been so kind to me. Just know that I loved you. I truly did."

"Don't talk that way," Jason breathed. The reality of her fate was suddenly becoming more real, and the thought of losing her was mortifying. "You're still here. Maybe he hasn't found out. We didn't do anything wrong. The Dragon is watching over us."

Saryan eyed him skeptically. She blinked a couple of times and said, "If you say so."

She rested her head on his shoulder as they danced. It was at that moment that Jason knew how terrified he was of the prospect of her gone. In his arms was the bravest girl he had ever known—his best friend, his truest love—and in his pocket was the key to having her forever.

So they danced. And inside, Jason battled with himself. She was still claiming to love him, even after she knew her life is in danger, but that wall that sprung up inside him was thick. She was sent to seduce him—the mission of a temptress. But she didn't want to, and they didn't do it after all. It was for her father. King Barnabas forced her. Everything she had gone through in the past several months... and she would definitely pay a price for her failure. He would miss everything about her, and when she was gone, that wall would come crashing down and his heart would have an even bigger hole than it already did.

If he didn't ask her, he knew in some later day he would regret it.

"Saryan," Jason whispered.

She pulled back and looked up into his eyes. Jason gazed back into them, his heartbeat accelerating.

"I love you too. Truly. I'm *so* sorry about your father and what you were required to do. If I could, I would just command all the pain and the uncertainty to go away. You're the bravest person I know. And I don't know what I would do if I were to lose you."

He reached in his pocket and extracted the ring. When Saryan saw it, her hands went to her mouth and her eyes grew wide, glistening. Jason swallowed.

"Saryan—."

BLAM!

Everybody in the room gasped and flipped around where they stood. Against the wall, the main doors had been flung open violently, revealing a small mob of Nezmythian soldiers. Every guest in the hall remained deathly still. Jason's fist clenched tighter against his chest and he bared his teeth behind closed lips. Saryan reached her hand toward Jason as she stared at the soldiers, her eyes ripening with fear. Jason took it tenderly. They knew why they were here.

The soldier at the front scanned the room fiercely, his eyes darting in his sockets under his metal helmet. No one breathed.

"Saryan and Tarren!" He called. "You know who you are, step forward!"

The people's heads swiveled on their shoulders as they surveyed the crowd, looking for the two perpetrators. All color left Jason's face. It was finally happening. Tarren and Saryan were being hauled away. The knowledge he had prayed would never reach the King had indeed reached him, and on a day like this.

With a gulp, Jason squeezed Saryan's hand and hesitantly let go, pushing through the crowd. Every pair of eyes fixed on him as he went. His palms became sweaty and his knees jittered. When he reached the rim of the wedding-goers, he didn't look the soldiers in the eye, but managed to mutter:

"What is their charge?"

"That is none of your concern," the soldier's booming voice echoed through the hall again. "We have orders directly from His Majesty, King Barnabas, to apprehend them immediately. They will be cast into prison."

If it were possible for the crowd to become any more deathly silent, it happened. Jason looked back behind him. He saw Saryan, standing all alone in the crowd and looking all sorts of horrified with wide eyes and a hanging jaw. Even from a dozen yards away, Jason could see her hands shaking. Tarren poked up through the crowd and joined Saryan at her side, his eyes filled with steaming rage.

"I'm innocent of anything!" he shouted. "This is injustice! But you know all about that, don't you? Stealing from starving Nezmythians—the people you're supposed to serve and protect. For what? A handful of Blocks in your pocket every month? The Kings of old look down on you in shame, along with the Sacred Dragon that built this kingdom!"

No one breathed. Tarren slipped his daggers from the holsters on his pants, his eyes fixed white-hot on the band of soldiers. Every word he spoke was full of venom.

"*You'll take my bloody, lifeless corpse, you devils!*" He bellowed. "If you can even manage that! *Come at me!*"

Jason was upon him. He grabbed Tarren by the collar and forced him to look him in the eye. His words came in frantic whispers.

"Don't make this worse than it already is!" he seethed. "There's nothing you can do, Tarren—there's a dozen of them. Do you think your father wants to come home to a dead son?"

"My father could be dead for all I know," Tarren didn't take his eyes off the soldiers.

Jason didn't have a response. It could be true. He could very well be dead. No one was allowed to communicate with the slaves at the eastern mountains, so they couldn't know for certain. Meanwhile, Saryan's eyes were glossy and blank, staring into nothing as if she had just seen a ghost. Her hands shook by her side.

It was the capstone to his nightmare. At this point, King Barnabas had successfully punished everyone Jason loved because of his Foreordination. His mother had been miraculously healed, but Jason held no hope of releasing Tarren and Saryan from the nefarious prison that awaited them. The only chance he had would be to survive his Year of Decision and immediately order their release, but the likelihood of that was dwindling.

Jason's eyes fell to his boots. "I'm sorry... I'm sorry for all of this. I wish there was more I could do."

They didn't have time to respond. The soldiers were upon them, forcing them and jostling them toward the door and tying up their hands as they went. Saryan managed to turn and make eye contact with Jason one last time before the double doors on the end of the hall slammed shut.

He never forgot the look in her eyes.

* * * * *

Jason's eye twitched in his sleep. The full moon made the curtains glow with an eerie haze. All was still. It was getting harder to sleep, and the pale moonlight blazing through the window didn't help. He was grateful that his room at Saryan's home had curtains.

Jason twitched again. The floorboards at the end of his room creaked. The curtains that blocked the moonlight had opened somehow, and the window softly creaked on its hinges. A soft, whispering wind crept into his room. Jason involuntarily pulled the covers tighter, and after a few chilly moments, his eyes fluttered open. He scanned the room, blurry and incoherent, and after spotting the open window, he groaned softly and sat up in his bed.

I thought I shut that? He thought.

He stalked over and grabbed the edge of the window, twisting a hook on the edge of the windowsill to seal it tightly. He yanked the curtains shut. Right as he turned around to retire back to his bed, his eyes shot open with alarm. His mouth froze with shock and ice water spilled through his veins.

Standing in the middle of his room, right at the foot of his bed, was the Person in the Dark Cloak. Its hood hung clear over its head, hiding the eyes. Jason squinted and his heart beat shakily. He remembered this figure. It had saved his life just months ago as King Barnabas tried to run his blade through him.

His eyes darted to his sword, which was on the other side of his bed. That was when the Dark Cloak spoke in the familiar deep, deathly voice.

"There is no need for that, Jason. I am a friend."

Still, Jason couldn't find his tongue. This being was perhaps as powerful as the King—the only thing that had paused him—and it was standing, talking to him in his own room. The fact that he meant no harm to Jason gave a dose of comfort, but the presence of the Cloak alone had an unmistakable ominous aura.

The Dark Cloak spoke again, "I know what you are, Jason. In less than two months, you could be the next King of Nezmyth."

Jason felt his blood freeze again. For a second he thought he was having a strange dream, but after feeling a sharp pain when he dug his fingernail into his palm, he concluded this was real. Or he was just mad.

"...Why are you here?" Jason finally croaked.

"To be a voice of assurance," the Cloak said. "I have been watching over Saryan's father while he is in prison. It has come to my attention that your two closest friends have been thrown into prison for your sake. I shall do what I can to protect them, although my powers are limited."

Jason's eyebrows bent. The strangeness of the event was undeniable. He continued to contemplate his own sanity after all that had happened recently, but only for a moment.

"Wait," Jason said. "Who are you, really? Why have you decided to help me?"

"In a moment, you will fall back asleep," said the Dark Cloak. "Good luck, my young friend. Believe, and all will be well."

"Wait! How do you know about...?" Jason's voice trailed off and became slurred as his vision became blacker and blacker. Unaware, he had limply fallen back onto his mattress in a sound sleep.

The Dark Cloak had vanished.

26 THE MOUNTAIN

Dusty sunlight spilled through the window onto Jason's bed. Saryan's home seemed so much emptier without her, even though she was just one of the four people who lived there. His parents had gradually grown to love her, as she would prepare them all breakfast each morning and go on outings with them. Kara especially became good friends with Saryan—any distrust she had melted away after a matter of days as they swapped stories in front of the fire. But neither Tomm nor Kara knew about Jason and Saryan's night together weeks ago. They couldn't, and for great reason.

Jason sat cross-legged on his bed. The thick sheets and plump mattress just wasn't as comfortable as they used to be. In his fingers, he rolled around the ring that he almost handed Saryan at the Melding Hall last week. The silver and sapphire still twinkled, despite their loneliness.

This should be on her finger right now, he thought bitterly. *But instead, she's got shackles on her wrists.*

He thought of Tarren, too. At this point, his entire family had been destroyed because of a corrupt King. His mother was driven mad, his father condemned to slavery, and he sentenced to prison. Jason wondered how many other families had been ripped apart in similar fashion. He tried not to think too hard about it.

On a cedar nightstand, directly by his bed, a rolled-up piece of parchment sat next to a lantern. It was tied up with an orange ribbon, handed to him from Master Ferribolt not long after his home had burned down.

"What's this?" he had asked him.

"This is a copy of your Blessing of Fate," Master Ferribolt responded. "I have every Blessing of Fate for every man in the kingdom stored away in this house. I assumed that your copy was destroyed along with your home, so I had this copy transcribed for you. You should read it often and heed the things it says. Please."

Jason remembered not knowing what to think as he extended his hand and took it from the Chief Patriarch. Ever since he was twelve, he hated the fact that the rest of his life was spelled out on that piece of parchment. He even hated the sight of it, from the blazing orange ribbon to the way the parchment crinkles and smells of old ink.

But now, Jason found himself in a different house, a month away from his Ordination as King. Things were different now. He had grown in a lot of ways over the past seven months, and now that Blessing didn't frighten him nearly as much as it used to.

He set down the ring. Carefully, he unraveled the ribbon on the Blessing of Fate and unrolled the parchment. The handwriting was different. Master Ferribolt wasn't rushing to copy down the words of a Patriarch like a Blessing Scribe would, so it was clearer and more legible. However, the words on the page were identical to what Jason remembered.

His eyes scanned each line from left to right, soaking in each word and phrase. He recalled tidbits of information, like admonitions to grow in goodness and nourish his relationships with his loved ones, but ultimately, he was waiting to read the last paragraph:

You will be a magnificent light that shines upon the world of Wevlia. You will imprison the vulture. You will restore the kingdom of Nezmyth to harmony and peace. Your blood is the blood of the next King of Nezmyth.

He read the paragraph over and over, and the last sentence echoed in his mind every time. *Your blood is the blood of the next King of Nezmyth.*

Jason paused and let that phrase sink in. In one month, that phrase would not only be a prophesy, but reality. His thoughts filled up a silence that echoed off the walls. He was so close, but what could happen in one month? In the past month, Tarren had nearly discovered his secret, Saryan had confessed her awful mission, and both of them were hauled off to prison. What would the King be planning now that he was so close?

...Is this really worth it? He thought to himself. *So much has happened to my loved ones during this year. And for what? Am I really prepared to lead a kingdom?*

Jason tightened his jaw and rolled the Blessing back up. After he tied the orange ribbon back on, he pushed himself off the bed and threw his sword onto his back. He lashed his tired, worn boots onto his feet and marched out the door.

Kara was busy sewing a new dress as Jason came down the hallway. Small spectacles, perched on the bridge of her nose, made it easier for her to see the needle. She looked up as Jason stormed by. Her focused, quiet expression turned to concern.

"Is everything alright?" she asked.

"No," Jason said blankly, thinking of Saryan and Tarren.

Kara paused, not sure how to reply, as Jason walked by. When he was finally at the door, she asked:

"Where are you going?"

Jason didn't look at her. He twisted the handle and pulled the door open, speaking half to himself and half to her.

"I'm not sure yet."

Jason closed the door behind him. He hadn't bothered to put on a jacket. The fading drift of winter still nipped at his nose and bare arms feebly as he made his way down the Upper City street. The snow had almost entirely disappeared and the trees were becoming greener with every day. Time passed quickly. As Jason was consumed in his thoughts, it felt like only a moment that he had absently wandered beyond the Southern Market Street and found himself on the rim of Lower City.

He passed by the corner where his flat used to be. All of the ashes were gone—likely blown away by the wind over the past two months. What was in those ashes? His old straw mattress? All of his old clothes? There was also no sign of rebuilding. What was left was an empty lot with two lonely trees and a stone walkway leading into nothing.

The cold dirt crunched under his feet as he continued on through Lower City. After a while, he passed by his house—the one his father and his coworkers were rebuilding. At this time in the afternoon, they were all still at the printing shop. The small cabin was almost completed. All it needed was some windows and a door. Jason didn't go inside, but he was sure it still needed a stove and furnishings.

He stood there, gazing at the new house—an exact replica of the one he grew up in. It was such a contrast from the home Saryan lived in. Saryan's home had separate rooms, padded furniture and animal fur rugs. Jason's old home was one room, with only an iron stove, one straw mattress and a table. He realized how lucky he had been to live in Upper City for the past two months. How do the people in the southernmost parts of Lower City feel? What did they live like?

He had never actually been there, he had only heard stories. None of the soldiers went there except on the day of the Harvest to collect what little the people had. Bands of street urchins constantly pilfered from each other. The homes were barely homes at all. Is life really like that down there?

With that thought in mind, Jason turned on his heels and walked south.

The walk into the slums of Lower City was a long one. The deeper and deeper Jason delved south, the darker the atmosphere became. Pairs of soldiers became less frequent. Small cabins turned to huts, which then turned into petty shacks and lean-tos. The people's expressions turned colder... weathered... dim. Hacking coughs accompanied the dirty faces and haggard clothes. Their eyes were void of any sparkle or sheen and they all seemed to stare at the ground absently.

At one point, Jason simply stopped and looked around. One hut to his right looked like it could collapse at any moment, and outside the door, a grimy-looking fellow was unconscious in a chair. Empty bottles of wine gathered at his feet. In the distance, Jason heard the frantic squawking of an angry woman, likely in a disagreement with a neighbor. A child, with a dirty face and no parents, drew pictures in the mud. The child spotted some bread crumbs in a patch of grass next to him and picked them out carefully.

One person amidst the crowd caught Jason's eye. An older lady carrying a heavy sack over her shoulder, her back bent forward, shuffled down the derelict street. Her hazy blue eyes ran deep with the struggles of past and present. Smudges of dirt and distress were smeared all over her face... but she had strong hands. She adjusted the burden on her back and continued to walk.

She finally came to a small shack just bigger than Jason's bedroom. As it stood, breathing filthy smoke out of a makeshift chimney, a small posse of children darted out of the edifice, shouting with delight and throwing their arms around the mystery woman. She stroked their hair lovingly and threw down the heavy sack by the door.

Jason kept his eyes on the sack, and he noticed the drawstrings around its mouth loosen as it hit the ground. A small piece of firewood toppled quietly from the top of the sack into the dirt.

Immediately, one of the boys from the group hurriedly dashed to the fallen bundle. He reached down, picked up the splintery wood and placed it carefully atop the others in the sack. He struggled with the drawstrings, seeing as the sack's mouth was barely out of reach. The woman walked up and tightened the sack shut, smiling gently at the boy before bending down and kissing his head. The rest of the children had retired back to the hut. Holding the small child's hand, the mother disappeared through the door.

Jason stood with mouth agape, his eyes stinging and a lump lodged in his throat. His gaze fell to his feet, and the back of his hand rubbed misty eyes.

"This is just small piece of what's happened in the past twenty years," a shaky, elderly voice came from behind.

Jason turned around. The guabo man stood with his cart of fruit rolling along behind him. A guabo was also in his hand, extended toward Jason. He took it silently. The man's cheery expression was gone, his eyes bleak, and his wrinkly jaw jutted out.

"I used to live in Upper City with my family," he said. "That was back when King Thomas reigned, may the Dragon give him rest... Lower City was a lot smaller. I was a Commander in the Nezmythian Army over the Upper City division of soldiers. When King Barnabas took the throne, I was forced out of my position, and I struggled to find another livelihood. When it looked as though we needed to move to Lower City, my wife left me and married another nobleman. The children followed after her... they missed their house and their horses and their expensive toys..."

Silence. Any response felt weak. Finally, Jason quietly asked, "...you had horses?"

The guabo man nodded silently. Jason spoke to the ground. "I'm sorry."

"Don't be," the guabo man sighed. "It happens to the best of us." A grin crept onto his face and his eyes sparkled faintly. "If it weren't for you, I don't think I'd still be around!"

"But this place is a disaster..." Jason said, scanning the landscape. "How could you be so grateful for this kind of life, especially after the one you lived?"

"There are worse things than poverty, my boy," the guabo man continued. "Riches are fleeting. They may grant you toys and trips, but none of those things grant lasting happiness. Your free will... your identity... your *integrity*... none control those but yourself, and when you find joy in those, *that* is when you are truly happy."

Goosebumps had risen on Jason's arms and legs with the wind sliding around his body. The sun would set over the distant mountains in just over an hour. He caressed the sheath on his back.

"You saw that woman come home to her family," the guabo man said. "Her children were dressed in rags—they didn't even have shoes—but they weren't any less happy. That's what some of these people have learned to live with as their numbers have grown over the years. The Dragon knows how long these people have been waiting for someone to turn this mess around..." he spoke quietly, even though no soldiers were in sight.

Jason's head turned to the guabo man. He tried to imagine a Nezmyth City without Lower City. That single mother would be living in a nicer home with room for her children to grow and learn in. They would have more space for their studies (*Do they even go to school?* Jason thought), more toys, maybe even more friends. Maybe the guabo man would even be back in Upper City.

"You're a good man," Jason said.

"You are too, my boy," he said. "Every time I see you, I can't help but think that you will do great things. I wish you the best of luck. But I need to get home and drop off this blasted cart... I'll be seeing you."

Without another word, the guabo man continued down the dirt street deeper into Lower City. Jason stood, feet planted, at the same spot he had been in for the past few minutes, reflecting on what had just happened. The guabo was still in his hand.

These people deserve so much better... how could a person even as arrogant and blind as King Barnabas turn a cold shoulder to this...?

An idea popped into his head... a wonderful, inspired idea. He spun on his heels and hustled back up the street toward Center Court. But before he did, he handed the guabo to the little child playing in the mud.

He passed more people as he made his way up the street—there were less people out and about as the evening grew older. The familiar orange and purple shades of twilight were splashed across the Nezmythian sky.

A hill in the far distance caught Jason's eye. He could travel all the way up into Center Court, then make a right and walk east for over an hour to his destination. He took a shortcut through Lower City, making his way to a hill on the eastern edge of Nezmyth City... Grace Mountain.

Jason massaged the sheath of his sword. The shacks and lean-tos were gradually turning back into simple houses. The glowing candles in the windowsills were becoming more visible in the dimming light. He looked at the ground as he walked, then looked at the sky, then he looked at the ground again.

He saw the rooftops of the Southern Market Street buildings a little farther northward and walked almost parallel to them, alone. His boots on the dirt path made the only sound in the evening air. Soldiers marched by occasionally, but made no confrontation with him. The nipping breeze was getting colder and colder as the sun glided down the skyline.

After a long while of thoughtful walking, the houses dispersed and grew farther apart. The urban landscape of Nezmyth City waned and relinquished to the rural fields and cottages of the agricultural edge of town—Eastern City. In the far distance, a small mountain stood majestically with a winding stone path leading up to the peak.

Jason glanced around. Some cows, horses and sheep were still out in the birth of night, some resting on the soft, cool grass and others retiring to their barns and stables. It wasn't much longer before the houses disappeared along the path and the landscape gave way to endless fields and trees. He took a deep breath—the air was crisp and fresh. The breeze caressed his cheek. All was quiet.

It was another long while before the dirt road abruptly transformed into a smooth stone path and wound its way up the landscape to Grace Mountain. Night had fallen upon Nezmyth. On the left side of the path, a vast field of thick, swaying grass rested at the foot of the mountain. The perimeter thereof was fenced off by a tall iron gate. Within the caged field, tall, wide grey stones were dotted everywhere in rows and columns. Jason spotted the entrance gate. It was tall and wide enough for a carriage to enter. Jason walked through when he reached it. Above the gate, words cut out of iron read: NEZMYTH CITY CEMETERY

The gate led to a separate stone path that cut straight through the Cemetery. That central path kept straight and constant, with several other paths breaking off of it like small stone rivers cutting through the field. Jason walked and walked until he had reached a secondary path exactly perpendicular to the central path. It only existed for about one hundred yards before it came to another fenced section.

Jason's mind wandered as his feet absently moved him forward. He thought of Saryan and Tarren cooped up in a small jail cell, trying at this time to desperately fall asleep on a miniscule patch of hay after a meal of stale bread and water. His forehead creased. *What else is the King going to do now that it's so close?*

He reached the fenced section and stopped. The gate was winding, elegant, and constructed of the finest steel. There was a sign just above his head.

COURT OF THE KINGS

Below those characters, he recognized some Ancient Nezmythian writing. He squinted his eyes and read, "*May the Dragon give rest to these Foreordained.*" He entered.

Jason's eyes went from left to right as he gazed on the resting places of past Kings of Nezmyth. Each grave stone was chosen by each King throughout the centuries. The first ones Jason saw were still written in Ancient Nezmythian.

One gravestone looked like a commoner's—obviously a more humble King who loved the people dearly. Some raised clear above Jason's head and had letters that wound around all sides. He kept down the path until he reached the last gravestone... the most recent.

King Thomas. The gravestone was flat on the top, as tall as Jason and as wide as his arm, perfectly square at the bottom. Mounds of flowers both fresh and wilted were strewn around the base. Jason gazed at it as the stars came out in and blinked against their black canvas. The writing was thick and clearly legible, even in the dark.

KING THOMAS
MASTER OF CHARITY, LOVE, AND JUDGEMENT
AS HE SO LOVED THE PEOPLE OF NEZMYTH,
SO WAS HE LOVED BY THE DRAGON
FIND PEACE IN ETERNITY
BIRTH – 4.3.2.5001
DEATH – 8.2.5.5042

He was forty-one years old... Jason thought. *And he died almost exactly twenty years ago. King Thomas...*

Jason's gloved hand found the hilt of his sword by his ear. Slowly, he pulled the blade out of its sheath and flipped it around to where his thumb was next to the pommel. He gazed at the sword, then the grave stone.

"How am I going to be like you...?" He thought out loud.

He shoved the point of the sword into the ground between his feet. As his blade stood erect, he rested both of his hands on the pommel. Jason muttered to the breeze as his eyes remained fixed on the grave.

"Everyone talks about you," Jason said. "You reigned over Nezmyth before I was born. You sound like you were so perfect—so honest, and just, and kind. But the King right now is the complete opposite. And I know that anyone would be better than him, but I'm only a month away, and I

still don't know why *I* have to be King. I just wish you were
here to talk to me. Maybe you would have some of the
answers I need."

The gravestone stood against the wind, firm and
unshaken. Jason stood quietly for moments, waiting, hoping
that some sign, some voice, a breath would come to comfort
him. But it was not to be. Jason withdrew his sword from
the ground, slowly slipping it back into its sheath and gazing
at the array of flowers around the King's grave. Jason's eyes
reverted to Grace Mountain, just above him. He sighed, gave
one last respectful glance at the resting place of King
Thomas' mortal body, and departed back down the path.

He retraced his steps: exiting the Court of Kings... down
the path... back up the main path... and back onto the stone
road leading to Grace Mountain.

As he resumed his present course toward Grace
Mountain, the grade of the hill gradually became steeper.
Jason's feet were becoming sore from so much walking and
his legs were pulling at him from the steep climb. The stars
danced in the black sky as they stared back down at Jason
from infinity. The breeze clung to him, making him shiver.
His gloved right hand remained warm.

The climb wasn't a short one. His breathing became
deeper as he made his way up the winding path. Finally, at
the top of the peak, the pathway spread out to a creamy white
plateau. One enormous monument stood out in the middle
of the grounds—it was the reason Jason had walked so far.
The increased wind whipped at Jason as strode toward it.

From Grace Mountain, Jason had a full view of
Nezmyth City—even Upper City and the castle. Thousands
of dimly lit windows emitted candlelight like pinpoints
underneath the brilliant moon and glittering stars, creating a
sea of orange and black in the valley. Jason marveled at the
sight. He thought about this fantastic world that the Dragon
had created—every grain of sand and drop of water working
together.

The monument he had come for wasn't difficult to make out in the nighttime. It was square at the base and very tall—twice as tall as Jason. The workmanship around the base was elaborate and although it was very large, its size isn't what stood out.

On top of the square base, a sculpture of the Holy Dragon wound and twisted its long, scaly body. Its head gazed down to the onlookers and its powerful claws clutched the edge of the stone. The sculptor had done a wonderful job of giving the Dragon an appearance of power while filling the eyes with the endless understanding of the eternities.

Jason blinked at it and inhaled, letting the breath seep back out his nose. He stood in the spot where the sculpture of the Dragon looked directly into his eyes. It was a little unsettling, but strangely, in a way, calming.

Grace Mountain, Jason thought, *The spot where the Holy Dragon first reached out its claw to piece together the world of Wevlia... the highest point in Capitol Valley. This is a sacred place.*

Jason remained where he stood, his feet planted. He gazed back into the eyes of the stone Dragon as if searching for something untold... some secret that might bring rest to his uncertain heart and the weary people of Nezmyth. He could almost hear its smoky breath, rumbling deeply in the distance.

Just like he did at King Thomas' grave, Jason extracted his sword from his sheath. But this time, he didn't thrust the sword into the ground. The sword rested horizontal in his hands, and he gently lowered it onto the stone as if giving an offering. He kneeled down, his elbow propped on one knee, and he bowed his head. Quietly, the words came.

"Holy Dragon... I come before Grace Mountain, the birth place of Wevlia and the kingdom of Nezmyth, seeking answers to my heart's questions.

"O Dragon... doubt overtakes me. This year has been harder than anything I have imagined. I feel that I'm constantly being watched, my friends and family have all suffered for my sake, and they don't even know it. King

Barnabas rules with no mercy, and as I stand on the threshold of my ordination, I don't know what to do.

"Is this all worth it? I know that the kingdom needs a King—a good King—but does it have to be me? I don't know anything about ruling a kingdom. What am I supposed to do?"

He stopped and listened, not with his ears, but with his spirit. After a long moment, he felt nothing... just the chill of the wind. He felt no inspiring words, no soft burning inside him, just... nothing.

Jason bent his eyebrows. "Holy Dragon, what should I do *right now*?"

At that moment, something twanged inside him— something dark. His eyes shot open on the alert and his body ran icy cold. One word rang through his entire body and entered into his mind:

RUN.

Everything hit Jason at once. The night had darkened. The sun was completely over the distant mountains, and he was all alone on the edge of the city. If there was a perfect time for the King to kill him, it would be now. He had been gone for hours—how long would it take for the King to send another assassin his way?

Jason didn't hesitate. He snatched his sword off the ground, rammed it into its sheath and bolted down the mountain.

His heart pounded. He picked up his feet as fast as his legs would allow as he soared down the winding stone path to the foot of Grace Mountain. The Nezmyth City Cemetery lay dormant to his right.

Jason shot glances all around him as he ran. He knew once he was in the urban landscape of Nezmyth City, an assassin could be anywhere. He passed the rural farmland. Sweat poured down his face and onto his filthy shirt. The houses were progressively becoming denser. The fields of Eastern City lay behind him. The cobblestone of the Southern Market Street was wide enough that no one could drop in on him abruptly. Nonetheless, Jason kept his concentration sharpened.

Suddenly, a large, black blob flew down from a rooftop several yards in front of him. Jason's eyebrows furrowed and he gritted his teeth. He came upon it within a few sprinting strides.

Jason tore out his blade and slashed it in front of him. The loud clang of blade connecting with blade rang through the endless starry night. The moon shined its bright light into the streets, allowing Jason to see the foe. The image he saw in front of him was almost identical to the one he fought more than a month ago—a tall figure garbed completely in black.

Jason thought with lightning speed. As soon as he had blocked the vertical slash from the assassin, he swung his sword aside, pushing the opponent's blade out of harm's way. He raised his left hand.

"*Cayloon!*" He shouted with fervor.

The white ball erupted from his palm with a *crack* at point-blank range, finding its mark directly in the sternum of the assassin. The assassin soared backward at breakneck speed for only a second before it crashed into a tall stack of hay outside a shop. The bails toppled down to the ground, burying the unconscious foe in dry, prickly hay.

Jason wasted no time. He darted into an alleyway toward Center Court, inwardly praying that this one would be the only one he would encounter on his flight home. Just as he disappeared into the mouth of the alley, he felt a jeroki zip behind his head.

He forced himself to run faster. After just a moment, he felt more jerokis shoot passed him, missing him by less than inches. He didn't turn around—he knew it was another assassin charging him down, and he knew it was probably gaining on him. He shot onto another pathway to his left.

Jason dodged in and out of alleyways until he eventually broke into Center Court. Here he knew he was a fish in a

barrel, but it was the fastest way to his temporary home in
Upper City.

A dagger clanged at his feet just as Jason tore by the
enormous statue of King Barnabas. He flipped around to
face the attacker just as it was hurling a jeroki at his head.
Jason swiped and managed to dissipate it. The assassin
stormed toward Jason, hurling one jeroki after another until
one finally collided with Jason's shoulder—his previously
wounded shoulder.

Jason cried out in agony and fell to the ground, his sword
clanging just out of reach. The assassin darted forward,
flaring its dagger and ready to pounce.

He had no time to scramble for his sword—the assassin
would be on him in a flash. In a hasty decision, he threw out
the quickest, most powerful magic he could muster. For the
first time, he thrust both his hands forward and focused on
intense heat, the scorching breath from the mouth of the
Dragon.

"*Mohlah!*" He shouted to the sky.

It was like an eruption from his hands. Blue beams shot
from his palms, pushing him into the ground. It felt like two
raging pythons were attached to his wrists. He forced the
beam forward with all of his mind and spirit, and they found
their mark in the assassin's chest. The black clothing gave
way to charred, smoking flesh as it cried out to the sky. It
dropped its dagger and fell to the ground, curled up and
shaking.

Once again, Jason wasted no time in scooping up his
sword and bolting toward Upper City. Sweat dripped from
his hair and covered his face and chest. He peeled onto the
Northern Market Street and ran for the street leading to
Saryan's home.

But will I even be safe there? Jason thought. *What if there's
another one waiting for me just inside? Is there anywhere safe at all
right now?*

He ran and ran, and it wasn't long before it finally hit him.
Master Ferribolt!

It was his one safe haven from the eyes of the King. He knew he could find refuge there. But what was the chance he could make it beyond the gate and the front door before being ambushed again? What other choice did he have?

As he turned onto the Upper City street leading to the Chief Patriarch's mansion, he froze. His mouth went dry and his knees became water. In his way stood a positively enormous man—the size of Bobby the Brute, and then some. In each hand, a ball with metal spikes hung from a chain. The giant was completely masked in the familiar black cloth, another assassin.

Jason's heart dropped into his stomach, but he tried to remain calm. With any luck, Jason would be faster than him and could simply run around him. Men these sizes typically aren't quick at all.

Not the case. The foe bent down and charged at Jason with just as much speed as the last two. Jason threw two jerokis at it as it charged, but they did as much good as balled-up pieces of parchment.

The brute raised its weapon to the sky. Jason had just enough time to dive out of the way before it came crashing down, leaving a crater of soil and stone in its wake. The foe swung its other spiked ball at Jason's head. Jason ducked without a blink of time to spare.

He lifted his blade to attempt a crippling slash, but the brute thrust out an elbow that caused Jason to topple onto his back. When he hit the ground, he had just enough time to roll out of the way before another ball came crashing down on where he was.

Jason had already sprinted all the way from Grace Mountain and had battled two assassins previously. His knees jittered and his heart thrashed inside him in a way it never had before. He felt himself teetering on the brink of exhaustion, but he couldn't stop now. He was so close.

Mustering all the strength that he could, Jason slashed at the brute's leg just as he had narrowly dodged another blow. His blade made contact. The giant cried out, and blood immediately began to seep down its leg and foot. Its knee shook, but it stayed standing.

With what time he had, Jason swiped his hand across his blade and cried out, "*Mohlah Eelohda matah!*" Immediately, the sword burst into flames. He reminded himself that the fate of Nezmyth hung in the balance. He focused his thoughts on his love for his family, including Saryan and Tarren.

He had to survive tonight, for everyone.

With that, Jason brandished his sword, ready for the next move. When he did, a burst of fire leapt from the tip of his sword and travelled through the air. The brute lifted its arm to shield its face from it. Jason spent only a second gawking before taking advantage of the new power. He slashed and swiped at the air mercilessly as if fighting an invisible force right before him. The sword spat fire every direction it swung until the foe was completely bombarded with fire.

Jason breathed hard. He lifted the blade over his head, and with justice raging in his eyes, bellowed to the air:

"*For Nezmyth!*"

The last slash was the brightest and most intense. An enormous wave of fire leapt over the assassin and settled on its garb. Within moments, the brute was completely engulfed in flames, like an enormous, burning phantom. It dropped its spikes and chains and bolted down the street, yelling and heading for a fountain outside of a Northern Market Street building.

With what little strength Jason had left, he ran for Master Ferribolt's house. It wasn't long until he had reached it. Miraculously, the gate was open just a crack, just enough for him to slip through. After he had leapt up the walkway and onto the porch, he grabbed for the doorknob. Once again, out of divine providence, it was unlocked. He threw it open and jumped inside, closing it behind him.

As he sank to the floor on the other side, he let his sword clang to the ground. Breathing came in great, frenzied breaths. Even his mind felt exhausted from using so much magic in one night.

Suddenly, the door clicked as if to lock shut. It was only then that Jason noticed that Jerem was standing directly beside him, looking down on him oddly. What was even more peculiar was that Master Ferribolt had moved his favorite chair into the main hall, facing the door, and he was sitting in it, wearing his night robe and peering at an Ancient Nezmythian book through his spectacles.

Jason gawked at both of them, not sure what to make of the situation.

"Well," Master Ferribolt began. "When I prayed to the Dragon today, I asked what I could do to better help you in your journey. I suddenly felt inspired that I should leave the gates and the door unlocked this evening. Strange…" he chuckled. "Is it really a wonder that we don't find answers to our questions until the most unexpected moment?"

Jason still didn't know what to say. His breathing was still frantic, and his eyes wild. Master Ferribolt simply ogled at him amusedly.

"You look like you've had an eventful evening," he said.

27 THE OATH

The vulture's rustled feathers were the result of dozens of sleepless nights as time ate away at its energy. The afternoon sun scraped at its icy, irritated eyes. It scowled with an inner loathing that came directly from its twisted soul.

The dusty wasteland that stretched to the horizon was interrupted only by an enormous tree that stood healthy, erect and green to the sky some miles away from the dead tree on a hill. The tree's branches reached out in every which way with thick, luscious leaves rustling in the breeze. The tree, merely a sapling a year ago, had grown into something mighty.

The vulture growled. The highest branch on the writhing, dead tree on a hill had grown weary of its ungrateful talons clutching to it so desperately.

Several feet below, the eagle looked onto the tree with pride. It wouldn't be long now. The eagle decided not to speak - it didn't need to. After all, it knew what was churning in the vulture's mind.

The vulture let out a controlled cry of rage and leapt off the branch. It fell for dozens of feet before, as it was about to hit the ground, it flapped its wings roughly. The vulture landed with a deep thud, its sharp talons clutching the dry dirt below. It paced back and forth. Its head hunched over and its powerful breasts rising and falling with every fuming breath. Back and forth it went, muttering.

The dark eagle watched the scheming vulture from above.

"If you're considering your options," the eagle said. "The best one is to give up."

"*Silence!*" the vulture spat at the eagle, its eyes wild. "It is *not* over! It isn't over until that tree is shriveled and twisting in agony where it stands! I've gone too far to be removed from my place by an insolent sapling!"

"But it seems as though that time has come," the eagle said. "I find it interesting how, after so long, you are still hesitant to give up this miserable wasteland. Maybe it is finally time for more flowers to spring from their roots. Perhaps it is time for the grass to cover the dry, cracked dirt—."

"*I said, silence!*" the vulture shot with a twitching eye. "This land is *mine!* I fought for it, and I live for it! Something a creature of privilege like you would never understand—."

"You live for it?" the eagle echoed heatedly. "You believe it lives for *you!* Do not lie to yourself as you've lied to countless others, you coward!"

The vulture wanted to say something cutting and offensive, but conjured nothing. It merely snarled its beak at the eagle, who took no thought of it. The eagle sighed.

"I've protected this tree for years," the eagle said. "Now that it is so close to fulfilling its potential, I will make sure that you do not do *anything more* to corrupt it. You shall not leave my sight."

There was a short, deathly pause before the vulture let out an unfiltered bellow of rage. It echoed through the night, finding its journey through oblivion. The vulture turned and flew up into the tree, darting directly for the eagle.

The dark eagle braced itself for the attack.

* * * * *

The sun was just cracking over the mountains and Jason could see his breath flowing out from his lips. The nipping cold of early morning hadn't yet relented to the cozy, spring afternoon warmth, and the Southern Market Street was currently devoid of any shoppers. His index finger traced the hilt of his blade as his eyes shifted from left to right across the street. The soldiers patrolling the streets eyed him as he walked by. Jason tried not to return their gaze with heat—it was difficult not to since Saryan and Tarren's imprisonment.

He turned and walked towards a modest building, twisting the handle and entering. The machines in the shop were already activated. Golan was shuffling about the room, busying himself with some recent orders. He looked up as he heard the door close.

"How's the married man doing?" Jason called.

The corners of Golan's mouth stretched and he returned to his work.

Jason didn't immediately walk beyond the front desk, but simply stood at the door. His eyes dreamily scanned each board in the ceiling... the table that had hosted so many lunchtime conversations, laughing employee discussions and hundreds of design plans. He gazed at the crunching, belching machines that had served alongside him and the others for these years they had owned the shop—there were minimal problems with any of them.

There wasn't much work to be done today. Jason would have less work than usual. He didn't hang up his jacket on the coat rack, and he didn't even bring a glove for his left hand. He approached Golan.

"How's Tarmanthia?" he asked.

"She's doing really well, thank you," Golan said brightly. "My father purchased a house in the lower portion of Upper City, almost right by the market street. Everyone is asking us when we'll start a family, but we want to wait a while... until it feels right, you know?"

"That's great," Jason grinned. "So it would probably help if you were making more money each year, wouldn't it?"

"I suppose…" Golan said quietly. "Speaking of yearly things, isn't your eighteenth birthday coming up soon?"

"Yes, but that's not important," Jason said. "Golan, I want to talk to you about something that is."

Golan lobbed him an inquisitive look and blinked. "Sure."

Jason took a breath. *How am I going to say this…?* "Remember when Kristof was training all of us as his apprentices? This place wasn't doing too well. With the taxes and the four teenage boys he had to train, he had lot on his plate. That was a rough day when he finally had to leave, wasn't it? It was hard for all of us."

"Yes, I remember," Golan said reverently. "I still miss him. It's hard to believe that it's almost been two years."

"I agree," Jason sighed. "Life travels quickly. The bottom line is that some things are coming up in my life, Golan… big things. I'm not going to be around here much longer."

"Oh, why? What's going on?"

"I can't really say…" Jason looked at the floor. "But this is why I asked you to come early today. Bertus and Jaboc are great friends, but I know they wouldn't take this as well as you would. They would try to talk me out of this when I really don't have a choice anyway."

Jason took his keys from out of his pocket. He circled through the few keys he had and found the set to the front door of the shop. Golan looked on with glassy eyes. Jason held out the key to him.

"I'm leaving the shop for good," Jason said. "I want you to find an apprentice to replace me—a boy from Lower City, just like me. Teach him everything we learned from Kristof, and give him a job and a chance for a better life."

Golan looked into Jason's eyes, then to the keys in his hand, then back at Jason. This came out of nowhere. He hadn't warned any of his coworkers previous that he would be leaving the shop. It could have led to explaining the reason why, and that of course was confidential.

"…You're serious?" Golan almost looked hurt.

"Yes," Jason said. "I'm not coming to work today—probably not ever again. It's hard, but this is how things need to be."

Golan reached out and gingerly took the key from Jason's grasp as if they were something holy. The humming machines provided the only sound in the shop other than the creaking floor. Jason adjusted his jacket as the chilly air nipped at his fingers and nose.

"It won't be the same not having you around," Golan said.

"Thank you," Jason said. "I'll miss you all as well. I'm sorry I didn't warn you. This was going to happen eventually."

"We'll still see you every once in a while, right?" Golan said. The keys were still lying in his open hand. "You can't be going far."

Jason paused. He thought about rolling up to the shop in a Kingly carriage pulled by a pair of white stallions. He would step out of the carriage with a billowing cape and a valiant stroll up to the door as his former-employees hailed him with reverence. *Me? Wearing a cape?* The thought was amusingly alien.

"Of course," Jason said warmly.

Golan grinned satisfactorily. They both took a step forward and exchanged a brotherly embrace.

"But honestly, where are you going?" Golan asked as they both stepped back. "Are you still going to be in Nezmyth City?"

"Yes."

"Doing what?"

"I can't say."

"Really?"

"Mmhm."

"Are you sure…?"

"Positive. Please don't ask me. You'll see soon enough."

Golan fell silent. He looked at the floor, decided not to pursue the mystery, looked up and said, "Thank you, Jason. It's been a pleasure."

"Thank *you*, Golan, for being the good man you are. Besides, without me, it means all of you will be making a little more money. And things will only get better from here."

"What do you mean?"

"Nothing…" Jason said. "Take care of this place for me, will you?"

Golan grinned brightly, "Of course. Take care."

Over the hum of the machines, neither Golan nor Jason said a word as Golan went to work and Jason made his way to the door. Just before he was about to twist the handle, he stole a glance over his shoulder.

The shop that he had called his own for the past two years, the shop that had paid for his rent, his clothes, his food… was now out of his hands… gone. As he gazed out, he could almost see the ghost of his younger self working alongside the strong and fatherly Kristof. He could hear Jaboc's teasing remarks, Bertus' comebacks, the endless laughs, the financial strains… they all combined into an experience he dubbed as priceless. And yet, those years were now fading into the caverns of history, never to be reclaimed.

Jason's throat tightened and his eyes started to sting. Under his breath, he spoke to the floorboards.

"Goodbye."

He unlatched the door and stepped out to the bitter spring morning, the resolution in his mind to venture to the library where he would spend the afternoon studying Ancient Nezmythian.

He didn't have the opportunity. Just as he had walked out the door, a familiar blue coach pulled by a pair of stallions was right in front of the store, seemingly waiting for him. The familiarity of the carriage wasn't pleasant. The last time he was in it, he recalled being knocked cold and tied up by a pair of soldiers. Suddenly, the door flung open, and out came the head of the Advisor, his searing red eyes fixed on Jason.

"Hello, Jason," he said mechanically.

Jason didn't answer immediately. "Good morning."

"Step inside," the Advisor instructed.

Jason caressed the sheath on his back. His first instinct was to run, but he knew that wouldn't be wise. Almost no one was on the Southern Market Street... no one to ask questions as to why he was being picked up personally by the King's Advisor in his royal coach. Jason breathed deeply and strode up to the carriage, forcing himself inside and sitting across from the Advisor.

There were no soldiers in the carriage, just him and the Advisor. The Advisor continued to gaze at Jason like an insect, and Jason didn't return eye contact. When the Advisor slammed the door shut, the stallions crawled to a trot, venturing toward the Northern Market Street.

"You have two weeks until your Ordination date," the Advisor said. "Congratulations."

Jason didn't look at him. "Thank you."

"Has the past year been difficult?"

It took everything Jason had not to return the absurd question with a scowl. He simply breathed deep and replied, "It indeed has."

"Of course," the Advisor said. "I am sure you are curious as to why you are being summoned. Seeing as your Year of Decision is reaching its climax, certain rites must be carried out. They will be explained further at the castle."

Of course, Jason thoughts echoed the Advisor's words as he stared out the window. As the morning grew older, more people were out on the Northern Market Street. Some of them turned and looked as they saw the royal carriage crawling up the street. If only they knew who was inside.

The rest of the journey continued in silence, and it was almost an exact mirror of what Jason remembered from seven months ago. They travelled the same Upper City streets leading to the castle. They passed through the same front gate. The castle grounds were just as dry and cold as they last were. Everything was the same... stoically, chillingly the same. It felt like no time at all before Jason and the Advisor were standing before the great castle doors.

The Advisor gave the order to open it. Three times the soldier slammed the door with his giant hammer. Jason remained where he stood, his hands still in his pockets and his sword slung over his back. He could hear each slam reverberate off the inside walls of the castle, and after a small wait, the monstrous doors slowly edged open as the soldiers grunted and heaved on the other side. The Advisor walked through first, with Jason following on his heels.

His heart thumped. He remembered that the last time he saw King Barnabas in person he was seizing the opportunity to kill him.

Maybe this will be another one of his attempts, he thought coldly. But inside, something told him that this wouldn't be one of those cases.

The long, red carpet stretched its way from the door to the throne platform and soldiers stood like statues around the perimeter of the hall. Everything was just as he remembered it from over four months ago. Thankfully, he wasn't strapped to a chair on the edge of death this time. At least not yet.

The door behind them finally edged shut proceeding the grunting of straining soldiers. He could see King Barnabas in the Throne, hunched over with his laced fingers touching his lips and his elbows on his knees. He only looked at him for a moment.

His fingers traced the sheath behind him. His heart thumped quickly. Finally, Jason stopped walking when he was a few yards away from the throne platform. He caught sight of King Barnabas' black sword leaning against the side of the throne and swallowed. He dropped to one knee and bowed his head reverently to the King, as he was supposed to.

When he stood, he noticed the loathing in King Barnabas' eyes was the only familiar thing in his countenance. His beard was thicker. His hair wasn't as tidy as usual. The Advisor took his spot at the right side of the Throne and turned about to face Jason.

"Shall we begin?" The Advisor said.

The King didn't acknowledge the question. Regardless, the Advisor gave a signal to a soldier, who marched up to him promptly. The soldier reached the Advisor and handed him a small sheet of wood with some parchment attached to one side. The Advisor thanked him with a nod and conjured a writing stick from his garbs. The soldier turned mechanically on his heels retreated back to its post.

Jason eyed King Barnabas, who was bearing his teeth at him from behind his hands. Jason thought he saw his eye twitch.

"As I have before mentioned, your Year of Decision is nearing completion," the Advisor continued. "Congratulations. In two weeks, if you follow suit as you have already done, we will ordain you King of Nezmyth. I will remain your Advisor, and His Majesty, King Barnabas, will step down from the Throne."

King Barnabas shifted his feet uneasily. He took his hands apart and sat up straight, trying with everything he could muster to keep a straight, undaunted face. His eyes bore into Jason's face like fiery coals. Jason frowned when he saw Barnabas' fists clenched so tightly his knuckles turned white.

"Naturally," Jason said.

"Have you considered what measures you will take as King if and when you obtain the Throne?" The Advisor asked.

"Yes."

"Go ahead," the Advisor said, readying his paper.

Jason looked at King Barnabas. He looked away from Jason as if he were an insect crawling across the floor. Jason eyes reverted to his boots and he picked at some of the ideas floating across his mind. He looked to the Advisor.

"I'd like to refrain from dictating what I will do when I rule this kingdom until after I've actually claimed the throne. For right now, I have only one request," Jason said.

The Advisor lifted his eyes to Jason's and blinked.

Jason inhaled. "I have some friends in prison that I would like to have at my Ordination Ceremony; my best friend, Tarren, my love, Saryan, and her father. They are some of my closest friends, and I can't imagine celebrating that occasion without them."

The Advisor nodded subtly and his writing stick scooted across the parchment. King Barnabas' breathing was heavy and his lip was trying not to curl. His fingers stroked the pommel of the dark blade, which leaned up against the side of the Throne. As Jason eyed it, a shiver slid down his back.

"Is that all?" The Advisor asked, not taking his eyes off the paper.

"That is all," Jason replied.

"Very well," the Advisor said. "We will announce to the kingdom the Foreordination of a new King shortly, but your identity will remain anonymous. We will send messengers to every village, town and city across the kingdom and alert them of your Ordination Ceremony commencing in Center Court two weeks hence.

"At the Ceremony we will issue you your royal cape, his Highness, King Barnabas, will officially step down from the throne, and the kingdom will recognize you as their new King. As usual, you must not reveal your Foreordination to anyone until that day.

"As for you, you must return here the fifth day of next week in preparation for the Ceremony. You will be instructed as to how the ritual will be carried out. You may go."

...Just like that? Jason thought. *No escort? Walk home? 'You may go?'*

He only thought on the peculiarity of the gesture before slowly turning on his heels and marching back down the red carpet. As he walked, he occasionally glanced at the soldiers lined against the wall, his back facing the Advisor and the King. Most of the soldiers looked ahead as if they didn't see Jason, determined to look disciplined and elite. But there was one soldier that caught Jason's eye in particular.

He and the soldier made eye contact. The soldier's eyes were deep, young, and they seemed to speak louder and more clear than any tongue could. They spoke of wonder. They spoke of hope. They spoke of times that they have for so long wanted to forget, but were not yet over. They spoke of advancing triumph.

Jason nodded at the soldier, who looked ahead as if nothing happened. It wasn't long before the soldiers heaved the ancient doors open and Jason walked out into the afternoon sun.

But as he did, a voice echoed through his head, a voice that filled his body with ice—the voice of King Barnabas. It sounded like he was whispering directly in his ear.

The whole kingdom will know of you, he said. *They may start to hope. They may start to foolishly think my reign is over, but I still have two weeks to fulfill my oath. You will die, Jason. No one will ever know who might have become King.*

The doors slammed behind Jason, and the King said no more.

28 THE STONE

During the daytime, Jason remained in areas that were public and crowded and showed little chance of standing out. During the nighttime, he slept with his sword and didn't leave his family's house in Lower City, which had recently been completed. He rubbed the sheath of his prized blade more often than he ever had since he had made it at age sixteen.

"Did you hear…?" Jason heard a man whisper to another as he stood by a cart on the Southern Market Street.

"Yes!" The second man replied excitedly. "A new King! After all these years!"

"Who could it possibly be?" The first man said with a growing smile.

"Who cares who it is as long as it's not *King Barnabas*…" the last two words were barely a whisper. "Anybody could fix the problems *he's* created… I'll bet ten Bars that the King tries to kill him before he can take the Throne… perhaps we shouldn't get our hopes up too quickly…"

Jason would shiver uncomfortably and walk away. He heard these low, excited conversations at least a dozen times a day. The soldiers had almost given up on silencing the whispering voices of excited Nezmythians. There's no possible way they could throw every Nezmyth City resident into prison.

Still, Jason couldn't shake that clinging notion of apprehension that latched onto his heartstrings. Passing the Year of Decision just is just one thing leading to another—ruling an entire kingdom. And there was only one week left. *The King said he still has this time to fulfill his oath. What should I be prepared for? Is the Dark Cloak able to watch him closely to make sure he doesn't try anything rash? Perhaps... but it's only a matter of time before he's able to slip something under his watch.*

Jason tried not to think about it, but he knew ignoring the thought would be unwise. Fear can sometimes be a safety net—it keeps men cautious and alert. His chest swelled as he walked down the Southern Market Street.

It was the fifth day of the following week of Jason's most recent visit to the castle. He turned onto the Northern Market Street and proceeded to a slanting street ascending to Upper City. He munched on a guabo he had received from the Lower City guabo man some minutes earlier.

The minutes dragged on. The houses become more and more elaborate. He raised his eyebrows and took curious interest as he passed Golan and Tarmanthia's house. The modest home grinned at the street with an elegant flare, a metalwork fence adorned the perimeter of the property and a well-tailored garden hugged the base of the house. The red bricks of the exterior wall were weathered with its veteran age, but still pronounced dignity and class.

Jason half-grinned at it and continued to walk up the street. An hour passed, and finally Jason found himself outside the castle gates.

"State your business," one of the soldiers ordered.

Without a word, Jason reached into one of his pockets and extracted a note with the royal seal on it. He had received it just recently upon returning home from a visit to the library. He briefly remembered that exchange:

Tomm and Kara were both sitting at the table, sullen and serious and supposedly waiting for him, when Jason had walked through the door. Jason knew what their expressions meant. When he closed the door behind him, he asked quietly, "You've heard the announcement?"

"Yes," Tomm confirmed as they both nodded. "Less than two weeks, then?"

Jason nodded, and a thick silence ensued. It was surreal and sobering, knowing that the calling Jason had been Foreordained to was coming up, let alone so quickly. It must have been a shock to them both. Besides, they were three of the few people in the entire kingdom who knew exactly *who* would take the throne, and none of them could speak a word of it.

"Some soldiers came by and dropped this off," Kara said as she held out a slip of parchment.

Jason crossed the cabin and took it. It was a card with the royal insignia on one side and a note from the Advisor on the other, permitting Jason entrance to the castle.

"What is it for?" she asked.

"I need to practice for the Ordination Ceremony on the fifth day this week," Jason replied quietly. "This grants me entrance to the castle."

"Is this why you've been so different this past year?" Tomm said. "You knew this was coming?"

Jason didn't say anything. He couldn't. But Tomm got the message anyway.

The soldier outside the castle gates examined the card carefully. With a nod, he thrust it back into Jason's hand and gave the signal to open the gates. They squealed open loudly and Jason marched through without further conversation.

The stone pathway leading through the castle grounds seemed farther on foot. He inserted his hands in his pockets to warm them up. The sun was in the peak of its daily climb and the azure sky conjured brief puffs of white clouds over Jason's head. The parched statue of an ancient knight stood with sword poised to the sky. Eventually, Jason reached the castle doors.

The soldier didn't say a word when Jason showed him his permit. He picked up the mallet and slammed the door three times. The door edged open inch by inch, accompanied by the usual grunting of soldiers. As Jason crossed the threshold, he noticed the interior of the castle had no torches lit. Instead, fresh sunlight streamed through the ancient windows, lighting up the dust particles that fluttered in the air and reflecting off the polished stone floor.

But the Throne was empty. As a matter of fact, the entire hall was—not even a soldier standing guard. Jason's every footstep was muffled by the red carpet, but no one was around to see or hear him.

"Hello?" he called.

No reply—just the reverberation of his own voice. He tensed, then slid his sword from out of its sheath.

Armed and cautious, he explored the ancient hall. He must have wandered alone for several minutes, scanning sculptures and paintings that had to have been hundreds of years old. He was analyzing a bust of a particularly masculine-looking King when a door on the opposite side of the hall flew open.

It was the Advisor. All he barked was, "Come!"

Immediately, Jason slid his sword back into the sheath and marched across the hall. The door the Advisor had flung open was between two suits of ancient armor. As Jason eventually crossed through the open door, he noticed that the room had no windows or furniture. All that stood in the room was a pedestal with a purple sheet hanging over it. Jason knew the Oracle Stone was beneath that sheet.

"If you will excuse me," the Advisor said as he walked passed Jason. "A pressing matter has suddenly arisen that I must attend to. I will be back shortly."

Jason didn't reply. The Advisor marched through the door without a second glance and slammed the door shut. As he did, torches on the walls magically combusted and dimly illuminated the room with a flickering red glow. Jason's only company in the room was the pedestal with the Oracle Stone.

Jason hummed and thought to himself, *A pressing matter?*

He slid into a sitting position against the wall. Several minutes went by. He wondered if this would be a proper place to practice some Ancient Nezmythian magic, but he didn't want to be practicing anything as the Advisor walked in.

He wondered many things as he sat. *How is the Oracle Stone involved in my Ordination Ceremony? When will the Advisor be back? Is this room just a cage so the King can more easily kill me?*

It was then that he noticed another door on the other side of the room. He pushed himself up off the floor and walked over to it. As he walked past the Oracle Stone pedestal, he heard a deep rumbling like the breath of a sleeping giant. He had heard that rumbling before—almost one year ago when he was first brought to the castle. The Oracle Stone had been in his hands at that point.

That rumbling breathing was so peaceful, he thought. *I could feel it more if I could just hold it.*

He tried to dismiss the idea. When he reached the door, he grabbed for the ornamented doorknob and twisted ever so slowly. He didn't want to disturb anyone that may be on the other side. But alas, the doorknob would barely turn.

Locked, he thought bitterly. *Stuck in here until he gets back.*

With that, he turned and walked back to the other side of the room. As he passed the Oracle Stone, he heard the rumbling breathing again.

He stopped. His Kinghood was riding on whatever color the Oracle Stone portrayed on the day of his Ordination. Master Ferribolt had elaborated on this:

A Foreordained King is Ordained at the end of his Year of Decision based on three factors: the opinion of the King and Advisor, the voice of the common people, and the color of the Oracle Stone. Undoubtedly, the King and the Advisor would be opposed to Jason taking the Throne, but the people of Nezmyth would be unanimously in favor. That left the Oracle Stone. If it stayed the same or darkened from its original color almost one year ago, King Barnabas would maintain the throne.

But had it gotten any lighter, despite Jason's best efforts?

He stood next to the Oracle Stone, staring at the purple sheet draped over it. The rumbling breathing seemed to reverberate inside his chest, leaving a wisp of warm glow inside him.

His eyes darted to each door. No sound was heard on either side. As he continued to stare at the Stone, his heart thumped inside him and he breathed deeply.

The Advisor might not be back for a long while, he thought. *Will one peek really matter? I won't even have to look at the Stone. If I could just see the color of the light it shines...*

Slowly, he placed his hands on the purple cloth on top of the Stone. Just as he remembered, the rumbling breaths filled his mind and heart and made him feel as calm as the sea. He stole another glance to the doors, then pinched the bottom of the sheet.

As he started to lift it up, the deep rumbling suddenly stopped. The room fell silent. It was then that Jason realized what he was doing.

I'm one week away from the Throne! He thought to himself. *And this could disqualify me!*

Immediately he released the purple sheet and jumped back. When he did that, the deep rumbling slowly started to return. He gawked at the Stone incredulously. It was as if the Dragon was aware of his actions and severed the peace that came from the Stone. Jason knew deep down that what he was doing was dangerous, and his curiosity almost cost him the kingdom.

It was then that the Advisor came bursting through the door. Jason's heart jumped into his throat. The Advisor ignored him and strode through the room until he, Jason, and the Oracle Stone made a triangle. Then he finally looked him in the eye.

The Advisor asked, "Shall we begin?"

* * * * *

Jason sat with his chin on his forearms. He leaned forward in the pew, staring at the podium ahead.

Thunder cracked outside. Bursts of light lit up the stained glass windows of the Cathedral. Candlelight warmed the stone walls that seemed to be asleep as the rain pelted the cobblestone streets outside.

Jason's body quivered slightly. The throne was so close he could almost feel himself sitting in it.

He sat alone for hours, staring ahead blankly in the silence. He thought of several things: his friends locked away in prison, hungry and cold... the numerous attempts on his life in the past year... the trials and struggles he had borne on his shoulders... utterly alone.

Finally, it was coming to an end... but what would lie ahead? He stared ahead at the enormous painting of the Holy Dragon at the front of the Cathedral, as if the answers to his soul could be found in its eyes. Hours of staring had brought no results.

Suddenly, the doors at the back of the Cathedral creaked open. Jason leapt to his feet and his hand shot for the hilt of his sword. As his eyes came around, he watched a hooded figure close the door. The slam reverberated through the hall, and as the hooded figure turned about to walk toward Jason, it lifted its hood back over its head, revealing its face. Instantly, Jason relaxed.

"I thought I would find you here," Master Ferribolt said as he walked toward the pew where Jason sat.

Jason didn't say anything. He released his sword and sat back down, looking forward.

"You've been spending a lot of time here lately," Master Ferribolt sat beside him.

"It's one of the few places I feel safe," Jason said quietly.

Master Ferribolt nodded, "For good reason. The King's jurisdiction ends inside these walls. The Dragon is your keeper here."

Jason inhaled and exhaled a feeble breath. He shivered again.

The both of them stayed silent for minutes, looking forward. Amidst the silence, Jason felt grateful. He felt grateful for Master Ferribolt's company. He felt grateful for the guidance and wisdom he had given him throughout the year. Even now, as the Chief Patriarch sat next to him, he felt as though there was another person to help him carry the weight on his shoulders.

Even after putting my trust in the Dragon, I don't understand why I'm the one to be King, Jason thought.

"I understand today is your birthday," Master Ferribolt said brightly.

Jason nodded.

"I have a present for you," Master Ferribolt reached into his pocket. "A lovely trinket. It has no value, but I'm rather fond of it—."

"Master," Jason turned and looked at him. "You didn't have to get my anything."

Master Ferribolt ignored Jason's protest and held out a bronze coin in his palm. The coin was marked with an equilateral triangle inside a circle. Inside the triangle, an inexpensive gem with a burnt orange hue glittered in the dim light.

Jason looked at it curiously. "It looks like the same symbol on the floor of the Melding Hall."

"It is," Master Ferribolt confirmed. "This was given to me by the Chief Patriarch during my training for Patriarchal duties. He gave it to me so it would give me strength and confidence. How? I'm not sure. But I've always carried it with me, and I believe it has. I want to pass it on to you."

Jason's jaw fell just a little. "Are you sure?"

"Very sure," Master Ferribolt's eyes twinkled behind his spectacles.

Jason took it reverently and let his thumb slide across the design. He could have crafted something like this in less than an hour, but coming from a dear friend and mentor... it was priceless.

"Thank you," Jason said.

Master Ferribolt grinned and patted him on his back. They sat in silence for several more minutes. Master Ferribolt occasionally stole glances at Jason, trying to get a feel for what he was thinking. After pondering, he finally said:

"Jason, we're not meant to know everything all at once. You'll be a fine King. I know you were hoping to find the reason why you were Foreordained sometime this year, but maybe that time hasn't quite come."

"Well, when then?" Jason shot him a look. His eyes stung.

"I don't know," Master Ferribolt conceded. "Sometimes our answers come in small nuggets of enlightenment... like when a Blessing Bearer arrives at your home in the dark of night, or when a worried, confused boy comes to your doorstep seeking guidance. It's my personal belief that the greatest wealth of knowledge comes from these small instances of enlightenment, coming together to form a beautiful, perfect whole." Master Ferribolt looked into Jason's uncertain eyes and said, "A sunrise doesn't happen all at once, does it? But watching it grow is one of life's simple pleasures."

Jason traced the back of the pew with his finger. He said, "What if the King kills me tomorrow? Or I survive, and I'm a terrible King? I don't know anything about leading a kingdom."

"The King *will* try to kill you," Master Ferribolt replied. "But I know the Dragon can protect you. And as for your Kingship, all you can do is your best. That is what the Dragon expects. That's what I've been doing for decades, and I believe that I have been blessed for that."

"You've been doing a good job," Jason said.

Master Ferribolt smiled feebly. "Thank you. I know you will do the same."

"How do you know?" Jason asked.

"Because I see a lot of King Thomas in you," Master Ferribolt said. "You are loyal, honest, humble, and you have a passion for justice… even if you need to be reassured of yourself every once in a while." He winked.

Jason's eyes stung, but he teased a smile. He tried to keep his voice from cracking, "I can't do this by myself."

Master Ferribolt said, "You won't have to."

29 THE RECKONING

The day had come.

Jason's heart beat ferociously. Every few moments he rubbed the palms of his hands on his already filthy pants. His mouth felt bone-dry and his head swam uncomfortably.

Center Court was packed. The excited people of Nezmyth City—and some Nezmythians that had traveled from the farthest corners of the kingdom—had all gathered to this central hub to witness this spectacular event. Vendors shouting to get people's attention sold fruit and candies as they pushed through the crowds. Jason saw fair-skinned dwellers of the western forests with bows and arrows slung over their backs. He also saw the strong, well-tanned farmers from the Southern region of the kingdom all gathered together to witness the event.

Right below the enormous statue of King Barnabas, the King himself sat in an elegant wooden chair with a pale face and frizzled hair. His black sword leaned against the side of the chair... waiting. The silent Advisor stood behind the right side of the chair with a face lacking any expression while a barricade of soldiers kept the townspeople a good distance from them in a large circle. Just a few yards in front of the King and the Advisor, the Oracle Stone sat on its pedestal covered in the usual purple sheet.

Standing next to Jason were his parents.

"Don't be nervous," Kara whispered as she squeezed her son's gloved hand.

Jason said nothing.

"We're right here behind you," Tomm said, who was standing on the other side of Jason. He nudged him gently.

"Thank you," Jason breathed.

Kara and Tomm didn't say another word, even though they both felt they needed to give some gold nugget of comfort to Jason's restless spirit.

People all around Jason were chattering eagerly except him. "I'm so excited!" "Who do you think it will be?" "A new King… and after nearly twenty years!" Jason thought about what he would be thinking if he were in their position, but the thought escaped him easily through his pulsing heart and quaking knees.

The minutes might as well have been centuries. Jason's teeth chattered. He fingered a small parcel in his pocket.

Strangely, every soldier was garbed in replicas of Ancient Nezmythian knight armor. Their golden helmets were perfectly round on the top with an encrusted triangle that came to a point between their eyes. Every aspect of the armor was gold plated, from the breastplates, to the shoulder guards, to the gloves. Jason assumed they wore these garbs for special occasions.

He looked around furiously, standing on the tips of his toes and peering over the crowd expectantly. He had been repeating this process for as long as he had been standing there, and had sunk back down to his standing position, crestfallen, every time.

"Who are you looking for?" Kara asked.

Jason didn't hear her.

Excited whispers rippled through the crowd as if someone important were making his way through. They sounded hollow and distant to Jason and he paid no attention. Suddenly, he felt someone squeeze his shoulder gently.

"This is a great spot to watch the Ordination Ceremony!"

Jason turned around to see Master Ferribolt standing directly behind him in his Patriarchal robes. People all around him greeted him with reverence, desiring to shake his hand and bid him hello. The Chief Patriarch complied happily, and when all those around him were satisfied, his eyes reverted to Jason. He winked.

Jason smiled feebly.

Finally, a vertical spear moved toward him amidst the crowd. Jason stood on his toes again and looked out to it. His heart leapt as he saw two blonde-haired heads and a black, graying one, accompanied by two soldier's helmets gliding along the top of the dense crowd. In no time, the soldiers and the three individuals were with Jason and his family.

"*Jason!*" Saryan leapt into Jason's arms. Jason nearly cried with joy as he felt those arms around his neck and that warm cheek against his face. Saryan's feet dangled in the air as he held her. After what wasn't long enough, he let Saryan back onto her feet and the two took their arms back from around each other. Tarren and Saryan's father stood just a little behind Saryan. Master Ferribolt pretended not to notice the spectacle.

Jason was extremely surprised at how good they looked. They were back in their normal clothes. The men had shaved. Saryan had her hair washed. They were all just a little thinner, but if he hadn't known better, he wouldn't have thought that any of them had been thrown in prison for any matter of days, let alone more than a month.

Saryan's father, a pristinely-built man with flawless posture and sharp silver eyes, hovered behind the five, patiently waiting. Tarren strode up and embraced Jason as though he were a long-lost brother.

"How are you?" Jason asked them as they stood close together, congested by the thickening crowd. "What did they do to you? What was it like? You look like nothing even happened!"

Saryan and Tarren exchanged looks. Saryan was the first to speak.

"We never got whipped or beaten. We weren't fed very well—father lost a lot of weight. I've seen what's happened in the Nezmyth City Prison... and none of it happened to us."

"But we watched it happen to others," Tarren's grin fell. "We were wondering why no one came to beat or flog us like they did all the other prisoners. It was very strange. We would wake up each morning wondering which one of us would get it first, but it never happened... after seeing some of it, I can see why my mother went mad."

Once again, Jason said nothing.

"And now we find out a new King has been Foreordained," Saryan's father spoke up from behind them. Jason was impressed with how his thick baritone voice resonated. "I must admit that I'm looking forward to working under someone other than Barnabas."

"Oh! I'm so sorry..." Saryan motioned for her father to come up. "Jason, this is my father, Garrit. This is the man I've been telling you about, father... the man I want to spend my life with."

Garrit put his hand out for Jason to shake, "Saryan has told me everything there is to tell about you. You sound like an honest man. Your parents must have raised you well. However, I am concerned with how you will provide for my daughter. She has said that you are a very capable fighter; we could train you to become a soldier so you could make double your salary."

Jason half-grinned and said, "I don't think that'll be necessary."

"Well, regardless," Garrit continued. "Your virtue and integrity is commendable. The Dragon always provides for those types. You will make a fine husband."

Kara and Tomm made it a point to introduce themselves to Garrit. Meanwhile, Jason and Saryan made eye contact. Her smile couldn't be contained. Jason's chest swelled and he found himself returning the smile. He reached into his pocket and pulled out the small parcel he had been poking at earlier with his thumb and forefinger. As he brought it into view, Saryan knew exactly what it was. She stopped herself from jumping up and down and clapping her hands.

As Jason held the ring up to her, he said, "I think I owe you this."

Tarren smiled broadly and pumped his fist discreetly while Kara, Tomm and Garrit smiled with sparkling eyes. Saryan took the ring and slipped it onto her finger. After that, and with an ear-to-ear smile, she leaned forward and slipped her fingers through the back of Jason's hair, her palms on his cheeks.

"That's not the only thing you owe me."

Their lips touched and Jason held her close. He hadn't once forgotten over the past several weeks how much he longed to have her in his arms. The doubt he held toward her after her confession had eroded away in her absense.

"*Hear ye!*"

The Advisor's voice boomed unnaturally loud from Center Court as he stepped out next to the Oracle Stone. The speed at which the deafening chatter stopped was astounding. The Advisor looked upon the crowd at all angles, realizing he was completely surrounded by Nezmythians and other travelers.

Jason then remembered how nervous he was. Saryan reached out and grabbed his hand. Jason's parents had returned and Kara had grabbed Jason's other hand from behind.

"*People of Nezmyth,*" the Advisor's voice sounded through the crowd. "*Welcome to the Ordination Ceremony of the new King of Nezmyth! For nearly twenty years you have been under the subjection of the noble King Barnabas.*"

The Advisor paused as if looking for something flattering or endearing to say about the King and the time of his rule, but conjured nothing.

"*However, as all things come and go, the reign of every King must come to an end…*"

Jason peered out and caught sight of King Barnabas. He was sitting as he usually did, with his fingers laced in front of his lips and looking as if he wanted to kill something small and vulnerable. His peppery hair was completely frayed and his teeth clenched in a venomous scowl—not to mention his eye twitched.

He's off... Jason thought while creasing his eyebrows. *He's held the throne for twenty years and now it's being swiped out from under him. There's no way he's going to give it up quietly.*

Jason inhaled through his nose deeply and exhaled shakily. If both of his hands weren't being held by his mother and Saryan, he would have rubbed the sheath of his sword. Saryan looked at him oddly.

"Are you alright?" She asked.

Jason didn't hear her. He tried to control his chattering teeth.

"*...the King and I understand the patience it must have taken for the new King's identity to be revealed, but today, you wait no longer. Today marks the beginning of a new era. Today, you look to a new ruler, a new guardian, a new advocate with the Dragon. Today, your new King is Ordained!*

"*So... without further introduction or interruption... Jason, son of Tomm the printer, step forward!*"

Gasps leapt from the lips of Saryan, Tarren, and Garrit. His mother squeezed his hand before Jason took a shaky step forward, gently nudging his way through the crowd. He rubbed the sheath on his back.

The crowd gradually parted as he made his way and all eyes focused on him even before he had even broke out into the open. Not a single person so much as breathed or shuffled their feet. Jason wondered if the people next to him could hear his heart beating. Cold sweat had built on his brow long ago.

King Barnabas kept his icy eyes on Jason. Jason felt nervous every time King Barnabas glared at him, but as he grew closer and closer, he noticed something in his eyes that filled him with dread... madness. King Barnabas' lips quivered and his teeth ground together as his body shook in his seat. The Advisor, amazingly, stood erect and completely collected not far away.

Jason stopped when he was a few paces away from the Oracle Stone. The Advisor took a few steps back so he, the King, and Jason formed a triangle with the Oracle Stone in the middle.

Jason swallowed, trying to douse his parched throat.

"Jason's worthiness for the Throne will be decided upon three factors," the Advisor continued. *"One, the opinion of the King. Two, the voice of you, the people of Nezmyth. And, three, the color of the Oracle Stone.*

"Your Highness, what do you make of the boy?"

Slowly, King Barnabas pushed himself up from his chair. Jason swallowed again. He gazed into Jason's eyes with icy heat and spoke to all of Nezmyth as he shouted.

"The boy is not fit for the Throne!" King Barnabas ranted. "He is too young and knows nothing of the governing affairs of the kingdom of Nezmyth! I would rather burn than allow him to replace me as King! Anyone who cheers for him will be—!"

Suddenly, his neck tightened and his face contorted. It wasn't until he dropped back into his seat that he gasped for breath. He choked and sputtered, gave a venomous scowl to the ground, then held his peace. Jason looked on shakily, along with everyone in Center Court, not sure of what just happened. The Advisor continued on as though he didn't notice the spectacle.

"Jason is only known by few," he continued. *"So as tradition states, the Chief Patriarch will give you his honest observation of the boy, and you, the people of Nezmyth, will vote in the affirmative or negative of his Kingship!"*

The Advisor nodded and Master Ferribolt came bustling through the crowd out into the open. The people of Nezmyth clapped valiantly for their leader under the Dragon as he shuffled along. His orange robe looked magnificent in the afternoon sun. He winked at Jason again.

"My friends," Master Ferribolt began as he clasped his hands together. "This is a very sacred, special day. Before us, we have Jason, a King Foreordained by the Holy Dragon itself. I've had the pleasure of meeting with Jason regularly throughout the past year. He first came to me as a frightened, confused boy… but what you see before you is a man."

He made eye contact with Jason.

"Jason still does not know why *he* was Foreordained to lead you. It's something that he struggles with deeply. Those of you who would merely look upon the surface would see but an average boy, but his greatness lies deep. This, I believe, is what makes Jason great…

"Despite his personal desires and self-doubt, he is willing to take the Throne of Nezmyth because of his love for all of you! He has seen your misery, your poverty, your fear… and he is willing to rise to his Foreordination at this time because he wants a better life for all of you!

"Is this not the quality of a noble King? Selflessness? But this is not all. His virtue is without parallel. He is wise and caring. He has endured all manners of trials and hardships this past year because he knew *this—is—his—duty!*

"Brothers and sisters under the Sacred Dragon," Master Ferribolt concluded. "Jason is a great man, and he will be a greater man as his time prolongs in the Throne of Nezmyth. The Holy Dragon has Foreordained him! *Let King Jason reign!*"

Thunderous applause and whistles were the kingdom's reply. Master Ferribolt glowed at Jason like a proud father as he melded back into the crowd. Jason sniffled, his insides warm and cozy, before the Advisor's voice brought him back to stiff reality.

"*All opposed, say nay!*"

Not a peep. King Barnabas shifted in his seat angrily. The Advisor continued:

"*All in favor, say yay!*"

"YAY!" All of Nezmyth shouted in unison. The sound almost knocked Jason to the ground.

"The voice of the people is unanimous in the affirmative!" The Advisor stated. *"Finally, the Oracle Stone will be consulted. If it has lightened in color since one year ago, Jason will reign as King of Nezmyth. If the color has remained the same or darkened, King Barnabas will resume the Throne."*

Jason, along with everyone in Nezmyth, held his breath as the Advisor strode up to the pedestal. His heart thrashed in his chest and the cold sweat on his brow grew thicker. Finally, the Advisor pinched the top of the purple sheet and gently lifted it off of the Oracle Stone.

It was beautiful. Jason distinctly remembered the glassy Stone containing curling smoke the color of an egg yolk. But now, the same smoke looked like puffy clouds with morning sunlight bursting out of the edges—brighter, emanating peace and warmth. It was lighter, not drastically, but obviously.

"The Oracle Stone has lightened!" The Advisor boomed. *"His spirit has become more attuned with the Dragon! According to the voice of the people and the hue of the Oracle Stone, Jason is qualified to reign as King over the kingdom of Nezmyth!"*

Suddenly, he turned on Jason and said, *"Jason, do you accept your Foreordination as King of Nezmyth under the Sacred Dragon, the creator of the world of Wevlia? In so doing, you covenant to protect and serve the people of Nezmyth until death or succession by Foreordination!"*

Jason took a very, very deep breath. With a shaky exhale, he said:

"I accept!"

The Advisor said, *"Let the royal cape be brought forward!"*

Jason dropped to one knee. Two soldiers—one in red armor and one in blue—appeared with cape in hand. Jason tried with failure to control his breathing through his nose as the soldiers quickly marched up to him. They each held one end of an elaborate crimson cape, holding it so the bottom of it didn't touch the ground, and as they reached Jason, they turned and laid it on his back.

One of the soldiers dismissed himself and the other remained to tie the laces around Jason's neck. Jason felt the soldier's nimble fingers tie the laces into a knot, securing the cape onto his back. When the knot was tied, the second soldier dismissed himself.

"*King Jason,*" The Advisor said. "*Arise!*"

Jason planted his feet to the ground and slowly, shakily stood up.

Eruption.

The cheers that filled the air were absolutely deafening. Shouting, whoops and whistles said the neglect, the gloom, the hopelessness of a wayward rule was finally over. Husbands held their wives. Children danced and screamed in expressions of joy. Even soldiers turned and clapped, smiling and holding their weapons in the air.

Kara and Tomm clapped with tears in their eyes. Master Ferribolt beamed satisfactorily in the crowd. Saryan and Tarren tried to cheer louder than anyone else. Nezmythians both young and old threw confetti in the air, making the afternoon sky shimmer with delight as the sun smiled down on Nezmyth.

A flicker of a smile graced Jason's lips. He ran his finger down the silky red cape on his back that symbolized his Kinghood, his success, his Foreordination. It was over. The Year of Decision was finally over.

But amidst the elation, a soul was retching.

"*NO!!*" Barnabas leapt up from the chair, his eyes wild and his arms shaking at his sides.

Center Court fell silent as quickly as it had exploded. Thousands of gleeful smiles fell from their faces to be replaced by shock and fear. Barnabas' eye twitched violently in its socket.

"*I will not accept this!*" His voice shook. "*I've gone too far, I've seen too much and I've been through too much pain to have my position swept from beneath me by a child! I deserve this!*"

"*Step down, Barnabas!*" The Advisor shouted with venom. Jason's jaw fell. "Two decades of your rule has been Foreordained completed! *King Jason reigns!*"

The crowd roared its agreement, accompanied by boos and hisses for the former King.

"*Fools!!*" Barnabas shouted. The crowd hushed again. "*I'm ten times the ruler this whelp will ever be! I've done—*"

"You've done *nothing!*"

Jason surprised himself. He hadn't noticed that his fists were clenched and his teeth were grinding together in his skull. Everything he had seen and experienced from the past year had bubbled into this moment, and now it all refused to be kept inside. Barnabas could have shot fire from his eyes.

"*...how dare you...?*"

"This kingdom is in shambles because of you!" Jason shouted. "How many people—how many families have been destroyed because of your relentless taxes and ignorant, self-absorbed rule? Have you even bothered to step foot in the southernmost parts of Lower City? People are starving! People are *dying* because of you! And I'm sure it's like that all over Nezmyth!"

Jason was astonished at his own audacity, but he finished his remarks with his most honest feelings. "I don't know why *I* have to be King at just eighteen years—maybe I'll never know—but I know that Nezmyth would have been better off if you never sat in that Throne! *Step down, Barnabas!*"

Once again, the people of Nezmyth roared in approval. Barnabas looked around, astonished at how his subjects had turned against him so quickly. The noise slowly transformed into something audible. Jason's jaw tightened and he brushed the sheath of his blade.

Barnabas' gaze fell to the ground in front of him, numb. His fists shook and his nose scrunched while Jason's heart beat so fast he thought he might faint. His mind reeled with the anticipation on the former King's next move. Barnabas lifted his eyes to Jason slowly, and as the iciness of his glare penetrated Jason's soul; every Nezmythian's cheers died. The tension was thick enough to taste.

"*I made you an oath one year ago, Your Highness,*" Barnabas seethed. "*Would you like to tell the kingdom what it was?*"

Jason didn't reply. Every part of himself tensed, bracing himself. His hand went for his sword.

"*No...?*" Barnabas said. "*Allow me to demonstrate!*"

Everything happened in a flash. Barnabas scooped up the black blade and dashed forward in a blur. Jason lifted his blade to block the blow, which he did, but the force was so strong that it knocked him to the ground.

He knows Ancient magic! He thought despairingly.

"Run!" The Advisor bellowed at the crowd. "The former King is mad! *Run!*"

Nezmythians pelted through the streets in a panic like sheep at the sight of a hungry wolf. Mothers scooped up their children as their fathers took their hands and ran with them. Soldiers did their best to control the chaos, but to no avail. Several soldiers ran forward to help Jason, weapons raised. But as they dashed, they all suddenly crashed and fell as if they collided with an invisible wall. The Advisor thrust his hand forward and shot fire from his palm, which stopped directly where the soldiers had crashed.

"Your magic has withheld me for too long!" Barnabas screamed and pointed at the Advisor. "But not today! Now he is *mine!*"

Jason tried to get up, but the former King kicked him down, laughing with sinister glee as his foot pressed on his chest. Beads of sweat trailed down Jason's face.

Eight months... he thought hopelessly. *And this is how it ends... I let Nezmyth down... everyone...*

Barnabas' eyes gleamed with madness as he looked down. "Even after all of your training, you are still *weak!*"

On the last word, he knocked the sword of out Jason's hand and thrust his blade into Jason's shoulder. Jason cried in agony as the blade ripped through his flesh and bones. Blood poured onto the cobblestone.

Barnabas laughed maniacally and lifted his sword to the air. Jason shook his head—tears that had welled up from pain now welled up from hopelessness. He tried to wiggle free, but it only made the former King laugh harder. Those terrible blue eyes hung over Jason with a ferocity that was ripe with victory and murder.

"*Long live the K—!*"

Jason didn't hear the last word. Barnabas swung his blade down and in the blink of an eye, everything went black.

30 THE KNIGHT

At first, everything was completely dark, cold, and hopeless, but just then, Jason heard whispering.

"He's Awakening…" one voice said. "It's too early."

"Peace, friend," another said. "The Dragon has foreseen this. A plan has been made. I will speak to him."

A slight pause hung in the air. "Then I shall wait outside with the others."

Jason heard the opening and closing of a door. The darkness from Jason's eyes gradually faded to light. He blinked several times as his vision adjusted. He was on his back, looking up into the posts in the ceiling of a small wooden cabin. Slowly, he pushed himself up. He realized he was in a bed he wasn't familiar with, covered in blankets that were warm and unnaturally soft and wearing clothes he had never seen before—a flowing cotton shirt and pants of spotless white.

His eyes darted about apprehensively. The strange cabin was small—just larger than old flat. Scraping white light was the only thing beyond the one window in the edifice. A stranger with curly black hair and a flowing red cape sat in a wooden chair by the door, looking over Jason curiously. His toned arms were folded over his chest and his brown eyes were soft. The man saw Jason's confusion and spoke first.

"Good morning, Your Highness," he said.

Jason said nothing at first. Words had escaped him.

"I understand you are a little confused. That is to be expected," the man continued. "I'm here to answer any questions you may have."

Jason looked around and then checked his injured shoulder. It was completely healed! He didn't know why he felt so warm, and although he had never been here before, this cabin had a strange feeling of home. His eyes fixed on the guest. Was he his guest? How did I know this cabin even belonged to him?

"...Do I know you?" Jason asked shakily.

The man returned the question with an amused smile. "You used to a long time ago. Before you were born, actually. I saw to it that I taught you everything that I could before you left. After all, you were born to fulfill a purpose that's very close to my heart."

Jason's eyes darted around the room. His sword was nowhere to be found. He looked into the stranger's eyes.

"I'm sorry, I don't follow."

The man gave him an understanding smile and a quiet sigh. "A long time ago, the people of Nezmyth called me—."

Suddenly, it sprang into Jason's mind. *I can't believe I didn't guess it before! Could it really be?*

He remembered a starry night several weeks ago when he shoved his sword into the ground and stood before the grave of one man he so deeply wished to be like. His heart leapt and he threw the blankets off him.

"King Thomas!" He gasped and scrambled to a kneeling position on the warm hardwood floor. "Forgive me Your Highness, I had no idea—!"

King Thomas chuckled with amusement at the sight. As his laughter simmered down he shook his head.

"Sit down, King Jason, there is no need for apologies!" He said with a smile. "Perhaps I should be bowing to you, considering your new position?"

Jason quickly got up and sat on the mattress, thinking to himself how strange it was to have one of the most beloved figures in Nezmythian history refer to him as *King* Jason. He forced himself not to smile. Considering where he was, that effort became easier very quickly. Thousands of questions started popping into his head as he looked around.

"Where are we?"

"The Third Life," King Thomas replied and his smile dropped slowly.

Jason felt the color leave his face. His hands shook and his throat tightened.

"You mean we're—?"

"Dead? In the mortal sense, yes," King Thomas replied. "And we were both killed by the same person, coincidentally, just twenty years apart. I was poisoned at the dinner table and left to die in my chambers some hour or two later... and you were beheaded in Center Court just minutes ago." King Thomas' tone became very somber. "I'm sorry."

The knowledge slammed into Jason. His entire body shook. His hand rubbed his neck as he imagined a blade slashing through his jugular. Tears welled up in his eyes quickly and he leaned forward on the side of his bed, propping his elbows on his knees and burying his face in his hands. He sniffed quietly. King Thomas held his peace as he watched.

"I failed..." Jason's voice shook. "All of Nezmyth was counting on me and I failed... killed right in front of them... after all that happened in the past year..."

King Thomas kept quiet as he watched Jason sniffle for a while. Finally, he adjusted himself in his seat, rubbed his knees and said:

"You know, failure is very, very malleable to the Dragon. Speaking metaphorically, it can take a crude nugget of failure and shape it into a gleaming bar of success. Even if it means bringing back the dead."

Jason's sniffles compressed for a small moment as he looked up into King Thomas' eyes. King Thomas adjusted himself again in his chair, this time taking his hands off his lap and folding his arms over his chest.

"Tell me about yourself, King Jason," he said. "What was your life like back in the Second Life?"

Jason's head swam. He wiped his eyes like a child and sniffled another time. He kept his elbows propped on his knees and laced his hands together in front of him. His voice quivered and he looked at the ground as he spoke.

"Well... I worked at a crafting shop... I had a woman I had planned to marry... two amazing parents and a loyal best friend..."

"What's that on your hand?" King Thomas asked.

Jason's face flushed. As he looked down, he suddenly realized he wasn't wearing a glove. He slapped his hand onto his knee, covering the mark from the world. *Out of all the questions he could have asked me... I can't lie to King Thomas. Is it possible to lie to someone in the Third Life?*

Jason swallowed. He rubbed his palm on his pants.

"I have a birthmark on my palm that's always kind of bothered me," Jason conceded. "Every time I look at it I feel like I've been marked for something... something I don't understand."

"Will you show it to me, please?" King Thomas said.

Jason hesitated before he uncovered his palm to King Thomas. He kept his eyes to the floor. He didn't see King Thomas break out into a sly grin.

"You have no idea what that is, do you?" he said.

Jason looked at his palm. The blazing orange triangle right below his forefinger shined in the light of the Third Life. Of course he had no idea what it meant. He had never seen anyone else with a mark remotely like it, and the only time he has seen something similar was mad coincidence in an Ancient Nezmythian book. Or was it?

"That's a very special mark, Jason," King Thomas said reverently.

He sat up straight in his chair. He turned his body slightly so his right arm was closest to Jason. With his left hand, he lifted up the sleeve of his shirt.

Jason thought his heart stopped. Could his heart stop in the Third Life? The hairs on his arms and neck bristled and what he saw caused his eyes to grow to the size of dinner plates.

On King Thomas' bicep, right below his shoulder, an orange triangle was blazed into his skin, identical to Jason's birthmark. A lump lodged itself in Jason's throat and refused to let out any words.

"Jason," King Thomas spoke to him in a dark tone. "You and I are Knights of the Holy Order."

Knights of the Holy Order? Jason's eyes fixed on King Thomas' shoulder, a reflection of what he had concealed on his palm for years. He looked at his right hand. He *was* marked for something... and he wasn't the only one. Dozens of questions started popping into his head, but he kept silent, assuming the King would explain.

"There are thousands of us spread throughout the millennia," King Thomas said, letting his sleeve fall. "Usually, we are Foreordained to positions like Kings or Advisors when we're in our mortal Second Lives, but we've had Knights of the Holy Order live their lives as humble blacksmiths, vendors or printers."

Jason thought briefly of his father hiding some mysterious mark and never letting him know about it. He shook the thought out of his head.

"So what does it mean?" Jason asked.

"It means your victory is secured as long as your good is stronger than his evil. He fights with his own strength, but you can fight with the Dragon itself," King Thomas' eyes flashed.

"But how?"

"With some faith... and the Blade of Nezmyth."

Everything came together in one fell swoop. The story of the Blade of Nezmyth was in the same book that contained a copy of Jason's peculiar birthmark. Now he knew it wasn't coincidence.

King Thomas asked, "You're familiar with the origin of the Blade of Nezmyth?"

He had barely understood the story when he tried to read it in that Ancient Nezmythian book. He shook his head.

"Then allow me to explain," King Thomas said. "In the First Life, the Knights of the Holy Order were the marked warriors that led the armies of the Sacred Dragon in the War Against Darkness. That's us, Jason. To aid us in our fight against the forces of evil, the Holy Dragon commanded that a sacred blade should be made for every Knight—blades that would stand for all that is good and be the bane of all that would oppose justice.

"When the War ended and we were allowed to be born into mortality, each Knight gave the Dragon their individual Blade. The Dragon took each Blade and forged a single Blade out of it, which would be used if ever a mortal Knight needed it. This is what is now known as the Blade of Nezmyth. If the cause is just, evil is ever present, and the Knight is fighting for the sake of justice, the Blade of Nezmyth will come and the mortal body will take on the appearance of an immortal Knight of the Holy Order.

"One of those days as come, Your Highness. You are a Knight of the Holy Order. Call on the Dragon for the power to defeat Barnabas and his tyranny. The Dragon will send you the Blade of Nezmyth, you will take on the form of a Knight of the Holy Order, and you will defeat him."

Jason could have melted where he sat. He saw stars. He put his hand over his eyes and bent down, his face toward the floor.

"I understand it's a lot to swallow," King Thomas said. "But this is what the Holy Dragon sent me to tell you as you arrived into the Third Life. And you'll be leaving soon—returning back to the Second Life to finish the job you were sent to do."

Jason fought the bile that was creeping up his throat. "You're going to send me back to fight Barnabas *by myself?*"

King Thomas sneered. "What did I just get through telling you? You won't be alone! Call on the Dragon and he will fight *with you!* This isn't a matter of you versus Barnabas, this is a matter of *Nezmyth!* Think of all the people you have fought for this past year. They need you. Now is not the time to fail them."

Jason didn't know what to say. The two sat in silence as Jason let everything sink in.

"There isn't much time left," King Thomas said. "In a matter of moments, we're going to send you back into the Second Life just before you were murdered. That will give you enough time to call on the Dragon for the Blade of Nezmyth and begin your battle with Barnabas." King Thomas stood up. "Good luck, Your Majesty."

"Wait!" Jason pleaded. "The Dragon... what is it like... to see it?"

King Thomas sighed, chest swelling and deflating heavily. His eyes read something that Jason couldn't easily discern before he shot Jason a glance out of the corner of his eye that was riddled with all sorts of emotions.

"It's like looking eternity in the face," King Thomas breathed. "If your spirit is dark, it's the most terrifying thing imaginable. If your heart is clean and you fight for what is good and just... it's like all of the pain, the misery, the uncertainty of mortality just melts away. You can experience it for yourself."

Jason's heart caught the ember of hope and it burned brightly in him for a few seconds. His eyes misted, King Thomas appeared hazy and the muscles in his chin tightened.

"All of the past Knights will be with you through this battle," King Thomas said. "There's a part of each of us in that Blade. Keep your faith burning bright, cast out all fear, and you will not fail."

Jason sniffed. Part of him wanted to stay with his new friend—his heavenly mentor—but something kept him planted on the mattress. The things that he had heard about King Thomas were true. He really was that kind and wise. Everything around him increased in brightness steadily and Jason felt his eyes growing heavier. King Thomas' valiant face became whiter and whiter until Jason fell back onto the mattress.

Jason heard him say as he fell into the abyss, "Nezmyth cheers for you, King Jason. Don't let them down."

31 THE ROAR

Jason's eyes jumped around in his sockets. *Did that really just happen?* He had been thrown back to where he was just minutes ago, standing a few yards away from the Oracle Stone, surrounded by Nezmythians at all angles. As he looked into Barnabas' confused and furious eyes, his own eyes sharpened.

"I made you an oath one year ago, Your Highness," Barnabas seethed. *"Would you like to tell the kingdom what it was?"*

Jason's hand shot upward and wrapped itself around the hilt of his own sword. King Thomas' words echoed in Jason's mind. Nezmyth was upon his shoulders. Twenty years of despair came to this one moment. Jason's eyebrows tightened and his heart beat soared like the Holy Dragon itself.

He uttered a prayer in his heart.

"No...?" Barnabas said. *"Allow me to demonstrate!"*

Jason ripped the sword out of his sheath and leaned forward as Barnabas pelted toward him in an enormous blur. The two swords clashed with a mighty *clang* as Nezmythians started to pour into the streets in a panic. The Advisor and soldiers shouted orders on where to go to find safety. Jason and Barnabas glared at each other venomously through the cross in their swords... but Jason's sword wasn't his own.

His heart jumped into his mouth. The fiery orange blade was brighter than the afternoon sun and his hand was wrapped around a hilt of the finest silver. A metal dragon wound its way around the cross guard while snarling an inanimate, fiery breath and a bright red ruby encrusted itself into the pommel. Its mere presence filled Jason with fire.

The Blade of Nezmyth...! Jason marveled.

Barnabas growled and grunted as he pressed down on Jason, who was having a much easier time keeping Barnabas' sword at bay. The former King's face contorted with bewilderment and fury as he pressed down on Jason. Jason's boots stayed planted below him, his hands shaking, the Blade of Nezmyth keeping death at bay.

"You once told me you could stab my Dragon through the heart..." Jason's voice reverberated and was overdubbed by a deep rumbling.

With a flash of light, Jason's entire body erupted into an inferno that shot Barnabas backward. He tumbled onto the ground some yards behind him, scraped and bleeding on his arms and head.

Jason's deep brown eyes scorched and singed until their hue was turned into a shimmering orange. Black, swirling marks snaked their way down his arms and legs. The leather glove on his right hand combusted and smoldered until it fell to the ground in a pile of ashes. The brown in his hair singed into a crisp orange that matched his shimmering eyes. His whole body radiated light.

Barnabas looked up with an expression of purest wonder and horror, his lips moving and his eyes wild, but nothing uttering. King Jason looked down at him with eyes like the sun.

Jason suddenly remembered speaking with Master Ferribolt in his lonely home almost a year ago. His heart was racked with uncertainty—why *he* had to be the one to be King. The words Master Ferribolt told him that day resounded in his heart once more.

"You'll discover it for yourself someday..."

Jason looked at himself, a Knight of the Holy Order, a chosen warrior of the Holy Dragon. He inhaled deeply, and as he released his breath, jets of murky black smoke billowed from his nose.

"*Now I know.*"

Clumsily, Barnabas scrambled to his feet and bolted in the opposite direction.

"*You'd better run...*" King Jason growled.

Then, suddenly, Barnabas bent his legs and leapt into the air. There was a loud pop as King Jason saw him soar higher and higher above the ground like an enormous, caped, speeding jeroki. He frowned.

"*He can* fly?" He thought aloud.

"*You can do it too...*" A voice echoed inside his head. Jason recognized it as King Thomas'. "*You're a Knight of the Holy Order, Your Highness. Let the air pull you.*"

King Jason didn't hesitate. He bent his knees and leapt into the sky. He heard the same pop and felt the air grasp his arms and legs as he shot through the air. The wind flowed through his hair and snapped at his cape as the air pulled him higher and higher into the sky.

Barnabas looked back as he sped through the atmosphere, expecting to see Jason still standing on the ground hundreds of feet below... but that's not what he saw. Jason's eyes had never been sharper as the houses and cottages of Nezmyth City became smaller and smaller. He brandished the Blade as he air pulled him closer and closer to the deranged former King.

Suddenly, Barnabas' face transformed into a determined scowl. He flicked his left hand and threw a great purple jeroki at King Jason. King Jason reflexively threw his left fist forward and it collided with the speeding ball of magic, sending it into oblivion. Barnabas continued to shoot jeroki after jeroki as he sped backward through the air, which King Jason sliced nimbly with the Blade of Nezmyth as he twirled and somersaulted.

Jason could feel the pumping through his veins. He could hear everything... see everything... anticipate everything.

"Don't become overconfident," King Thomas admonished in his head. *"You haven't won yet. Remember who you're fighting. "*

Jason shouted as he hurled his own jeroki at Barnabas. The small white sun flew toward the former King, and as his eyes widened Barnabas barely dodged it within an inch of his nose.

He spun a complete and hurtled toward the ground, soaring with the force of gravity. Jason silently commanded the air to stop him, and quickly, he slid to a halt in midair. He hovered for a moment, glaring down at the dot that was Barnabas flying farther towards the ground. Jason frowned, curled himself into a ball, and shot toward the ground with a deafening bang.

He commanded the air to pull him faster. The wind was deafening in his ears and his hair bent completely backward in the gust. He tightened his grip on the Blade of Nezmyth as closer... closer he came to Barnabas... until he was face to face with him, soaring toward the ground.

Barnabas gasped with wide eyes as he beheld those orange eyes just a foot from his face, then, shouting in anger, he lifted his demon blade.

The dark blade and the Blade of Nezmyth clashed in furious frequency, sending out bursts of light through the afternoon sky with every contact. When the space between the two warriors and the ground thinned, they pulled up, soaring parallel to the ground through the streets of Nezmyth City. The frightened Nezmythians only saw blurs and flashes through the windows as the two pelted through the air, blowing aside bits of hay and parchment that had lay abandoned in the streets.

Barnabas pulled up. Jason looked ahead of where he was soaring, and just as he did, he crashed through the wall of a market street building, sending splinters and debris raining into the streets. He shielded his face with his arms and blasted through the opposite wall, screeching to a halt in midair and rising above the skyline.

He hovered there above the rooftops, breathing heavily, covered with splinters and dust and probing the landscape for a possible sign of Barnabas. He spat some debris out of his mouth.

"*Feel his presence...*" a calm man's voice echoed inside him. "*He can't be far...*"

Jason took a deep breath and focused on Barnabas, feeling for his beating heart... his twisted spirit...

Just then, he felt and heard a loud crack from behind him.

He flipped around to see a purple jeroki the size of a carriage pelting toward him from an alleyway, whistling and hissing through the air. The Blade of Nezmyth disintegrated from his hand in white smoke and he held both of his palms toward the speeding projectile. Reflexively, Jason gripped the monstrous ball of magic in his hands, feeling the raw magical energy conjured from Barnabas' spirit. He kept the jeroki in his grip for a full three hundred and sixty degrees before launching it back at his attacker.

The jeroki sped with just as much velocity and heat back at Barnabas. But strangely, Jason didn't feel Barnabas' presence in that direction.

"*Behind you!*" Several voices shouted at him.

With a swish of his arm and a flash of light, the Blade of Nezmyth was back in his hand and he blocked Barnabas' attempt to behead him from behind. The loud clang sounded at the same time the monster jeroki connected with the corner of a market street, exploding a crater into the building's exterior. As they hovered in midair, Jason spun around, kicked Barnabas in the chest with a painful *thud* and sent him tumbling toward the ground.

Barnabas regained his composure just seconds before his spinning body hit the earth. The loud pop rang through the streets as he soared in the direction of the deserted Center Court.

Jason exhaled a frustrated smoky breath. As he did, he felt himself falter in midair. The markings on his arms faded slightly. He started to sink toward the ground.

"Don't get angry, be patient!" Another voice rang. *"Anger will only drain you of your power!"*

But Jason only got angrier and more frustrated as he began to sink. The color left his hair. His eyes became brown again. Finally, he sunk lower and lower until he fell to the rubble-strewn street below. The sword that clanged to the ground beside him was his own, not the Blade of Nezmyth.

Jason grabbed it and scrambled to his feet. His heart was in his throat and beat furiously. All was silent. He spun on his heels repeatedly, his blade at the ready, anticipating when Barnabas would fly in and try to attack.

I'm prey as long as I'm not a Knight of the Holy Order, he thought.

"King Thomas!" he asked out loud. "How do I get my power back?"

No reply.

"...King Thomas!" Jason shouted more desperately.

At that moment, a flash of purple smoke billowed in front of Jason, and there was Barnabas. He launched his fist forward and caught Jason in the jaw, knocking him to the ground. With bloodlust in his eyes, he lifted his dark blade to the air.

No, Jason filled with despair. *Not again...*

This image sent him reeling back to where he was just moments ago. The Third Life. King Thomas. The marking on his hand. The Knights of the Holy Order. The Blade of Nezmyth. *"Nezmyth cheers for you, King Jason. Don't let them down."*

For Nezmyth.

Time slowed down. Barnabas' blade swung, and King Thomas' voice echoed once again, *"Don't let them down."*

Everything became clear. It was the quietest, quickest prayer Jason had ever uttered, but it worked. He roared with all of his soul for the kingdom he was called to lead, and his body once again burst into flame. Barnabas shot backward. His hair, eyes and body transformed back into a Knight of the Holy Order, and in a flash of light, the Blade of Nezmyth was back in his hand.

With more fire in his soul than before, Jason bellowed, "*For Nezmyth!!*"

The entire earth shook. Barnabas, on the ground, looked about him, fearing the buildings around him might collapse. With an angry, twitching scowl, he vanished once again in a cloud of smoke. Jason exhaled a smoky breath.

Somehow he knew. *He's in Center Court.* He could feel him there.

"*You can warp your surroundings…*" A man's tenor voice rang in his head. "*Feel the energy in your environment and bend it to your advantage… The Dragon created everything, and Barnabas can't escape everything…*"

Jason leapt into the air, soaring above the rooftops. The Blade of Nezmyth again melted away from the King's hand in the sparkling white smoke. He took a deep breath and closed his eyes, stretching his arms out and feeling the energy of all the things the Dragon had created.

Barnabas hovered above Center Court, his eyes fixed on the dot that was Jason in the distance. His dark blade quivered in his shaking hand and his head jerked.

"What are you planning, Your Highness?" he muttered.

It was then that he heard a loud cracking, like ice breaking. He flipped around in the air. The statue of himself in Center Court was twitching. His eyebrows and his jaw fell. Then, with crumbling cracks and snaps, the statue leapt off its pedestal and hovered above the ground, silently towering over him. The statue shook and vibrated some more before, with numerous sickening snaps, the limbs snapped off the body like stale bread. The torso cracked in half and the head exploded into dust.

The mad King brandished his sword with brutal shouts while each section of his broken statue pelted toward him like angry hornets, one after another. The blade cut through several pieces flawlessly, but that just separated the pieces of his immortalized self into more angry, attacking projectiles. He frantically sliced and slashed through the air, and just when he thought he was going to collapse, each piece of stone melted into sand and fell to the earth.

Barnabas let out a shaky growl as he held his sword with both hands. Right as he turned about, Jason, soaring through the air, collided with him in a midair tackle.

Jason hit Barnabas so hard that Barnabas' sword flew from his grasp several yards away. The two plummeted toward the ground and smashed into the white, stone cobblestones of Center Court, shooting out bits of stone and debris onto the street.

Jason's fist made successful contact with Barnabas' right cheek—he could feel the teeth break inside his mouth. Barnabas put his palms into King Jason's chest and launched a set of jerokis at point-blank range just as he had shaken the stars from his eyes.

Jason flew backward through the air, landing nearly fifty yards away with a *thud*—face up. He didn't push himself up—it was like an invisible rope pulled him back onto his feet. He brushed himself off, shook his head slightly, and the pain disappeared.

Barnabas had already staggered to his feet and was now soaring desperately for his sword nearly a hundred yards away. The King pointed his palm toward Barnabas' target and shot five miniature jerokis at once—one from each finger on his hand. They each caught Barnabas' black sword right before he could wrap his hand around it, sending it farther and farther away from the fallen King.

Barnabas planted his feet on the ground and slowly stood up from his hunched position. He shot a sideward glance at Jason, spitting some blood onto the ground. Jason let the Blade of Nezmyth melt into smoke and motioned for Barnabas to come toward him.

"*We can end this right now,*" Jason's voice rumbled and shook with the force of the Dragon's. "*This doesn't have to end with blood.*"

Barnabas looked toward him, thinking... contemplating... considering... then, his face contorted.

"*Coward!*" he bellowed.

Barnabas lifted his arms to the sky and his eyes rolled back into his head. He started uttering things that Jason couldn't easily discern—it wasn't Ancient Nezmythian or any language he had previously heard. His eyebrows bent uneasily.

"*What is he doing?*" Jason asked.

"*He's casting a spell...*" King Thomas' voice sounded distressed inside Jason's mind. "*But it doesn't sound like anything I've studied.*"

Jason's blood turned cold, "*Tepnoh Edomah...*"

Suddenly, jets of sickly black smoke shot from every pore in Barnabas' body. The cloud of smoke swirled and gathered as it rose to the sky in its filthy murk. It took on the shape of a demon with long, curling horns, penetrating purple eyes and enormous, powerful claws. The smoky demon grew in size until it towered above their heads, as tall, if not taller, than an Upper City mansion.

Barnabas laughed with delight behind the demon as the smoke stopped pouring from his body. The demon reared its ugly head and roared into the sky like an angry boar, shaking the ground and the houses that every Nezmythian took refuge in, purple smoke billowing from its sickly lips.

Jason looked on in fearful awe. The markings on his body started to fade.

"*Don't be frightened!*" King Thomas shouted. "*That's what Barnabas wants! You can only fight as a Knight of the Holy Order if you have the faith and the hope to do so! Roar, King Jason! Roar like the Dragon!*"

Jason's mind raced. He clutched desperately at the ember in his heart and, taking King Thomas' counsel, lifted his eyes to the sky and bellowed with all of his soul.

The roar that escaped Jason's lips was not his own. It shook everything—the ground he stood on, the clouds in the sky, even the sun seemed to quiver at the sound. An enormous pillar of fire billowed from his mouth, burning orange and fearsome nearly twenty feet into the air. But through the fire, something took shape…

A dragon.

It snaked its way out of the fire, as if its home was in Jason's heart. Out of Jason's mouth it came—a head, a pair of claws, and a long, fiery body. Jason nearly fell to the ground when the blaze from his lips stopped and he beheld the dragon slither through the air, its glory and passion for justice shining from its noble eyes to its pronounced tail.

"*Now control it!*" King Thomas said frantically. "*Barnabas is controlling his conjured demon so you need to control your conjured dragon! Use your hands and mind to guide its direction and fight with it!*"

Jason lifted his arms and bent his eyebrows. Barnabas, hundreds of yards away, did the same thing.

The dragon and the demon made eye contact and roared. Jason tried not to shudder and cover his ears while the ground shook beneath him. Silently, he prayed for victory.

The dragon and demon clashed at each other, each swinging their claws and biting at each other for dominance in this battle of the Kings. Puffs of smoke and flashes of light lit up the air as roars and bellows were frequent. Jason breathed hard and sweat poured down his face. His filthy arms were matted with small chunks of debris from plaster to bits of stone. Barnabas growled and snarled hundreds of yards away, uttering dark curses in his mind, uttering more *Tepnoh Edomah* to keep his giant demon alive and fighting.

Jason struggled to stay vertical as he swung his arms and the fiery dragon in the air mimicked his movements. He felt his energy running low. His knees shook, and he fought desperately to keep himself standing.

Please, O Dragon, help me… he silently prayed. *I've fought for as long as I can, but I'm afraid my best might not be enough…*

There was a short pause while he waited for his answer, then it came.

The dying ember in Jason's heart exploded into an inferno. His brows bent and once more he let out a shout that erupted into a mighty roar. The dragon that fought the demon above his head roared along with King Jason, spewing blue fire onto the depths of the smoky demon.

The demon screeched in agony and Barnabas covered his ears. The blue fire carved into the demon's very center, and from the center, white light crept outward onto its oily skin. The light penetrated through its eyes, its mouth, and its nostrils until it exploded in a flash brighter than the sun, the smoke disappearing away into nothingness. The fiery dragon that had fought so valiantly for King Jason curled itself into a spiral and rapidly spun until the fire disintegrated into the afternoon sky.

Barnabas staggered, unbelieving of what had just happened, his energy completely drained. Jason swung his arm and the Blade of Nezmyth reappeared in his hand. He dashed forward the hundreds of yards between them in a flash until he stood in front of Barnabas, just feet away, looking him directly in the eye.

The fallen King stood with mouth agape, staring into the young man's shimmering orange eyes. His cape had torn and his armor had been badly damaged. Blood trickled down his chin from his previously broken teeth. His arms were scraped and bleeding and coated with just as much sweat and dust as King Jason's.

The two stood staring into each other's eyes and not speaking a word.

Then Barnabas' eyes filled with shock as Jason conjured his black blade, which had fallen by the wayside, and carefully held it out to him. King Jason gave Barnabas an intense expression of warning as Barnabas looked at the blade, eyes wide and jaw hanging. Barnabas took the sword slowly… almost as if waiting for something… but nothing came.

Jason didn't attack—he merely stood in front of Barnabas waiting for a response.

He got it. Barnabas' face twisted in arrogant rage once again and he raised his dark blade with both hands. King Jason planted his feet and gripped the Blade of Nezmyth tighter.

With a clang and a snap, their blades met. The Blade of Nezmyth remained intact, but the dark, terrible blade snapped in two where the Blade of Nezmyth touched it. The one half of the blade fell to the ground, lifeless, useless, as Barnabas held a handle with a double-edged stump in his hand.

Frustrated with his arrogance, Jason raised his left palm and blasted a blinding white jeroki into Barnabas' chest at a distance of mere inches. He flew backward at blinding speed perfectly parallel to the ground before he slammed into the pedestal that once held a statue of himself.

Barnabas twitched were he had slid to a sitting position below the pedestal, barely holding on to consciousness. As his eyes fluttered and slowly opened, he beheld the mighty Jason quickly approaching with that bright orange blade still gripped firmly in his hand.

Jason raised the Blade of Nezmyth and pointed its tip into Barnabas' chest, pinning him to the side of the pedestal. Barnabas raised his hands in the air shook his head frantically, his blue eyes wild and rapidly filling with tears.

The aura that surrounded Jason slowly dissolved. His hair turned back to its sandy brown hue, along with his deep brown eyes. The mysterious markings disappeared from his arms and legs. Jason blinked, and the Blade of Nezmyth vanished, replaced by his own prized sword.

"Go ahead," Barnabas muttered. "Do it. I would do the same to you."

Jason scrunched his nose and his grip on his sword tightened. Barnabas' eyes dug into him.

"Your Highness!" King Jason heard from behind.

He turned around where he was—still holding his sword to Barnabas' chest—and saw soldiers and the Advisor rushing toward him. Nezmythians cautiously followed as they came out of their strongholds into Center Court. The Advisor's eyes hardened as he looked intently at what was happening. Jason looked into Barnabas' icy, blank eyes.

"I would be doing the kingdom a service by running this blade through you," he seethed.

"Then—do—it," Barnabas breathed.

"Your Highness…" the Advisor spoke softly in the background.

Jason bore his teeth at the fallen ruler. He thought of the battle that had just taken place. How did Jason conquer the most seasoned fighter in Nezmyth? The Dragon fought with him. He held tight to faith and abandoned anger—the anger that was flooding through him right now.

He thought of Saryan. He thought of his parents and Tarren and King Thomas. His love for them all poured over the boundaries of his expression. He wanted nothing but the best for all of them. He looked into Barnabas' eyes, and saw nothing but a cold void. No love, no honor, just bitter loneliness.

Jason thought to himself as his heart rate descended, *Do I really want to begin my rule as a killer?*

With a deep exhale and a scowl, Jason lowered his sword. He turned about and his eyes locked on the nearest set of soldiers.

"Take him away!" He commanded. "Put him in the darkest, deepest cell in the prison and throw away the key! Give him the rest of his life to think about what he's done—."

Jason was interrupted by a mad yelp from behind him. He flipped around to see Barnabas frozen in midair with his hands outstretched in attack—that stump of a blade was just inches away from Jason's face.

Jason jumped back and looked behind him to see the Advisor's hand outstretched toward Barnabas and his red eyes burning fiercely. As he twitched each individual finger, a different part of Barnabas' body would jerk, sending him into odd convulsions as he hovered just inches above the ground. Finally, the Advisor stretched out his hand and Barnabas' body jerked into spread eagle. Barnabas' eye twitched at Jason and the Advisor. Every jaw was hanging in the thickening crowd of Nezmythians.

"We have had enough of you, Barnabas," the Advisor said, "Especially I. Twenty years of standing by and letting you rule this kingdom, as unqualified as you are, nearly drove me mad. King Jason and I will be working on repairing this kingdom that you have plunged into darkness. Enjoy your new home. We will surely be making new rules about recent guests at the Nezmyth City Prison."

With that, the Advisor dropped his hand, Barnabas' expression became blissful, and he fell to the ground as numbly as a ragdoll, his torn cape falling over his head. Grey clouds unexpectedly filled the Nezmyth City sky. One after another, the raindrops came as the King, Advisor, and the people of Nezmyth stood around the fallen King's unconscious body.

32 THE REVELATION

A carriage rolled up to a monstrous mansion just down the street from the castle. Rain pelted from the sky in a way the kingdom hadn't seen in years. Jason looked out the window as he remained seated in the perfectly dry, burning red interior of the coach. The flickering light from the mansion's windows were dull against the downpour but still clearly visible beyond the metal gate that wound itself around the fortress. The steady roar of the rain forced Jason to shout.

"Are you going to be alright, Lawrence?" King Jason called up.

"Right as rain, Your Highness!" Lawrence called merrily against the torrent. "I figure I'll just go down to the tavern and celebrate with some of the common folk! Why aren't you celebrating along with everyone else in the kingdom, Your Excellency?"

Jason had already stepped out of the carriage and into the downpour without waiting for Lawrence to open the door for him. His royal armor made soft clicking and clacking noises as he walked, and his prized sword was slung around his hip underneath his billowing red cape.

"Are you joking?" Jason looked up at Lawrence through the rain. "I'm King now! I can't go about getting drunk with merry hooligans like you! I have Kingly business to attend to!"

Lawrence threw back his head and laughed. "Oh, Your Highness, it's so wonderful to work under a pleasant King for a change! I'll be back in an hour."

"Lawrence!"

"Yes, Your Grace?"

King Jason cut him a sly look, "Don't get *too* drunk."

Lawrence slid Jason a wink before he snapped the reins and the royal carriage trotted out of sight.

"Good evening, Your Highness," the gatekeeper that had so often got used to seeing King Jason before his Ordination smiled genuinely and opened the gate. Jason gave him a nod as he walked quickly through the shallow puddles that dotted the walkway. He skipped every few steps when he leapt up the stone stairs to the mansion's porch. He shook his head when he reached the door, whipping the water out of his drenched hair. He grasped one of the brass knockers, clapping it against the door thrice.

The door opened and a butler revealed himself, bowing reverently.

"Good evening, Your Majesty," he said.

"Good evening, Jerem,"

"King Jason, thank you for stopping by!" Master Ferribolt popped up from behind the door and shook Jason's hand, pulling him into the mansion. "Can you believe this weather? I've never seen a rain so thick!"

Jerem shut the door and scurried back to a separate room as Jason and Master Ferribolt stood by and chatted. Their idle chatter reverberated off the pristine walls and polished floor of the hall. The rain provided a dull roar in the background.

"Come to my study," the Advisor said. "We wish to speak to you in private."

We? King Jason thought curiously.

Jason and Master Ferribolt walked side-by-side through the large arch in the wall and into the study. A flickering fire was lit in a large stone fireplace on the far wall.

Waiting for Master Ferribolt and Jason was the Advisor.

"Your Highness, I believe you are already acquainted with your Advisor?" Master Ferribolt asked cheerfully.

Jason cracked an uncomfortable half-smile, but tried to be polite. "Yes, we've met briefly."

"Good evening, Your Highness," the Advisor stood and bowed respectfully. He actually smiled. The sight was as familiar as a dog with two heads.

"Please, take a seat," Master Ferribolt motioned for Jason to sit down in the usual armchair. Jason slowly sat down in the comfortable chair as the Chief Patriarch walked over and sat in the identical one facing him. The Advisor sat next to him in an average wooden chair.

"How are you feeling right now?" Master Ferribolt asked with shimmering eyes. "Your Year of Decision is over. Barnabas has been cast out of the Throne. You have taken your position as the Foreordained King of Nezmyth, and the kingdom rejoices."

"You must be very happy," the Advisor said.

King Jason rubbed his hands together and stared absently into the fire. "I don't know if *happy* is the word. I feel like I now know why I was Foreordained, but there is still a lot I don't understand."

"Such as?" Master Ferribolt replied.

At first, Jason didn't answer. But after mustering up his courage, he shot a heated look at the Advisor.

"Why did you save me today?" King Jason said. "For the past year, you've been on Barnabas' side as he made my life a living nightmare. Then suddenly, you have a change of heart because someone else wears the crimson cape. Why is this?"

Master Ferribolt's eyebrows popped and his view changed to the Advisor. The Advisor was puzzled at King Jason's vehement questioning. He answered softly:

"I was never on his side."

"I'm not convinced," King Jason replied.

"Why don't you show him?" Master Ferribolt's question was directed toward the Advisor.

"Only if he'll allow it."

"Show me what?" King Jason said.

The Advisor stood from his seat. "If I may? I think it would answer your questions."

King Jason made eye contact with Master Ferribolt. Master Ferribolt nodded. King Jason sighed and conceded. With that, the Advisor strode up to his chair and placed three fingers on his forehead. The strangest sensation fell over King Jason. He felt as though he were quickly slipping into a dream. His body relaxed, he closed his eyes, and slowly, images started to form in the black.

Thunder cracked all around and rain pounded the streets of Nezmyth City. He was overlooking a street in Upper City, somewhere between Master Ferribolt's mansion and the castle.

Just at that moment, a carriage came barreling up the street, headed for the castle. Master Ferribolt was inside it. He kept looking out the windows anxiously—scanning, feeling for something or someone.

"Any luck, Master?" the man at the reigns yelled to the Chief Patriarch over the torrent.

Master Ferribolt didn't hear him. His eyes stayed glued to the window. He didn't notice that someone had suddenly appeared next to him in the carriage.

"You needn't worry. It's all taken care of."

Master Ferribolt let out a startled yelp and nearly jumped through the roof. The Advisor was sitting next to him, his grey hair soaked and his red eyes filled with urgency. Master Ferribolt clutched his heart and glared at the Advisor.

"I've told you to announce yourself before you suddenly appear!"

"Forgive me, my friend," the Advisor grinned sheepishly.

As Master Ferribolt's breathing settled, he shouted for the carriage driver to head back to his mansion. The carriage slowed to a crawl and turned around in the street.

"So you know about the boy?" Master Ferribolt asked.

"Yes," the Advisor replied. "The King relies on others to be his eyes and ears. Little does he know that they're mine as well. The spy promised not to breathe a word of it to him, but I erased his memory of this evening to be absolutely sure the boy's life is safe. We cannot leave a shred of a clue—not until the Dragon has prompted you that it's time for his Year of Decision."

"I agree," Master Ferribolt said. "But that could be years. We must be patient."

"Yes," the Advisor said. "It's a pity you and I have no evidence to convict the King of his treachery. He is the one who killed King Thomas. We could have ended this tyranny years ago."

"All of Nezmyth knows that, but this is a better way," Master Ferribolt said. "Nezmyth needs someone called from the Holy Dragon, not just another aristocrat or nobleman. We need someone pure—humble."

"Then we shall wait, then?" the Advisor said.

"Yes, we shall. Thank you, my friend."

The Advisor nodded, then vanished.

"I prayed today at the Cathedral."

The Advisor sat in an armchair in the Chief Patriarch's study sipping a cup of tea. Master Ferribolt faced the fire with his hands clasped behind his back. He watched the coals smolder in the flame as his restless mind churned.

"Is it time...?" The Advisor asked.

"It is," Master Ferribolt said.

The Advisor set down his cup and his eyes became stone. "The King will undoubtedly try to kill him."

"That goes without saying," Master Ferribolt replied. "But this means that the following year won't just be a challenge for the boy, but for us as well. The Year of Decision is an opportunity for rising Kings to grow and to learn—prepare themselves for the Throne. The King will likely construct counterfeit 'tests' in order to sabotage the boy. We must do everything in our power to protect him. I want to meet with him every week. I'll teach him the Ancient Language. If he's smart, he'll realize the wealth of power that comes from it and utilize it."

"Excellent," the Advisor replied. "I wish I could do the same, but I don't want the boy to know he has an ally directly in the castle. That could make him lazy. He is already so unsure of himself... he needs to grow. I'll cast dreams—let him know what's going on inside the castle without explicitly exposing us."

"He could catch on," Master Ferribolt said.

"I hope he does," the Advisor replied. "But as long as he sees an eagle and a vulture instead of me and the King, he won't know for sure. He won't know where the dreams are coming from."

"And you'll keep a close eye on the King?"

"Every moment."

"Good," Master Ferribolt said. "Then you'll fetch him tomorrow. It's time for Nezmyth to begin anew."

"Let the boy go. If he's guilty of anything, it's selflessness. Leave him be."

The Dark Cloak muttered as King Barnabas' face twisted with rage. He was inside the castle on the day of the procession. Jason watched himself from five months ago get blasted with a jeroki, then run out the castle doors. The enormous doors swung shut quickly, and Barnabas found himself face to face with the Dark Cloak.

The Dark Cloak uncovered his face, revealing himself as the Advisor. His red eyes could have burned a hole in the King. King Barnabas scowled, then erupted, howling with rage. He shot forward in a blur, his blade raised, ready to strike.

However, as soon as he was upon the Advisor, his forearm snapped into a right angle. His blade clanged to the ground and King Barnabas cried out in agony. Then, his forearm snapped back into place, and before he could do anything else, he was launched backward parallel to the ground. He soared into the Throne, then slumped down, disoriented.

"I warned you not to force me," the Advisor said, his tone icy cold.

King Barnabas twisted his arm satisfactorily and laughed. "You can't kill me. And as long as you don't, the boy's life will still be in danger. With your magic your strength equals even mine, but you lack the stomach to use it."

"The Throne has seen enough bloodshed with you in it," the Advisor replied. "And I've already stopped numerous attempts to kill the boy."

"But the year isn't over yet," King Barnabas sneered.

"And when it is," the Advisor said. "I won't be playing your puppet anymore."

Jason found himself looking in a dark room of the castle. Only two torches were lit in the whole room. The Advisor stood over a body that lay motionless on a table. The body was that of King Barnabas. A door flew open, and in bustled Master Ferribolt.

"What? What happened?" he asked.

"Jason will likely tell you of this tomorrow," the Advisor said, motioning toward the body.

"You still haven't answered the question."

King Barnabas' body was as stiff as a board, with his eyes fixed unblinking at the ceiling and fingers outstretched, as if groping on to life.

"He's not dead," the Advisor said. "He's been Overcursed."

"Overcursed?"

"It's almost impossible, especially with a warrior of the King's magnitude. The King tried using a powerful spell on someone—likely *Tepnoh Edomah* on our friend Jason—and the victim's willpower overacted the potency of the curse, countering it. The boy must have an extraordinary spirit. You're teaching him well."

Master Ferribolt fanned his hand over the King's eyes. They didn't blink.

"So why did you call me here?"

The Advisor smirked. "I wanted you to see his reaction when I wake him up."

He stretched his hands over the petrified body, took a deep breath, and uttered a series of phrases in Ancient Nezmythian. After a pause, the King gasped and sat up as if awakening from a nightmare. His eyes wildly darted around and his breathing was furious. When he saw the Advisor and the Chief Patriarch standing next to him, he went pale.

"I take it this attempt was as successful as the last?" the Advisor asked him.

Jason watched himself walk out the castle doors from two weeks ago. As soon as the doors had boomed shut, the Advisor opened his mouth.

"I heard what you said in his mind," he said. "Two weeks to fulfill your oath, is it? I'll admit several of your attempts have slipped through my fingers, but this time you will not leave my sight. And now all of Nezmyth will know. Can you imagine the consequences of killing two Foreordained Kings? There will be riots in the streets."

The King ignored him. Petty things. He can control some restless commoners. After all, he had done it for years.

"But alas, perhaps the boy doesn't need my protection any longer," the Advisor continued. "His faith in the Dragon is strong enough. I will protect him these two weeks, but on the day of Ordination, he will be yours."

King Barnabas turned his head and slid the Advisor a skeptical eye. "You will simply hand him to me?"

"The Chief Patriarch has prayed and feels that the Holy Dragon will protect his Foreordained servant on the day of his Ordination. You may try to destroy the boy, as you already have, but you will reap the consequences. Perhaps now is the time to change your mind."

The King sneered and looked away. "Nezmyth will remain in my hands."

"Your pride will be your demise," the Advisor said. "The boy possesses power that you haven't foreseen—the Chief Patriarch is aware of it. He has a special mark. And when the boy is King, and you in shackles, Nezmyth will be rebuilt. You cannot stop what the Dragon has set in motion. Savor the Throne while you may."

Jason felt the Advisor take his fingers off of his forehead, and he began to fade back into reality. He slumped in his chair, overcome. The Advisor sat back down and looked at Jason expectantly. All Jason could think to do was to gaze at him amazedly.

"I had no idea," he muttered. "So you were the Dark Cloak? You protected my friends while they were in prison?"

The Advisor nodded.

Suddenly, he turned on Master Ferribolt, pointing at the mark in his hand. "And you knew what this meant all along? And you didn't tell me?"

"It wasn't the right time to tell you," Master Ferribolt said. "I'm sorry, Your Majesty. I wanted to. But all things must be learned in their proper time."

"Do you know what this means, too?" Jason asked the Advisor.

The Advisor nodded. "Yes. It is extremely sacred. I would not recommend making idle conversation to anyone. It is honest to say that it is a birthmark.

"Your Highness," the Advisor continued. "I ask of your forgiveness. I understand that you must now feel some hostility toward me, but I want to do whatever I can to remedy that. I know that as we keep the interests of the people in mind, the Dragon will help us build Nezmyth back into a prosperous kingdom."

Jason drummed his fingers on the armrest. He had gone an entire year fearing this man along with King Barnabas. Even after seeing everything that he had, it was still hard to come to grips that he was a complete ally.

But he was. He was the one protecting him from the King all along. He was the one protecting his loved ones in prison. Wasn't that more than enough? He smiled, "You're forgiven. I'm just grateful that things are about to change. And you'll be there to advise me through it all."

"As Advisors do."

The Advisor, Master Ferribolt and the King stood up from their chairs and shook hands before walking into the main hall.

"I feel it's going to be a pleasure working with you, Your Majesty," the Advisor said.

"Thank you," Jason replied. "I'm grateful you told me what you have this evening. I appreciate your honesty. By the way… what is your name? I've always simply known you as the Advisor."

The Advisor smiled and said, "Nadiel, son of Will, the printer."

Jason beamed. "Thank you Nadiel. Anyway, Lawrence should be here any moment, and the Queen's patience with me is probably wearing thin by now. I should be spending more time with her on our wedding day."

"May the Dragon be with you, King Jason," Master Ferribolt said.

The instant Jason's hand wrapped around the door's handle, the steady roar of the rain hushed.

He opened the door and the smell of rain fell upon him, which he drank in through his nose. The clouds had disappeared as quickly as they had appeared hours ago and the moon smiled brightly on Nezmyth, content and blissful among the stars.

They all bid their goodbyes and Jason walked back down the stone pathway toward the street. The guard by the gate again tipped his hat and pulled a lever, opening the creaking gate slowly. Jason strolled through with a thankful nod toward the guard and waited at the side of the street, his bare right hand sitting on the hilt of his blade.

After several minutes, Lawrence and the royal carriage came barreling up the drenched street in frenzy. Jason almost laughed to himself as the horse, startled by the sudden yanking on the reins, screeched to a halt in front of him. Lawrence tipped his hat apologetically.

"Not a sip of hard stuff tonight, Your Grace!" He said proudly. "I would like to ask your forgiveness being late, though. There was this red-headed lady at the tavern with a charming pair of dimples..."

"Save it, Lawrence, nobody died," Jason said as he opened the door and stepped in. "Let's just go home. It's late."

"Right-o! Yip!" Lawrence cracked the reins and the carriage pulled up the street in a trot.

They passed the trip in silence. Jason watched the water trickle down the Upper City street, weaving through the cobblestones like rocks in a soft stream. As they approached the castle gates, the carriage didn't even stop as the elite soldiers on the gates beckoned them into the grounds merrily.

"Good evening, Your Highness!" one called.

"Hope you had a wonderful evening, Your Highness!" the other said.

"You as well," the King said as the carriage rolled on by.

"Your Majesty!" Lawrence called from outside. He sounded as though sweets were falling from the sky. "Your Majesty, look out the window!"

Jason's furrowed his eyebrows curiously and poked his head out of the window slowly. What he saw filled him with wonder.

The dark, charcoal-hued palace that King Jason remembered from one year ago had completely disappeared. In its place was a radiant white castle gleaming with nobility and majesty. White birds flew off in the distance behind the noble fortress, and Jason noticed a bigger stained-glass window above the ancient doors he hadn't before. It was a

Knight nobly pointing its orange blade to the sky, where the Sacred Dragon soared triumphantly.

"Miraculous," Jason uttered.

Lawrence snapped the reins and the carriage picked up pace. Jason smiled to himself and sat back down on the padded bench. He couldn't help but shoot more glances out the window, expecting more things to jump out and astonish him. He raised his voice:

"Lawrence, when we reach the statue in the middle of the grounds let's stop for a moment."

"Of course, Your Excellency!"

The landscape slowly shifted and the carriage wheels crackled against the ground as Jason waited for moments to pass. Abruptly, the stallions stopped their trot and the coach lurched to a halt. Jason threw open the door and jumping onto the white stone pathway below. He briskly walked by the carriage as he approached the inanimate statue, and as he did, his grin broadened into an ear-to-ear smile. Lawrence looked on with mild curiosity, reins still in his hands.

The parched mote at the bottom of the fountain had filled to the brim with crystal-clear rain water. His eyes traveled up the statue—up another immortalized depiction of a Knight of the Holy Order—until they met a small hole in the Knight's lips. As he focused his eyes, he noticed it was trickling water.

Jason nearly laughed through his teeth before he flipped around to walk back to the carriage, but as he did his eyes caught something small and green—almost unnoticeable. His jaw dropped and his heart leapt.

"Lawrence, come look at this!" the King said before he jogged over to the edge of the path.

Lawrence put his hands down and leapt off the driver's mount, hustling toward the elated King. Jason had squatted to the ground while looking at something in the black, moist earth. Both corners of his mouth were touching his ear lobes and his crimson cape fell in bunches onto the stone path. As Lawrence approached, he stood by the King and put his hands on his knees. He laughed approvingly.

"This night just keeps getting better and better!"

Through the soaked, black earth, a small green stem, no bigger than Jason's pinky finger protruded to the surface. A tiny leaf the size of a fingernail stuck out of the miniscule stem, greeting the world, having escaped from the parched, dead soil.

FOREORDAINED

SOME YEARS LATER...

At the western edge of Nezmyth, a canyon carves its way through the landscape, separating the dry, cracked wasteland of eastern Unbuntye from the forests of western Nezmyth. The wind whistles softly, carrying the whispers of Wevlians long past. They shudder as three personages appear.

One is human. His icy blue eyes lack any spark or glimmer and the edges of his lips have been permanently branded into blankness over the course of years. The breeze makes his eyes water, but he debates whether blinking is worth the effort inside the echoes of his mind.

The other two are towering, massive beasts. One lugs a battle axe on its side and the other, a spear over its back. Their faces are deformed—their grey skin has sunken into their skulls and their eyes and ears appear to be melting off their faces. Apart from their facial features, the rippling muscles on their tall bodies are as thick and hard as stone.

They stand on the edge of the forest, overlooking the canyon, and converse briefly.

"We're on Nezmythian land," the first beast states.

"Yes," was the only reply the human gave. His tone is as flat as his vacant stare.

The second beast's voice is harsh and raspy in contrast to the first's rocky, deep tone. "We're not causing trouble—at least not yet. If King Jason's reputation holds true, he won't mind us investigating a little. Wouldn't you agree, Your Majesty?"

The human doesn't answer. His hand strokes the bark of the nearest tree, and his breathing rattles like the organic quality gives him some twisted pleasure. He can feel the life even in this mindless plant. The corner of the human's mouth twitches slightly, almost teasing a smile.

"Everything we need is here," he says. "And it's mine."

"So let's take it," the second beast replies.

"No," the King continues. "Not now. Patience. It shall be ours in time."

"Of course, my Lord," the first beast revels, bowing timidly. "Nezmyth will know that you are its rightful ruler."

"Yes," The King replies. "But... they will still prefer King Jason."

"They couldn't *possibly* prefer Jason over you, sire," the second beast purrs. "You are powerful and wise. And if they do, we'll kill them. All of them."

A pause. Then, satisfied, the King turns on his heels and wordlessly walks away. As he passes the beasts, they bow in reverence, then follow behind him. A wall of purple smoke develops several feet in front of them, and as they approach it, it grows bigger. They step through it silently, and in a moment, they are gone.

ABOUT THE AUTHOR

Aaron N. Hall began drafting *Foreordained* at the age of fifteen and finished the final draft shortly after age twenty-two. Aside from writing, he is an avid musician, movie buff and New England lover. He lives as a full-time student in southern Utah.

Made in the USA
Charleston, SC
17 February 2014